# THE BELOVED

*To risk it all for love of a king?*

As England tears herself apart in the War of the Roses, Anne de Bohun lives far from the intrigues of cities and courts. Once King Edward IV's mistress, Anne has found safety with their son in Flanders, but now Edward himself is a hunted fugitive, while Anne's real father, King Henry VI, rules England again. Summoned by an enigmatic message from her lover, can Anne, with a child to defend, let her love for Edward threaten everything she has? Or will she need his help to protect her from the powerful enemies who mean to destroy her?

# THE BELOVED

# THE BELOVED

*by*

Posie Graeme-Evans

**Magna Large Print Books**
Long Preston, North Yorkshire,
BD23 4ND, England.

British Library Cataloguing in Publication Data

Graeme-Evans, Posie
    The beloved.

A catalogue record of this book is
available from the British Library

ISBN   978-0-7505-2696-8

First published in Great Britain in 2006 by Hodder & Stoughton
A division of Hodder Headline

Copyright © Posie Graeme-Evans 2005

Cover illustration by arrangement with Hodder & Stoughton Ltd.

The right of Posie Graeme-Evans to be identified as the author of this
work has been asserted by her in accordance with the Copyright,
Designs and Patents Act, 1988

Published in Large Print 2007 by arrangement with
Hodder & Stoughton Ltd.

Magna Large Print is an imprint of Library Magna Books Ltd.

Printed and bound in Great Britain by
T.J. (International) Ltd., Cornwall, PL28 8RW

For my daughter, Emma MacKellar,
with all my love.
When you were born I glimpsed the
meaning of existence. I am so lucky to be
part of your life.

# Prologue

There were eagles in the sky over London. Sea eagles, a pair of them. They rode the smoky air slowly, spiralling upwards on the heat from the early cooking fires – he with her, she above him. The king of birds, the queen of birds.

Beneath their wings the city nested tight behind its walls as, one by one, houses woke to the day. The eagles saw the people, tiny figures far below, as they issued from their doors – specks of restless colour channelled into streams by the dark streets.

The eagles called out to each other. Enough, said that cry. No food for us here. And they flew away towards the coast, towards the empty, clean sea without another glance.

But the people of London had no wings. Left behind, the dirty streets heaved and rippled with speculation. At first it was a whisper, neighbour to frightened neighbour, but terror spoke at last and named the thing out loud for what it was. War. War was coming.

None would speak *her* name though, for saying it, actually *naming* her, might bring the curse, bring her, to their doors.

That fearful knowledge hollowed out the day. The old queen, Margaret of Anjou, and the Earl of Warwick had become allies where, before, the deaths of many men had forged and sealed their enmity. Dread of that strange pairing flowed over

11

the walls of London and drifted through the gates like grey fog, chilling the unwary.

And rumours spread as sweating sickness does, mouth to mouth. Troops were massed on the other side of the water; all the horses in Normandy had been requisitioned by her knights; the masts of her fleet were thick as forest trees. This, and more, was proof that she was backed by the power of the mad and terrible French king, Louis.

It was certain, people whispered. Margaret had sworn to take the kingdom back for her lack-wit husband *and* her loose-born son, and God help them all when she came. She would not pity them when her troops entered their city. London, and Londoners, had betrayed her before and all the prayers in the world, all the pleas for intercession, would be as nothing for the old queen's memory was long. She'd been driven from this city and her kingdom years ago. Exiled now, she waited for revenge. She was Edward Plantagenet's Nemesis and at last, at last, her hour had come.

The citizens of London shivered as they whispered, and terrified the children who heard them talking. And they mourned as they prayed without hope.

They mourned for their king, their Summer King, and for his queen, Elizabeth, as lovely as the Empress of Heaven descended down to Earth. The Yorks had had their brief summer, a summer of hope, of optimism, and soon this young king and his silver-gilt queen would be gone, swept away with their little princesses on the tide of history, never to return. None doubted it.

Least of all Sir Mathew Cuttifer, mercer of the

12

city of London.

Stoically, hour after hour, he knelt as if on knives whilst the silence of his working room in Blessing House – his London base – grew thick as dust. Mathew too prayed for deliverance.

First, his prayers were for the kingdom of England; next for his king, Edward Plantagenet, and all his family. Then he prayed for his city and its frightened people. He asked intercession for his wife and their grandson, his household, his business and for his own personal survival, if that were God's will.

Lastly, he prayed for the safety and wellbeing of Anne de Bohun, the girl he called his ward, over the seas in Brugge. The girl whose destiny had come to be so bound up with that of his family, his house and, truly, the kingdom of England that her very existence seemed an omen. Whether good or bad, it was impossible to tell. It had always been impossible to tell.

And though Anne was safe where she was, soon, very soon, the dark fingers of the turmoil in England would reach out over the water and touch her with their taint. Of that, Mathew Cuttifer had no doubt.

'Master?'

The voice was muffled by the door, four inches of ancient oak bound by iron.

Mathew frowned. He was praying; the household knew that. On his explicit instructions, the sacred was never to be interrupted by the profane concerns of everyday life. He muttered an Ave and ignored his knees; he would not recognise the pain. And he would not respond to the man

13

outside the door. The servant would go away. If he was sensible.

There was silence once more. Motes danced in the cold slant of light from the single high window.

Then it came again: a rapid knocking. 'Master? Can you hear me?'

Mathew crossed himself and breathed deeply.

'This is not the time. Go away.'

'There is bad news, master.'

Mathew knew himself to be a rational man, a calm man. His friends, his trading colleagues all agreed. Mathew Cuttifer was always staunch in a crisis, they said; always good for wise, detached advice and clear analysis of a problem. Not today.

'What news?'

The door was wrenched wide so fast the hinges yelped. Leif Molnar, chief captain of the burgeoning Cuttifer fleet of trading vessels, stood outside. Anxiety had made his seaman's cap a shapeless mass in giant hands.

'Warwick and Clarence have landed in the west, master. Jasper Tudor is with them. They're being supported by the people. Some of the lords as well. Too many.'

Mathew Cuttifer's face was plaster-white. He gestured for the man to enter, waved him to the high stool in front of his working desk

'So, it's finally come. Does the king know?'

Leif lifted massive shoulders in a shrug. 'It's said he's still in the north. York, perhaps. They're rioting in Kent already. News travels faster than men do.'

Mathew crossed himself. 'God defend us then.'

Kent was troublesome no matter which king sat

14

on the throne. Always opportunistic, the men of Kent; they'd looted London on a rumour of trouble before.

'We'll need to shore up defences here. Those who are not friends of the king will think they've been given a licence to sack the city.' Mathew gathered his old-fashioned houpelande around his shanks as he hobbled from the room. Sudden energy freed up his joints remarkably – the operation of fear. 'Come with me, Leif. There is much to be done.'

Leif was an oak-like presence in that low-ceilinged room. 'Master?'

'What?' The word was flung back over Mathew's shoulder.

'The Lady de Bohun?'

Mathew slowed his pace and allowed Leif to catch up with him 'She's safest out of this. Best she stays where she is.'

'But her connections might be useful – to the king and his cause?' Captain Molnar did not add, *And to you, master,* but that's what he meant.

Mathew turned so quickly the Dane cannoned into him, treading heavily on his master's gouty toes. Instant, breathless pain, and the merchant's face collapsed around his missing teeth.

'Connections? What do you mean?' Hissing the words, Mathew moved his mind away from the agony of his feet, though his eyes watered.

Leif was embarrassed. Only on the deck of his ship was he graceful. Or in a fight. 'The sister to the king, the Duchess of Burgundy, she is Lady Anne's friend because of the affection they both share for...' He swallowed defensively as Mathew

15

glared at him. 'It is common knowledge, master, that Lady Anne and the king have a ... connection.'

Mathew snorted. 'Common knowledge! Gossip, you mean. You disappoint me, Leif.'

He hurried away, leaving his captain wallowing, discomforted, in his righteous wake.

But later that night, after a lengthy conversation with his wife, Lady Margaret, whose judgment Mathew Cuttifer deeply respected, as well as much searching prayer on the matter, Mathew came to a decision that surprised and frightened both husband and wife. He would send Leif Molnar to Brugge.

The Dane would survey and secure the trading operation of the House of Cuttifer in Brugge, and report back. Mathew didn't doubt the worth of his steward there, Maxim, and Meinheer Boter, who controlled his accounting-house, but with war beckoning, chaos would shortly follow, and a prudent man did what he could to protect what God had so graciously given.

Leif would also visit Anne de Bohun. Mathew's ward *did* have links to the Burgundian court at the very highest level and she would be asked to obtain information regarding the intentions of Charles, Duke of Burgundy, in the coming war. Such intelligence would be of great worth to the future of London, and of England. And to the Yorkist cause.

Both ends against the middle – that was the game Mathew Cuttifer played now. And Holy Mary help them all, for he'd been in this place before with Anne de Bohun and her terrifyingly high 'connections'. Once, Anne's links to the court of England, to the king himself, had almost cost Mathew his family, his business and his life.

And in sending Leif Molnar to Anne at this time, and on such a mission, Mathew Cuttifer placed them all in danger once more. In the end, though, what else could he do?

His prayers had told him the truth in this matter.

It was the will of God.

# Part One

# The Shadow

# Chapter One

Snow was falling again. Soft, lazy flakes. She tasted them. Held up her hands to catch them. They touched her like a kiss.

There were footprints in the fallen snow. Large. Not hers. Marks made by a man. But they were old, the edges of the outlines rounded, blurred. The man was long gone.

She looked down at her own red shoes. Would she fit her feet within the marks the man had made? They led away across the white field towards the fence of trees that was the edge of the forest. Stark black trunks, limbs burdened, clotted with snow. Yes.

Suddenly convinced she hurried forward, the deep, soft powder creaking beneath her Spanish slippers, but she was hot, not cold, as she stepped into the hollows of the footprints in the snow. She had to stretch to match his stride – he'd been tall, this man – and she could feel it in her thighs, her knees.

And then she was amongst the trees, breathless, starting to hurry, trying to run, trying not to flounder, stumbling on though her skirts were wet and heavy. Her mantle was a burden. Throw it away, that was best – she would not be so hot. Impatiently she dragged at the cloak pin, a gold dragon with milk-white eyes of pearl. It ripped the heavy velvet as she tugged, but she didn't care; she threw the precious garment down beside a naked hawthorn tree, the last blood-dark berries shrivelled on the twigs, some caught into icicles, the fingers of winter. Perhaps she would come back and find the blue cloak later. Only perhaps.

She was strong, she knew that, but every part of her was in pain as she struggled to be faithful to the marks in the snow, her chest heaving with the effort of moving forward, ploughing forward. The footprints led her on. She allowed herself to feel hope now, to believe that she was close. That soon, if only she ignored the agony in her knees, her side, her throat, she would find him, the man who'd made them. She was clear on that: she wanted that. She must find him, ask him why he had ... what? Gone on this weary journey, of course, when all the world was deep asleep, locked in the depths of rigid winter.

And it made her happy, knowing she would find him, so happy that suddenly nothing else mattered. She would see this man, touch him, hold his face between her hands. She would feel the sharp day-old stubble on his skin, she would taste his mouth softly, and he would hold her.

Not concentrating, Anne stumbled, falling suddenly into the cold, soft snow. She laughed. She liked snow, liked the feel of it, only it was important to brush it off quickly so the cold did not travel to the skin. First she would sit up, then she would stand and then...

She saw the wolf. Smelled her. This white world had no smell, but the wolf did – a rank, dog-slobber stench. The creature was yellow-eyed, all sinew, no fat this deep in winter. Ravenous, and pregnant. Anne was fresh meat – a happy bonus in the frozen world of the wolf.

Anne heard herself scream, the sound given up from deep in her chest, as the wolf sprang. The animal's weight hit her and teeth, hard yellow teeth, ripped and connected within her throat; blood, blood was everywhere. White pain, white snow and blood, a sea of blood, soft red blood. How could blood be so soft?

The wolf was shaking her now, shaking Anne's shoulder. Addressing her, whilst ripping at her tender flesh.

'Anne? Anne, all is well. Anne?'

Yes, perhaps all would be well. Dying was easy; she'd always known that.

Anne sighed. These were the last things she would ever feel; she allowed her hands to pat the soft red snow as her body flopped this way and that, shaken by the wolf as the creature went about her work.

'Anne? Wake now, sweetheart. Wake!'

It was the counterpane – red silk and goose down, that was all. Her hand was white against it and there was no blood.

'No blood?'

Deborah, Anne's foster-mother, swallowed acid fear as she held the girl tight against her own body. 'No blood. All's well now.'

The dream had gone but the forest had not quite left Anne. She still saw the footprints leading her on. Old footprints, lost in the snow. The girl closed her eyes against tears as Deborah kissed her brow, soothed damp, tangled hair back from her face.

Anne knew who the man was now. Edward Plantagenet.

'Will you pray before the break-fast?'

Deborah's tone was carefully brisk, formal, as she tidied the bed. Anne was glad, suddenly, that her foster-mother – her housekeeper in the eyes of the world – was practical. She was right. It was time to begin the day, time to leave the night world, and there was much to be done as autumn approached winter. They must also think about protecting the farm from brigands, in these uncertain times. For that they would need money.

Anne sat up, huddling the bedclothes around her bare shoulders. It was dark still but the branch of candles on the shelf beside the fire made a brave show of challenging the gloom, as did the fire itself on its newly built hearth.

'Yes, I should like to pray with the household. But I've slept late. Perhaps I'm the last down and they're all about their work already?'

Deborah, splashing hot water from a ewer into the washing bowl by the fire, smiled at the girl in the great bed.

'Do not distress yourself – we've all been working hard these weeks with the harvest. You most of all and–' She'd been about to say, 'you needed a good sleep' but stopped herself. There'd been far too many nightmares recently, as this last night showed.

Anne was determined the wolf's shadow would not enter her daylight world. Slipping down from the high mattress, she groped on the boards beneath the bed for her felt house-slippers. 'And little Edward?' Anne shivered, naked, towards the fire and the comfort of the dressing mantle – an extravagance from her former life.

'In the kitchen. A matter of new bread, I think. He could smell it when he woke.'

Both women laughed and the dark air moved and shifted with the sound. Anne's son, the boy she called her nephew, was three, though tall for his age, quick and speaking well. She was proud that many people, first meeting him, thought him at least five. She would laugh and say, 'Ah, yes. It's the good food he gets here. He grows like a weed outside the town. Boys need space.'

There was always comfort in the ritual of washing and dressing for Anne and Deborah. It was almost the only time during the day that they could expect to be alone together; that was, if the noisy boy they both so deeply loved was not bouncing around on the great bed, demanding that they both hurry, hurry, down to the kitchen and break-fast.

'House dress, or fine?'

'House dress, Deborah. We've much to do today.'

Anne avoided her foster-mother's glance. Their current situation was her responsibility and it weighed on her. Hoping for greater freedom outside the narrow life of the city, she'd brought them all to this little farm beyond the walls of Brugge. Yet now that war, rumoured and actual, was spreading through Europe she could not avoid the uncertainty of their situation. There were hard questions to be asked. And there were no easy answers.

Preoccupied, Anne washed herself quickly in the

warming air. Light from candles and the fire touched her body like a loving hand. She was gracefully made, with curving hips, a straight well-muscled back, high delicate breasts with tawny rose nipples – larger for having had a child – and strong, slender arms and legs from all the work she did.

Deborah sighed and turned away to find the girl a house dress. There were so many things they did not speak of any more. Marriage, that was what Anne needed. A real flesh-and-blood marriage, not an insubstantial, passionate dream that receded, day by day, into enchanted mist. Marriage was an alliance, a contract designed for mutual aid and support between a man and a woman; such a contract would protect Anne and the boy and her household as the constant dangerous wrangling between Burgundy and France escalated. It was a shame, and a waste, that nearly two years since their last meeting, her foster-daughter still yearned for the one man she could not have. Edward, the English king; Edward Plantagenet, her son's father. A thousand miles away over the sea, but closer than thought to Anne – always closer than thought.

But things changed when they needed to and there was an unexpected cause for new hope in their lives. Last night, very late, Leif Molnar had arrived from Sluys – too late to talk, except to say he'd come from Sir Mathew. Perhaps Leif brought Anne a solution? Perhaps they would all go back to London, to Sir Mathew's house, until the wrangling between France and Burgundy resolved itself? Yet England too was in turmoil. There was even talk that Edward Plantagenet might lose his throne. Perhaps nowhere was safe any more?

Deborah took a house dress down from its peg on the wall and shook it vigorously. Concentrate on the moment, banish gloom with hard work. 'The worsted? It's clean still. Which sleeves would you like?'

'You choose, Deborah. I don't mind.'

The kirtle was designed for work and not for show, but it was still a pretty thing. Dark red, it had several pairs of sleeves that could be swapped depending on mood. Deborah, thinking the day would be sullen, chose a set in cheerful crocus yellow, piped with blue to match the blue lacings of the dress. She knew that Anne liked colour, particularly as the days drew in. The older woman also found a linen chemise for her daughter. Anne appreciated the warmth and durability of her own good woollen cloth, but was sensitive to its itch against her skin. She always had been, even as a little girl.

Footed hose, a practical luxury, were laid up in a fruitwood coffer. These would be tied beneath the knee with ribbon. Lastly, there was an apron of forest-green serge and a thick shawl, its warp bright blue wool with a startling weft of yellow silk.

Helping the girl dress, Deborah worked, crab-wise, towards her design for the future. 'So, what do you think our neighbours will ask for the plough land?'

As Deborah laced the kirtle, Anne stared out towards the first faint light in the east.

'I'm not certain. Perhaps I'll not offer much coin at all. An annuity might be better – for them

27

and for us.'

Deborah tied the blue laces into a serviceable double bow where the bodice joined the skirt.

'Do you think mother and son will agree? It's her dower land, isn't it?'

'I don't know what Meinheer Landers' mother expects. He'd be more interested in money paid now, of course. But if I can bring them to accept an annuity, she'll have an income against her expenses now that she lives in his house. That will help them both and we will not have to give so much when we sign the contract. I have plans for that land – it will return the value of an annuity tenfold when it's used properly. River land is always good soil.'

Deborah finished dressing her daughter and returned to pummeling the high goose-down pillows energetically. She was determined to be positive. Perhaps speaking of the future of the farm would open a way to talk more broadly about other things. 'What will you grow there?'

Anne looked up from tying the ribbons on her stockings. 'Crocus. Saffron crocus. I believe it will do very well: good soil, water close by. There's always a ready market for saffron and the flowers are so pretty. Perhaps we can increase your physic garden too? Comfrey, and the plants that like rich soil. Angelica? That would sell well if we candied it in honey. We can use the knowledge you've given me.'

Anxiety flashed into Deborah's eyes.

Anne laughed. 'I mean the plant lore. I've already talked to the potter in the village. I want him to make me little bottles with stoppers. And little pots. We can make face washes and creams for the ladies of the court here, such as I made for the queen, and sell them.' Briefly she paused, thinking of Elizabeth Wydeville, the queen of England. Her enemy. A flicker of compassion touched her. It would not be easy being queen in England now.

She shrugged, moving on with an effort, smiling brightly. 'Beauty will come from beauty, you'll see.'

Deborah nodded as she finished smoothing the coverlet on the bed. Anne made the most unlikely farmer. She'd bought her farmstead last spring, after some months of haggling. The River Zwijn formed one of its boundaries, but the farm buildings and the home orchard had been shamefully neglected. Nevertheless, Anne saw the value of the access to Brugge that the river would give her and had walked every chain of the land, carefully noting the deep soil, the dense woods – good foraging for pigs in autumn – and the south-facing meadows.

The previous owner, a wealthy peasant, had bought individual strips of this good land long ago from his own impoverished lord and combined them into substantial fields – a forward-thinking departure from usual practice. But age and sickness had meant the old man had lost interest and the farm had slid into neglect and debt, both of which his son had inherited with the land when his father died. Yet Anne had seen that cows did well on these meadows and where cows were happy, wealth came from the earth. But Deborah knew none of this would have been enough for her foster-daughter if the place had not been beautiful also.

'Well, it is a good plan if you can bring Mein-heer Landers to accept it on behalf of his mother. Now, there is another matter of which we should speak–'

A loud crash came from below, followed by a woman screaming, then the terrified howl of a child.

'Edward!'

Anne ran from the room and down the wooden stairs to the kitchen, where she found her son hiding amongst the skirts of the cook, Lisotte. He was sobbing but unharmed.

It was another matter for the stranger lying on the flagged floor, blood a veil for his face.

'He came through the door so quickly, with a sword, and there was the boy...' The cook was wavering on her feet from shock. 'And I had this, so...'

Lisotte saw the moment again, all too vividly. She'd been using the long poker to stoke the fire under the three-legged pot when the stranger threw the door open, entering from the dark with a drawn sword in his hand. Her first thought had been to protect the child. The result lay before them.

Edward ran to Anne. She scooped him up and he hid his face in her neck. She felt his heart pound in the fragile chest though he'd stopped crying. 'There now, my darling. I have you, I have you.'

She kissed her son and held him tight, wrapping his small body in her arms and using her own to shield him from the sight of the man on the floor.

'Now, Edward, you must go with Deborah. I need to speak to Lisotte. Sit, Lisotte. Come, here on the settle.'

Edward patted Anne's face, concerned. 'You alright? You frighten?'

Anne's heart lurched with love. He was terrified of the man and what had happened, but he was more worried for her. *Please, never let him lose that kindness. Let him grow to be a kind man.* It was a silent, passionate prayer as Anne carried the boy to her foster-mother.

'Take him. And find Leif Molnar. Quickly!'

'I am here, lady.'

Three strides from the open door and the Dane was kneeling beside the intruder. The man's sword lay where it had fallen. Leif Molnar removed it and glanced towards Deborah. 'Take the child, woman. Go!'

Deborah did not think to contradict him. Scooping the boy up on her hip, she hurried away.

Leif looked at Anne. 'Lady, we must speak with this man. He cannot die before we know more.'

Lisotte gave a horrified sigh and slumped off the settle in a faint. Anne just managed to catch her before her head hit the flags.

The girl nodded. 'Do it. I agree.' There could be no pity in these war-plagued times.

Outside the kitchen door, a butt collected water from the red-tiled roof. Leif removed the plank cover quickly, smashed the first thin ice of autumn and filled a leather bucket. He was back beside the unconscious man in a moment and threw the freezing water full into his face and

31

open mouth. The effect was instant and violent. The intruder vomited red water and jerked on the floor like a fish in a boat.

Anne turned away, close to retching herself, but when she looked back the stranger's eyes were open, though he was groaning.

'Who are you? What do you want?' Leif spoke quietly to the man, but he'd hauled him to a sitting position, his knife against the stranger's Adam's apple.

The man swallowed and coughed, straining away from the blade as he tried to speak.

'I come from the king for Lady Anne de Bohun. Urgent. No time. Must speak, must...' His eyelids flickered and his eyes rolled upwards.

Anne leapt to her feet, pulling Leif's knife away from the man's throat.

There was only one king in Anne's life.

Edward Plantagenet.

'Sweet Christ, he's a messenger! Ah God, no, he must not die. Leif, more water. Quickly!'

As the Dane ran to the door, Anne knelt beside the man. He was a soldier; she could see the ringmail beneath his surcoat. Unwittingly, Lisotte had struck at the only place a woman could have damaged him: his unprotected face and head. Light from the fire showed an open gaping crescent above the man's right temple; amongst the blood, it was possible to see the broken white bone of his skull.

Anne searched the man's body, looking for a written message. There was nothing. The realisation was a bitter one: this man carried information for her, certainly, but it was in his head. The head that Lisotte had broken like a nutshell.

'Oh, please wake. Do not die. Tell me what he said to you. Tell me, tell me...'

She rocked the man's big body as she knelt beside him, as if he'd been her own child; pressed one corner of her apron hard against his wound to stop the blood. Light from the fire touched the edge of a small medal on a chain around his throat. A crucifix?

'Thor's hammer, lady.'

Anne looked up. 'Thor? Who is Thor?'

'One of the old gods. My people worship him still, though the church thinks otherwise.' For a moment Leif grinned, though it was a mere flash of white teeth and did not reach his eyes. 'This man is Thor's servant.'

Surprise replaced fear. To worship other gods than the Christian one, to be a pagan in these times, was not only remarkable, it was very dangerous. Anne and Deborah lived with that knowledge each waking day of their lives.

'But he is English. He's wearing York colours.'

The seaman shrugged as he inspected the filthy tunic, murrey-red quartered with blue. 'Lady, it is the truth. English or not, this man belongs to Thor. He would not wear the hammer, otherwise.'

Anne looked more closely at the medal. It was crudely made, but yes, it *was* a hammer, not a cross, though the shapes, quickly seen, were similar. The fire sparked and belched smoke; she coughed and turned her head away. And, in that moment, something glittered beneath Leif's half-opened shirt.

'You have this sign as well?' Anne's eyes were very wide.

Leif smiled at her amazement. 'It was how I was raised. I am his servant also.'

The man in the girl's arms stirred and spoke, though his eyes were closed. It was as if a corpse had spoken. 'As are we all his servants when war comes. But, lady, you must help the king.'

'How? How can I help the king?' Anne pleaded. 'What does he want from me?'

'Truth, from those who deal in lies.'

One breath more and the man was still.

'No! No, come back to me. What do you mean? Come back!'

Leif bent and lifted the messenger out of Anne's arms. Big as the soldier was, Leif looked like a man carrying his sleeping son.

'No use, lady. He spoke from the fields of death. Now he has gone farther and we cannot call him back.'

Anne clasped her hands together to stop them shaking. 'How can I answer this riddle?'

Leif turned back to her, the soldier in his arms. She could not see his face because he was silhouetted in the open doorway.

'We all seek truth, lady. I will help you find it.' Then he was gone.

Anne's knees shook when she tried to stand. What now? What should she do?

And how could she help the King of England?

# Chapter Two

It was close, too close, and it happened in sight of land.

The freezing wind locked Edward Plantagenet's jaw so tight it was difficult to speak, but he tried to look defiant for his men – the way a king should look going into battle. Of course he didn't know if he was, technically, a king at the current moment. Were you a monarch still if you fled your kingdom?

During the last mad days it had seemed the right thing to do. At the end of a week of crazy riding, little food, less sleep, he and his youngest brother, Richard of Gloucester, had commandeered a cog, the *Norwich Lass*, in Kings Lynn – they'd fought their way across the country to the coast and the sea beckoned as a way of escape. What choice did they have with Warwick at their backs?

And here and now, right or wrong, they were about to fight again: on sea this time, not land. And none of them could swim. Was this the last, fatal, mistake after a campaign filled with mistakes? The one that would kill them all?

The *Norwich Lass* was sturdy but a cog is no seabird and she was wallowing now, trying hard to put about as the mighty Hanseatic carrack bore down upon them, having won the tacking duel in sight of the Dutch coast. How could he have for-

35

gotten that the ships of the Hanseatic League patrolled this northern sea so vigorously, seeing off English and French ships alike – or taking them as prizes?

What was done was done. Gutted from their days-long flight – running from Warwick and his other, turncoat, brother, George of Clarence – Edward Plantagenet summoned a last reserve of energy as he flexed stiffened shoulders, bracing his back and thighs for what would come. Then he found the words he needed and the means to say them.

'Richard, form them up! Archers, here, before me – fire only on command. Hastings and Rivers, the rear if you please. Gentlemen, swords. And now … Captain, we are ready.'

His voice was loud and clear and the hand that held his father's sword against the sky did not shake. A miracle.

Will Conyers, captain of the *Norwich Lass*, was exasperated. It was all very well for the king to say he and his tiny band of followers were ready to fight the appallingly obvious might of the Hanseatic League, but that wouldn't help much when the vessels came together. This contest was idiotically unequal. They were doomed.

The king, however, was apparently indifferent to their impending fate, as were his men. Obediently they shuffled themselves into a compact group on the slimy deck – a party of twenty or so, including no more than ten archers. None of them found it easy to catch the rhythm of the bucking ship but they drew their swords anyway and nocked their arrows, the archers praying the strings had not

36

been slackened by the flying sea.

Will shook his head and turned away from their folly. He could only muster a hasty 'My thanks, sire' before roaring for his men to haul on the yards harder, *harder*, and abusing the tillerman: 'Bring her round, round, you nun's bastard. I said bring her ROUND!' Made furious by terrified ineptitude, Will grasped the tiller himself and began to haul with all his considerable strength.

Slowly, so laboriously, the *Norwich Lass* finally answered, began to turn as she caught the wind. Sail suddenly taut, she leapt as if alive and bit down into the running sea, more nimble than Will Conyers had ever seen her. Perhaps she knew what faced them all and was trying to escape in her own way. But the captain had no time for gratitude.

'Guns! They've opened the ports!' came the cry.

Indeed they had. The *Danneborg*, immediately to starboard and four times the cog's size, had bronze bombards poking out in a line along her mighty flank.

'Down, all. *DOWN!*' Will roared.

Edward ignored the captain. 'Archers?' The men stood straighter, trying to brace themselves against the lurching deck. 'On my mark, high and fast and ... LOOSE!'

A good archer fires fifteen arrows in the space of one minute, and these were good. The last of Edward's own Welsh guard, they'd made the mad dash from Nottingham across Lincolnshire beside him, in company with his most loyal friends and supporters: his brother, Richard of Gloucester; William, Lord Hastings, High Chamberlain of England; and his brother-in-law, Lord Rivers.

Now here they were, facing death once more, even so close to the coast of the Low Countries and safety.

The English arrows hit the deckmen of the Hanseatic carrack with a sighing, lethal whine, proving what Edward already knew: his archers themselves were the true weapons, not their bows. At one with the yew as it bent and sang, they fired as regularly, as rhythmically, as the workings of one of his mechanical clocks. And they did enough damage for their opponents to falter, for some of the cannon crew to misfire. And then, when the helmsman was hit on the castellated deck and the captain winged where he stood bellowing orders, the carrack lurched and lost the wind.

It was enough, just enough, and not a moment too soon, for the archers had loosed nearly all their arrows.

Will Conyers crossed himself, astonished, and, for a moment, thought of his wife waiting at home back in Lynn; she'd be none too pleased by this adventure. Even as he bellowed at the crew to trim the sail again and swung the tiller hard to port, he made himself a promise. He'd sell the *Lass*, go in with Nan's dad on the alehouse. He'd had enough of the sea. Yes, there was a message in this mad adventure with Edward Plantagenet. Be damned if he'd lose his ship or his life for a man who'd gambled his throne in this gathering disaster of his own making!

All the while, as Will hauled the *Lass* about and more surely into the wind, he talked to her as if she were a horse or a woman. She was a tricky thing and might be offended by his traitorous thoughts of selling. 'Come up, my girl, that's the way. Now bite down, bite down harder and ... take the wind!'

And as she did, the men on board cheered and stamped, hoarse with relief as the little cog left the carrack wallowing in her modest wake, their shouts drowned in the slap of the sea, the howl of rushing air in the full belly of the sail. There, less than a league away, was the little Dutch port of Alkmaar and never was a sight more welcome.

Edward cheered with the rest of them and felt the fear leach away as his heartbeat slowed. Their luck would turn now, please God. Charles of Burgundy, his brother-in-law, held the Low Countries as part of his dukedom. Soon they would be amongst friends and have time to think their way through the puzzle that England had become now that he'd fled the country. He would need money, men and arms to restore his patrimony, restore his throne.

And for all of these, he needed help. Someone to intercede with Charles on his behalf, to make his case for assistance.

A messenger had been despatched from York more than ten nights since. Had he found her? Dear Lady in Heaven, had the man found Anne de Bohun?

# Chapter Three

'I will not go. No! Not until I know where the king is and if he is safe.'

The scene in the queen's rooms at Westminster Palace was chaotic. Elizabeth Wydeville's chamber women and her lady companions stumbled over each other, cursing, as they shoved clothes, veils, linen and jewels into coffers and boxes, terror making fingers clumsy and tempers short. The queen herself sat immoveable on her chair of state, her straight back rigid with defiance.

'But, Your Majesty, we have word that the army is outside the wall. The Londoners and the city will not hold them for long. Earl Warwick and–'

The queen's personal chamberlain, John Ascot, gulped and, swallowing air, choked into a fit of coughing. It was the stress of this terrible day – and the fact that he must tell the queen the truth.

'Clarence? Go on, man, say his name. My husband's brother, *that traitor Clarence*, is with him, isn't he? *Isn't he?*'

John Ascot was pale and sweating with the effort of persuading his pregnant mistress to leave the palace. For her sake, and his, one of them had to stay calm, though it was hard.

'Your Majesty, I understand that the duke does accompany the earl. This may be a good thing–'

'A good thing; master chamberlain? *A good thing!*'

The chamberlain winced at the queen's tone but forced himself to meet her frigid glance. He bowed as deeply as he could and spoke the shocking truth; there was no time for niceties now.

'The duke is popular with the London commons, Your Majesty. That may buy us a little time. But you must come with me immediately. For the sake and safety of the prince still to be born. And his father.'

Elizabeth Wydeville closed her eyes so the chamberlain would not see the sudden tears. Unconsciously, her hands clenched around her greatly swollen belly. The child kicked vigorously beneath her fingers.

'There is no other place?'

She spoke so low, John Ascot had to lean forward to hear her words. His mistress was a difficult woman, little loved by those who served her, but unexpectedly he was touched by more than duty. There was despair in that whisper.

He shook his head. 'I dearly wish I could offer you another refuge, but you and the prince to come will be safe there. The holy abbot, Dr Milling, has offered his own personal quarters to Your Majesty and...' – he looked around at the women in the chamber, all of whom were now listening breathlessly – '...some of your women.'

Elizabeth opened her eyes at that and skewered him with her glance. 'How many?'

'Five, Your Majesty.'

There was instant of stricken silence, then a low agitated tide of noise rose higher, and higher.

'*Five?* That is impossible!' The queen's tone was implacable.

41

John Ascot turned to face the queen's women. 'It must be so. There is no room for more.' He caught the eye of the queen's mother, Jacquetta of Luxembourg, with a pleading glance. *Help me!*

The duchess, who had been supervising the queen's women as they packed, was not the daughter of a great nobleman for nothing. She clapped her hands for silence, and was rewarded. Her, they respected.

'Very well. You, you and you. And you – and you, there, holding the green veil.' Jacquetta pointed around the room at individual women. 'You five will accompany the queen and myself.' A bright glance stopped John Ascot who had been about to protest. Jacquetta made six. 'Hurry now, we must finish packing for the queen and leave immediately for sanctuary in the abbey.'

The train of the duchess's black velvet gown was encrusted with silver embroidery and very heavy; normally at least two ladies were required to hold it up as she walked. Now, she swept the material up in one hand, as if it had been silk sarcenet, and held out the other to the queen.

'Come, my daughter. It is time. Let me help you; lean on my arm.'

The queen exhaled a deep breath; the sigh became a sob between clenched teeth. 'I can't. I can't stand.'

'Chamberlain?'

One on each side of her, Elizabeth Wydeville's bulky body was levered out of her Presence chair by her mother and John Ascot.

As they helped her walk slowly from the bed chamber, past rows of kneeling, crying women,

Elizabeth cast a glance back towards the massively carved chair. Who would sit in it next?

And would she ever see the king, her husband, again?

## Chapter Four

'Master Conyers, I thank you for the service you have given. But I am embarrassed. We left Lynn so quickly that I have no coin.'

Edward looked at the small band of men clustered around him on the sturdy wharf at Alkmaar. The land still tipped and swung; it made no difference that the earth lay quietly beneath their feet. The king didn't want to beg money from his friends; they'd need every groat, penny and angel in the next little while.

'Which would you rather have? This?' Edward pulled a ring from his right hand, a heavy gold band set with a bevelled jasper in which had been carved his crest, a rayed sun in splendour. 'Or this?' The king swung his riding cloak from his shoulders. Cut from expensive broadcloth dyed a rare, lively blue, the garment was lined with winter marten, with the same fur forming a deep band at the hem. It was joined at the throat by a chain of silver gilt studded with emeralds.

Will Conyers hadn't wanted to come on this voyage but what did a man say to a bunch of lords who stepped onto his boat one blustery autumn morning, slung around with weapons, and demanded, 'Take us to the Low Countries'? Nothing, unless he was a fool.

So, he'd let them on board his modest trading cog and put out to sea, though Nan, his wife, hearing of it, had run down to the harbour too late to stop them. There'd be a lot of explaining to do once he was back. If he got back.

And now here they were and they couldn't pay him; not properly.

Yet gold *was* gold – that seal ring would be worth some sort of price to the Jews – and the king's cloak was a very fine thing also. Certainly he could sell it, if he chose. And if he didn't, what a fine sight he'd make at home on market day. If Nan allowed him to keep it.

He laughed suddenly and Edward, trying not to shiver in the brisk wind from the sea, laughed with him. 'Well, master, which is it to be?'

The captain of the *Norwich Lass* found himself bowing and was surprised. He'd never felt any real allegiance to this king in faraway London, even though the Rivers, the queen's family, had connections in Lynn. Maybe, in the end, that slender thread of affinity counted for something.

'I'll take the cloak, liege. I've a mind to dress like a king when I get home.'

There was a moment's shocked silence and then they found themselves laughing, the whole of Edward's party, at the man's audacity. Laughing, almost sobbing, after the tension, the fear, the fury of the last weeks. It was good to laugh, for now the future must be faced. A future as exiles.

'I count it a fair bargain now that you have brought us to this place. Alkmaar, you called it?'

44

The captain bowed. Then, as the king dumped the cloak into his hands, the man nearly dropped it with sudden knowledge of his own temerity.

'And what do the people of Alkmaar do?'

The king was determined to sound cheerful as he cast his eyes around the little town huddling at the water's edge, amongst dunes that stretched away north and south.

Master Conyers spoke cautiously as he measured the weight of the cloak. 'I believe they make cheese, sire.'

The king glimmered a brief smile. 'Ah, well then, that would explain the smell. And I had thought it was rotting fish!'

His men laughed again, giddily. Their ribs ached. Edward, too, guffawed and clapped a few on the shoulders as if he'd made the best joke in the world.

A girl, a servant, out early to collect bread for her family also giggled as she passed the group. They looked so odd: filthy, and yet well dressed at the same time. But their weapons made her nervous.

Her laughter triggered the image of another girl's face for Edward Plantagenet. *Anne*. It was a sigh that found a name before the king could prevent it. Could she see him now, if he sent his thoughts to her?

'Did you say something, Your Majesty?'

William Hastings, Lord High Chamberlain of England, suppressed a grimace. Already it sounded false, calling Edward a king.

His master, alert to the quickly disguised uncertainty, smiled brightly. 'I must be tired, William, when thoughts speak aloud.'

45

Edward inspected his sword and wiped the blade against his surcoat; he could not allow treacherous sea water to linger on the steel and damage its edge. 'Form them up, William. But first, has anyone a spare cloak? This wind is cutting.'

'A cloak for the king?'

The party of men rummaged amongst their few remaining possessions. Richard of Gloucester, Edward's youngest brother, hauled out a spare riding cloak. He'd managed to hang on to his saddle bags when they'd boarded the cog in Lynn; the whole party would be grateful for their contents in the days to come.

'Have this, brother. It's sadly creased, of course, but serviceable. Not up to your usual standards, though.'

The brothers shared a look and a laugh. Edward was famous for his love of clothes.

'Oh, I don't know, Richard. Green has always suited me, so I'm told.'

As Edward swirled the heavy garment around his shoulders and slid the chain through the eyelets at the throat, the softness of the fine cloth, the waxed silk of its lining and, most of all, the deep forest green brought more pictures into his mind – Anne dressed in green. Anne reaching out to him. Anne kissing him. Anne lying with him as he...

'The party is ready, sire.'

*Ready for the future*, said Richard of Gloucester's confident tone. *Ready for you to lead us, brother.*

Edward smiled just as confidently and turned to face his companions. 'Well now, here's a pass.'

Men raised their heads to catch the king's

words and those who'd been sitting on the walls of the dock scrambled to their feet.

'And I'm very annoyed.'

One or two laughed at the ironic sally.

'Yes, very annoyed. *Mortally* annoyed.'

The king's tone was savage and his sword hissed out of its scabbard in a flashing wheel of light, startling the seabirds, crying, into the bright air.

'We will take our country back, hand over hand.'

Less than twenty men to regain England? Edward's spell was strong; not one of his companions looked around in doubt.

'We have friends, good friends. And we've been driven here by traitors. Traitors do not prosper. But in the future, you who are here with me today will want for nothing; neither shall your families.'

The king turned back to Will Conyers. 'Captain, I thank you for your help and for your courage. And for your fine crew,' Edward raised his voice so the men on the *Norwich Lass* could hear what he said. 'You too, all of you, will have cause to be thankful for this voyage. Return home. And spread the news of our imminent return.'

Edward slid the sword back into its sheath and stalked off towards the town, his men falling in behind him, a compact and purposeful group.

Will Conyers shrugged uneasily as he watched Edward Plantagenet stride away. Lynn, where he came from, was a quiet place and the people of the small, prosperous town were unused to the tide of politics, but it was lapping high now, right to their very doors.

The captain crossed himself and turned back to face the sea. Perhaps he'd let folks know where

47

he'd been, perhaps not, though it would be harder to stop the crew talking. He was troubled. Would the new masters of England let him and his men lie safe in their beds if they heard he'd helped the former king?

Unconsciously, he stroked the precious cloak. Perhaps he could sell the knowledge he had? Then he discarded the thought. Dangerous to play both sides. Best lie low.

Will shaded his eyes against the sun rising in the east and turned for one last glimpse of Edward Plantagenet. The king and his party had almost reached the town square, where they were attracting astonished glances from the townsfolk for their fine clothing and their grim looks. But where would they go? And who would aid them? Brave words were all very well, but this king would need his friends, and plenty of them.

Twenty men couldn't take back a kingdom. Could they?

## Chapter Five

Duchess Margaret of Burgundy was missing her husband, away on campaign again against the French, always the French. She was doing her very best to appear calm and happy, which was hard. Her flowers had appeared again this morning.

Married for more than two years and still no pregnancy. This month she'd been so hopeful for she'd been nearly three weeks late, but bloody sheets this morning had withered those hopes. It must be that she was barren. Charles had already proved himself capable of children, with a daughter, Mary, from one of his previous marriages. Swallowing hard to prevent self-pitying tears, the duchess tried to concentrate on what her friend, Lady Anne de Bohun, was saying.

'...he died. There was nothing we could do. But he had a message for me, from the king, your brother, Duchess. Have you heard anything more?'

Margaret shook her head and signalled for her ladies to retreat a little so that she and Anne could speak privately.

'All I know is that England is in chaos. We had word from our ambassador in Westminster some weeks back that things were increasingly bad. Warwick is expected to land with his forces at any time.'

Why was it that Edward had never appreciated the extent to which he'd alienated Earl Warwick when he married Elizabeth Wydeville in secret, Margaret wondered. It had all begun then, and the animosity had only deepened with the descent of the queen's enormous and rapacious family onto the court. Edward had been a fool, led by lust, and now Margaret feared her brother would lose his kingdom for that mortal sin committed all those years ago.

'Ah, Lady Anne, I've felt so powerless at this distance. I had a letter from my brother a month ago, and even then he was quite certain he would engage with the earl and win. Duke Charles is away campaigning, as you know. Perhaps he will have more recent news when he returns.'

Margaret shook her head sadly. One of Edward's greatest qualities, and greatest weaknesses, was unfettered optimism: he believed everything would right itself in the end. Some called him unwilling to act because of it, but Margaret and Anne de Bohun both knew the king better. They knew he had faith that he could negotiate his way out of most problems. Often he was right. Now his sister prayed every night, most deeply and faithfully, that he was safe and his luck still held.

She smiled at her guest. 'You look weary, Lady Anne. Are you well?'

Anne shook her head. 'I have bad dreams so often these nights, Duchess.'

A thread of soft, cold air sighed through the cheerful room and the duchess felt its chill. She took a shaky breath and turned to look out over the gardens of the Prinsenhof, the fanciful, elegant castle in the centre of Brugge, which housed Charles of Burgundy's court when he or his duchess was in residence. Then she turned back to glance at her friend.

'Do you see my brother in your ... dreams?'

Friendship over several years had brought the duchess knowledge of Anne's unique gifts. Dangerous knowledge. For them both.

Anne nodded and spoke very quietly. 'Yes, Your Grace. I do.' She gazed down at her hands clasped gently in her lap, tried not to twist her fingers with fear. The strain shadowed her face.

'What do you see?' Margaret's tone was urgent. 'Anne, tell me. Please!'

Anne released a long breath, her eyes far away.

The hairs on Margaret's arms stood up. 'I am fearful of what I see, Duchess. Danger, all around him. Blood. Every night lately and…'

She looked down again, trying to smooth all expression from her face, but the duchess was too quick for her.

'Is it just dreams, Anne? Or do you see him at … other times?'

Sorcery. The word hovered unsaid, with the power to ruin both their lives.

'I do not ask for this, Duchess. It comes unbidden.'

Margaret, Duchess of Burgundy, was well-liked by her subjects, but she had been one of the 'Ladies of England'. Command, when she chose to use it, came effortlessly.

'Therefore, Lady Anne, it must come to advance God's purpose for us all. Tell me what you see. Is he alive?'

Anne shivered. 'Yes, he lives. But he was hurt. I think he nearly died…'

How to describe the moment? She had been standing in her farmyard, stirring cloth in a vat of mordant, when it happened. Instant darkness, sand and salt water in her mouth – and his. Choking, vision failing, she'd tried to suck air into lungs collapsing beneath the weight of the sea. Men's distant screams as everything, all sight, all sound, was absorbed by the violent water. Then … agony! Hauled upwards by the arms, the limbs nearly jerked from their sockets against the strength of the tide that held her – his – legs and feet with the strength of death.

'Where? What happened?'

The duchess's tone was sharp and the soft hum of voices around them paused. Margaret looked up quickly and laughed. 'Come, ladies. I'll tell you all Lady Anne's delicious gossip in a moment.' An answering tinkle of laughter ran around the room as heads bent back to embroidery. Margaret turned her strained and brilliant smile towards her friend, murmuring, 'And so?'

'Men were riding very fast down a beach as the tide came in. The king was with them. They tried to race the sea but the king's horse floundered and he fell. There was quicksand and–'

Anne could not stop the tears of terror and anguish. She turned her face away to hide her distress while Margaret, sensitive as always, said loudly, 'Yes, a very early autumn, I fear. Who would have thought it after the great heat of the summer? The first frost has turned all the roses quite black.'

Anne stared into the sun outside the casements, hoping the light would burn back her tears. Why did she feel like crying all the time? Fear's bony fingers gripped her. Perhaps she was denying knowledge of Edward's death? Was that what the tears truly meant?

'We must send to him,' Margaret whispered. 'Find him. Find out what has happened.'

Somewhere from the distance, a tide of sound washed towards the duchess's private quarters. Shouts and running feet. A moment later there was a thump on the solar door and a voice outside announced the last man on earth the duchess expected to see.

'Your Grace!' Margaret jumped to her feet. Only

years of training suppressed the passionate need she felt to run to her husband and leap into his arms.

Brown as good leather, bright-eyed and filthy from the long ride, Charles of Burgundy smiled at his wife, a glancing, complicit look that said 'I understand'. He advanced into the room, bowing charmingly left and right. 'Ladies, sweet ladies, I must ask you to leave the duchess and me alone.'

Then he noticed Anne. 'Ah, Lady de Bohun. Perhaps you might stay?'

Charles of Burgundy herded his wife's laughing women through the solar's double doors before closing them himself. The brightness in his face ebbed and he looked like the man he was – exhausted, stretched beyond bearing.

'I wanted to tell you myself. I did not trust a messenger.'

Margaret sat suddenly. Outside, in the garden, a gentle wind was nudging leaves from the trees. The last bees of summer lent an air of false, busy contentment as they robbed pollen from the fading flowers.

'Is he dead?' Anne spoke Margaret's thought, unbidden.

Charles shook his head and strode over to a table where a silver flask of wine and goblets were arranged. 'No, not that. But he's lost the country. He fled England more than a week ago. I've had word that he's landed and is marching south towards the Binnenhof at s'Gravenhague. I've sent people to find him and escort him so that soon he will be safe with our governor there, Louis de Gruuthuse. No doubt Edward means to rest his men at the Binnenhof before continuing his journey to us. We shall see...'

He swung back to face his wife, a brilliantly polished beaker glinting in his hand. The room was silent as he swallowed the wine to the lees and belched discreetly.

'And?'

Margaret was white with strain and Anne forgot to breathe as both women waited to hear what the duke would say.

Charles of Burgundy closed his eyes. He had been riding for most of the night. He wanted his wife's counsel, and her body, but first, perhaps, food and sleep might restore his judgment. He sighed deeply.

'Ah, wife. I know what you want me to say. And you, Lady Anne.' Charles knew Anne still loved Edward, though he had no idea if the king reciprocated her passion after all this time.

'Edward has always been good to Burgundy, husband.'

'Indeed he has. That is certain.'

Briefly, wolfishly, the duke smiled as he looked at his wife – his gift from the kingdom of England. She was beautiful, and he enjoyed her body and her company, but that was a bonus. She had brought Flanders as a dowry when they married; even more importantly, she was the living symbol of his duchy's alliance with England through her brother, the king. Now that alliance was gone. Finished. The pieces on the chessboard of Europe would rearrange themselves once more and it might be beyond his power to control the direction of the play.

Earl Warwick had driven Edward Plantagenet out of England, which gave France the power to interfere with English politics – through Louis XI's manipulation of the vain and insecure earl. A very dangerous situation indeed. England and France banded together in a new alliance would pose a truly powerful threat to Burgundy. A threat he might not be able to counter. So would he help his brother-in-law regain the English throne? Would he? Or was it already too late?

'Therefore, will you assist King Edward, Your Grace?'

Charles laughed, an unexpectedly happy sound. 'Ah, Lady Anne, why am I not surprised by your candour?' He shook his head, avoiding an answer, instead addressing Margaret almost casually as he yawned. 'Louis must be enjoying all this, wife. He's got what he wanted.'

Louis XI, King of France, was Burgundy's – and the duke's own, very personal – enemy. For it was Louis who stood between Burgundy as a duchy and Burgundy as a kingdom, with Charles its king. King Charles I of Burgundy. It had a good ring to it. But without the help of England as his ally whilst he waged a slow war in the Lowlands against France, would it ever happen?

Charles must choose his next move very carefully. How strong was Warwick, now that he had caused Edward to flee with Louis's help? And would the magnates and the baronage of England support the earl if he put that fool, George of Clarence, Edward's turncoat younger brother, on the throne? Warwick had at last succeeded in marrying his whey-faced daughter Isabel to the young duke, hadn't he? That was a throw of the dice towards creating another royal family for the country to follow.

Yet what about Margaret of Anjou and this new alliance with her old enemy, the earl? She had borne a son to the former king, Henry VI, and now that boy would be reinstated into the succession of England as Prince of Wales, most assuredly. Where would that leave Edward's brother, Clarence, married to Isabel or not?

Charles closed his eyes for one weary moment but the automatic speculation did not stop.

Would it advantage him, and Burgundy, to support Edward or should he desert his brother-in-law and try to make peace with Warwick, Margaret of Anjou and Clarence? Would that be the wisest course for Burgundy in the long run? Would it keep Louis at bay a little longer? The duke yawned deeply and blinked, the image of a man exhausted past all knowing.

Margaret hurried to his side. 'Ah, husband, what you need most now is your bed.' She did not say sleep; she was hoping for more than that.

Anne de Bohun watched as the duchess put her arm around her husband's shoulders. Perhaps it was the concern of a wife, or perhaps it was because Margaret yearned to touch Charles, touch any part of him, since she'd hungered so long in his absence. Anne understood that. She picked up the skirt of her gown and walked behind the duke and duchess towards the solar's doors. The question had not been answered, though it hovered in the air like phantom thunder. They would have to wait to learn more of the duke's intentions.

Anne tried to be glad for her friend as she paced behind her and the duke. Margaret's husband had returned to her unharmed and that was a joyful thing. Why then did she, herself, feel such sadness – indeed, envy – as she saw the duke slip his arm around his wife's graceful waist? In truth, she knew the answer.

Some years ago, she had chosen to leave England, to go into exile. She had left Edward Plantagenet behind and, gods knew, though it had been a wrenching choice, she'd believed it was the right one. But seeing lovers together again after a long absence was hard. She was young and she yearned for her man, just as her friend the duchess did.

And then Anne remembered what Charles had said. Edward was now within the duke's domains.

Hope bloomed in her heart. Dizzy, fluttery hope.

She would see him again. Soon. If she allowed that to happen.

And if she did, she would meet once more the three companions who walked beside her when she was with Edward Plantagenet. Fear and joy. And love. Which would be strongest this time?

## Chapter Six

'Where are we, Hastings? This is charming countryside, but I've had enough of it.' Edward was cold and hungry, as they all were, but he kept his tone light.

William Hastings, swaddled to the eyes in a stained hunting cloak, turned back and grinned at the king, his white teeth flashing in the gloom.

'There is good news, my liege. We're close. Only five leagues or so south down the coast to the walls of the Binnenhof and a warm welcome from the Sieur de Gruuthuse. This man says there's a good track all the way, with only a few fishing villages on the dunes. We can avoid them easily.'

The weary party of men had just reached an intersection of the farm track they were following with another. The light was fading rapidly and Hastings had been pleased to see a farmer trudging home from working his strips of land. It had been an odd conversation, an exchange composed of the few crumbs of Dutch possessed by the Englishman plus scraps of old High German and the farmer's one or two French phrases, but it had told William what he needed to know. By the Grace of God, they were close enough to s'Gravenhague and the Binnenhof, the erstwhile seat of the Counts of Holland, to reach it tonight.

William crossed himself gratefully. It had been a risk to ask for directions, but their case was urgent enough to gamble on information of their presence spreading, even from this most isolated place. If they could just get to the Binnenhof ahead of the news of their arrival, it would be worth it. He'd had little to trade for this welcome information, however, and that worried him. He'd given his last piece of coin to the man, an English threepenny bit, but it might not have been enough to buy a night's discretion. The coin had been good silver, though, that was something.

Truly God *did* move in enigmatic ways. In his previous life as England's chamberlain – such a short time ago – William had reformed the English currency against the abuse of corrupt coin dealers, who 'clipped' the edges of legitimate coins, mixing the stolen metal with lead or tin and issuing false coin. Such activities had caused confidence in the currency to plummet, with disastrous results for England, and for trade. But Hastings' work had put a stop to the practice, and the Dutch farmer, after biting the coin to test it for hardness, seemed to approve. William had almost laughed. Perhaps God had guided him to improve the metal weight of English coins just so they could command one night of silence from this Dutch farmer?

Amused by the oddness of the thought, William moved through the party of men, taking stock of their resources. There were only five horses amongst them all and that meant slow progress, even though the end of this weary journey was now so close. By their looks, and their silence as they waited for orders, the men were dangerously tired. After weeks of cold and dangerous fighting in England, they'd endured the hardships of a sea voyage and then walked south for two days with little food. Mostly they'd travelled at night – the nobles, including the king, taking turns to ride while the rest walked; during daylight hours they'd slept under their cloaks amongst the dunes, huddling together like dogs for warmth, not daring to light fires. By this morning what food they'd had was gone and the king had taken the decision to travel by daylight as well to make all speed. Perhaps the boldness had paid off. William fervently hoped so, but only the last leagues ahead would tell the case truly.

'So, my liege, if you would give the order?'

Edward slid down from the bony gelding he'd been jolting along on for some hours. 'Your turn, William. Up you get.'

Hastings protested. 'No, Your Majesty. I will not ride while you walk.'

'My legs could do with a stretch.' Edward smiled. 'Here, let me help you up.' He cupped his hands so William could mount more easily.

What he did not say, as he swung back to face his weary bunch of companions, was that he was more than grateful to ease his aching arse as well; the gelding's gait was particularly trying at a slow trot, which was all that could be managed if the men were to keep pace with the horses.

'Not long to go. My good friend the Sieur de Gruuthuse will make us a noble welcoming feast in his hall tonight.'

It was the slithering hiss that alerted them – the sound of steel being drawn from a metal scabbard – but too late. Edward's hand flew to the pommel of his own sword but he knew it was pointless.

'Drop your sword, messire.'

Edward's heart hammered painfully as he made out the number of men surrounding his own small band. How could they have been so careless, and so stupid? The crossroads was ringed by trees, many still in last leaf. It was a perfect hiding place for armed men and now they were caught.

His assailant repeated the request. 'Your sword, sir, if you please.'

Edward nodded reluctantly and carefully

extended his sword arm, his mind racing. The man had spoken in courteous French, presuming he was understood, and Edward was suddenly hopeful. Perhaps their captors did not know whom they had bailed up.

The Frenchman leaned down from his horse and twitched the blade out of the king's fingers. His eyes glittered in the gloom when he saw what he had.

'But this is a very good sword, messire. Where did you get it?'

The Frenchman spoke quietly; perhaps he did not want his men to hear. Suddenly it made sense. These men were outlaws, wolvesheads. Perversely, that gave Edward confidence.

'I will give it to you, and more besides, if you will help us.'

The leader of the wolfpack laughed heartily. *'If you will help us?* Us, help you! Now, that is the strangest thing I have heard in all the days of my life.'

Suddenly the man's sword was at Edward's throat. English hands went to English swords in a dangerous breath.

'I do not think it is for us to help you, messire. On the contrary.'

Confident he was backed by his men, the Frenchman leaned from his horse again and ripped Edward's expensive sword belt and scabbard from his body. Richard's riding cloak was about to follow when Edward whispered, 'Do not be a fool, my friend. You'll get more money in letting us live. *Draw!*'

Edward's bellow rang through the gloom and in

an instant the English were clamped around their king, knee to knee in a dense mass. The over-confident outlaw leader was suddenly in *their* midst, on his increasingly panicked horse. He was ringed by drawn blades, English blades, and the air was dizzy with the promise of blood.

The Frenchman sat back in his saddle and removed his sword from Edward's throat. 'Ah. *Touché*. Clever. And well disciplined.'

Edward held out his hand. 'My sword.'

After a moment, the Frenchman gave it to him, though his men protested loudly. He had no other choice.

'But this will not save you, sir, because, as you see, my condition as your ... guest can only be temporary.'

The outlaw had courage and Edward liked that, especially since he now had his own sword point at his former assailant's neck.

'Get down.' The king said it mildly, but when the Frenchman appeared not to understand, he repeated it in a frigid tone. 'I said, get down.'

The Frenchman shrugged and slid from his horse's back. 'And so, what now, Englishman?'

Edward smiled as he mounted the outlaw's horse. It was a much better animal than he'd been riding for the last few days, though thin. 'You depress me. I thought I spoke your language without accent.'

'Speak French like a Frenchman? Bah! English arrogance.'

Even off his horse, the little man was cocky, a bantam with formidable spurs. That too made Edward smile.

'Tell me your name, Frenchman. I should like to know it.'

'Before you die, Englishman?'

They were bantering now, quite enjoying themselves, while the men from both sides waited tensely to see what would develop.

'Hold him a little tighter, if you please, Richard.' The king gathered up the reins of the outlaw's rangy bay and settled himself comfortably into the saddle, adjusting the short stirrups to accommodate his own long legs. 'I repeat, messire, what is your name?'

'Julian de Plassy.' It was said with pride and the small Frenchman held himself straighter, puffing out his thin chest.

'Well now, Julian de Plassy, you bear an honourable name but you are engaged in a dishonourable occupation. Would you like me to help you change that?'

The Frenchman threw up his head, surprised, and the sallet he was wearing caught the light from the rising moon. His men pressed forward a pace, uncertain.

'No! Back,' he commanded, and the men paused.

'They obey you. You lead them well, it seems.'

The Frenchman nodded, his confidence undimmed. 'I repeat, Englishman, how can you help me?'

Edward laughed. 'Oh, I might know someone, who might know someone else. You know how it goes. But first, you must be our escort to s'Gravenhague tonight.'

The outlaw's eyes narrowed. 'And what would

our reward be if we agreed to protect you?' He said 'protect' with the most subtle of sneers.

The English pressed tighter, the points of their swords nudging the Frenchman in a way that was distinctly unfriendly.

'Your life will be your reward, Julian de Plassy. And the freedom of you and yours. I shall have the attainder against you lifted. I'm sure there is one.'

Julian de Plassy bowed ironically, in recognition. 'My lord is wise beyond all telling.'

The king grimaced. 'Not so wise as you might think. Yet I can tell you what the future holds, on this occasion. If God decides to call you home to his loving embrace, I can arrange that as his instrument on earth. However, a long life is better than a short one and God is merciful, even to you. You have this choice. Which is it to be, Julian de Plassy? Choose now.'

## Chapter Seven

Anne shivered. It was cold and dark in the still hour before dawn. She was on her knees beside her bed, praying for help and guidance.

Almost every silver penny, every English Angel, she possessed from her trading days in Brugge had been sunk into her small farm and its rebuilding. There were some precious furnishings in her house, including her bed and the great devotional portrait she'd commissioned from the German painter Hans Memlinc, but much else had been sold to buy the plough horses, the seed, the expensive wheeled plough and the labour she needed to work her land. She'd had plans, big plans, to make her farm prosper and to live a good and quiet life raising her son. All that seemed pointless now.

Last evening she'd had word from Duchess Margaret confirming that Edward *was* alive but that Charles of Burgundy had declined permission for him to come to Brugge. Worse, he'd forbidden his wife from going to her brother or aiding him in any way.

Anne opened her eyes into the candle-wavering darkness. Why? Why had Charles turned against Edward, his brother-in-law and friend? And what should she do – what *could* she do – to help Edward?

With the king deposed, perhaps she and her son would be safer in London. Elizabeth Wydeville was no longer queen and so perhaps, now, she would not hover in the darkness of Anne's dreams, an ever-present threat to the child Anne called her nephew?

But if Margaret of Anjou came back to England and Anne's own father, Henry VI, was restored, would Anne be welcome in her native country? Her half-brother, another Edward, would reign, but would Margaret acknowledge her husband's baseborn daughter, the granddaughter of Henry V, in her restored kingdom? Anne knew it was Margaret who had tried to kill her own mother, Alyce, all those years ago when she'd heard Alyce was pregnant with her husband's child. And now

Anne herself had a son with a king.

It was all so tangled. Anne closed her aching eyes. What should she do? What could she do?

'The timing is wrong.'

Anne slewed around towards the voice. Deborah was standing in the open doorway, a lantern held high.

'What makes you say that?'

Deborah looked back over her shoulder before she closed the door. She went to the fireplace and knelt to arrange kindling over the straw. 'Politics. And the news about the king last night. You must wait to hear more. Now is not the time for decisions.' She struck flint to the laid fire.

'But I need advice, Deborah. Badly. It's all so very complicated.'

Deborah smiled. 'Well then, here is my advice. First we dress. Then we eat. These things are simple. And after that? Then, we think.'

Anne's tiny workroom was the only truly private space in her busy home. Now, as a pale sun struggled to bring light to the world, Deborah arranged their breakfast on a low table in front of the sputtering fire there. The table was just large enough to support a deep bowl of fresh goat's-milk curd, a piece of hard cheese, a stone jar of pickled walnuts from Anne's own trees and fresh-baked flatbread from the brick oven Leif Molnar had just built in the kitchen yard.

Anne drew up a joint stool and held her hands to the flames; each morning now was a little colder than the last. She was glad of the warmth.

'I think of Edward all the time, Deborah. He

needs troops and money. And if the duke will not help him, I must.'

They were words that would seem scandalous if overheard. An unmarried woman yearning for her lover. Her married lover. For Edward was very married, to Elizabeth Wydeville, the queen of England, who had tried to murder Anne some years ago. Something of a tradition for the queens of England where their husbands' lovers were concerned.

Deborah held out her hand to her foster-daughter. At last Anne's silence had broken. 'Troops and money? These things cannot be my concern, or yours. Love is another matter.'

'But, Deborah, Edward needs money most of all, and soon, if he's to strike back at Warwick. He sent the messenger to me, remember? I feel so responsible that the man died before he could tell me what the king wanted. Whatever it is, Edward is relying on me. I have to think through this puzzle. I will not let him down.' Anne took a deep breath and turned to her foster-mother. 'I must sell the farm.'

Deborah, concentrating on filling horn beakers with their own ale, heated, spiced and brewed with honey from the hives in the old orchard, only half registered the words.

'What did you say?'

Anne spooned curd into Deborah's bowl and handed it to her, avoiding her eyes. 'I said, I must sell this farm.'

Deborah was deeply upset. What difference could the price of one small farmstead make in helping Edward's cause? 'But what about all your

67

hard work? And the boy? What will become of little Edward – or, indeed, you – if you sell this place?'

'Deborah, the king will succeed and we shall receive the price back, and more, when he takes back his throne. It must be done. We must get the money to him.'

'Mistress?' A gentle cough outside the workroom door was followed by a discreet tap.

'Yes, Vania?'

Vania was little Edward's nursemaid and helped Deborah run the house for Anne. She was a calm, plain girl with a strong back and kind eyes, who, having been brought up a dairy farmer's daughter, knew all there was to know about cows and goats. She sounded distinctly flustered.

'You have a visitor, lady. She's in the hall, waiting for you.'

Anne, mystified, rose to her feet. These were certainly odd times. 'Please finish your breakfast, Deborah. I'll return very shortly.'

As she hurried the few steps towards the hall, Anne could hear Lisotte singing in the kitchen. She smiled, worried as she was, when she heard Edward join in. It was a song about lambs losing their mothers then finding them again. If only real life were so simple, thought the mistress of Riverstead Farm – the very English name given to this most Flemish of places.

She pulled aside the heavy cloth covering the doorway into her hall and greeted the stranger seated by the hearth. 'You are welcome to my home.'

The lady was cloaked and hooded, so her face

was in shadow, but as Anne spoke she jumped and the hood fell back.

'Your Grace!'

Margaret, Duchess of Burgundy, rose and hurried forward. 'No! Do not call me that, Anne. No one knows I've come. Not even Charles. He thinks I'm on retreat praying for a son.' The duchess smiled, strained and pale. 'I've come to ask a favour. A very great favour. One only you can grant.'

Anne was bemused. 'I had made up my mind today to ask one from you. And here you are.'

The women sat together and spoke in urgent whispers.

'Your Grace, I must sell my farm to raise money and I need your help to find a buyer. Perhaps one of the duke's followers?' Anne clasped Margaret's hands.

'For my brother?' the duchess asked.

'Yes. He will need every groat and every penny he can find.'

Margaret nodded, she understood that this woman loved Edward Plantagenet too. 'Of course, but this farm is nothing near the answer to his needs. And he would not want you to lose your home. He cares about you, and the boy. If you will help me, however, perhaps we can bring him a much greater sum than the price of this place. And men besides. That is his real need if he's to beat Warwick. And ... George.' It was hard to say the name of her brother, the Duke of Clarence. The traitor. 'Charles has forbidden me to help Edward. Or even to go to him. But you could, Anne, if you chose to.'

The duchess held up a bulging leather bag. 'I have this for him – money, and a letter from me. He needs to know what he's facing. Charles will not help.'

The duchess was very pale. She had sworn in the cathedral at Damme that she would obey her husband, but now she was betraying that oath made before God. She had also sold some of the York jewels, including the crown she'd worn on her wedding day – a double betrayal since they were part of the dowry she'd brought to Burgundy. It was a bitter choice – loyalty to blood rather than to the man she loved – but in the end she'd made it.

'My husband means to trap Edward at s'Gravenhague. He will hold him there until he makes up his mind about what should be done. Perhaps, in the end, the duke will hand my brother to the French.'

'No! He would not do that.'

Margaret gripped her friend's hand passionately. 'Listen to me, Anne. With this money the king can buy a proper escort: arms and men and horses. My husband will try to avoid meeting Edward. He says he must be seen as uncommitted to either side – the French or the English. But England cannot face another civil war, which will happen if Margaret of Anjou takes back the English throne. Charles is the key – he *must* meet with Edward and support him, if only to spare the English people. For that, the king must come south. Once he is here, I am certain I can make a meeting happen. But I cannot leave Brugge. You can, however.'

Margaret knew what she was asking. If Charles found out, Anne would suffer for her disobedience of his implied command. And it was a long and dangerous journey on the edge of winter across provinces ravaged by the constant fighting between Burgundy and France.

'There is no one else I can trust. Or who Edward will trust. You will never betray him. He knows that and I know that.'

There was a fluttering buzz in Anne's belly as she nodded. Not because she had agreed to go, but because the duchess was right. She was the logical messenger.

A hand touched hers in the dark, and a man laughed. Him. He was laughing. She turned her head and saw him; he looked down at her so lovingly. Saw him reach out for her; felt it as he kissed her deeply; saw his fingers as they undid the lacing on her gown and...

'Will you go? Anne?'

Anne clenched her fingers into fists, nails puncturing her palms. The image of the king had been so real, she could even smell his scent: orris root, sandalwood and his own personal smell – leather, fresh sweat, linseed oil from the reins he handled every day of his life...

She sighed and shook her head. 'We nearly destroyed each other, your brother and I. I want to help him, dear Christ, so much, and if I sell everything I have, that must be enough. My coin will add to yours. You must find another messenger, Duchess, and I will find another home.'

It hurt so badly to think of selling her farm, but, in the end, it was a better way, a stronger response to the hand she'd been dealt. And, this way, she need not face the temptation of seeing the king again.

'But, Anne, the king must be told what only I can tell him: he must know my husband's plans or England *will* be lost. My husband and my brother must meet, they must renew their friendship. Edward has no other allies. You must go; you must. Please consider what I ask.'

Anne de Bohun looked down. There were tears welling in the eyes of Margaret of England, Margaret of Burgundy, and she couldn't bear to see them fall.

There was a long moment of silence, then Anne released a pain-filled breath.

'Duchess, I will pray for an answer. If I am told in my prayers that I must go to your brother, then I shall. If not, then I will not be the one to carry this message. And I will sell my farm.'

The duchess rose and Anne saw how sad she was, how lost. Margaret of Burgundy was unused to begging.

'Then I shall pray too,' she said. 'For you and for me. And for him. May you receive guidance you can live with.'

Anne curtsied, shivering, as the duchess left her hall. She watched in the gloom of early morning as Margaret mounted the palfrey that her companion, Aseef – a deaf-mute moor and her husband's most trusted servant – held for her. As they cantered away into the rising light, Anne shut the door of her house and leaned against it, her heart lurching like a creature imprisoned in her chest.

Yes, she must pray again for the guidance she could not supply for herself. This time, perhaps, other gods would give her the answers she sought. Wrapping her shawl tightly around her body she hurried away.

Leif Molnar had been waiting patiently outside the plank door of Anne's workroom to speak to her, but as she walked past him, preoccupied, he hung back in the shadows. He watched her retreating figure thoughtfully. He'd heard every word of the conversation between the two women and he was filled with fear for Anne.

He had been given a task by his master, one he had only partly fulfilled. Certainly, he had vital information now about the duke's intentions towards Edward, and he would make sure that Mathew Cuttifer received it, by the fastest boat to England he could find. But he knew that the duchess's message *must* reach the king in exile also, for that would surely influence the course of the coming war in England. One woman's life was a small thing to consider at such a time. But Anne de Bohun's life, and her safety and happiness, were not small things to Leif Molnar.

And, over the last few days, he'd come to see they never would be.

## Chapter Eight

Lodewijk, Sieur de Gruuthuse, governor of the province of Holland on behalf of Charles, Duke of Burgundy smiled at his 'guest', the former King of England, and shrugged apologetically.

'Sire, I am sure that you do appreciate the help these men gave you, but please understand my position and that of the duke, my master. He trusts me with governing this place for him. I keep civil order but for that, the people must have confidence in my rule. How would it look to them if I granted what you ask?'

Edward's bargaining position was weak, he knew, yet whilst he had lost his throne, he was still a knight. Knighthood, even in these rapacious times, still warranted some obligations – when convenient.

'Governor, these are good men made turbulent by violent times. The Frenchman who leads them is a brave man and bears an honourable name. His only foolishness is to have trusted Louis of France. One king has cheated him of his place in the world. This king would restore it.'

The Sieur de Gruuthuse bowed. Edward, as gravely, bowed in return. They were old friends, these two. Lodewijk de Gruuthuse – commonly called Louis – had been Burgundian ambassador in England several times over the last twenty years and had known the Earl of March, as Edward once had been, since he was a little boy. He'd liked him then, and continued to like him as a man, exiled king or not. Though Edward's current situation posed more than a few problems for him, of course – and burdened him with a secret he could not share with his guest.

For his part, Edward was greatly heartened that Louis was Governor of Holland and therefore so close to Charles of Burgundy, his brother-in-law. Aristocrats in England had often sneered at the elegant Louis: he might look like a noble, they said, yet he'd made his extraordinary fortune from brewing beer. He'd bought his nobility, rather than earned it on the field of combat. Yet Edward, always interested in trade and merchants and their intriguing creativity, had felt Louis de Gruuthuse had a great deal to teach him about the world. Unlike so many English nobles, Louis did not despise learning for its own sake; he collected books and pictures, and his house in Brugge was more splendid, warmer and more luxurious than most English palaces. He lived as opulently as a king and Edward, during his various visits to that great trading city, had learned much of civilised living from the man. Tastes which he'd taken back with him to London and which showed in the eventual adornment of his many houses and his own person.

Now these two old friends found themselves sparring over the fate of a ragtag band of French and Flemish outlaws.

'My lord, this man and his followers would augment your own personal guard with distinction, I feel certain of that. They have provided me with their service, at some cost to themselves, and I wish to reward them for it by making their lives useful again.'

Edward grimaced slightly as he spoke. The wound on his left forearm ached. It was a just reminder of the minor mêlée he and his followers had been involved in during the early hours of this morning. The little Frenchman had shown great courage in that same fight.

Julian de Plassy and his men had agreed to

provide an escort for the English to the Gevan-
genpoort, the outer gate of the Binnenhof, to
increase their chances of reaching the Sieur de
Gruuthuse safely. But Louis's men had happened
on the English and their escort only two leagues
outside the walls of the town. Mistaking them all
for outlaws in the half light, they had fallen on
the party.

It was brief but hard fighting, in which Julian
de Plassy, Lord Hastings and Edward had found
themselves hand to hand against Louis de
Gruuthuse's men. Then Edward had shouted, in
English, 'A York, a York, to me, to me', upon
which the baffled Flemish guard had faltered and
the English had pressed their advantage into
what threatened to become a rout, until the
captain of the Flemings had called out in French,
'Lord King? We are your friends.' Strange words
to use, Edward thought now, when surrounded
by groaning, bleeding men.

Now, Edward sat, newly bathed, perfumed and
dressed in borrowed clothes according to his
station – a sweeping black, damasked gown,
belted with a gem-heavy, gilded girdle and worn
over part-coloured hose, one leg red, one leg
blue, and soft black kid half boots embroidered
with gold thread – in the private chambers of
Louis de Gruuthuse.

'I cannot free them,' Louis said. 'There would
be an outcry, Lord King. You must see that?
Many things I can grant, but this – I fear not.'

Edward settled himself more comfortably
against the padded back of the carved chair he'd
been given. Louis sat in its twin; the chairs, each

76

with a Cloth of Estate, had been arranged so that Louis's chair was on a dais slightly lower than that occupied by Edward. The king found that a delicate compliment, considering his current situation.

'Give them to me therefore. All those whom I gather around me now will have cause to be grateful for the rewards they will receive ... later.' He laughed but the laughter was not pleasant.

'Very well, it shall be so. When you decide to return to England, they shall accompany you and I will see that they wear your livery then. However, in the meantime, to placate my people, they must remain in our prison.'

Edward nodded. It was a reasonable compromise. He would make sure the Frenchman and his band were well fed and well housed. He did not want good men made sick by prison fever. They would be no use to him then.

'Could Your Majesty allow me to understand how the situation in England developed?'

Edward grimaced. Ten days, was it? Ten days, and he had no throne?

'Warwick and my–' He'd been going to say 'my brother', but it still hurt too much. 'Warwick and Clarence – you must know it's been going back and forth between us for these last three years and more. Clarence ... well, he's proved to be more amenable to Warwick and his plans after the earl found he couldn't control me. Warwick has even married Clarence to his daughter now. Something I could never agree to, for obvious reasons.'

Marriages of the great: they were always rife with the heaving possibilities of dynastic struggle. Had

77

not Earl Warwick himself been shamed when Edward, his then protegé, secretly married the English lady Elizabeth Grey, née Wydeville, a Lancastrian knight's widow? Louis well recalled that the earl had been planning a grand French marriage for the young king at the time. Furious at being made a fool in the eyes of all Europe, Warwick had quickly turned his attentions towards a more grateful quarter. Rumour said that he'd promised Edward's disgruntled younger brother, George, Duke of Clarence, a tilt at his brother's throne. And now the marriage between Isabel and Clarence had cemented that ambitious plan.

'They've gone too far this time, Louis. And it won't get Clarence what he seeks.'

Louis de Gruuthuse sighed. 'No, indeed. Rumour has it that Earl Warwick wants to restore the former royal family to the English throne. Is this so?'

Edward swirled the wine of Burgundy in his Venetian glass goblet; it was closer to black than red in this light.

'Yes. Warwick's reinstated Henry, and Margaret's son is back in the line of succession, Edward. Another one.'

He grimaced and, for a moment, almost mentioned Anne de Bohun, Henry's other child. But then he stopped himself. Very few knew of Anne's royal descent. Or of his feelings for the girl. He would not discuss her now. He looked at his host with the glimmer of a smile.

'Can you imagine it, Louis? Warwick joining forces with the woman whose husband he and I tried to kill at Mortimer's Cross and Towton? As for brother George...' Again he laughed, a grating sound. 'What chance the throne for him, now that the old queen has Warwick to back her? And, as we said, there's her son, Edward, the grace-given boy.'

Both men chuckled. It was ancient scandal that marital relations between the previous, now restored, Lancastrian king, Henry VI, and his French queen, Margaret, had been anything but warm. So chilly had they become, in fact, that when the queen's son was first placed in the king's arms he'd piously said the child must have been fathered by the Holy Ghost for he could not see how the boy was of his own get. Yet this same boy – son of his father or not – was now the Prince of Wales once more, and Warwick, in swearing fealty to the old queen, must, of necessity, have sidelined Clarence's own ambitions to sit on the throne of England himself.

'Your master, Charles of Burgundy. Will he help me, Louis?'

Louis de Gruuthuse had been a diplomat for many years and his response was elegant. 'Your Grace, I feel sure that my master is most agonised at your plight, bound together by family as you are. I am instructed to aid you in any way that I can, and to house you fittingly whilst you consider your future.' Elegant, but not direct.

Edward frowned. He was tired and less in command of his expression than usual, or he would not have been so unsubtle. 'Well, let us see what this aid of yours consists of. However, it is imperative that I speak with Charles face to face. We must move quickly if we are to beat the French as they conspire with Warwick to hold

England. King Louis wishes to isolate me, but there is much at stake for your master too. I need to retake my kingdom so that England can, once more, be the duke's strong ally against the French. He must see that.'

The Sieur de Gruuthuse rose and bowed. 'I am certain that my master sees all, Your Grace. But these are matters we should speak of when you are properly rested. Come, we have prepared a feast of welcome and entertainment to amuse you and your party. A little music and more good wine will help the world seem brighter.'

A credible facsimile of delight brightened Edward's face. 'A feast? Charming thought! Dancing, music and pretty women – these three will make us all feel better. I declare that I could eat the wretched gelding I've ridden these last days if you would only serve him up! Come, my friend, lead the way.'

Louis clapped his hands sharply. The two bronze-bound doors, with their allegorical scenes of the labours of Hercules, were instantly thrown back and the palace major-domo, flanked by at least fifty attendant gentlemen, including the English party of lords, sank down on one knee, heads bowed, to honour the governor and his exalted guest.

Louis and Edward, matching their pace as if taking part in a courtly dance, entered the mighty space of the Ridderzaal, the Knights' Hall. This handsome cavernous chamber had been built by the unlamented Count Floris V, to adorn the castle which began as a hunting lodge two centuries earlier. It was a jewel-like setting for courtly

80

festivities, designed to show off the wealth and power of its now-supplanted owners. Perhaps there was a message in this, but that night, as all watched the English king laugh, compliment the dancers and the mummers, and distribute largesse when he left the feast for his bed (with coin provided discreetly by the governor) no one doubted for a moment that the situation in England was anything but temporary. Power, in the person of Edward Plantagenet, would be restored to its rightful place.

Edward, when he closed his aching eyes in his bed chamber, finally let all pretence of mastery drop away. 'Did my messenger find you, Anne? Will Charles help me? What must I do?'

William Hastings heard his master's mumbled words through the open door between his room and the king's. It was a question William also wanted answered.

It was unlikely Charles would help Edward's cause without great inducement, because Europe and Burgundy were most delicately poised right now. Duke Charles had achieved a cessation in hostilities with the French – a fragile peace, but one that was holding for the moment. To actively assist his Plantagenet brother-in-law would most likely cause Warwick and Louis of France to move together against Burgundian territory in the prosperous Low Countries – perhaps even the very citadel in which they slept tonight. The balance of power in Europe, relatively stable for a few short years, was beginning to teeter, and disaster loomed.

Yes, Hastings too hoped the king's messenger had reached Anne de Bohun in Brugge. She was close to the court, close to the duke. Charles might listen to Anne as a go-between, where he would be suspicious of his own wife's opinions and intentions, as she was Edward's sister. Lord, let it be so, let the man have found her. Let her have agreed to help the king's cause with Duke Charles.

Surely Anne de Bohun would see that was her duty, whatever history had been between them? Surely she would help Edward Plantagenet?

## Chapter Nine

There were secrets about the farm Anne de Bohun had bought. And one of them was in the oak grove on a small hillock near the river.

Flanders and the countries about it were not called the Low Countries for nothing. The land, once covered by the sea – as evidenced by the seashells found so often in the good soil – was nearly completely flat, levelled by water long ago, most probably Noah's flood it was said. But there were still one or two pieces of raised ground close to Brugge, and the small hillock on Anne's farm was one of them.

It was deep in the night, with a rising wind and a new sickle moon, and all the lights in the farmhouse were out. Even the carefully banked embers on the kitchen hearth gave out no active flame, though the ashes glowed fitfully as night air sighed and stirred in the chimney's throat.

Hour after hour, the new moon mounted the sky, until, in the darkest part of the night, when it had finally begun its long, slow setting, two figures stole out of the back door of the farmstead house and moved as quietly as shadows through the yard, past the animals sleeping in the winter byre. So softly did they tread that not even the geese wakened, nor the lurcher, kept to bring the cows in from the fields for milking. He slept before the kitchen embers peacefully, because Lisotte was kind to him now that the nights were cold.

As the wind dropped, frost settled out of the still air and the two women found the going easy because the mud in the ploughed fields hardened in the freezing night. Moving as quickly as they could, they hurried towards the distant river at the bottom of the home pasture. They could see their destination if they strained their eyes – the dark shape of the hillock with its almost leafless trees reaching into the sky above them.

'Are you sure you have it?'

'Yes, Deborah. Of course I have it.'

Anne and her foster-mother reached the very end of the plough land and came to the stile in the hawthorn hedge that gave entrance to the hillock ground. There was only the last faint starlight abroad now, but it was enough: they could see the path in front of them, winding around and around their little hill, up to the ancient oaks crowning its top.

Deborah had been the first to recognise the path for what it was: an ancient track cut into the face of the hill which led, by a spiral path, right into the heart of the grove. Its discovery was the final omen Anne needed to convince her to buy her farm. Local legend said the little hill was not made by God, but man, a long, long time ago. It might even be the grave of an ancient king. Deborah and Anne did not doubt it when they saw the overgrown path around the hill.

This place had seen much life in its long past, well before the city of Brugge was founded or formed – or so Deborah believed. Neither woman had done anything to clear the path on the hill – so that none but they would know they came here – and the place had become another church for them.

Silently they hurried now along the spiral path until the darkness of the trees swallowed them up.

From a distance, there was nothing to say the two had passed this way. But then the wind rose again, sighing. Something knew. Perhaps it was the earth.

'What was that?'

It was unlike Deborah to be fearful of the night, but for a moment it had seemed as if the ground beneath her feet, in the depth of the oak grove, had moved.

'I felt it too.'

Anne was uneasy. Something smelled strange up here. A storm coming – was that it? And yet the sky was clear, so clear they could see the setting sickle of moon and the morning star beginning its rise in the east. They would have to be quick.

With cold fingers, Anne fumbled in the little bag slung from the belt around her kirtle. 'Here it is, mother.'

She only called Deborah 'mother' at moments like this, when the kinship between them became an even stronger bond. If one Seeker ventured out into the night world alone, another must remain behind to call the Voyager back. Mother and daughter, daughter and mother – so it had been for many generations. So it was tonight.

'Very well. But we must uncover the circle first, then we can light our way.'

Anne and Deborah hunted amongst the trees to find the collection of stones they'd previously laid out in a circle and then covered in fallen leaves. They were mostly rounded white quartz, water-smoothed, secretly and laboriously brought up from the river over the months since summer.

'Help me, child.'

Deborah was trying to carry the largest stone into the centre of the circle. It was the size of half a woman and similarly shaped, even to the suggestion of arms, legs and vulva. Surmounting the form was a 'face' sketched by the line of a nose and a slit for the mouth. This stone was black and too heavy to lift alone.

Breathing hard from the effort, Anne and Deborah placed the woman-stone upright in the centre of their little circle. Traces of wax could be seen on the head of the stone pillar; they'd dribbled down in such a way as to suggest hair. Anne shivered when she touched it.

The stone was bedded into a dimple hastily scraped in the earth floor, then Deborah flint-lit a wax candle; the 'click' as she scraped sparks from the metal was very loud in the night. When the candle was alight, she handed it to her daughter who carefully dripped new wax onto the old. It would form a bed in which to sit their light tonight.

Eyes closed, Anne cupped her hands around the wavering flame as it grew from a point. She could feel the warmth on her palms as it settled, sending a tiny trail of smoke up into the freezing air. The honey smell from the wax was a faint breath of summer.

'Are you ready, daughter?'

Anne nodded. 'I am ready, mother.'

Silently Deborah leaned forward and unclasped the pin that held Anne's hooded cloak together at the throat; it was gold, a little dragon with blind eyes of pearl, the same colour as the last of the stars. In one quick movement Anne shrugged herself out of the cloak. She was naked. The cold night touched her skin and she sobbed one sharp breath, as a swimmer does upon entering freezing water.

Deborah, clothed though she was, felt the cold in her own bones but suppressed pity and fear. This was important, for the sacrifice must be willingly made. 'Now?' she said.

Anne nodded and the women joined hands, kneeling down on either side of the stone pillar, their arms stretching around it completely.

'The sacrifice.'

Shaking, Anne extended one hand towards the candle flame. Deborah brought an awl from the bag hanging at her belt. Quickly she pricked the girl's outstretched Jupiter finger so that one fat drop of blood, then another, fell into the transparent heart of the flame. A hiss like a cat, the smell of burning iron, and then the flame burned up again, clean, faintly blue. Unwavering.

Deborah, whispering, began a chant. 'Mother of All, Mother of All, hear us, hear your children.'

Anne, her teeth clenched against the gripping cold, tried to sink herself in the darkness, fixing her eyes on the shape of the candle flame, echoing the words. Her hands were numb, and her mouth was stiff as she tried to frame speech. *The flame, concentrate on the flame.*

'By the four winds and the seven seas, hear us. By the sun, by the moon, by the stars, hear us. We are your children and we cannot see in the dark. We ask you to bring us light, so that we may know what is needful, understand what is permitted. Mother of All, Mother of All...'

Nothing. There was nothing. Anne had stopped shivering but was still and cold as stone. Closing her eyes, she saw the red image of the flame behind her lids. Perhaps she was becoming stone herself, would turn to a rock and be left here for evermore? That was sad. As a little girl, she'd always felt so sorry for statues in winter. Worried about them in the dark sleet of winter, the snow and the frost...

Now it was black. Deep and dense. There was nothing to see, no flame, not even the ghost of its image. But she was comfortable in the velvet darkness. Perhaps she was no longer cold? Yes, her hands, her fingers, even her face, were all warmer, just as if she were beside a fire. It was odd, though, if that were so, because her back was cosy also. Anne giggled. Astonishing! Normally in winter, if you warmed the front of your body at a fire, you had to keep turning or the side away from the warmth of the flames froze.

*Lady Anne?* It was a man's voice. And that was strange, for they'd called on the Mother, hadn't they?

*Lady Anne?* The voice was anguished.

'Yes. I'm here. Who are you?'

*I am nameless now, though I am Thor's servant, first and last. But once I was the messenger of a king.*

Anne was suddenly frightened. 'Thor's servant? But ... you died.'

*There are things to be said. I have come to say them. Question me. It is your duty.*

Blindly, in the blurred, soft dark, Anne turned towards the sound of the voice. There was a shape, black on black, and a buttery thread of light was creeping, growing, outlining a head, a shoulder, an arm...

Dread crawled towards her out of the dark like a living thing. Anne knew that if the thread became brighter, spread faster, she would see the man's face, see his gaping death wound.

'What was your message from the king?'

*To ask for help.*

'I have said I will give all I can.'

*That is not enough. You must give without hope, without count of cost, without thought of reward. Eyes where he has none, ears for what he cannot hear, a tongue to speak when all he knows is silence and betrayal.*

'But I was right to turn away from him. That was the greater good.'

*You must turn again. You cannot see the pattern, or*

88

*the measure of the dance, but you dance just the same. You must take my place.*

Cold bit at her, working its way upwards from her feet, towards her heart, as the light grew brighter. Thor's servant, dressed in red ringmail, was glowing so brightly, with such heat, that the billets of iron he held in his hands began to melt. And the thought came to her: this was a waste, for the iron could be forged into ... what? A sword?

'Am I stone, that I can withstand what is asked of me?'

There was something beyond words here; something she understood but was frightened even to think about.

*You must accept all that is. Acquiesce.*

The cold reached her heart and, with the last of her breath, Anne screamed. But no sound disturbed the still air. She lay on the frozen ground of the oak grove, wrapped once more in her fur-lined cloak, her eyes glued shut.

Deborah chafed her hands, held her, shook her, called out: 'Child! Hear me!'

Anne sensed words, but there was no sound, no sight. Just pain. And fear.

'Anne!'

Deborah's voice burst in her ear with the percussive force of a bombard. The girl jerked upright, nauseated. Vomit hit the leaves on the floor of the grove. She retched so loudly that sleeping birds startled on the branches and flew up into the changing light, protesting.

Deborah was crying as she held Anne's shaking body while the girl emptied bile from her gut.

'Enough of this. Enough! You nearly died!'

'But I did not.' Wearily Anne shook her head. 'I have to go to the king.'

It had come, this thing they both feared so much.

'Can you stand?'

Anne straightened her back and absently patted her foster-mother's hand.

Poor Deborah. She had performed similar rituals all her life, but was fearful of the cost of the knowledge they brought to the living. Drawing the cloak around her body, Anne turned shakily towards the east and the growing light.

'We must go, or we'll find the household awake.'

The two women carried the centre-stone back to its hiding place in a tree hollow, then covered the quartz circle with fallen leaves and dead furze.

Anne turned to Deborah. 'I'll do what the duchess asks. I'll take her message and find a way to bring the king back to Duke Charles. I cannot escape this.'

Sometimes, when you finally face the thing you are frightened of, it seems less than it is. Deborah heard herself as she spoke – she sounded calm, she *was* calm. 'And then?'

'I do not know.'

Was it a new beginning or an ending? Anne could not tell. Was that ignorance a blessing or a curse?

# Chapter Ten

'Mother? Mother!'

Jacquetta woke in the dark with a jolt and snatched up the lighted candle at her bedside. 'I'm coming, daughter, I'm coming.'

It was years since she'd risen to a fretful voice in the night and now, unfamiliar with her surroundings, the duchess stubbed a naked great toe on the edge of a coffer. Agony hissed out on a breath through the 'lucky' gap between her front teeth, but the pain roused her from half sleep. Pulling her cloak over her shoulders, she fumbled at the door latch into her daughter's room.

The queen struggled to heave her bulk upright when she heard her mother. She lay on a narrow bed in a narrow room – the abbot's own personal cell – and the mattress was thin and lumpy as a sack filled with acorns. As a poor Lancastrian widow she'd slept on worse, but that was a very long time ago and now the deposed queen of England was frightened. What if this was all that was left to her? What if the rest of her life was to be this uncomfortable, this bleak. This hopeless.

'Mother, where are you? I can't see you. I'm frightened!'

'Now, child, all is well. I am here.'

Elizabeth reached out and gripped her mother's hand. Jacquetta yelped. The ague in her finger joints was pain itself in this cold season.

The queen wailed suddenly and covered her face, tears seeping between ringless fingers. 'The baby... I have the gripping pain. He wants to be born, but I will die and he will die, and the king will never see his son.'

The duchess heard the panic in her daughter's voice, but there were no courtiers now to flurry round and soothe her. Jacquetta held her candle higher. 'Look at me, Elizabeth!'

Her voice was harsh and it shocked the queen. She gulped back tears and her voice trembled. 'Why are you not kinder to me, mother?'

Jacquetta's irritation with her difficult daughter ebbed away. Once she'd been an enchanting little girl, a child who'd laughed and kissed her mother sweetly. Occasionally, as now, the vulnerability of that child flickered still in the eyes of the adult she'd become. Jacquetta sighed and huddled down beside her daughter.

'Because that will not help you or me – or the baby. Come, let me aid your sleep. You need strength for the time that is coming. Do you not remember what I taught you? Concentrate ... here, follow the flame ... follow the flame as it moves.'

The queen clutched the turned and patched sheets around her cold shoulders and did as she was told, sniffing. In the dark, her pupils grew to a great size, so great the blue was drowned in black and a reflection of the candle flame wavered in their depths.

'Yes, that's better, my daughter. Much better. Now, you will listen to me and repeat what I say...'

'*Repeat what you say.*'

Jacquetta smiled. 'Good, very good. Watch the

flame, keep watching the flame. The baby is well and so am I...'

*'The baby is well, and so am I...'*

'He is not yet ready to be born, so I can sleep...'

*'He is not yet ready to be born, so I can sleep...'*

The queen, eyes fixed on the small flame, suddenly yawned and her eyelids fluttered. The tense lines of her face softened.

'All will be well. I know this to be true...'

*'All will be well ... I know this to...'*

Elizabeth Wydeville sighed and the last of the words drifted away. She slept, one hand placed protectively across her belly.

Looking down at her daughter, Jacquetta expelled a long breath. Every weary year of her life was written on her own face, yet once she'd been as lovely as the queen. To be beautiful was a useful thing, but also dangerous. Gently, she tucked Elizabeth's other hand under the counterpane.

'All will be well?'

The duchess looked over to the abbot's unadorned prie-dieu in the corner of the room. She resisted the urge to kneel on it and ask for help, for reassurance. At moments such as these, friendless and nearly alone while the enemy roamed the streets of the capital, it was hard to believe God even existed.

A blasphemous thought. And in the abbot's own cell. She would be punished for this sin.

Fearfully, Jacquetta hauled at the chain around her neck, pulling out the crucifix that hung from it. Kissing the body of Christ, she knelt beside her daughter's bed and prayed to a God she did not believe in for relief and comfort that had never truly been hers, in all her long life.

And, as self-administered penance, she decided to give up the warmth of her own bed. And somehow her resolve, formed by guilt, kept terror at bay as the weary night wore on and she listened, telling her beads, to the deposed queen, her own daughter, as she groaned in her sleep.

If there was a God, he might hear her as she prayed this long night. What did she have to lose? What did any of them have to lose that was not already gone?

## Chapter Eleven

Louis XI, King of France, had courtiers who swore he was the most handsome man on earth. He knew they lied and sometimes, if he was feeling cheerful, it amused him to see how far their obsequiousness would extend when they wanted his favour. And as they all wanted his favour all the time, when he asked them to describe his appearance, they frothed that he was an Adonis, a veritable Apollo. Unfortunately, the game palled quickly, for whilst Louis delighted in human stupidity, since it conveyed advantage, eventually he became annoyed by their implied contempt. Did these fools not understand he knew exactly what he looked like?

He did not enjoy the sight of his own face and, for that reason, avoided mirrors. It was the length and size of his nose that particularly offended him, but what could one do about such things? The nose he had been born with would accompany him to the grave – unless leprosy took it from him; he had a morbid fear of leprosy amongst many other such terrors. At the thought, the king crossed himself and touched the finger bone of St Louis, his own ancestor, which hung around his neck in its little green malachite box bound in gold wire. Unlike others – Edward Plantagenet, for instance – Louis was not greatly troubled by lust, yet he was a man as others were. And as his wife did not greatly attract him, he, as most men did, risked disease from the occasional women he consorted with.

If any of his courtiers had been brave enough to point out to Louis that the source of his ever-present desire to crush his two chief enemies – Edward Plantagenet and Charles of Burgundy – might be caused more by envy of their famous good looks than by lust for their territory, well, the king would have laughed heartily, ironically, and changed the subject. But, of course, it was true.

Louis – secretive, pious, clever Louis – *was* jealous of his rivals, of their looks, their famous, radiant charm; and, since he'd schooled himself to a cold heart and low expectations of the behaviour of those around him, he had no problem convincing himself, his court and his allies that Edward the Usurper and Charles, the traitorous duke, his cousin, both deserved to be utterly destroyed. It was simple: they opposed his will, the will of the sanctified King of France and of the French. And there had never been a better time than now to scoop up both of them in the one mighty net. Edward had been driven from his kingdom, and Charles was thus fatally weakened by the loss of his chief ally against the French.

That was good. That was very good, yet Louis felt no real or lasting pleasure in these facts, though he'd personally worked hard, and his servants harder still, to bring them about. In truth, he had little pleasure in anything. Life remained wearisome and annoying, just as it always had been.

'This is intolerable! I have ash in my eye!'

November had arrived and with it dark winds from the far north. Louis angrily furled his robes more closely around his body and bellowed for men to fix the smoking fire.

Famous for his restless year-round processionals through the kingdom of France, Louis was currently roosting in the primitive – at least by Parisian standards – castle of his provincial capital, Reyns. His bored and fractious courtiers were heartily sick of the lack of even basic comforts as winter settled over the land. They were desperate for distraction of any kind to break the endless monotony of their days.

At last it arrived.

Rumour swept the draughty old castle: a messenger had just ridden in, was being ushered, exhausted, into Louis's presence. Perhaps the news he brought would be a distraction to the king, lifting his petulant gloom. His courtiers certainly hoped so. If the news was good, entertainment might be ordered and that would cheer them all.

But Louis was not thinking cheerful thoughts; pessimism was his native mood and nothing had happened to shake that so far today. He drew down his long upper lip and sniffed hard; smoke from the stubborn fire made his eyes stream tears and his vision blurred as he inspected the man before him.

'Enough!' he commanded the tribe of servants fussing with increasing panic over the fire. 'I shall conduct this audience and then dine. By the time I return to this chamber, I expect the fire to be working. Properly. Now, go!'

It was miraculous, really. A certain tone in his voice and men scattered like leaves. Louis found the effect gratifying – even after a reign of nine years – but odd that his least word was taken so seriously. It would be far too easy to take it for granted, but one had only to think of the fate of others – Edward Plantagenet, for instance, or his own father – to remember that even the mighty, even a king, could fall. One must be on one's guard for treachery all the time. Tedious, but necessary.

Louis turned to the slightly higher flames in the chimney breast and rubbed his hands together in their feeble warmth.

'Well, man, speak. What do you have for me?'

The glassy-eyed messenger, Riccard of Polignac, was exhausted and dazed from his long and freezing ride. Now, ushered into the king's presence, terror oozed down his back seeking his twitching sphincter, and turned his legs to boneless sacks of flesh. The sound of his heartbeat filled his ears and he yearned for the moment when he could exit the Presence and sink back into the obscurity of the guard command in Paris. That was, if he survived the news that he carried.

'Sire, the success of your campaign in Picardy and the Maconnais is glorious. Your troops mass on the borders of Burgundy itself even now and await your word to advance. But I have urgent news concerning the fate of the former King of England.'

As the man spoke, Louis breathed in too deeply, trying to mask his tension, and took a great freight of smoke into his lungs. For a moment, he could not speak but his face turned a deep brick red and sweat stood out on his forehead as he tried to catch clear air into his mouth.

Without thought, Riccard lunged forward and thumped the king heartily on the back. That was a shock to both of them and, for a moment, each man stared at the other in terror. The messenger had laid hands on the sacred person of the monarch. He could be expected to die a nasty and protracted death for such effrontery.

Understanding instantly the graveness of his offence, Riccard slumped to his knees, hands covering his head, eyes wild.

'Ah sire, your pardon! I beseech your pardon!'

He knocked his forehead so energetically on the flags that a bloody smear was left on the limestone.

The king regained his breath and marvelled at the absurdity of it all. Of course he'd flinched when the man rushed at him – he could have been an assassin – but as the lurching thump of his heart returned to normal, he was glad of the messenger's service, for the fear had squeezed his chest, driving out the smoke.

'Get up. Get up, you fool!'

Riccard, still dazed, stumbled as he tried to stand and grasped at the edges of a tapestry on the wall for support. With a ripping groan, the rotted arras parted company with its hooks and soon the messenger was completely engulfed by *Moses Parting the Red Sea*, a heaving, twitching lump of foolishness at the feet of the king.

'What is the message?' shrieked Louis. 'Tell me, or I swear you shall join your ancestors' bones in the pigsty they reside in. Speak!'

Poor Riccard. If instant death would have eased his plight he would gladly have obliged the king, but it was not to be. Closing his mouth against the dust of years trapped in the cloth, he found a way towards a little patch of light and slithered out from beneath the arras on his belly. Heaving himself free, he saw the terrible eyes of the king upon his own. For a moment he had no voice but then it came in a rush and he blurted his message as fast as hail drumming on a roof.

'The English king, sire, or the Earl of March as he is now – he is in the Ridderzaal with the Lord de Gruuthuse, Governor of Holland. The earl is the governor's prisoner, but does not know it.'

Louis was not without pity, though he rarely showed it. Therefore he kept his eyes trained like an arrow on the bowed head of Riccard of Polignac, ignoring the blood dripping onto the floor at the man's feet.

'And? There is more?'

The man's voice trembled. 'Yes, sire. But it is contained in this cipher which will need translating. I was entrusted only with the outline of the facts.'

Riccard held up a stoppered brass tube in one shaking hand. The king leaned down and snatched it. 'And I can see why,' he snorted. 'A greater fool I have rarely encountered. Out of my sight! Go!'

The king's merciful release of him confused poor Riccard. He had heard that Louis was very cruel and that his favourite pastime was hanging prisoners in metal cages from the battlements of his castles. They were left there in all weathers, with no food, no water, until at last they died and their bones swung in the wind, sometimes for years and years. Riccard backed, hobbling, from the king's presence before Louis could change his mind.

The king, watching the oaf depart at speed, permitted himself to smile briefly, naughtily, as he stroked the small canister containing the promised cipher.

Perhaps, at last, he was beginning to corner his dear cousin Charles, but the fate of the erstwhile English king was very much in play. Divide and conquer, divide and conquer, Louis thought. A sound maxim for which he thanked another monarch, though a Roman one of ages past.

What he needed now was for his Doctor of Divination to cast a chart, perhaps the chart of England itself, to see what the future held. Yes, that might help him decide what to do next.

Was it possible that the Fates, those three implacable sisters, had ordained that he, Louis de Valois, would be their instrument in the ultimate downfall of Edward Plantagenet?

He very much hoped so.

# Chapter Twelve

Edward Plantagenet and his host, Louis de
Gruuthuse, rode out in the crisp November days
in search of stag. They were in a private chase,
given to Louis, as Governor of the Lowlands, for
his entertainment and which had once been part
of the giant hunting preserve of the Counts of
Holland. But Edward was distracted.

'Something's not right. I know it. Why haven't
we heard from Charles? It's been ten days or
more. Enough time for my messages to reach
him, and for us to have had a return. This freeze
will have made the tracks firm.'

Edward's horse shied under him, nervous at
some imagined shape in the bushes as the two
men waited for the hounds to raise the quarry.

'Alas, Your Majesty, I thought I had provided
you with a better mount!' Louis was annoyed, his
concern genuine. The king had been given a bang-
tailed grey stallion with a deep chest and long
delicate legs. Speed rather than weight-carrying
capacity. Perhaps that had been the wrong choice.

'No, he's a fine animal. Good heart, I suspect –
just a little young and flighty. He'll settle when I
shake some energy out of his legs.'

Louis patted the polished neck of his own
horse, a stately bay, which stood calmly waiting
for the call to advance. 'Perhaps I may suggest
you take my animal, Lord King, and allow me to

"shake out his legs" for you myself. It is the least I can do.'

'No, Louis. I can manage this animal – and I appreciate, very much, you offering me such fine entertainment – but my men are restless and so am I. Time disappears as the weather worsens. Why has Charles not sent us word of his intentions?'

Deep in the chase the halloo began and the Sieur de Gruuthuse was spared the need for replying as both horses, champing, dancing from foot to foot, took all their riders' strength to hold them.

'Come, sire, there may be news when we return to my halls. For now...'

The chase was arduous and unexpectedly long, and, in the end, unsatisfying. The stag, an excellent animal with at least twelve points to its antlers, disappeared into a stream, outrunning the hounds and the court party surrounding Edward and his host. The king felt responsible for the loss, for he had led the riders and at one point his flighty mount had become distracted by the noise of the hounds and baulked the jumping of a log, causing confusion amongst those who followed. And in that moment the stag escaped.

It was an especially sharp blow – he'd always had success before at the chase – and Edward was privately dismayed, though he laughed it off at the feast that night.

'Ah, Louis, my cunning at the hunt must have suffered after all the alarms of the last weeks. Your red monarch lives to fight another round with your hounds – and I take that to be an excellent omen for my own case!'

Louis de Gruuthuse laughed along with the rest at the high table in the Ridderzaal, but secretly he dreaded the close of the feast. He had finally received despatches – despatches he was yet to share with the king.

Drink deep, and deeper yet, he told himself, and perhaps it would give him courage for what was to come.

Edward sauntered towards the fire in Louis's private quarters, joining his brother, Richard of Gloucester, and William Hastings as they warmed their backs, beakers of honeyed wine in their hands.

It was a cold night, with the first real snow of the season falling silently outside the thick glass of the casements. Edward, accepting more wine from his host, kicked at the great log on the hearth. As if to answer such impertinence, a gust of wind sent sparks and smuts belching into the room from the chimney's throat. The king turned away from the fireplace, wiping-soot from his eyes.

'Damn it, Louis. Does no one understand how to build a chimney in this country? Everything smokes!'

'I heartily agree with you, sire! There are never such good builders of fireplaces here as you have in your country. I brought an Englishman to Brugge to make all mine for me in my new house.'

'And may we stand before our own fire in the great hall of Westminster before Advent is done, brother!'

Edward swung to face his younger brother, smiling. 'Admirable sentiment, Richard. Excellent aim! Come, Louis, let us drink to that. London and the greatest Yule log any of us has ever seen!'

'Amen, Your Majesty. Amen to that!'

A hearty swallow and robust belches from all four men, followed by laughter, made all things seem possible for the moment; only the moment, however, for, as the laughter died, Louis strolled forward and extended a roll of vellum to the king.

'I think you should see this, my lord. It arrived earlier this evening, while we ate. I have read it.'

A pleasant smile fixed itself to Edward's face as he took the document from Louis's fingers. He turned towards the fire and bent down to milk light from the flames.

The other three were silent, apparently unconcerned, though Richard stole a glance at his brother's face. Edward's expression did not change in the few seconds it took to read what was written; once finished, he dropped the parchment onto the fire, silently watching the skin curl up and turn black as the letters were consumed. Then he looked at his host, his eyes deep holes in his face, unfathomable.

'Fair words from Charles, Louis. But nothing of substance. Would you agree?'

Louis de Gruuthuse shrugged, most uncomfortable. There were soothing things he could say, but they would not be the truth.

'Your Majesty, you must give my master a little more time. As you know, he is placed in a most difficult situation. The French king has his army knocking at the very doors of Burgundy and–'

'Time!' Now Edward allowed a little of what he was feeling to be seen on his face. 'Time, dear Louis, is what I do not have. And Charles knows it! He is foolish if he thinks that the King of France will skulk away. That will happen only if I retake England. If Margaret and Warwick consolidate their power, then Burgundy is lost. Louis will pick off Charles's territory province by province, and he will not have England to take up his cause.'

Privately Louis de Gruuthuse agreed with his guest, but now was not the time to speak such truth. It was his duty to play the game the way his master, the Duke of Burgundy, wished it to be played. Carefully.

'Why will your master not at least allow me to come to him in Brugge?'

Louis smiled gently. 'Ah, sire, I suspect he worries for your safety with the French around and about the country everywhere. You would be a rich prize indeed.' And then, seeing the king's sceptical expression, his hard eyes, Louis sighed and spoke the truth. 'Perhaps, also, he does not wish to be overwhelmed. You are a difficult man to oppose in the flesh.'

Edward snorted and bared his teeth for a moment, an imitation of a smile, then dropped his shoulders and turned back to look into the flames. 'Well, we are no further forward, but no further back either. Nothing is lost. There is still some hope in this for our cause.'

There was silence, except for the crackle of the fire as the last scrap of the parchment flamed and turned to a thread of smoke.

'Does it please Your Majesty to rest?' Louis de Gruuthuse bowed as he spoke.

The deep respect he offered was small solace to Edward for now he must give heart to his men. It was an easier task in battle – a reflex operation to swing a sword or an axe in response to years of training; the fear snuffed out in action. No time to wonder what was right, only time to act. This slow game of politics was different; this was thought above physical strength – and a truer test of who he was in many ways.

And so Edward raised his head and smiled warmly at his host, a real smile this time. 'Certainly it does, dear friend,' he said, yawning, and linked his arm through that of Louis de Gruuthuse. 'You know, Louis, this will make a great tale in the telling when you visit us in London,' he went on. 'How the king went to bed one night and, in the morning, woke with the solution to his little problem.'

Edward laughed, and his genuine lightness of tone drew relieved chuckles from his brother Richard and William, his closest friend. Their spirits lifted. There would be a way; there was always a way...

But later that night, alone in the great bed, Edward lay with eyes open in the darkness and his mind turned and churned on the fair, safe words from his brother-in-law. Could the man not see the danger if he allowed Edward to swing on the gibbet of chance. Or did he not *want* to see?

And was his sister, the duchess, true to her family's cause, or had her great love for her husband distorted her loyalty to her original home? Edward frowned as he remembered the wedding so little time ago, his sister's hand trembling as he'd placed it in that of her new husband after the nuptial mass at Damme.

And Anne. His Anne. Why did he still yearn to see her, to touch her, when so much else was at risk?

Perhaps the itch of the flesh was a useful distraction and his dreams of her, the clear heat of his thoughts when he remembered her face and her body, was God's kind way of giving him relief from the endless tension of his days. Blasphemous thought! The priests would be shocked if he confessed such things. But still, could it be so?

Yes. God *was* merciful, for Edward's last images before deep sleep took him were of Anne – laughing, reaching out a hand to touch him, kissing his mouth – rather than the harrowing spectres of loss and disgrace that had haunted these last days.

## Chapter Thirteen

Leif placed the first split log on the fire he'd started in Anne's workroom, and then another, carefully lifting the kindling beneath so that air rushed in and made the flames leap and catch. The room was cold but, because it was small, would warm rapidly if he built the blaze well.

At first light he'd occupied himself in cutting wood for all the fireplaces in Anne's home. Everywhere he'd looked on the farmstead there was work half done in preparation for winter. Anne needed more men to help her – and someone to oversee their work, or she'd be taken advantage of. He did not like to think of that. At some very deep level of his being, he wanted the mistress of this house to be warm and safe. He shook his head; he was avoiding the truth. He could stack all the logs he liked, but there'd be no warm, safe winter for Anne de Bohun.

Standing in the open doorway unseen, Anne watched Leif and found herself smiling. For such a large man he did his work neatly, taking pride in the neat stack of logs he'd built beside the hearth.

'Thank you for the fire, Leif, and all the wood you've cut. It will be very useful.'

The seaman spun around, startled. Anne smiled again as she sat on a joint stool and picked up her carding comb. There was a mass of unspun wool in a basket by her feet; she bent to select a hank of it. 'The year has truly turned. It's cold today.'

Leif nodded as he fed the fire, watching from the corner of one eye as she teased the wool into long strands, readying it to spin. She had beautiful hands; he hadn't noticed that before. Anne looked up from her work and caught his glance.

'And so – overland? Or a sea journey? Which is best, do you think?'

The seaman shrugged his shoulders, cloth straining as the formidable muscles moved. 'Easier by sea, except for the season. The alternative, well...' Many days' journey in cold weather on half-made tracks with mercenaries everywhere was what he meant.

'You are right,' Anne said. 'The sea road will be better for us. How soon can you be ready?'

She was businesslike, her tone implying the thing was settled, but of course it wasn't. The *Lady Margaret*, presently docked in Sluys, the

108

nearest seaport to Brugge, was under Leif's command but she was a valuable merchant trading vessel and not Anne's – or Leif's – to dispose of. The cog belonged to Sir Mathew Cuttifer, Anne's patron and former employer, and both were acutely conscious of that. Silent for a moment, each stared into the fire.

Leif leaned forward and added another, superfluous log to the bright flames. 'We are loaded nearly to the gunwales with cargoes my master is expecting in London. I'm just waiting for the last bales of damask and crates of majolica now.'

He was caught between his declared duty to Mathew Cuttifer and his undeclared fears for this woman. And when he thought of the ex-king, coals of red rage flamed in his gut. Edward Plantagenet did not know, did not care to understand, just how many lives he placed at risk with his ambitions and his carelessness, Anne's included. And the girl felt something for the king, Leif sensed it; she dropped her eyes from his when they spoke of Edward Plantagenet. The gossip was true, then.

Leif glanced at Anne's profile as she stared into the flames, her hands idle. He sighed. If this girl was really determined to go, so was he. So much for the firewood.

Exasperation made his voice harsh. 'If I have to answer your question, the sea road is a little better. And though I don't like this, I will agree to help the king. My master is Edward Plantagenet's friend, and he has few enough of those left now. Earl Warwick has seen to that.'

Sudden tears dripped onto the spindle between Anne's fingers. Her voice shook and it was hard to breathe.

'You are a good man, Leif Molnar. I am grateful for your help.'

She said 'I' unconsciously; she should have said 'we'. Embarrassed by the slip, Anne put down her spindle and hurried from the room. Not for the first time she thought, guiltily, that if Edward did not exist then this man, this good man, might have meant more to her. She liked him, and some said that was enough. And Anne de Bohun knew, better than did Leif himself, that if she once stretched out her hand to him, Leif would clasp it and he would not let her go. Ever.

She shook her head, banishing the image. She would not allow that picture, that fantasy of a safe and happy home and a real father for her son, be given life or strength, not even for a moment. She had enough emotional confusion in her life without adding more.

Once given, Leif's word bound his actions.

In the days since offering Mathew Cuttifer's trading cog to the cause of Edward Plantagenet, the Dane worked harder than a chained slave to find warehouse space in Sluys for his master's cargo until it could be retrieved. Leif might borrow the ship but he would not risk more than that. This was no easy task. Trading goods from Brugge were building up in storage ahead of resumption of seaborne trade in the spring and warehouse space was expensive and hard to come by. Also, Leif had to buy or find other goods to fill the cog's hold as cover for their voyage.

In the end, bolts of Anne's own woollen cloth

were stowed in the belly of the *Lady Margaret*, plus willow-wood tubs of good white butter from Riverstead Farm. To the navvies of Sluys it seemed odd to ship butter and cloth north to other Lowland provinces, which had a more than plentiful supply of their own such goods, yet the captain of the *Lady Margaret* refused to be drawn by their jokes. Setting his face and urging them to load faster, faster, he promised a bonus of Gruuthuse beer at the end of the stowing, if they did it in a day.

It was a cold and sad departure when the little ship slipped out past the breakwater of Sluys on a sullen November dawn. On her deck, Anne was red-eyed from crying, though she'd managed to save her tears until after her departure from her son, who would remain safe with Deborah.

Somehow the little boy had understood, no matter how hard she smiled and reassured him, that Anne was leaving for a long time.

'Don't go. No. Stay!' he'd cried when she put him to bed in her own room the night before she left. She'd loved that flash of defiance, but had tried to respond in a sensible, 'parent' voice.

'But you can sleep here, in my big bed with Deborah, until I return. You'll like that, my darling.'

'No. Stay with Edward. Stay!' His sobs tore at her resolve.

'Ah, there now, there now, don't cry. I'll bring you a present, a special one.'

The little boy had perked up at that; he loved presents.

'I want a blue horse.' He'd said it very firmly, looking her in the eye through his tears. 'A *giant*

111

blue horse. All for me. I'm a big boy now.'

'A blue horse? Very well.'

The tears subsided into gulps. 'Really? A truly blue one? Where will you get him?'

'I have some very clever friends. We'll find him, your horse. What will you call him?'

Edward had yawned and burrowed under the covers. 'Oh, I don't know yet. He will have a splendid name.' He used the big word proudly, but his eyes were drooping closed. Anne had sat beside him all that night, stroking his high, pure forehead, her heart breaking. Perhaps she would never see this child again.

Recalling her son's request now, as a rising sea rushed past, Anne smiled and shook her head. A blue horse? Why not? If she could make the impossible happen, if she could bring Edward back to Brugge to meet with the duke and survive, physically and emotionally, perhaps finding a blue horse would be easy.

Then she shivered as a physical pain beneath her ribs took her next breath.

*If I die in this journey, let the child survive. Ah, Mother of All, please let the child survive.*


## Chapter Fourteen

'When did this happen?'

'Five days ago, sire.'

'And where, my dear friend, did this so felicitous birth take place?'

Philippe de Commynes felt his nervous heart skip painfully. He lived in a capricious world. How often, in the end, did the messenger get blamed, no matter how valued he might be, how esteemed?

'In the sanctuary of St Peter's Abbey at Westminster, my Lord King. The queen – that is, the wife of the usurper, Edward, the Earl of March – laboured through the night and the boy was born early on the fourth day of this month. Of November,' he added helpfully.

Louis, King of France, looked hard at the man kneeling before him. 'I know the names of the months well enough, Monsieur de Commynes. Do you have proof?'

Philippe was sweating; he could feel the dank trickle under both his arms even though it was very cold in the Presence chamber. He swallowed and drew a deep breath, yet his words shook slightly as he exhaled.

'Nothing but the account of a witness, Lord King. A woman that my master, the duke, maintains amongst the ex-queen's women.'

For once Louis felt warm; perhaps it was suppressed choler heating his blood. His words smoked on the air as he spoke.

'And does your master know, Philippe? Hmmm.'

The young Monsieur de Commynes blushed at the king's sly tone. 'Of course, Your Majesty. Or else I should not be here.'

'So dignified, my young friend. So righteous.'

Louis drew the skirts of his heavy, fur-lined robe tight around his meagre shanks as he stood. He had conducted the audience in the Presence room, which was both formal and pompous, but

113

the throne itself was increasingly uncomfortable; the sharp edges of the seat cut off the circulation behind his fleshless knees and numbed his legs. That annoyed him. However, he bestowed a wintry smile upon the young man in front of him. *It is good for Philippe*, he reflected, *that I find I like him.*

'I have a message for your duke, Philippe. Tell him that word reached me two days ago that Edward Plantagenet has a son. And, unlike your master, I have proof that this rumour is correct.'

Pulling off a darned glove and exposing one wrinkled hand, Louis removed a ring from the smallest finger.

'Observe! This ring came from the finger of Elizabeth Wydeville herself, after the birth. She sent it with a message to her husband. But I have both the ring and the message. And the messenger. And thus I, also, know where Edward Plantagenet is hiding.'

The last word was defiled by spittle as the king spoke it, showing obvious contempt. A foolish response, thought Philippe de Commynes. Could it be that Louis underestimated Edward Plantagenet? He surprised himself with the treacherous idea and, for a moment, forgot to be afraid; suddenly he saw this king as he might be perceived by eyes not filmed with terror.

Louis was an unheroic sight. A face where the flesh had settled into blotched and raddled pouches; a barrel of a body, swaddled with fat, sitting like an apple above thin legs, with stick-thin arms attached. And an unfortunate stoop which had settled the head on a neck like that of a tortoise. As Philippe stood waiting for Louis to say something further, a treasonous image captured him. This king was a spider, a fat spider, pregnant with bile, ready to project poison if his belly was punctured by–

A sound like a dog vomiting interrupted Philippe's thoughts as the king spat onto the gleaming tiles of the Presence chamber. Again Louis gathered phlegm and hawked it up. A lipless smile split his face.

'Tell your master, Philippe, that his intelligence was of little use to me since I had it already. Burgundy will not become France's friend by the gift of second-hand information.'

Philippe couldn't help himself; he spoke without invitation. 'Sire, my master is a true subject of France and wishes only peace between his realm and yours.'

The king snorted. He slid the ex-queen's ring back onto his finger and held it up to the light for the younger man to observe. 'A ruby.' Malice almost made him merry 'So sentimental. A good and constant wife, her price above rubies, offers hope to her noble husband in exile with the news of the birth of his son, and so on. Such nonsense.'

The king wriggled gleefully on the Presence throne.

'Sadly, children, especially the newly born, often die in these dark months, do they not? It may be this little child will have been taken to his ancestors even before the ex-king, his father, hears of his birth? Ah, to be friendless and alone, as Edward Plantagenet is. How sad. But then perhaps this is the will of our great and gracious Lord.'

Piously, the king crossed himself and kissed the relic ring on the middle finger of his right hand.

Philippe de Commynes shivered. He was aware of the withered bits of flesh, the various splinters of bone, that the king kept dangling about his person. Devout as he was, they still gave Philippe the creeps. However, he also did not doubt the power of the French king. If he chose to stretch out his arm, perhaps his hand *might* reach into the Sanctuary of Westminster Abbey so far away across the sea.

'And so, my friend, pleased though I am to have seen you once more, your journey here was wasted. Go back to your master and tell him that France needs nothing from Burgundy.'

Another man, a man more given to bluster, might have shouted these last words, but not so Louis Valois. He spoke mildly, quietly, and yet they shivered in the air as if a trumpet had sounded beside Philippe's ear.

The young man bowed, the tippets of his sleeves brushing the floor.

'I shall convey Your Majesty's words just as they have been so graciously spoken.'

The king chuckled. 'Ah yes, I am certain that you will. You have proved your courage to us before and we live, yet to this day, as testament. Our court is the poorer for your departure, Philippe.'

Philippe did not raise his eyes as he backed away from the Presence chair. He knew that Louis was acknowledging their special relationship, yet other men stood about the chamber and they would be avid to see or hear anything they could report to ... who knew? Polite behaviour, however, demanded he respond.

'Your Majesty is too kind, indeed, to remember my trifling service. It was my duty, as a guest in your court.'

It was nearly two years gone since he, Philippe de Commynes, had saved the life of this same French king. Attending court with his master, Charles of Burgundy, on an official visit to the Louvre the year after the duke's marriage to the Lady Margaret of England, Philippe had seen a page empty the contents of a poison ring into the sauce around the king's dish of cinnamon-spiced tench. Philippe had raised the alarm immediately, though discreetly, whispering into his master's ear.

The result had been both blessing and curse. A blessing because the page had been caught and, after the sauce had been tested on a dog – which died in convulsions – had been racked for more information. They'd been too zealous, however, and the boy had died before revealing who had hired him to do the deed. For some days, paranoia had stalked the French court and suspicion, in the end, had fallen on Charles of Burgundy. There in lay the curse, and a froideur had underlain the relationship between Philippe and his master ever since.

Courtiers gossiped that Philippe was now more France's servant than Burgundy's. Desperate nonsense; nevertheless, his previously favoured existence at the right hand of the duke had become complicated and smeared by suspicion. Now, to prove his devotion for all to see, he had personally volunteered for this dangerous mission to the French king in these uneasy times.

If he could just safely depart the Presence chamber…

'Philippe, one last thing.'

'Sire?'

'What is this amusing name I hear you are called now?'

Philippe blushed. He would not say it; it was too humiliating. 'Name, sire?' He could not control his voice. Was he a child, close to tears, that it shook so?

Observing his discomfort, an almost palpable stirring moved through the court as wind through wheat.

'Boothead? Is that it?'

Philippe heard snorts of laughter, suppressed into coughs, all around him. He squared his shoulders, straightened his spine and dared to look the king in the eye.

'A joke, sire. It pleased Duke Charles to make a joke after an accident. We all laughed merrily.'

He bowed with dignity and removed himself from the Presence chamber, his ears painfully hot. He could still hear the titters as they closed the doors but he determined to ignore them, all of them.

Yes, a hunting boot had been thrown at him, one of the duke's, and yes, it had hit him in the head. Had it been a deliberate insult or just a slip, as can happen? He'd laughed along with all the rest of Charles's suite at this misfortune, but the duke had compounded the injury by referring to him by the repellent name, 'Boothead'. It had stuck. And now they knew of it here in France. The *king* knew of it. Philippe felt his heart swell and harden.

If he were not appreciated in Burgundy, plainly there were other openings for him. Perhaps, if his duke and the Burgundian court did not believe in his loyalty, if they continued to mock him, he might become Louis's servant in truth, not just rumour.

'A son? The queen has had a son?'

Louis de Gruuthuse nodded. 'It was a good birth, sire. And the boy, your heir, is healthy and well.'

The party of men had been returning from another day at the chase, weary and mud-flecked but successful this time, when they were joined, at the gallop, by their host. The king had reined in his horse sharply, startling the stallion he was leading – across whose back the body of the elusive stag from the day before lay slung – fearful of bad news. But the knowledge of this birth changed everything. Everything.

Edward Plantagenet was joyous. His elation caused him to curb his horse so tightly that the animal snorted and fought the bit; then, slowly, regret chased rapture from his face. The Lowlanders put it down to his separation from the queen at this time, but William Hastings and Richard of Gloucester knew better. They knew his thoughts were with another little boy. And with his mother, Anne de Bohun, the woman who had given the king his real firstborn son.

Hastings, determined to break the king's sad mood, called out, 'The country will rejoice with you, sire!' He brought his horse close to the king. 'Wriggle all she likes when she comes to it, but

Margaret of Anjou's son has never been accepted as Henry's legitimate get. The new prince will give the lords someone to rally to. This is a most fortunate day for our cause, Your Majesty.'

Richard crossed himself fervently. 'Amen. A legitimate prince.' Briefly he caught his brother's eye.

'What name has the queen given the child, Louis?'

'Your own, Your Majesty, so I understand. Edward.'

'And so, Louis, if my brother-in-law has sent this news himself, how long ago did it happen?'

'Perhaps as much as eight or ten days?'

But Edward hardly stayed to hear the answer. Dropping the reins of the horse carrying the stag, he spurred his mount and wheeled it back in the direction of the Binnenhof.

'Edward?' Richard called after his brother. Then, being ignored, he kicked his own mount into a gallop to follow the king, as did William Hastings.

Louis de Gruuthuse, caught by surprise and mud-spattered, was left to lead the stallion and the stag home. The time for caution was at an end, and he knew it.

## Chapter Fifteen

The waves were mountains and the valleys between them deeper and darker than the night fast coming out of the west. Amongst the chaos of wind and water, the shrieking power that threatened destruction to the *Lady Margaret* and all aboard her, the treacherous thought came unbidden. *A woman on board. What should a seaman expect?*

But the Dane dismissed the superstition immediately, settling in to fight the sea. Freezing water in his face, darkness coming on, terror nesting in his bowels, he remembered that other voyage, years ago, when he'd taken Anne and Deborah to Whitby on the *Lady Margaret*. His own fear, and that of his men, had been groundless then, in that storm, and they'd be groundless now. He'd not give in or give up, because he wanted to live. And he wanted her to live. He'd fallen in love with Anne on that first voyage and nothing had changed in the years since. He'd bring them to land. He had to. He'd won against the wind and the sea before and he would again. Today.

Through the fast-dying light, he knew it was there, the coast. They were nearly in safe harbour, nearly, if they could just hold on, hold the *Lady Margaret* from breaking up.

'Bail! Bail – all hands. BAIL!'

But the cog's bow went under again, and she had only just struggled up, shrugging off the weight of the water streaming down her high, planked sides, when yet another black hillock hurled spume towards them and the mountainous crest toppled down.

Leif had been lashed to the tiller hours ago but even he felt numb as he saw what was coming. He had trimmed the sail as tightly as he could, leaving only just enough for the helm to answer.

But now, as he hauled on the tiller and hauled again, there was an almighty crack – the sail on the mast below the sterncastle shook loose and bellied wildly, yards trailing and whipping.

Leif bellowed without thought, 'Let it fill, then lash it *tight*. HARD!' The few men who remained on deck leapt to obey. This was life or death and they were all in it together.

Willing hands hauled at the sheets and Leif breathed in, a great swallow of cold air, and hauled on the tiller again with the strength of the desperate as the wave bore down towards the prow. But she answered, the helm answered, and the *Lady Margaret* began to tack across the face of the wave, diagonally, and up! And then she was at the top and sliding down, planing down into the valley below without being swamped. A miracle!

*Praise be!* For before the *Lady Margaret* journeyed down into darkness, Leif glimpsed heaven. Last light and a gap in the flying spume showed him what he sought: the breakwater of the port of Delft. His strength would serve; he would make it serve.

'Captain!' The shout came from his mate. 'Another one!' Another giant crest, and the *Lady Margaret* was heading straight towards it.

'*Get below!*' His voice was great enough to be heard above the storm and he knew they would obey him; there was nothing the men could do now that the sail was lashed. This was for him now, him alone.

As the wave barrelled towards them, the howling dark personified, he began to count, 'One, two, three,' as, measured, careful, powerful, he wrenched the tiller around once more...

Anne, below, bailing beside the men and up to her thighs in water, did not have time to pray, but she felt no fear. She would not die here. Not yet. This was only bad luck and the wrong season.

She had not served her purpose.

Yet.


When the *Lady Margaret* entered the pool at Delft, she was listing and damaged. The last part of the blow had swept two men from the deck and broken away a section of the rudder; it asked much of Leif to bring her to the quay without causing havoc to the carracks, hulks, cogs and even one great caravel already docked there.

But Delft was serene in the clear night as they tied the *Lady Margaret* to the wharf by what was left of her sternpost and a line from her bow. And Anne, after the fear and the cold of the storm, turned her mind to the next part of their journey. At least she was feeling warmer, having changed into her one dry travelling dress. Her clothes were good without being showy – the kind of garments a lesser merchant's wife might wear. She turned towards the exhausted captain.

'Leif, I have much to thank you for, and amends to make. We stand here tonight because of your great skill and strength. I am very grateful.'

Leif did not speak, his gaze sweeping the deck of his ship. It was a painful sight, one that offended him. He shook his head. 'Skill? I doubt my master will regard it as such.'

The *Lady Margaret* was a mess. Giant hands had tried to rip her body apart and, being frustrated, broke all that could be found on deck, most principally the upper structure of the sterncastle.

'Leif, I know the damage will take money and time to mend. I can provide the coin.'

He turned on her, dark-eyed with fury. 'I hope he's worth it to the country, lady. And to you. Men died for him today.'

Anne said nothing. The Dane was right: his men had died so that she could reach the king. That was her burden to carry. Another one. But she was exhausted too and felt a spasm in her jaw as her teeth clattered together. They needed food, warmth and sleep.

'We will speak of this tomorrow. And find men who can do the work whilst we are...' she stopped herself from naming their destination, '...away. Now, do you think we might find an inn that is even a little respectable?'

Leif guided her down the gangplank, the fingers of one hand laced with hers. 'Depends on your definition of respectable, lady.'

Anne laughed, she couldn't help it. 'Seaports. I remember Whitby some years ago. Don't you?'

He wished she'd not said it, not made him recall; he'd banished the knowledge of what he felt for her while fighting the storm.

Now, on the dark quay, with light spilling from a noisy alehouse as a drunk fell out of the door, abusing those within to whoops of laughter, there was a moment when Anne looked into Leif's eyes.

And accepted – as she'd not allowed herself to before – that this man was hers, body and bone.

She had to tear her eyes away from his, and found her fingers still clasped in his own; big, strong and scarred. Hers were tiny in comparison.

'I am so sorry for all the trouble, Leif. And for your men.' She uncoupled their hands gently and tried to joke, though there was an odd edge in her tone. 'I did not raise that storm. Please believe me.'

She intended to be ironic, but her voice broke and suddenly she looked what she was: young, vulnerable and crushed by responsibility.

Pity and compassion fused within the sailor's heart and almost stopped him breathing. Without thought, he reached out to enclose Anne within his arms – to give comfort, to seek comfort – but one look from the girl stopped him.

'Food. And warmth?' Her voice was almost under control.

She would not let herself take what was offered. To do that would destroy ... what?

Too much, that was all she knew. Too much. Herself included.

## Chapter Sixteen

'But why not? Why will you not allow an escort? Five days' hard riding – less, perhaps – and I can be in Brugge and this nonsense will be cleared up. Ten men, Louis, just ten of your men. Or I could take the Frenchmen we brought here. There, you see? An answer that serves us both.'

Louis de Gruuthuse was in a difficult situation. He understood the king's point of view entirely, and all the feasts, all the hunting, all the dancing in the world were not enough to hold Edward Plantagenet now that his son was safely born.

'Sire, my master has asked you to have patience. It is not the right time for you to attempt this journey. The road is far too dangerous and a handful of wolvesheads added to your own men cannot protect you properly once you are past my lands.'

Edward looked at him cynically. 'Your lands, Louis? Does my brother-in-law's most loyal servant now think of himself as something more than a *steward* of the Lowlands?'

He was deliberately provocative, determined to disturb the self-possession of his host with any weapon he could find. He succeeded.

A blush seeped upwards from beneath Louis de Gruuthuse's high collar; for once his patience broke and he glared at the king. 'That is unjust, Your Majesty. I am honoured to hold this country for my lord, the duke, your brother-in-law. I *am* his honest steward, overseer of his lands. I seek nothing more.'

'Oh ho, Louis, so stuffy, so righteous. You count Flanders amongst your duke's lands and yet my sister brought that to him as her dowry. Perhaps, since there's no help from him or you, and our old alliance is clearly at an end, I should turn freelance and take it back? I need a base, since neither you nor he will give me one.'

The king was deliberately working himself towards anger. He would break Louis's resolve with

126

whatever tools he had to hand.

The Sieur de Gruuthuse knew well that he was being provoked, but his innate courtesy was sorely affronted and he took the bait. 'Oh yes? And that would mean, let me see, thirty men to take a province?' His voice held just the hint of a sneer.

Real fury brought blood to Edward's eyes. 'Thirty men to take a kingdom, if you will not help me, Sieur de Gruuthuse. But, beware. Fail to assist my cause and Burgundy *will* be crushed!'

The Plantagenets were famous for many things: long legs, great height, great charm; but it was also said they had descent from the Devil's own consort, Melusine, through the female line. Stared down by red eyes in a marble pale face, Louis felt certain that the legend must be true.

The king placed his hand on the great sapphire set in the pommel of his sword. 'Choose, Louis. Choose *now*.'

Louis de Gruuthuse was neither a coward nor a weak man, but he knew of the berserk fury that Edward found in battle. A fury that some said was a gift from God, and others a curse from another source entirely. That engorged rage was personified before him. Edward, on his feet and furious, was a terrifying sight.

Slowly Louis lowered himself to one knee, though he did not bow his head.

'Your Majesty, you do yourself no honour in this. I am not your enemy. But you are not my lord. I owe you nothing.'

There was a moment's aghast silence in the room; a silence that hummed like swarming bees.

127

Louis heard the quiet hiss of steel withdrawn from scabbards.

'Yet my lord, Duke Charles, is bound to you by blood. By marriage. I will serve your interests, and those of your family, as I serve his, but I may not give what is not mine to offer.'

'Leave us.' Edward said it quietly, then, since no one moved, bellowed 'LEAVE US!' Primal and percussive, the roar bounced off the walls and men shook their heads to clear the ringing.

Louis nodded to his outraged companions, waving them towards the great doors. Edward, after a moment, tossed his sword to Hastings, who caught it neatly in mid-air. The king wished peace. For now.

The two groups of men backed from the hall, silent, dangerous and watchful. Edward Plantagenet might not be a king any more but the ferocity of his actions, his utter certainty, told that no one had discussed that fact with him very recently.

'Oh, get up. Go on, man. Rise!'

Louis got to his feet cautiously, his eyes never leaving the king's. Somehow he'd retained an appearance of detached calm, but how he yearned to sob breath into lungs that had almost collapsed from fear and anger. Suppressing that urge, he spasmed into coughing. The king banged hard on his back as he lectured his host.

'I was serious, Louis. If your duke will not see me, and you will not supply me with men, I fear I must take what I can from this country. You cannot expect me to stay mewed up and patient after all this time!'

The last words were screamed into the chill air

of the chamber and accompanied by a final hearty thump on Louis's back which hurt like a blow. The world held its breath; all sound outside the room ceased. Louis closed his aching eyes. He could see them all in the anteroom as vividly as if he were with them: the English staring at the Flemish, each group daring the other to make the first move.

'Your Majesty, I can do little. It pains me, but it is the truth. You must give my master more time. I beg you, please, do nothing rash' – by which he meant, nothing stupid.

The Binnenhof had once been a great fortress for the Counts of Holland. There were dungeons here still and, though he felt sick at the thought, Louis might yet be forced to offer Edward Plantagenet lodging in one of those deep windowless chambers; an acknowledged prisoner at last, not just a frustrated guest.

Would he do it? For a moment, an image of this magnificent man chained to a wall and starving flashed into Louis's head, but he knew the answer as he knew his duty to the duke. Yes, he would do it, if he had to.

The king gripped Louis's shoulder painfully and thrust his face close. The governor's head swam. He would faint! Then a film of pain descended over the brilliant blue of the king's eyes. 'Louis, I beseech you.'

The words were whispered; the men outside, straining to hear, caught nothing.

The silence filled them with dread; the same emotion that infected the blood of their masters.

De Gruuthuse shrugged and his mouth was stiff

as he tried to smile. 'Edward, you must be patient. There is nothing more I can offer you. I am your friend and my master wishes to be your friend also. No!' The knight held up his hand as Edward's eyes flew open in rage. 'It is the truth! And you must understand. Now is *not* the time for sudden action. We need more information, all of us, about Louis's plans. You must govern yourself in this, Edward. Nothing would please that spider more than to see you ride out from here, under-attended, under-armed, so that he may scoop you up and destroy you! Where would your country be then?'

'My country? My country does not want me or need me. My people will not care, perhaps.'

It was said. All the fear, the uncertainty and the terror had found a voice at last.

Louis smiled. The kind of smile a father gives a beloved son when the boy first challenges his sire's physical powers. 'Lord king, that is not true. You and I both know that the greater magnates of your realm will wait, very patiently and carefully, to see if it is worth committing to the cause of Warwick. Especially now you have a son and the succession is safe.'

It puzzled Louis de Gruuthuse that the king burst into laughter at those words, laughing until he gasped and nearly choked.

'Yes, I have a son. The son I've always wanted!'

The tone was odd; it seemed that the king was desolated by loss, rather than joyful at his good fortune. Louis ignored the strangeness; Edward was, after all, at breaking point.

'You must trust my master. If you can find faith

in his goodwill towards you, there is much to hope for regarding his support. Come, I feel certain that the feast is prepared. Perhaps you are hungry? I believe I could eat, if only to settle my stomach.'

Louis attempted this little joke to raise the king's spirits. But Edward Plantagenet had other thoughts. He shook his head.

'No, Louis. I wish to pray. Can you arrange for a priest to say a mass?'

'A thanksgiving mass for the birth of your son? I thought we were to do that tomorrow?'

The king nodded. 'Yes, tomorrow we will give thanks for my new son. This mass is for me, now. For strength. And that I may bring confusion to my enemies. Of which I have more than all the grains of sand in the sea.'

## Chapter Seventeen

'Which way is s'Gravenhague, young sir?'

The goose-boy was attempting to drive his reluctant charges through to the gates of Delft, yet he was flattered to be called 'sir' by this giant man with the kind eyes.

'Follow the road along the strand, Meinheer. It's not far. With brisk walking you should be there before they close the gates tonight.'

The big man's wife – a small woman wearing a travelling cloak, her face well hidden by its hood – held out an English penny to the goose-boy and asked, 'Is the strand road safe, young master?'

The boy puffed out his chest; he'd never been called 'young master' before either. 'There is little traffic on the road, dame, in this season. The Lord de Gruuthuse keeps order well in his domain. Wolvesheads do not dare operate between here and s'Gravenhague; he hangs them and leaves them turning in the wind.'

'We thank you.' The woman curtsied and hurried on after her man as he strode towards the line of dunes curving away to the north.

It was a cold morning, with a low sky, and the clouds were soft steel-grey. The boy was already late getting his geese to the poulterer, but he stood for a moment and watched as the two figures got smaller and smaller in the distance. He was puzzled. In these times there were few strangers on the roads, and yet this woman was plainly foreign, as was her man. The husband had spoken like a northerner, but his wife's accent had been odd; French was it, or something else? Hard to tell. Perhaps they were dangerous and he should warn the authorities in Delft? He snorted even as he thought it; would they listen to a goose-boy?

Besides, since when did spies have such gentle ways? The woman's hands had been soft; he felt the tips of her fingers where she'd put the penny into his palm still. He wished he could have seen her face. She'd have to be pretty, surely, since she'd gone to such pains to hide it, probably on her husband's instructions. Or perhaps she was grossly deformed. Was that it? Could she have been a leper even? The boy shivered, suddenly fearful. Could he really have been touched by a leper?

A sudden hissing and a volley of honks brought

him back to reality to see his flock broadly scattered; looking for forage and squabbling over what little there was. Three or four of the biggest birds were pecking at each other – wings up, necks stretched – over the desiccated clumps that remained after the first severe frosts of winter. The noise drove everything else from his mind. His geese did not know that this was the last meal they would taste on earth and, at another time, he might have let them sort it out amongst themselves, for pity's sake, but now he had to get his flock to the poulterer, and soon, or he'd catch more than leprosy!

Anne heard the boy shouting as he chivvied his flock together. She smiled. How simple that child's life was. So few concerns, so few duties. Just the geese and getting them to market.

Her concern, in the meantime, was keeping up with her companion, who was striding ahead. 'Leif? Leif! Slow down, *please!*'

When the sailor stopped, finally, and turned towards Anne, his heart squeezed tight in his chest. The hood of her cloak had blown back in the sea wind and, unusually, she'd not covered her hair beneath it, not even with a kerchief; the unexpected sight of glossy bronze tendrils floating in the breeze hit Leif with the force of a blow. It was a provocation, her uncovered hair, and it was not fair of her, not decent.

Anne was intimidated by Leif's scowl. Perhaps he was still angry with her about the damage to the *Lady Margaret?* Her voice shook when she caught up to him, though she masked it with a cough. 'What's wrong Leif? Are we lost?' She had thought they were friends, but now something cold touched her. Perhaps she'd been wrong. If so, her situation was much worse than difficult.

'Leif?'

He didn't reply, busying himself with checking the soles of his sea boots.

'Leif, is it the *Lady Margaret*? I thought the men you spoke with seemed honest. I am sure they'll do as you asked in repairing her, and their price seemed reasonable to me.' She had her voice under control now. It was important not to sound afraid.

Leif bit back hard words. How would this girl know honest from dishonest amongst shipmen? 'We'll see,' he said. 'Hard to bargain when something must be done fast.' He was gruff, patronising.

Anne coloured; a flash of anger spoke before she could choose the words. 'You forget that I managed Sir Mathew's trading fleet with Meinheer Boter in Brugge. I have a little knowledge in this area.'

He was abashed but her defiant glance provoked a self-righteous response. 'Cover your hair, woman. If we should meet other souls they will think it strange that my wife goes about so brazenly.'

Anne had never seen the easygoing seaman this way before. 'I had no time because you said we must leave so early. And everything was wet from the storm, even my kerchiefs. But if you think I should, "husband", I will do it, certainly.' She attempted a little joke to lighten the atmosphere between them.

'Don't call me that; it is foolish. Worse than foolish.'

Anne saw the hurt in Leif's eyes and quickly bent to open her pack, rummaging through her small bundle of belongings to cover the moment. 'Ah, here it is. Damp, but it'll do. You're right, we should do nothing to arouse suspicion.'

Deftly, she bound the white linen around her head, completely covering her hair. 'There. Respectable again?'

The sailor grunted. 'We must hurry, we've a way to walk before dark.'

Anne wrapped her spare kirtle around the heavy purse she'd been given by Margaret of Burgundy and shoved it right to the bottom of her bag once more. Her spare undershift and favourite shawl – the cheerful blue and yellow one she wore when working around the house – went in next. At the very top, she carefully placed a precious bone comb and a second pair of warm stockings; the ones she was wearing had helped with the blisters forming on her toes in the new willow-wood clogs, but if she needed extra padding she'd wear these as well.

'I'm ready.' She stood beside Leif, head held high, composed and tidy. Her leather pack, buckled closed, was back on her shoulders. 'Lead on, my friend, I'll do my best to keep up this time.'

For a moment, his face worked and it seemed as if he would reach out...

But Anne had turned away to gaze north, into the future, and the hand he'd begun to extend did not reach hers. He snatched it back before she could turn and see.

'Very well. We'll rest from time to time, but we must walk briskly or we'll find the gates closed against us.'

For luck, and to keep storms away, he kissed Thor's hammer on the chain around his neck. He would need more than the strength of the God of thunder on this journey, though. Loki's cunning was required if they were to survive, plus the speed of Sleipnir, mount of Odin; and, to see the future, to choose the right way, he must seek the wisdom of the All-Father himself.

And so they trudged on together into a bitter wind from the northeast; a freezing wind that whipped sand from the dunes into their faces and was as cold and sharp as shards of glass. But not once, in the next few hours, did Anne complain.

And not once, even if she stumbled, did Leif offer to help her.

She knew why. Of course she knew why. And so did he.

There were bells again, always bells, and though Edward tried to ignore them, they had become a severe trial for they measured out the agony of these uncertain days in pitiless bronze.

The town of s'Gravenhague was still crammed with people celebrating the first Sunday of Advent. Darkness closed in as the Haguers wandered home in noisy groups and, one by one, lamps were lit in the houses like so many small stars. Edward and Richard rode quietly through the narrow streets, murmuring plans to one another as their horses ambled along.

Since Edward's last painful interview with Louis de Gruuthuse, his resolve had stiffened. The birth of his heir would give his supporters in England heart; the tide would be turning in his favour even now. Money or no, supporters or no, tomorrow, at dawn, he and Richard planned to cut their way through the town gate and make for Brugge. This was the focus now of all their urgent, whispering talk, all their plans. The how, the what, the when.

Charles must be made to listen and, God willing, the rest would follow: men, money, armaments, and England.

But then the bells came again, clamouring, calling out, instructing. *Return to the palace, return to the palace, for if you do not, our master's men will search you out. Go now, for the gates of the town must be closed, the streets must be emptied and chained against the night. Go now, whilst you are still safe, protected within the sound of our voices...*

Bells and men know about the night. The time of shadows is a time of unexpected things, a time when souls can be lost to the snares of Satan, to the uncontrolled wiles of the flesh. A time when the great wheel of fate begins to turn...

'We should return to the Ridderzaal, brother, or our most saint-like host will become alarmed. We must be careful not to rouse his suspicion today.'

Edward snorted. 'Ha! At least we could supply Louis's men with a little sport if they tried to chase us through these lanes amongst the people. By God, I know London's streets are narrow, Richard, but these are absurd. And dangerous.'

They were riding slowly behind an obedient

137

crowd of Haguers hurrying home when some-thing caught the king's eye. Or someone.

He noticed the man because he was so tall; it was hard to tell in the fast-dropping dusk, but perhaps he and this stranger might even be of a height. Edward Plantagenet was used to being the tallest man in any gathering; to find another who matched him piqued his interest. The big man was striding away purposefully, followed by his much smaller wife, and walking so fast that the gap between the couple and the king was becoming greater by the moment.

Edward pointed. 'That man. See, brother? He looks useful.'

Richard craned to look and nodded. 'Seaman's boots. We'll need seamen. What do you think? Two-man press gang?'

That was enough for Edward; the king spurred his horse, hurriedly bowing left and right as the animal leapt forward to not a few shouts and oaths. 'Your pardon, dame, and you sir ... forgive us but...' Soon he was the length of his horse behind the tall man and felt safe to call out, in French, 'Sir, would you pause for a moment? Sir?'

Perhaps it was the press of people in the narrow street, or a last belligerent clang from the bells, or perhaps because the king's voice was very loud and that startled his skittish horse as he called, 'You, sir, you there. Stop!' – but what happened next would stay with Edward Plantagenet until the moment he died.

The tall man paused in his stride, then turned fast, defensively, an exposed knife glinting in one hand as the other was flung out, automatically, to defend the small woman at his side. She, surprised, turned back towards the king, seeking the source of the command, but slewed around too quickly. The cobbles of the roadway were greasy after rain and in that moment, with that sudden movement, the girl lost her footing on the filthy surface.

Down she fell, down, but she saw him, saw the king, and he saw her, her face a white blur as the hood of her cloak fell back, bronze hair suddenly freed as the kerchief fell from her head, and she called him, called out his name, 'Edward!'

And then she was gone, trampled beneath the hooves of Edward Plantagenet's unreliable horse. Anne!

'Ah, God, God!' He didn't remember flinging himself from the stallion's back, didn't remember pushing the rearing, frightened animal backwards into the outraged crowd. But in his dreams, his nightmares, once that terrible day was gone, he saw what happened next over and over again.

Anne, plucked up from the filth of the roadway, lay limp and broken in his arms; Anne, silent, as, frantic with fear, he held her against his chest, willing breath into her small body; Anne moaning, blood seeping into her hair; Anne opening her eyes, sorrowful, shocked, confused when she saw his face so close to hers...

But then came the blessing. She smiled. He always remembered that, dreamed of that, her smile at that moment. 'Ah, love; my dearest love,' she whispered, and one finger reached up and touched his face lightly, his mouth. Then she sighed, and closed her eyes. And he thought she

139

was dead; that he had killed her by his careless-ness, his ambition.

And in life, as in his dreams, Edward Plant-agenet stood like a rock in the angry, confused crowd as it eddied and swirled around him; stood there, holding Anne's frail body cradled against his chest and howled like an inconsolable child.

He had killed the woman he loved.

## Chapter Eighteen

The Binnenhof exploded with noise and rumour as people ran to accommodate the sudden crisis.

'Is she alive? Who is she?'

'Yes, just. I don't know. No lady, by her clothes.'

Gudrun and Hawise – two of Louis de Gruut-huse's kitchen women now pressed into different service – went about their work efficiently, each hurrying past the other in the Ridderzaal. Gud-run had just left Anne's room with a load of soiled clothes, and Hawise was running to supply the third-best guest chamber with clean, blanched bedlinen.

'Anyone else know anything?' Hawise hissed.

'No. Not even a name.' Gudrun flung the words over her shoulder 'But for a no one, she's being treated like she's someone, that's for certain.'

She was indeed, thought Hawise, as she rushed, panting, up the massive main staircase to the range of rooms that had been built into the walls of the old fortress. Normally, she would have used one of the twisting sets of back stairs, but there was no time to observe social niceties today.

She knocked softly on the door of the bed chamber and, hearing nothing but the low murmur of male voices, eased open the door and sidled through the gap.

Anne was lying, coma-deep, on one of the biggest, finest beds in the castle. She'd been cleaned of the filth from the roadway – Gudrun had seen to that – though she was paler than the milk-white dressing-gown Gudrun had robed her in.

*Very odd!* thought Hawise as she curtsied and placed her load of linen on a chest drawn up beside the bed. It would stay there until someone, anyone, gave her permission to change the bloody covers on the bolsters. Why was this humble woman – *very* humble, if the clothes taken from her bruised body were any guide – being waited on like some fine court lady? Witness the Lord de Gruuthuse's very own doctor, a grave look on his face, currently attempting to find the girl's pulse and not having an easy time of it.

And the English king. There he was too, pacing up and down, up and down, beside the bed and looking so anguished as he gazed at the girl, you'd think he'd killed a member of his own family.

'You!'

Hawise froze. Lord Louis had entered the room; the maid dropped a deep curtsy, her skirts crumpling in folds as she dipped.

'Yes. I meant you. Can you sew?' Louis was brusque.

All the men in the room turned and looked at her. Hawise blushed and fixed her eyes on the

141

floor, unused to the attention. 'Yes, sir, I can.' At another time, the girl might have boasted she was as neat with her fingers as any lady, but her lord's stern tone, the sense of things unsaid, frightened her.

'Very well. Master Jacobi – you hear? You have a confederate. What do you need?'

The doctor gently placed his patient's hand on top of the embroidered coverlet of the bed where it lay small and white. Unmoving.

'Spirits of wine, liquid honey and cobwebs; the first to clean, the second and third to seal the wound. Then silk thread. Are there ladies in this castle? Ladies who embroider?' He ignored what the servant had said, naturally.

Louis de Gruuthuse met Edward's eyes and shook his head. 'No, Master Jacobi, the Binnen-hof is a masculine world. We are an area garrison.'

Edward was suddenly beside the doctor. 'You must be able to use something other than silk, surely? Horses' hair, from their manes. It's used in field hospitals – I've seen them use it!'

The doctor shook his head. 'Sire, many men die in battle, but many more from poor doctoring afterwards. I do not find horse hair efficacious. I must have silk because it is strong; preferably silk thread which has been boiled.'

'What nonsense is this? Boiled? How can that help? There is no time for this, even if we had such thread–'

Hawise was very brave – and, yes, reckless, as she came to consider afterwards – when she interrupted the English king. 'Sire, I have a little silk.'

They all turned to look at the maid, astonished.

142

'I sew, as I said. A little. The nuns taught me. I make things for them. Altar clothes,' she added hastily. It was against the sumptuary laws for a girl such as she even to think of dressing in silk – that was for ladies, and only court ladies at that. But Hawise had the guilty secret of a red petticoat; something she'd been making recently. When it was finished, she intended to wear it under her kirtle to the spring fair. For luck, she'd told Gudrun, just for luck.

'Praise be, girl!' said the doctor. 'Go and find your silk and boil it well, for the time it takes to count to ten, ten times; that will soften the thread for my purposes. Do you understand?'

Hawise nodded. She couldn't count well herself, but there'd be someone in the kitchen who could. Perhaps the cook, since he kept the tally sticks for the larder. Without another word she ran from the room, not even stopping to curtsy.

The doctor's words followed her: 'And send the other one back with a pannikin of boiled water. And the honey. And cobwebs too. Hurry!'

'Doctor?' Edward spoke hesitantly, his eyes fixed on Anne's face. 'What will you do for her?'

Master Jacobi looked up briefly from his work as he probed with gentle fingers amongst the matted blood on Anne's skull, moving the strands of her hair aside.

'The horse trampled the girl, here...' he displaced the neck of the dressing-gown for a moment; the bruises on Anne's shoulders and chest were violent and extensive, '...and here I think too, on the side of the head. Just above the ear. Do you see?'

Edward, used to the gore of battle, had learned emotional immunity from the shock of seeing bone, flesh and blood mashed together, but a great wave of nausea swelled into his throat as the Jew lifted a flap of skin from the side of Anne's head, the hair still attached.

'One or two ribs only are broken, and one of her fingers also. I can do nothing for the ribs except strap her chest, but she must be kept still whilst they heal. I can bind the finger too, so that it sets straight. Then we must clean this wound on her head and sew the skin back in its correct place. The lady...' there was the merest hesitation before the word, 'is young and strong, sire. There is every reason for hope since I cannot find any fracturing of the bone of the skull. That was my chief concern.'

Edward sat down abruptly on the chest beside the bed, pale and sweating. Somehow he forced the words out. 'She will not die, master?'

'What must be done is delicate, but no, I do not think she will die.'

Before he could say more, Gudrun arrived carrying a leather bucket of steaming water in one hand and an earthenware pot in the other. She curtsied awkwardly to Louis de Gruuthuse. 'Honey, master, and boiled water? Hawise said–'

The doctor frowned. 'And cobwebs? I need cobwebs!'

The girl looked at him blankly. Irritated, he motioned for her to place what she carried on the chest beside the king.

'Since you have no cobwebs, girl, this must serve. Rip up one of these fine sheets as quickly as you can – thin strips, if you please, but not too long. Shortly your friend will return and then, when I tell you, I want you to dip the linen in the honey. Do you understand?'

Gudrun nodded obediently, thinking the man was mad. Cobwebs? Honey? On *bandages?* What for? Still, being young, and not pert – unlike Hawise – she said nothing and did as she'd been told.

'Lord Edward, and you, Lord Louis, I will need your help very soon.'

The doctor examined the head wound closely again, using a candle since most of the room was dark except for the light from the fire. 'And more candles here, quickly, so that I can see!'

Louis strode to the door. Outside, a small number of men guarded the entrance to the chamber. Leif Molnar was there as well, growing increasingly angry with fear.

'You! Go to the pantler – bring candles quickly. As many as you can carry.' One of the guards bowed and hurried away.

Leif looked Lord Louis directly in the eye. 'How does my wife do, lord?'

He spoke clearly, calmly, and Edward, inside the bed chamber, heard him. His face drained white. Anne was married?

Louis de Gruuthuse was surprised as well. He'd not had time to question Edward since the flurry and drama of the king's arrival back at the Binnenhof, the filthy, bloodied girl in his arms and the Duke of Gloucester shouting for assistance, but clearly the woman currently lying unconscious in the third-best bed chamber was very important to the king. The agony of great loss was in Edward's eyes, and on his face.

Edward strode to the chamber door and looked searchingly at the man who claimed to be Anne's husband. Implacable, as if on guard, Leif Molnar stared directly back. For a moment, the king was intimidated; there was a spark of red in his rival's eyes, he'd seen it quite distinctly when the man first turned and looked at him.

'You are her husband?'

Leif nodded but did not bow. Now he knew, with utter certainty, that he hated this man. King or no king, duty or not to his master, the fate of the kingdom of England – none of that mattered to Leif Molnar any more.

'I want to see my wife.' No hint of deference, no plea.

Edward stood aside silently as the Norseman strode past him; he'd been right, they were of a height.

The room was quiet except for the fire's crack and sputter. The doctor went about his work silently, washing the last of the blood from Anne's face. Leif's own face was rigid, a mask of control, as he walked towards the carved bed on which Anne lay. For one wrenching moment it seemed he was looking at a corpse, but then her chest rose, microscopically, and she opened her eyes.

'Leif?' She managed to mouth the word, and even smiled as she swallowed painfully. 'Give Edward what we came with,' she whispered; then her eyelids quivered and closed and she was still again.

Leif wheeled around. Edward was watching

him from his place by the fire. 'You did this.'

It was more than a flat accusation, it was a curse, and its contempt was an affront to Louis de Gruuthuse. Distraught husband or not, this could not be tolerated.

'Guard!'

'Wait!' Edward's voice cracked through the room as Louis's men appeared. 'What did she mean?'

There were tears in Leif's eyes, which added to his rage, his humiliation. 'She has nothing to give you. Nothing!'

It took four men, six, finally eight of Louis de Gruuthuse's bodyguard to remove Leif Molnar from the chamber, but in the end, remove him they did, ignoring Edward's protests.

Louis de Gruuthuse was glacially polite. 'This woman's husband he may be, Your Majesty, but I cannot permit such insolence to your person in this house. He will not be harmed. And when his wife has recovered, he will be released and they can both go home.'

During the flurry of the ejection, Hawise had returned with a wooden bowl holding a mass of wet silk thread. She was followed by two soldiers, each carrying standing branches for candles the height of a man, made from forged iron. Each guard also carried at least a gross of thick candles made from precious summer wax. When they were lit, the scent of honey filled the room; the breath of grace.

The candle stands were positioned on either side of the bed so that the doctor's work would be lighted from both sides and from above.

'Now, if you would just help me?' Doctor Jacobi

147

motioned for the maids, Gudrun and Hawise, to draw back the sheets so that he could move Anne across the bed.

'No! Do not touch her.' Edward strode forward and the women pulled back, frightened. 'I will lift this lady.'

He gathered Anne gently against his chest and, tender as a father with a sleeping child, lifted her from the surface of the bed. He leaned down to place her flat upon the mattress as the doctor had ordered, and her hair, the colour of amber, spilled between his fingers into the light. Russet and gold glimmered against Anne's white face, and then, oh how he remembered.

'Your Majesty?' The doctor was nervous. The king still held the girl in his arms above the surface of the bed as if he would never put her down.

Louis de Gruuthuse cleared his throat noisily; it was enough.

Edward laid Anne on the mattress as carefully as if she'd been made of glass. And in a sense she was – milk glass; her face was almost translucent in the candlelight, with blue shadows at her temples and under her eyes.

'Come, Lord King, we should permit Master Jacobi to be about his work. The court will be waiting for its supper.' Louis winced as he saw the doctor lift the flap of skin from Anne's head once more, momentarily exposing the bone of the skull beneath. Perhaps food was not such a good idea after all.

Gudrun held Anne's head immobile whilst the doctor began a line of tiny stitches along the girl's scalp, for all the world like the edging on a blanket.

Louis de Gruuthuse swallowed his gorge. 'We can visit this young lady later, when the doctor has finished his work and she has recovered, my lord?'

But Edward was standing beside the bed, fascination lending momentary detachment. He had seen enough doctoring in the field to realise that this man had superb technique and his earlier squeamishness dissolved in gratitude. Doctor Jacobi was sewing Anne's scalp back together as carefully and neatly as any duchess about her embroidery, though the red silk thread was an ominous note against the white skin.

After many minutes of careful work, the doctor exhaled a sigh, straightened his back and turned to Lord Louis and the king. An undemonstrative man, he was almost smiling now. 'In the end, it is a simple wound. We must wait for the morning now to see how she fares.'

The king nodded, his eyes fixed on the still figure in the bed. 'I will remain here, Lord Louis. Forgive me, but food is not what I need now. What is needed is prayer for Lady de Bohun, and that I can supply, by her bedside.'

Louis was astonished. This was the legendary Lady de Bohun? How had he not recognised the woman who had passed like a meteor through the trading community of Brugge three or so years ago? Waving a dismissal to the now very curious doctor, Louis de Gruuthuse hurried forward to the bed, delicate sensibilities forgotten. And then he understood.

In Brugge, he'd never seen this woman in anything but the clothes of a courtier and certainly never with her hair loose, as it was now. And earlier this evening, when she was carried into his castle by the king in the midst of a panicked crowd of courtiers and servants, her face had been obscured by blood and she'd been wearing clothes that were anything but lavish.

'Yes. It is Lady de Bohun. I see that now.'

He and Edward locked glances. Louis de Gruuthuse now understood everything. He bowed with the grace of the born courtier.

'I shall see that you are not disturbed, Your Majesty,' he said, and backed away reverently, gently closing the door as he left.

In the silent room, Edward Plantagenet leaned forward and delicately brushed a strand of hair from Anne's face. She did not move. He picked up one pale hand and held it to his face. Her skin was cool, and soft.

'My darling girl. I'm here. I'll be with you all this night. And tomorrow – as long as you need me. But, if you can hear me, tell me, what do you have for me, Anne?'

There was no answer, just the crack of the fire as a log dropped and sparks flew up the chimney.

But in that sudden flicker of light, Edward saw Anne's small leather pack. It had been cast without thought into a corner of the room and now an edge of bright blue with a flash of yellow caught the king's eye.

'Forgive me, my darling girl.'

In two strides he had picked it up and un-buckled the straps that held the bundle together. And there, inside, wrapped tightly in a kirtle beneath a shawl of finely woven blue and yellow, he found what he was looking for.

150

The milk-pale girl in the bed remained still and silent as Edward Plantagenet stuffed the letter from his sister into the front of his jerkin; he would read it later. He weighed the heavy purse of coins in his hands and gazed at Anne's closed eyes, the bandages around her head.

Anne had paid for his freedom. Was the price worth it?


## Chapter Nineteen

The baby whimpered, hungry again. Duchess Jacquetta picked the prince up from his cradle and rocked him, but it was not enough. Even one of her fingers to suck made no difference. 'There, there, little man; soon, soon.' Wails turned into a healthy bellow.

'Mother?' The voice from the bed was sharp. 'It's no good, I cannot sleep; the poppy they gave me did not work. Give him to me. At least one of us will be happy.'

The baby was swaddled tightly, arms bound to his sides. *Just like a little silkworm*, thought his grandmother tenderly as she took the boy who should have been born the Prince of Wales over to her daughter.

Elizabeth Wydeville struggled to sit up and uncovered one breast, swollen and proud now that the milk was well established. Taking the baby in the crook of her right arm, she tapped him on the cheek so that he turned his head towards her.

151

Smelling the milk, he fastened his tiny open mouth around the nipple. The wailing stopped as, urgently, the infant sucked and snuffled and sucked again, so fast that he choked. An indignant roar filled the small room.

'No, Edward, not so impatient. Really. Just like your father, sometimes...' Elizabeth looked up and caught her mother's amused glance. The glimmer of a smile curved the queen's mouth, the first of many weeks. She rocked her son, settling him with the ease of an experienced mother. 'Here, yes, like that ... slower, no gulping.' She relaxed as the baby's suckling found a rhythm and he closed his eyes, concentrating.

'I'm sorry we couldn't get you a nurse, child.'

The queen shook her head. 'I'm not. I haven't done this before. It's ... different. I'm glad I'm giving this child suck.'

The duchess was curious. 'But your breasts, daughter. Are you not concerned your son will wither them?'

A hard expression marred the queen's lovely face. 'I don't care. Let him suck them to dry husks. He'll suck my rage into him. He'll suck my desire for justice into his bones. It will make him stronger. Besides, what does it matter if my breasts turn to empty bags? I'll never see the king again if Louis has his way, and then beauty won't matter to me ever again.'

Jacquetta smiled. 'Perhaps you will change your mind, in time. Besides, I think there's a way to go before Louis gets what he wants. I've heard some interesting news.'

Her daughter's eyes sharpened on hers. 'What?'

'Charles of Burgundy is wavering. He doesn't know what to do, which side to back. In that fact, there is opportunity.'

Elizabeth Wydeville snorted with derision, disturbing her son. As he yelled, she swapped him to the other breast, and he subsided into earnest silence as he fed once more.

'Who says this?' she demanded.

'I've had a communication – a message from Sir Mathew Cuttifer. He says he has a reliable source in Brugge. A friend of the duchess.'

The queen's face darkened. 'Why should we trust what he might say? He, and his house, have never been our friends. That woman, Anne de Bohun, was his servant. She tried to steal Edward from me.'

Patiently, Jacquetta shook her head. 'Tried, and failed. Ah, daughter, daughter, this is all in the past. Do not distress yourself. The king has not seen Anne de Bohun since his sister's wedding. She has disappeared from our lives for good. But information is useful, whatever its source.'

The baby sighed deeply at his mother's breast and his small red mouth softly detached from the nipple. He slept, his little face flushed rose-pink from the effort of sucking. Automatically Elizabeth rocked her son back and forth, back and forth.

'And so?' her tone was sullen.

'Don't you see? If Charles is uncertain what to do about Edward and England, then he may be influenced. Influenced to our cause; influenced to help the king. But first, we must deal with Louis.'

'How can we do such a thing?'

153

There was little light in Abbot Milling's cell, even though it faced east. Elizabeth Wydeville squinted and leaned forward to inspect the thing her mother was holding towards her; something Jacquetta had fetched from the pocket-bag slung from her girdle.

'What *is* that?'

Jacquetta held the object up in the light from the one, small, high window.

'A toy for the baby?'

The duchess shook her head and spoke softly. 'Look closer, my daughter. This is no toy.'

Gently placing the sleeping child on the counterpane of the bed, the queen held out her hand to inspect the object. It was a doll-sized man, mounted on a little wooden horse caparisoned in blue cloth. Painted in gilt on the cloth were miniature fleurs-de-lys. The doll had a tiny gold circlet around its head.

'Who is this, mother?' She might ask the question, but Elizabeth Wydeville knew the answer.

Jacquetta looked around. The door was closed and they were alone. She leaned towards her daughter and whispered one word. 'Louis.'

The queen gazed fearfully at her mother. Jacquetta had something else in her fingers now: two tiny silver daggers, blades as sharp as thorns.

'Hold out your hand, my daughter.'

The baby whimpered in his sleep and twitched, frowning. Both women turned to look at him.

'We have no choice, my daughter. For your son's sake. He will be king one day, but only if we help him now.'

Elizabeth looked down at her infant and

nodded. Slowly, she extended her hand and took one of the wicked little knives from her mother's fingers.

'Together. We must do this together. Now.'

There was an instinctive rhythm to what happened next. One breath, two, and on the third, the deposed queen of England plunged the little knife deep into the straw breast of the doll; at the same instant, her mother stabbed hers into the effigy's groin. There was a sound like breath escaping. Perhaps it was the wind.

The baby woke, screaming, as is the way of a fractious child when his mother is tense. But try as they might to comfort him, mother and grandmother both, the distraught baby did not close his eyes for the whole of that day, nor the night that succeeded it until Thomas Milling, the abbot of St Peter's Cathedral Church, touched his brow with holy water.

Then he slept.

## Chapter Twenty

Louis XI was not an athletic man, and he didn't like riding because horses didn't like him; a feeling that was mutual. This was not only an inconvenience, however; it was a scandal. The King of France, after all, was expected to be Le Grand Chevalier. Well, this king wasn't. He preferred to travel by litter.

And so, on a freezing evening just after the

second Sunday in Advent, Louis de Valois arrived at an obscure hunting lodge he favoured, huddled behind the curtains of his shabby litter. He was accompanied by a small party of guards and a scant few annoyed and wet courtiers. He was grumpy, tired and in pain from his belly – a not uncommon occurrence.

The king favoured this place for its unfashionable anonymity. Cramped and uncomfortable as it might be, the lodge was close enough to Paris for intelligence to reach him if he required it, yet sufficiently hidden away to be discreet and therefore safe.

Louis didn't like his capital, Paris, for it contained many unhappy memories of the father he'd loathed and been frightened of. As a consequence, he was suspicious of the city's loyalty and avoided it whenever he could. Paris was also where the nobles liked to congregate, especially now that Advent had begun, and the palace of the Louvre was Queen Charlotte's most favoured residence. If Louis went there, he would have to speak to her, even go to her bed, since it would be scandalous if he did not.

This last, and the fact that the magnates and lesser lords would even now be gathering to petition him for this thing and that as seasonal boons, made up his mind. They would all have to wait. He didn't want the distraction of dealing with their plots and counterplots for there was urgent work at hand.

Tonight he'd received news that worried him; perversely, he blamed his functionaries in Paris for that. They should have told him sooner! It was their job to find him, to track his progress around the kingdom. He would have no excuses!

Edward Plantagenet and his men had disappeared from the Binnenhof.

Sitting down to dinner, Louis called his advisor to go over the details once more.

'How many of them?'

'We are uncertain of their numbers, sire.'

Olivier le Dain – called 'the barber' due to his humble beginnings in the court as Louis's valet – was extremely nervous but hoped he did not show it. Born under the sign of Saturn, le Dain lived up to the stereotype, being dark, quiet, cautious and dangerous. But this king, to whom he had become a useful advisor, reduced him to a fearful, sweating jelly, much to the secret joy of his enemies.

It was the spectre of the 'cage' that did it.

Two years ago le Dain had displeased the king – he still did not know in what way – and had spent an appalling winter hanging in a cage over the battlements of Nantes, exposed to the wind, the sleet and the snow, wearing only what he'd had on when arrested. He'd nearly starved and both his little fingers had frozen black and fallen off, but eventually – praise be – he'd been forgiven his sin, whatever it had been. But what if he should offend again? How would he know?

Le Dain watched nervously as Louis turned his attention to the food. The king attempted to gnaw on a goose leg, but even at this distance the advisor could see it looked slimy – the sign of putrefaction. He blanched as, grimacing, the king threw the leg down on the silver charger.

'Too much pepper. They've burned my mouth!

The cooks are idiots, did they think I would not notice? This meat is putrid. Do they plot to poison me? Le Dain! I want answers. Now!'

Le Dain hurried forward to the table; he was sweating, giddy from fear. He would have to distract Louis, and quickly, or God alone knew how far the king's paranoia might run.

Tonight, the king was dining in a small room at the back of the hunting lodge, completely alone except for five servants and the barber. Wiping greasy fingers on the sleeve of his gown, Louis waved the food away, scowling, and belched foul breath full into the face of his advisor. Then he winced. He'd been troubled by pain in his guts all day; it was getting worse.

Another scowl, this time at le Dain. 'Why are you uncertain of the Englishmen's number, Olivier? It is not useful to me if my servants know less than I expect them to.'

Le Dain resisted the urgent desire to piss himself as he ran through the best way to present what he knew. Plainly this was a night when the king's digestion would be a trial to both master and servant. The barber would accept any kind of reprimand for poor performance, just as long as it did not end in the cage.

'Sire, the facts are these. Edward the Usurper, Earl of March, crossed from England nearly a month ago with a party of some twenty men. It included his younger brother, Richard, formerly Duke of Gloucester; his Great Chamberlain, Lord William Hastings; the Lord Rivers, his brother-in-law and a number of archers and–'

'I know all this! Why tell me again?'

Le Dain swallowed and sucked a deep breath into his lungs. *Calm. Stay calm.*

'It seemed useful to recap the names of the nobles, sire, because they too are missing. As are the earl's Welsh archers. He had only a few, but they are formidable fighters.'

Louis grunted, and signalled for le Dain to continue as he picked at the uneven stump of one black tooth with his knife; a morsel of gooseflesh had become trapped – he could feel it. The puffed and tender gum sat proud of the damaged tooth and prodding it disturbed a fragile balance within the king's mouth; there was a sudden eruption of pus and blood. Louis yelped and spat the foul matter onto the floor rushes at his feet. The barber fell silent, unnerved. Irritated, the king signalled for him to continue as he mopped at his mouth with the edge of the tablecloth.

'It seems that the Sieur de Gruuthuse did not approve of his guest's departure. We know this because on the morning that the king ... er, the earl that is ... was found to be missing, several parties were sent out from the Binnenhof to find him.'

'And then?' Louis's voice was muffled as he tried to staunch the blood and pus now oozing freely from his gum. The tooth had surrendered its tenuous hold under his ministrations and had left an inflamed and angry hole. The pain was eye-watering.

Le Dain glanced warily at his master. The king was moaning and snorting now, tears running freely from closed eyes. He hurried on, since those had been his instructions. 'Alas, the earl could not be found. Louis de Gruuthuse has since sent urgent messages to Duke Charles at Brugge. We know this because we managed to fall in the way of one of the messengers.'

'Only one of them?'

The king was inspecting the remains of his tooth as he spoke, holding it up to the light as if it were a gem, or a pearl of great price. He glowered as he turned it round and around. 'This is the fault of the cooks. That goose was a disgrace!' Suddenly he threw the little black pebble into the heart of the fire. 'I've only got six of my great teeth left now. And perhaps they will not survive to the spring. I shall have to live on gruel. Or have my food chewed before I eat it.'

A repellent and gloomy thought, but Louis was not seeking pity; he was angry. He wanted someone to blame for growing old. There was a sudden *pop* from the fire as the tooth exploded and the foul smell of rotted, burning bone wafted into the room. That made the king even angrier.

'Send me the man who cooked that goose!'

Le Dain backed out of the king's presence at speed, bowing, blessing the rotten tooth as a diversion from the discomforting news of Edward Plantagenet's disappearance.

Not for all the estates he coveted in the Loire would Olivier le Dain go willingly into the king's presence again whilst Louis was in this mood. Luckily for him, the hapless cook would most likely draw the king's ire down upon his head, and he, Olivier, would have another night's sleep in a bed, rather than on the freezing metal bottom of a cage. Tomorrow would be another day. And to-morrow, he felt sure, he would find out where Edward Plantagenet was hiding. But when would that be?

Olivier le Dain stood in the hall of the hunting lodge and bellowed. It gave him pleasure to see how many of the king's party came running to see what he required.

'The goose cook! I want the goose cook! And so does the king!'

The unlucky chef was ejected from the kitchens and into le Dain's presence, where he fell on his knees, head bowed.

And then it came to him. He, Olivier le Dain, would deliver the head of Edward Plantagenet to his master on a platter; just as this man, grovelling before him, had served up the goose. Then he would be rewarded with the pretty estates he coveted in the valley of the Loire.

Fearfully, the cook dared to raise his eyes, hoping against hope that he had earned the praise of the king for the meal that had just been served. But then all hope died. He saw his fate written in the eyes of Olivier le Dain and moaned.

The barber was pitiless. 'My friend, you have just cooked your last goose.'

## Chapter Twenty-One

They were moving dangerously fast across a silent, white world. Leif Molnar had been right: a sea voyage, treacherous as it might be in winter, was much to be preferred to a land journey.

161

Horses are fragile creatures, despite their size, and a landscape obscured by winter hides many obstacles – holes in the track, frozen puddles, black ice. Every step the horses took risked their riders' lives at this speed.

But Anne de Bohun did not consider any of these things as she rode pillion behind Edward Plantagenet. Her concerns were of the future beyond this cold journey – that, and the immediate past.

It was less than ten days since she'd been trampled beneath the hooves of Edward's horse and, though she was strong and had recovered quickly, she was still frail and in pain. Under the hood of her riding cloak, her head throbbed in time with the jolting hooves, as did her tightly bandaged ribs and finger.

Was it the wounds knitting together that caused the pain, or was it her conscience? It had not been her choice to leave Leif Molnar behind. Why then did she feel such pain when she thought of the captain, saw his face in her mind?

Edward, his men and Anne had fled the Binnenhof some three days and nights ago. Anne had not been asked if she wished to accompany them. Edward had entered her room in the dead of night, kissed her awake – she'd thought it was a dream – and, taking her from the warm sheets, had dropped clothes over her head to cover her shivering naked body. All that time he had said nothing, though he'd kissed her again, so longingly.

Together they had stolen, hand in hand, through the sleeping castle to where the horses and the men were gathered, restless and silent in the starlight. Her knees had given way then, from fear and physical weakness, but also from the sudden knowledge that her future had just lurched into being, fully formed.

Edward caught her before she slumped to the ground. Quickly, he'd vaulted into his saddle and she had been handed up to him. He did not trust her to ride alone until he knew she had the strength to hold a horse in check. They'd wrapped her in a thick riding cloak, over the many layers of clothes Edward had insisted on dressing her in before they fled her room. He had even advised on two pairs of hose, and his own long fingers had tied the ribbons beneath her knees.

Now, three days into their journey, Anne blessed the king's foresight and his care for her, but it was impossible to stay warm, especially riding pillion. She burrowed into Edward's faintly warm back, sensing the heat of his body even through his layers of clothing and her own.

He glanced over his shoulder at her, smiling. 'My darling is brave. We will rest soon. When it is dark. How is your head?'

His back was very broad and to sit behind him, pressed up against him, was intoxicating after two years of deprivation. Anne's feelings were a rolling mass of confusion, and they were not helped by this proximity.

'Better, I think. But ... Your Majesty, I feel sure that I could ride by myself now. We would travel faster, if you'd let me?'

The king laughed, and the vibration passed through her chest, between her breasts. Unconsciously, her hands tightened around his waist.

Edward felt the circle of her arms and a slow, hot ache warmed the pit of his belly. He covered her hands with one of his, the other controlling the horse with practised strength.

'I don't want to travel any faster then we're going now. I want every moment of this. Every single moment of you.'

Only she heard the whispered words. She bowed her head and the hood slipped forward obscuring her face. She said nothing.

'Anne? Did you hear me?'

She sighed. 'Yes, I heard you. But I've been thinking of Leif.'

Leif. Edward Plantagenet frowned. He wanted, so much, to know if Anne had married the Dane, but then again...

'Will he be alright, do you think? Leif, I mean.'

The question hovered between them in the frozen, rushing air. Edward heard the shame and the guilt in her voice. He ignored both as he lied calmly.

'Of course. Why would Louis want to harm him? They'll have let him go by now, I should think. Why feed one extra mouth in winter, if you don't have to, even if he is your husband?' He almost choked on the last word, fishing for a response. Anne did not reply.

Around and ahead of them, the party of men travelled at a rough canter across the hard ground. The earth was frozen so rigid that it drummed beneath the hooves of the horses. And the wind, if Anne looked around and past Edward's torso, was bitter. Better by far to press herself into his back, head snuggled between his shoulder blades. That way she could pretend to be warm, pretend this was all a dream, pretend that Leif was not a prisoner in the dungeon of the Binnenhof.

The movement of the horse was seductive, it rocked her. She was tired, so tired. Nearly asleep...

'Anne?'

'Yes, Lord?' She spoke dreamily into his back, his spine.

He felt the sound travel through him. It was delicious, but he shook his head. 'I am not your lord. I am your lover. Perhaps you had forgotten.'

She shivered. She'd been so afraid of this, knew she'd not be strong enough when the time came. She did not answer.

Edward narrowed his eyes. Half of him was doing the job he was used to – scouting the landscape automatically, alert to pursuit or threat of any kind – but the other half was a starving hound. He was alive with every sense to this girl; she was his most tangible desire and now they rode through the world together as if tied. He could feel her ribs as she breathed; the firm pressure from her breasts as they moved up and down with the motion of the horse; her thighs, her knees, lying behind his own in the pillion. He had only to drop one hand behind him to...

'Are you his wife?'

What should Anne say? The truth would be no protection. But if she lied, perhaps it would give her the strength to...

'Tell me, Anne. Did you marry that man?'

She spoke into his back again, the sound

165

muffled by the layers of cloth between them. The words buzzed through his flesh from his spine to his heart. 'You've been a long time gone. Is it so surprising?'

He knew her well and even laughed then. 'Nothing about you will ever surprise me.'

The king reined his horse tighter and the animal responded, picking up its pace. This was good ground now, the party could make more speed in their flight.

'You're being evasive. Tell me the truth.'

She sighed shakily. 'I will tell you the truth. But not now.' She grimaced even as she spoke. It was a stupid answer; only exhaustion could have formed those words.

They were riding due south and the world was empty of people. As the season of Yule approached and the weather turned colder, work in the fields stopped. Winter was the time for indoor enterprise: chair-making, carding and spinning, telling stories beside the fire. And the women nursed the babies born in late summer, each mother hoping there would be enough food to make enough milk so that her little one lived to see the spring...

Edward and Anne were excluded from that warm world with its fug of family and hearth. They were both outcasts now, fugitives. It was the irony of fate: Edward was now living as Anne had once done, when he exiled her from England, pregnant with his son, nearly five years ago.

Richard of Gloucester cantered up beside his brother and matched his horse's pace with the king's. He smiled briefly at Anne – he liked this girl, liked her courage. She asked no more than the men, refused special treatment when they camped at night, and ate less than the rest of them. Yes, he admired her spirit. But there were harsher things to concern him now than one woman's welfare caught up in a man's quest. He was anxious.

'Edward, there's a farm ahead. A big one.'

The light was dropping fast as the brief afternoon fled. Edward slowed his horse from a canter to a trot. Anne's thighs, behind his, clenched to help her balance with the change of pace. Richard was right. Ahead in the gathering gloom was a substantial huddle of buildings: a large hall-house with barns around it. A light shone in one of the narrow windows.

'Halt.' Edward called the word softly and Richard picked it up, echoing his brother's order down the line of men. The Welsh archers and the mercenaries that Margaret's money had bought as escort slowed their horses carefully. This road was not much travelled and last night's ice was still on its surface almost a day later. Haul their horses to a stop too fast and disaster beckoned.

'Form up.'

The response was instant: the king's companions shuffled their horses into an orderly line, two by two. The aristocrats – William Hastings, Lord Rivers, Richard of Gloucester – had often been part of Edward's 'riding court' in England and followed him without question, trusting his judgment; the archers had learned, through the wild ride across country to Lynn, that Edward's instinctive leadership was vital to their survival. The mercenaries responded to whoever paid them; none of them questioned the order.

'We will sleep warm tonight, my friends. For a change.' There was a flash of the king's white teeth and a laugh – which spread amongst them all. His confidence was heartening. They were used to campaigning and living off the land, even in winter, but they would all welcome respite from another freezing night camp in open country such as this.

'I see our hosts expect us. How kind.'

Another light blinked up ahead, a lantern perhaps, illuminating the outside stairs that led up from the farmyard to the second storey. It was clear that the farmstead was expecting visitors, but not those who were about to arrive.

'Quietly now. Richard? William?'

Signalling his brother and his chamberlain to take the lead, Edward dropped back into the middle of the train of men. He would not expose Anne to unnecessary risk.

As they reached the base of the small rise on which the farm stood, the party could see the place was even larger than it had seemed from a distance. Whoever had originally chosen this site had a good eye for a defensive position. The barns that surrounded the farmhouse formed three sides of a quadrangle – the family dwelling made the fourth – and all were massively walled from good stone, not brick.

When they looked more carefully in the half light, properly constructed arrow loops could be seen beneath the tiled roof. There was only one way to arrive at the farmer's living quarters and that was through the iron-banded great door that

168

barred entrance to the farm's inner yard. And the door itself was positioned in a recess in the walls, with arrow loops looking down into the narrow entranceway.

Edward hooted like a barn owl. The Duke of Gloucester turned back in his saddle when he heard it, and rode fast down the line to his brother.

'Well, Richard?'

'It's very well defended for a farmhouse.'

Edward glanced over his shoulder at Anne. He was tempted to press on, for in seeking entrance they might be buying into a fight and he could not afford to lose a single man, but he sensed that the girl behind him was exhausted. He could feel that she was straining to hold herself upright in the pillion.

'Well then, perhaps we should breach those defences. Gently.'

Richard looked at his brother, confused. 'Gently?'

Anne spoke so that only the king and his brother could hear. 'Let me call on them to open the gate. They'll be less frightened by a woman's voice.'

She was right, but the duke saw the king's concern. 'Brother, it may be the only way if we wish to take this place "gently",' he said. 'And sleep undercover tonight.'

Edward looked around at Anne. 'I do not wish to place you in danger.'

She smiled at him. 'I know that, my liege. But I think it must be done. For all our sakes.'

## Chapter Twenty-Two

The householder of Red Farm – so named for the colour of the ancient roof tiles on her barns – heard a strange sound. The voice of a woman calling over the clonking of the cow bell attached to the outer gate.

'Is anybody there? Can you hear me?'

Dame Philomena was old – she had seen forty-seven winters and summers, each marked as a nick on an ivory stick she kept in her bed chamber – but she was not stupid. What business had a woman outside her gates?

Unless…

The owner of Red Farm tried to ignore the wild way her heart was beating. She had asked them to light the lantern tonight as they did every night, so there would be a beacon, but she had given up hoping long, long ago.

But now … yes, there it was again.

'Hello? I'm very cold, and hungry.'

A girl's voice. Could it be?

'Mark, hurry! The gate. Send to open the gate!'

But Mark, the reeve who had run the farm for the old woman since the death of her husband, was fearful.

'Dame, this is dangerous. What woman would be out alone in the night?'

'Can you hear me?' The girl's voice was fainter. Exhausted.

Dame Philomena was certain now. It was her daughter who called. It was Ysabelle!

'I'm coming, child. I am coming!'

So much for the protests of Mark and the four or five other workers and servants who had just settled down to eat before the fire. Dame Philomena left them, running for the first time in years, and they did not catch her, though they tried.

'Ysabelle! I'm coming. Mother's coming.'

She reached the gate crying with both tears and laughter, unlocked it, raised the iron bar and pushed it open. 'Oh, child, I have waited and waited. But you are home now, home...'

But the woman on the other side of the gate was not her lost daughter. Dame Philomena saw that too late as the girl reached up and gently took the wildly swinging lantern from her hand and pushed the door wider.

'My name is Anne. And I thank you. My friends and I are cold, and beg lodging only for tonight. We will not hurt you.'

The words washed over Dame Philomena, meaning less than nothing. Her heart broke; she felt it, as a bone might suddenly give way against impossible pressure, and she could not breathe. This was not her child.

The lantern, the light to show Ysabelle the way home, had conjured up another girl from the darkness. A stranger surrounded by armed, mounted men.

'Mark!' the old lady called.

But the reeve was a pragmatist. When he'd seen his mistress run to the gate and unbar it, he'd hung back, wary. And then he'd seen the girl and

171

all her followers. What could four or five farm servants do against these men? Pulling off his hooded cap, he knelt in the muck of the yard as the men rode through the open gate and past him in an armoured mass, iron-shod hooves clicking busily on the iced cobbles.

But he'd kept hold of his knife from supper. He hid it quickly. Best these men not see it; they might think he'd offer resistance. He wouldn't. None of them would. Perhaps they'd escape with their lives that way. He bowed his head even lower until it touched the cold ground.

At the great gate of the farm, Anne was very distressed. The woman who had let them in was sobbing so pitifully she could not catch her breath. She had fallen to her knees and would have beaten her head on the cobbles if Anne had let her.

'Dame? Lady? We will not hurt you.'

The king gestured towards the house and the barns, and his brother peeled off with four or five men, swords drawn, to carefully inspect each of the buildings for hidden assailants, unlikely as that might seem.

Edward slipped down from his horse, trusting it to stay where he left it, and hurried back to Anne who was saying, over and over again, 'There, lady, there. All is well, all is well, I promise.' Anne was nearly crying herself, so great was the woman's sorrow. Edward was alarmed and confused. This was very strange. The woman was not frightened of them; she was wild with grief and heedless of anything or anyone.

'Come, lady, it is cold. Let me help you.'

The king bent down and, as gently as he could,

pulled the woman to her feet. She was limp and heavy as a sack of barley. Between them, Anne and Edward carried Dame Philomena past her terrified reeve, who was now on his feet and babbling at the unexpected visitors in a language none of them could understand. He managed to indicate that they should take her up the outside stairs into the main hall.

William Hastings was there before them, and had rounded up the few men and one woman who had been eating there. The servants were now gathered in a corner, large-eyed and silent as they watched Edward's men scour the building for any further inhabitants.

Amongst the efficient pandemonium, Anne dragged a settle over to the fire. 'My lord? Bring her here.'

Edward Plantagenet, feeling very awkward – one did not usually assist the owners of places that were raided, much less dry their tears – attempted to sound confident and kind at the same time. He hoped it would stop the wretched woman weeping. 'Here lady, here is your fire. A good one!'

He looked at Anne helplessly as he deposited the sobbing woman on the settle, where, leached by emotion, she collapsed like a lump of punched-down dough. Anne saw what was needed and sat beside her, one arm around her shoulders, offering the hem of her shift to staunch the tears that fell as thick as blood.

Edward, relieved, hurried over to Hastings. He'd always been uncomfortable around crying woman. 'Any more of them, William?'

Hastings was not especially concerned by the

farm workers, or the reeve, who'd just been hurried into the hall by one of the archers and deposited amongst his fellows. He was more worried that the extent of the farm buildings might mean other workers could be lurking, having gone to bed early when the light went from the sky.

'We'll know soon enough, liege.' He cast a quizzical glance at their reluctant hostess. 'What's wrong with her?'

Edward shrugged. 'Well, I don't suppose she's happy we've arrived, but it does seem an extravagant response.'

William nodded. He would swear that not one of the men had laid a finger on the old woman. In fact, she'd received nothing but kindness from them. He shook his head. What was the world coming to? It was Anne's idea to come here. She'd caused all this chaos. It made him uneasy.

'What orders, sire?'

Edward responded promptly. 'Bar the gate again. Now. And then I think we should set them,' he nodded at the farm workers, who huddled together, terrified of his glance, 'to cooking. Hot food. Now there's a thought!'

William Hastings grinned, showing white, sound teeth in a brown face – one of his most attractive features. 'Certainly, sire. I think we can arrange that. Malken!'

One of the archers, who'd been deputised to watch the dame's servants, hurried over to the chamberlain and saluted. William ordered, 'Food! They will cook it. Fast! You're to watch them. And find ale for the men.'

Edward, standing quiet amongst all the bustle

around him, looked across to where Anne sat murmuring words of comfort to Dame Philomena. His heart lurched; he actually felt it move inside his ribs. All the women he'd had, the few he'd thought he loved, and none did this to him but Anne.

His yearning for her – a hunger only just kept under control, a physical appetite – stirred and stretched. She looked up, caught his glance and flushed; turned her head away.

He smiled. Tonight they would have time alone together, he'd see to that. And then they would find out, husband or not, what remained between them.

## Chapter Twenty-Three

Margaret of Burgundy was cold. Nights in November in the Lowlands were often cursed with fog, dank and soup-thick, especially in the cities where the smoke from wood fires deepened the frigid murk. Parts of the night chamber *were* warm, it was true, but these were the areas nearest the fire, which had been well laid and fed to a roar in the deep fireplace. But in the shadowed depths of the great room the air was like iced bone, and although the glowing braziers dotted around the huge chamber looked cheerful, they made little real difference to the temperature.

'Hurry! My lord duke will join me shortly and I wish to be done with this.'

Margaret was referring to the elaborate preparations that her woman insisted on before she went to her bed. First her hair must be loosened and brushed one hundred times from root to tip with a horsehair brush before it was rebraided for the night. Then her face and hands and feet must be washed with scented warm water. The warmth was notional; the contents of the washing bowl were frequently as cold as well-water by the time it arrived from the distant kitchens.

Lastly, the duchess vigorously cleansed her teeth using her own fingers. Pumice, ground to a flour-like fineness, was mixed to a paste with sweet almond oil and lemon juice – rare and very expensive at this time of year – and rubbed onto her teeth and gums. Margaret spat the grit out of the window when she'd finished, and rinsed her mouth with rosewater.

And now, tonight, there was something new. Something Margaret had only recently agreed to because she was wearied by the nagging of her women.

Margaret had slept naked all her life, like everyone else, until this point. One wore a dressing-gown for modesty amongst kindred and in front of servants as one was dressed in the morning, however the current rage was for light silk *sleeping*-gowns fashioned from yards and yards of semi-transparent fabric. This new fad had swept north from the courts of Italy and taken hold amongst those desperate for the latest fashions, no matter how unsuitable such garments were to the frozen winter-world of Burgundy.

In Perugia, Venice, Florence or Rome, how

176

perfect such a garment would be for warm summer nights. And how alluring. So far the duchess had resisted this new and, to her eyes, idiotic trend, but tonight she had given in to the entreaties of her women. As they cajoled her into a delicate sleeping-gown made from corn-coloured silk voile, sprigged with tiny green, white and blue flowers, the duchess could only reflect how silly a thing it was, if pretty, and how signally it was failing to keep her warm. Further, how could one expect to sleep swaddled in such a length of material? Surely it would tangle around her legs and ride up if her sleep was restless?

'Ah, Madame, you look entirely charming. The duke will be ravished. Ravished!'

'Will he? Step aside that he may see for himself.'

None of them had seen or heard Charles of Burgundy saunter into his wife's room. He clapped his hands and the women scattered, laughing, into the shadows. They knew they should leave, but each was hungry to see how the duke reacted when he saw his wife.

They were not disappointed.

'Well, now...' He stopped just inside the wavering pool of radiance created by the candles in the brass candelabra above their heads.

Margaret was unaware as she turned towards him, smiling, that the light from the fire made the sleeping-robe all but transparent. The duke sucked in a breath. 'Yes. A very pretty effect. Very pleasing.' His voice was a tone or two lower than normal. Almost a growl. Margaret's spine prickled and she found she was trembling slightly.

'Are you cold, my darling?' The duke breathed the words softly, for her alone, and strolled towards his duchess, prolonging the moment until, at last, he was close.

The duchess shook her head, then nodded. 'No. Yes! This silly garment ... it has no warmth.'

She smiled provocatively as she held up the silk of the gown for his inspection, allowing the delicate fabric to run through her fingers like water. Charles was staring at her face, her throat, dropping his eyes down the length of her body so deliberately it was as if he touched her with his fingers. She blushed and murmured, 'Stop, Charles. You're embarrassing me.'

'Dismiss them.'

A sensible man did not order his wife to do anything. But Margaret was not displeased. She shivered at his tone and obeyed, though she had little breath to speak with.

The women left, giggling, calling out wishes for a 'good night'. The room was suddenly very quiet. The duchess was not cold now.

'It is a happy thought, this gown.' Her husband still had not touched her, though he was standing closer now and closer again.

'I'm pleased you like it, Charles.' The duchess tried to keep her voice evenly modulated, but it was hard, for her breathing, and his, was a little ragged.

'Yes. Particularly because...' And now he touched her, one finger tracing the line of embroidery at the neck, which led to the loosely tied ribbon between her breasts, almost as if it were meant as a sign, an indicator. He untied the ribbon, slipped one hand inside the loosened garment, searching. '...it's transparent.'

His wife gasped. 'Oh, but that's so–' The rest of her words, her embarrassment, were smothered as he kissed her, pulling her body hard to his, both hands holding her hips against his own.

'Mmmmm. You smell delicious. And you taste ... divine.'

How busy his tongue was, teasing her, licking the inside of her lips; his mouth nibbling her with tiny little bites, her ears, the column of her throat and down, down to her nipples.

She gasped as he slid the dress off her shoulders and she stood, naked, in a puddle of silk, her eyes closed. Tears pricked behind her lids from intense, melting desire. She wanted him, ah, God and Mary, how she wanted him.

'Lie down.'

There were sweet new rushes on the floor. Not for Margaret of Burgundy the bare tiled floors of the north. Gracefully she knelt naked before him and then, allowing him to watch, lay back, pulling the silk of the despised night-dress beneath her so that it formed a golden coverlet over the rushes. She saw, in her mind, what he must be seeing and was astonished she was not ashamed.

The light from the fire flickered over her perfect skin, her virginal body, unmarred by time or childbirth. Charles was dazzled.

'A maiden, lying in a meadow,' he said.

The duke was a sensualist and a connoisseur of women. Before he had wed Margaret, he'd been certain that their marriage, contracted for dynastic and political reasons, would be, at best, pleasant.

179

He had taken two other wives previously, for similar reasons, and one had given him his daughter, Mary, now a teenager. He had felt little desire for either of the women, though he had been careful, of course, to honour them scrupulously, not least in sharing their beds from time to time. But Margaret of England was different. Very different, for he had fallen in love, and lust, with the Lady Margaret when her brother, Edward Plantagenet, had placed her hand in his two and a half years ago in Damme Cathedral. And he loved and lusted for her still. That was a record for a man who had, hitherto, sought his pleasures outside the marriage bed.

Charles looked down at his lovely girl now as she, catlike, stretched and yawned delicately. He laughed, undoing the buttons on his jacket.

'Tired, Duchess? Perhaps you need to sleep?'

Now his jacket was gone, dropped behind him on the floor, and his shirt. He stood above her, bare-chested, unclasping his belt, dressed only in black velvet hose. She could see every defined muscle in his thighs beneath the gleaming surface of the tight cloth. Her throat was so dry she swallowed. Tried to speak, but could not.

The duke smiled. His experience of sensuality was much greater than hers – he had been her only lover – but she held much charm for him in spite – perhaps because of – that. Her response to him was direct, unfiltered. She lusted for him as he lusted for her – and that was a gift from God.

Margaret watched the muscles gather and slide under her husband's skin as he bent to remove his hose. Then he stood. Naked. Magnificent. Hers.

'Is my wife cold, that she shivers so?'

Charles was grinning at her now as he knelt, his hands sweeping up the inside of her feet, knees, thighs. Higher. She gasped, and for a moment he straddled her hips with his knees, then, with exquisite control, he lay full length upon her, his knees nudging her own apart.

'Speak to me. Let me hear your voice,' he whispered into her ear as he entered her body. The shock was piercing, centred, and she felt herself tremble and melt and open around and beneath him.

'Ah, Charles, I fall apart. I am split like a willow wand.'

The building pleasure was intense and she dissolved into it. Molten, it gathered, hot and dark and urgent. He moved fast, faster. Pinning her arms apart, bracing himself against her wrists, his full weight behind his pelvis. He felt himself harder than oak inside her, and she was so soft, so buttery soft.

She keened as she stared into his eyes, her own open and wild, holding her hips up to his, higher and higher, moving them to match his rhythm. For him, the intensity between them was teasingly unbearable and, as she called out, he smothered her mouth with his, ate her scream, taking the sound deep into his body, his chest, down into his groin ... and that was his release. And hers.

As deep as tears, rich and sweet, the joy they gave each other on that cold night would stay with them both as long as each had breath. They lay before the fire, naked as children, he curled protectively around her body, and for a little time

181

both drowsed.

But the fire had reduced to embers, and the chill lapped inwards from the walls to find them. Shivering, Charles stirred and kissed Margaret's shoulder.

'Come, little heart of mine. Time for bed or we shall both freeze!'

Margaret yawned as she struggled to sit up, her whole body relaxed and loose. For modesty's sake, she scooped up the silk bed-robe and held it against her body. It made Charles laugh as he tossed logs onto the embers to revive the fire.

'Charles, do you think we will have made a child tonight?'

He heard the courage in her deliberately light tone and he reached down to help her stand. 'Well now, if we have not, it will not be for want of trying, wife.'

They both laughed as he pulled her to him, kissing her on the brow; then he found her hand and led her to the tented bed that stood against one wall.

'There, climb up, my love. Perhaps the sheets will still be warm.'

Margaret's grimace said otherwise as she clambered up and wriggled beneath the counter-pane. Shivering, she pulled the sheets and blankets high around her chin, trying to stop the chattering of her teeth. 'Not even a ghost of the warming pan, I'm afraid. Perhaps I should have worn the bed-dress after all.'

Charles quickly scuttled to the foot of the bed, then jumped up and vigorously burrowed into the bedclothes, tunnelling across the vast acreage of the mattress to seek the warmth of his wife's body. Finding it, he clamped himself against her, belly to spine. 'We will warm ourselves, never fear, my darling.'

Margaret laughed. Her rump against his belly, she could feel him stir against her.

'And how does Your Grace intend that blessed state to occur?'

She was demure and that piqued his lust again, though he was tired, so tired. He could not stop himself. He yawned. 'Ah wife, I fear I must sleep.'

She smiled in the darkness as he snuggled against her, one hand on her breast, the other gripping her by the waist.

She was close to sleep herself but then she remembered what she needed to ask him.

'Charles, have you heard anything of Edward? Charles?'

She was too late. Deep, even breathing said the Duke of Burgundy had been claimed by Morpheus.

The duchess sighed, and closed her eyes. But not before praying, briefly, that her brother and Anne might have found each other. And that each of them was well and safe.

Soon Margaret of Burgundy, the former Lady Margaret of England, slept. But her husband, the duke, did not. He had heard her question and he had an answer to it. But it must wait for the morning.

Terrified, he forced himself to wake, but there was no comfort when he did, only fresh despair. He had dreamed again, had seen her face covered in

183

blood, the gaping wound in her head. Had seen her go down once more, screaming, beneath the horse's iron-shod hooves. Every night, again and again, he was too late to save her. She died because it was his fault. He had not guarded her well enough.

Slowly, the jolting of his heart settled and faint shapes emerged from the noisome dark, black against charcoal grey. He was thirsty, and so cold that every joint in his body ached. They had left him water – if he chose to reach out his arm, stretch his fingers and feel for the edge of the wooden bucket – but, as always, he would not drink. He would wait for the small beer of morning. Drink the water in this foul place and he would die of gaol fever, nothing was more sure.

Anne. Was she alive still, or had she truly died after they brought her to this place?

Metal scraped against metal. The Dane sat up. Someone was turning the key in the lock!

'Oy! You in there?' It was a voice Leif knew, the only human sound he'd heard in many days.

'Do you come to torment me, gaoler?'

The other man laughed and hauled open the cell door. The light was dazzling after all this time in the dark. 'If going to a better place is torment to you, then yes, I'm your man.'

Leif struggled to stand, pain fizzing as the blood moved through his cramped limbs. 'A better place? Heaven – is that what you mean?' He swallowed his fear. Perhaps his time had come. He hoped his death would be quick.

The other man laughed again as he unlocked the manacles around Leif's ankles, the iron rings that chained him to the wall. 'Man, you're a fool. Come.' He poked Leif into a stumbling walk in front of him, up the steps and out of the cell.

'Tell me, does she live?' the captain pleaded. 'Did my wife survive? *Tell me.*'

'Keep walking, my friend. Just keep walking. You'll hear soon enough. Soon enough.'

And that was all the answer Leif Molnar obtained that night as he followed his gaoler through the groaning, freezing darkness beneath the Binnenhof.

## Chapter Twenty-Four

Relaxed, well fed and warm for the first time in some days, Edward Plantagenet was fighting sleep beside Dame Philomena's fire. Around him, his men lay amongst the deep straw that covered the floor, twitching like so many hounds as they dreamed.

The king yawned and stretched, nudging Hastings who was slumped down beside him, head on the board they'd eaten at.

'Anne. Did you see where she went?'

The chamberlain sat up in a scramble, hand already on the sword at his belt; half awake but more than ready to kill. 'What? Where?'

The king laughed, entertained by his companion's automatic response. 'Formidable, my friend. But we have no need of the sword. Anne. Where did she go?'

The chamberlain shrugged, blinking, and ran one hand through hair matted from days in the saddle.

'Perhaps she's with our hostess. The kitchen?'

Both men grimaced slightly. 'Ah, yes. Our Lady of Sorrows. Well, perhaps I should find them...'

William Hastings said nothing in reply because there was nothing to say. It was the king's affair if he chose to seek out Lady Anne de Bohun, with or without Dame Philomena.

Edward smiled as he stood. 'Sleep, William. It will not be dawn for many hours. Rest is important. We've a day or so of hard riding still to come.'

Lord Hastings nodded and sighed. Rest. Sleep. Such lovely words. His head fell to the board once more, and he was snoring before the king had reached the stairs that led down to the kitchen.

'Anne? Anne, are you there?'

The house breathed quietly in the cold night. Thick walls and small rooms held the heat of the evening and the banked fires well. The low-ceilinged kitchen was still haunted by the ghost of the dinner that had been cooked for the English, and it was a comforting, domestic-smelling silence that greeted Edward when he found his way there. Abruptly, he was homesick. The smell of roasted meat made him think of Windsor and the Christmas revels. Would he ever see another?

He forced himself to banish the fear.

'Dame Philomena?' he called.

'Shush. I've managed to get her to sleep, poor thing. Her story is very sad. Her daughter was taken by brigands as she walked home from a fair.

186

Dame Philomena thought I was she, returning.'

The king swung around at the sound of Anne's voice. 'Where have you been? I've missed you.'

Anne stood in the shadows of the kitchen, holding a lamp high. The light was soft, enchanting; it poured dark gold onto Anne's hair. Quickly the king strode over to her and, twitching the lantern from her grasp, enveloped her body with his arms.

'Ah, my darling, my darling girl.'

He could not have enough of her mouth, and when she tried to speak, he ate her words with kisses. Anne gasped and, like a drowning swimmer, struggled towards breath, towards speech, but he held her tighter.

'No! I don't care if you are his wife!'

'Edward, please!' She was pulling at his hands, his iron arms. But he would not let her go – until she caught her breath in a sob.

Then he dropped his hands and they stood together, not touching, each stricken by the presence of the other. Edward was breathing hard, striving to control himself. An onlooker would think him ill, perhaps in deep pain from an unseen wound.

Now, when she needed words most, Anne could not speak either. She shook her head.

'You have ceased to love me.'

It was a flat statement, desolate, and the last thing the king expected in response was laughter. But, once started, Anne could not stop. Until she cried – and that was all the answer he needed.

Sighing, Edward took Anne in his arms, gently, softly, this time. Picking her up by the waist with both hands, he deposited her on the kitchen board, a sturdy, high trestle, and stood with his knees between her own. And when he kissed her, that was gentle too. Sweet, chaste almost. Almost.

He nuzzled Anne's neck and felt her shiver. Then, pushing the hair back from her face, he stopped, surprised. 'Your hair is wet. And you've taken the bandages off.'

He sounded so alarmed, Anne found herself soothing him. 'It's healed well but I was so dirty from the ride I couldn't bear it any longer. I washed myself, and my hair. Dame Philomena is a good housewife. She has dried soapwort and rosemary water.'

Edward was worried 'But the night air? This is dangerous!' He touched her scalp lightly, feeling for the stitches. In the uncertain light, it was hard to see the site of the wound amongst her hair. 'Does it hurt you, my darling?'

Anne shook her head. 'No, not now. It itches a little, which I think must be good.'

She yawned and leaned against his chest with her eyes closed. She was tired, so tired. Her body ached from the long ride of the last days.

'I have so much to tell you,' she murmured. 'Things you must know. But perhaps it can wait until the morning?' She yawned more deeply still, setting the king to fighting sleep himself. 'No one's going anywhere tonight.'

He slipped an arm around her waist and found himself rocking her as Anne snuggled into his shoulder like a trusting child. 'Come. Sleep is what we both need.' Edward knew there were other rooms in the upper part of the house besides the hall. One or another of them must have a bed in it.

Anne opened her eyes and smiled at him. 'Can we sleep together, Edward?'

He knew what she meant. 'Yes, my darling. Like brother and sister.'

And so the dethroned King of England and an ex-servant girl, lately a merchant of Brugge, stole hand in hand through the kitchen, across the hall filled with snoring men and up a further staircase, almost as steep as a ladder, until they found a room high beneath the red tiles of the roof.

The little chamber smelled of apples and the straw that stored them, and there was a bed. Not wide and not long, but deep and soft enough with its wool-stuffed ticking mattress so they could sleep together in perfect peace, with Edward's fur-lined cloak for covering.

And sleep they did. Wrapped warm and tight in each other's arms like two children. Tomorrow was another day, and they would think about that then.


'Husband, is there any news? Jassy told me a man had come.'

Mathew Cuttifer looked up wearily as his wife entered his workroom. He was standing at his table before a stacked pile of ledgers, a branch of candles providing uncertain light. Too restless to sit as he worked, he was exhausted past all counting. He'd not slept for three days – could not, for formless terrors stalked him when he closed his eyes – and his whey-pale face told its own story.

'No, wife. Nothing of consequence. News from

our northern lands. All seems well there with my daughter and her husband, praise God. Nothing from Leif.'

Margaret went swiftly to her husband and picked up one of his hands. 'Dearest Mathew, you're doing all you can.'

The merest glimmer of a smile stretched his mouth. 'Ah, but is it enough? All we know is that Leif has disappeared, and the *Lady Margaret* with him. Privateers, perhaps? Who can tell.'

His wife nodded soberly. 'Come, sit with me.' She held out her arms and, with a sigh, he followed her obediently to a bench beside the hearth. The fire was banked low, the ashes a white heap with a red heart providing an illusion of heat. Margaret shivered; in truth, the place was tomb-cold.

'What did Leif say in his last note to you? Tell me again.'

Mathew's head buzzed and throbbed. It was hard to concentrate. With an effort, he forced words out of his mouth. 'He had visited Anne and was staying at her farm. Her news was that Charles of Burgundy was vacillating. Not wanting to support the king in any obvious way. Since then – nothing. Nothing from either of them.'

Margaret tried to bolster her own heart, and his, against despair. 'Leif is more than competent, Mathew; and Anne will have her reasons for silence, also. We shall hear something soon, I'm sure of it. And we must make plans, husband, for it will be good news. I'm certain of it!'

She patted her husband's hand with new energy. 'And if you're to take advantage of the tide turning, you must rest, my dear. Lack of sleep makes all things seem black. Come, I have the bed warmed and a camomile posset brewed for you. Tonight I feel sure you will rest dreamlessly.'

Mathew crossed himself and stood. Perhaps his wife was right. Perhaps tonight there would be no night terrors. Please God, let it be so...

## Chapter Twenty-Five

How was it that news could travel faster than a man, even when the tracks were good?

Two days after leaving Dame Philomena's house the king's party arrived at Anne's farm on the banks of the Zwijn. It was just after dawn, yet a woman was waiting by the gate on the road that ran parallel to the river's edge.

'Anne!' The old woman hurried forward in the half light, eyes like candles lit for thanks, as the girl slipped down from the horse she was riding – a horse so black it was nearly blue in some lights. The two embraced, cheeks wet with happy tears.

Richard glanced to the king, his tone cool. 'A happy meeting, brother?'

Edward spoke quietly. 'Happy, yes. But...' He caught his brother's eye and motioned with one hand.

Richard nodded and made a sweeping gesture with his own mailed arm, holding up three fingers. Tired as they were, the men immediately shuffled their horses quickly into neat lines of three, blocking the road and surrounding the king and his brother. Archers nocked arrows to bows.

Deborah was suddenly rigid in Anne's embrace. The girl wheeled around to confront a solid wall of men, arrows aimed at Deborah's heart.

'My lord? What does this mean?' Anne might have laughed if she hadn't been so angry.

Edward shrugged unhappily. 'Lady Anne, this woman seems to have expected us. How can this be so?'

Deborah mustered a dignified curtsy.

'Sire, my name is Deborah. I come to the gate at dawn every day and have done ever since my mistress, Lady Anne, went away in your service.' There was the merest stress on the word 'service'. 'We had no word to expect your party, I can promise you that.'

Quickly her thoughts flashed to the Sword Mother, Goddess from the West, Goddess of War. *Mother protect us here*, she prayed. The runes had told her that these men were coming, and that there was danger and transformation. The runes did not offer words; they brought dreams, pictures of the future, for those who could read them. And they never lied.

Edward grunted, embarrassed. As the light rose, he saw Deborah clearly and remembered her now. They had met before.

Anne's face was carefully blank but Edward knew her well. She was angry. And very hurt.

William Hastings broke the moment. 'Ah, war – lies become truth, and truth? Truth is very strange. Lady, I must crave pardon for this momentary uncertainty, yet I know you understand. As does my lord, the king.'

The chamberlain was interrupted by a yell that might have come from a much bigger chest than that of the butter-haired little boy now hurtling towards them at a run. 'Wissy! Wissy! You're back. My Wissy's home!'

The small missile hurled himself from ten paces at Anne's legs, still yelling. She caught him just before he fell beneath the hooves of her startled horse, moving as fast as a juggler at the fair – a fact much commented on later amongst the archers. And, slight though she was, and tall for his age though *he* was, she managed to throw the boy up in the air as if he'd been a fairing himself.

'Edward! Oh, my darling, I've missed you! But look, here is your blue horse.'

'Where?' Little Edward raised his head and looked around, eyes enormous. He'd never seen a blue horse.

Neither had the archers, and one or two crossed themselves just in case a fairy animal was lurking about. Couldn't be too careful in foreign lands.

'Here he is!' Anne placed a hand on the animal she'd been riding.

The little boy looked puzzled. 'But he's brown. Like mud!'

Anne laughed. 'No, you wait. When he's clean and all glossy, he's so black, he's blue.'

Edward Plantagenet smiled down at his son and spoke softly. 'Yes, Edward, he is. A horse fit for a prince. Perhaps you can ride him home? And then you can keep him.'

Anne caught the king's eye and a slight smile destroyed the last of the tension between them.

'Your Majesty is generous. My nephew is very grateful.'

Little Edward nodded with great certainty. 'Very grateful! Now, may I ride? Please, Wissy?'

So it was that laughter swept the party into Riverstead Farm, not tears. And, coming home, Anne was glad that Edward Plantagenet saw what she saw. Her security; the security she had built for herself without help from anyone.

And he had seen her son again.

The boy they had made together.


## Chapter Twenty-Six

'I will not see him. I absolutely refuse. Your brother is here against my express wishes and command.' Charles of Burgundy had disappointed his wife, bitterly. But he was unrepentant. 'No! It is not possible. Louis de Valois will know – very soon, if he doesn't already – that Edward has found his way to Brugge. It could be disastrous. *Disastrous* for Burgundy – and for you and me – if he heard that we had met.'

'But, Charles, you must hear Edward out. He needs–'

'Must! What is this must? You belong to Burgundy now, wife. Not England. Shall I remind you where your duty lies? Or is it too late for that? Did you help your brother, madame?'

Margaret's eyes filled with tears. It was rare that she and Charles fought on any issue, but to quarrel over Edward and the survival of her brother's throne in England was unbearable. Words hurried out of her mouth as she ignored the question.

'But, Charles, you have often said that Burgundy needs England to stand against France; you *must* have Edward's help as King of England if you, too, are to become the king you should rightfully be. Yet England will be our enemy – *our* enemy, my lord, not just yours – if Warwick successfully joins with Margaret of Anjou. She will land her troops very soon – you've told me that – troops supplied by Louis de Valois. Edward is your last hope, as well as mine, to make England a counterweight to France once more. I will speak the truth to you, husband, even if no one else dares to. That is my duty also.'

Charles answered with icy calm. 'Women have no place meddling in statecraft and no right to oppose their husbands' wishes or commands, in any way. Heed well the words of St Paul, wife: "Let a woman be silent when her husband speaks". It is not your place to teach me how I may or may not run my duchy, or to usurp my place as head of this household and your superior in every way. Must I beat you to make you understand this?'

Margaret swallowed tears of shock. He meant it; he really would beat her if she continued. And it was his right; he was her husband.

The news of this humiliation would spread through the Prinsenhof more quickly than smoke. They might be alone, but fifty or so avid courtiers waited outside the door of her solar, without numbering her husband's guard or her own men. Soldiers were the worst gossips of all.

Did Charles now despise her because she was English? Did he no longer love her for herself, only for what she had been once: a princess of England, a useful counter on the board? Desperate thoughts, but they could be true. Most royal marriages were not about love, or even affection; they were about duty. And if theirs were the same, in truth, what then? Would he banish her because she could not conceive and was therefore of no further use? Or send her to a convent cell – locked up and left to starve as that abomination, a woman who wilfully disobeyed her husband and was made to pay the price?

The Duchess of Burgundy linked trembling fingers in a knot in front of her belly and dropped into a very deep curtsy, head bowed. If swallowing this furious misery, this injustice, this terror, could help her brother and her country of birth, well, she would do it.

She forced meekness into her voice. 'I am sorry, my lord duke and husband. I had thought to please you with the news that King Edward, my brother, is within your domains. I know that you like and respect him. However, I was wrong to have questioned your judgment in this matter. Correct my mistakes and I will bear your discipline gladly.'

Charles was pacing, agitated. He would not look at his wife.

'Have you seen him?'

'Lady de Bohun brought me news of him.'

The duke swung around, glaring at his wife suspiciously. 'Lady de Bohun? Why would she know anything? And where has she been? I have not seen her in these many weeks.'

The duchess gulped. 'As you know, Lady de Bohun and my brother have had...' She came to a halt, searching for a word that would be correct yet not brutal, 'An association. They remain close.'

The duke interrupted her. 'How do you know? How could they remain close, after all this time?'

That was too much; the Lady of England spoke without thought of the consequences. 'Because love lasts, Charles. It is not easily thrown away when it is real. At least not by my brother. Nor by Anne de Bohun.' She was glaring back at him now.

There was a moment's frozen silence, then, abruptly, the duke laughed. 'That's better. I wondered where my real wife had gone for a moment. I thought she'd been replaced by a stranger wearing her clothes.'

Margaret gasped with rage. Then relief flooded her eyes and tears dripped down her cheeks. 'Oh, Charles.'

She ran to him and he pulled her against his chest. He was shaking slightly but his ragged breathing slowed eventually, as did hers. Taking her hand he led her to a window seat, a finger to his lips, shaking his head and pointing with his other hand towards the door of the solar.

She was puzzled and then understood all in a rush. He was concerned they were being spied upon. Of course!

'Is Your Grace hungry? Or thirsty perhaps?' They were the first words that came into her head and she felt silly saying them, but she spoke loudly, clearly enough to be heard outside the door of the solar. 'See, my lord, here are damsons twice-stewed with honey, and sweet almond biscuits. They will taste well, together, with this hypocras...'

All the while, Duke Charles was whispering directly into her ear. 'Not here. And not now. Later – tell him that. It's too dangerous for us all until I know more of Louis de Valois's plans.'

Could he go on stalling his wife? Perhaps; only perhaps.

'Very well, my lord. I will see if the kitchens have other food that may tempt you more.'

The duchess stood and he joined her, smiling. 'Yes, wife. I should like that.' He made a little shooing gesture towards the door, nodding.

Margaret, Duchess of Burgundy, turned smartly on her heel and marched towards the door of her solar, filled with energy and determination. They would meet, Edward and Charles, she would see to it. Anne de Bohun would get her wish.

Charles watched his wife's departing back and the smile dropped from his face. Would he allow his duchess to have her way? Would he meet with Edward?

And if he did, what then?

## Chapter Twenty-Seven

'If you could have one thing above all others, what would it be?'

Edward of England and Anne de Bohun were sequestered together in the great barn amongst the summer hay, avoiding the household in Anne's now overpopulated farmstead.

'We have spoken of this before, Edward.'

The king rolled over onto his back and laughed. 'Perhaps. But tell me again, Anne. Humour me.'

Anne sucked pensively on a piece of straw and didn't answer. He glanced at her.

'Very well, since you are so stubborn, I shall tell you in one word what I want. You. I want you, lady. No more parting. Ever.'

It was said seriously, without emphasis. The words fell into silence.

'And this is the part where *you* say, "Edward, that's what I want too."' The king propped his head on one hand, looking Anne directly in the eye. 'Or, rather, that you want me. That I am your dearest wish and always will be.'

Anne closed her eyes. He was far too near to her, his own warm musk competing with the green smell of summer from the straw they lay on.

'I have no need to speak since you know my thoughts.'

'Do I, Anne? Do I know your thoughts...?' One hand crept out to circle her waist, and suddenly hauled her body to his so that they lay against each other. '...as I know you?'

Anne tried to sit up. 'You are dangerous, Edward Plantagenet. Very dangerous.'

He released her. 'I cannot believe you've turned into some kind of tease in the time we've been apart. Tell me, Anne. Tell me you feel nothing for me!'

'Do not torment me, Edward!'

She was suddenly furious, and then came terror

199

for the mote-filled light of the barn was suddenly gone. Ink-black dark lapped her close.

'Edward?' Was that her voice? Or someone else's? 'Edward!' No, *she* was calling out. But there was no answer. And then she felt something move, close by. Very close. Her skin crawled and, though she could see nothing, nothing at all, she stumbled to her feet and tried to run from that sound, the dry insistent rustle of someone, *something*, moving towards her in the dark. But her legs, her feet, were so heavy she could not make them function.

Her senses, all her senses, strained to understand what was happening. Then a thing like a feather touched her cheek. Soft, smelling of dust, faintly sweet. And she understood, as she was meant to. Grave clothes – that was what she felt against her skin. She could not see them, but the picture was there: a pale, fine shroud filled with formless dust. The dust of the dead.

She tried to scream, but an object brushed against her throat and the sound stopped as uselessly it began.

'Look.'

No voice spoke that word, but a light burned in the dark and Anne saw it. Saw what it was. A disembodied hand, each finger flaming at its tip.

'See.'

The burning hand beckoned, once, twice, and then a third time. Anne felt herself pulled forward and her legs jerked, trying to move of their own accord. She did not want to approach that flaring, sulphurous-smelling thing.

But she *was* walking, closer and closer to the hand. It was beckoning, beckoning her closer.

Now she could smell the fingers as they burned and smoked. Like a pig on a spit, like pork meat.

Anne's belly heaved and vomit filled her mouth. She stumbled, nearly fell. She willed her legs to stop; they disobeyed her. The hand crackled as the flesh of its fingers was consumed before her eyes. She felt the heat on her face. Now there was only bone, held together with glistening, blackened, twisted sinew. Then the bone itself was flame, a bunch of twigs, cracking and popping.

At the last, what was left revolved in space and pointed at her. 'Be warned.' Then it was gone, the fire extinguished, though Anne could still smell the greasy smoke.

'Why be warned? I do not fear you, Anne.' Edward was lying in the straw, amused, confident. Waiting for her to come to him.

Anne collapsed against Edward's chest as if her own bones had been consumed in the flames. She lay there, heart bruising her ribs, breathing like a forge bellows, but grateful, so grateful, to be out of the dark. She could not speak.

'Tell me, my darling. What am I to be warned against? This?'

He slipped one hand down the bodice of her dress and found her breast. 'You burn me, Anne,' he whispered into the hollow of her throat. 'You burn my hand where it touches you.'

His words shocked her, but then she heard her own voice respond. 'Oh, my love.' Her mouth spoke her mind.

'We'll get through this, together. Charles will help us because he must, and when it's all over, you'll come back to England with me. For good.

Promise me that. I want your word. No prevarication.'

Edward gazed at her, both hands gently cupping her face as he spoke, soft and low. 'Am I still your king? Will you obey me in this?'

She was saved from reply by a man's cautious whistle. Then his voice. 'Liege? Are you there?'

Putting a finger to his lips, Edward kissed Anne once, hard, then laid her gently back on the straw. 'Your Majesty?'

Edward wriggled forward to the edge of the loft. 'Yes, William. I hear you.' It was a large barn and the threshing floor was fifteen feet below as Edward looked down on his shabby chamberlain.

'Lord King, you must come at once. An important development.'

'So mysterious, William. But first, do you know how dirty you are? My chamberlain looks like a hayseed.'

William looked down at his filthy boots and muddy breeches. The king was right. Somewhat fruitlessly, he slapped at his leather jerkin, raising dust. Edward, meanwhile, descended the hayloft ladder with the unnerving speed of a cat.

'Have you seen Lady Anne this morning, William? Is her presence also required for this "important development"?'

William, apparently engrossed with stamping mud off his boots, kept a miraculously straight face. 'Most assuredly, Your Majesty. Mistress Deborah is searching for her now.'

Above, in the straw, Anne felt terrified still by the burning hand, but embarrassment now blurred the edges of that grim vision. Then such

202

a gust of laughter swept up from her chest she had to stuff fingers in her mouth to stop it. How would she exit this barn unseen?

'Let us go then, William. I see my criticism of your clothes could as well be applied to my own. I must change.'

As the two men hurried out of the barn, William's words floated off into the morning breeze. 'There's also the matter of the straw, Your Majesty. In the hair...'

There was silence for a moment. Then another voice; Deborah's.

'Anne? Anne, you must come down. Immediately. We have a visitor.'

## Chapter Twenty-Eight

The Duchess of Burgundy was spoken of as having 'the common touch', and it was true. It had never been better employed, this gift of making all she met feel important, than sitting today in the parlour of Anne's farmhouse, waiting for her brother and her hostess to make their appearance.

'This is delicious, Dame Lisotte! These curds have the consistency of cream. Yet so light and agreeable. And such a pleasing flavour. What can it be?'

Deborah had deputised the cook to wait on the duchess with anything that could be conjured up from the kitchen or the stores, whilst Anne was searched for. And the king.

'We make them ourselves, Your Grace, from the milk of our own cows. I flavour them with candied elderflowers from the bushes in the kitchen garden. My mistress is fond of them.'

'And that is God's good truth, Your Grace!'

Anne entered the parlour, a picture of neat composure. A high-waisted dress of violet velvet – the sleeves lined with a shade of green damask between moss and dark emerald – glimmered with muted splendour in the winter light.

'Your pardon that I was not here to greet you. I was still being dressed.'

'And I, dear sister. I was also. Being dressed, that is.'

All three women in the room curtsied as Edward Plantagenet strolled into the parlour. For a moment, his eyes brushed Anne's. Raised brows asked the question: 'How did you change and get here before me?'

She smiled demurely, dropped her eyes from his, as was proper, and watched with delight as Margaret and her brother embraced tenderly.

'Ah, dearest sister, you have bloomed in your marriage. That gives me great joy.'

'And joy has been my lot, Your Majesty.' The duchess made a punctiliously deep court curtsy.

'Such formality for your long-lost brother? No. You can address me as a king when I have earned the title once more.'

However, matching her in ceremony, Edward bowed to his sister, motioned that she should sit, and sat beside her himself on a settle near the fire. Deborah, Lisotte and Anne remained standing. It was expected.

Edward smiled at Anne. 'This lady, Your Grace, has been my kind friend. And saviour. She found me and delivered your most generous message – with its welcome inclusion – that I should come here to you, to Brugge. And so we did, once Lady Anne was recovered.'

Margaret glanced at her friend and back at Edward. 'Recovered, brother?'

Anne blushed and carefully inspected the toes of her embroidered velvet slippers. Pain shadowed Edward's face for a moment. 'Yes. I ran the Lady Anne down with my horse and she nearly died.'

Margaret did not know how to respond. In the small, embarrassed silence, Anne signalled for Deborah and Lisotte to leave the parlour.

'I have a strong constitution, Your Grace,' she said. 'And it was an accident. Perhaps it was God's will,' all three crossed themselves automatically, 'that we should meet again in that way?'

Margaret held her hand out to Anne. 'Sit here beside us, Lady Anne. You must have had a long and very cold ride. Louis de Gruuthuse, good man that he is, has sent me personal despatches, just very recently arrived, telling me of your ... departure. He did not tell me, however, of the accident.'

'But the question now, Your Grace, is will the duke, your husband, consent to see the king?'

Anne asked the question for Edward. Perhaps it was best to confront the unspoken issue. She hoped so.

Margaret looked uncomfortable, and was prevented from answering by a soft knock at the door.

'Come.' Anne's tone was sharp, which was unlike her, and Deborah shot the girl a worried look as she edged into the room, followed by Lisotte. Both women were burdened with food: good bread, white cheeses, little cakes stuffed with currants, the pastry yellow with saffron, preserved plums and quince in honey syrup. There was enough for a platoon of hungry archers, let alone three people who had no appetite, knowing what they did.

After the two women had departed, Margaret spoke calmly, hiding her anxiety well. 'My husband, the duke – your brother-in-law and friend,' she said, careful to emphasise the relationship between Edward and Charles, as it gave her confidence, 'is very worried indeed about Louis de Valois. But, I am certain that the duke *does* want to see you.'

Edward was pacing the small space of the parlour. He stopped and faced his sister.

'He does, brother, he truly does, but the timing must be right. You can understand that?'

Edward's nose was so pinched from rapid breathing that the bridge was a sharp white line in his face. 'I have heard nothing but the importance of the "timing" of our meeting for this long month past. But Charles is foolish, Margaret. Every day's delay now is a day longer I am out of my kingdom. He needs me strong, in Westminster, and with an army around my throne if he intends his duchy to survive against Louis de Valois.'

This was too much for Margaret; she too stood, anguished. 'I know that. And I have told him so many, many times. Sometimes he agrees with me, and sometimes...'

Edward finished the sentence for her. 'And sometimes he wonders if he is better to make peace with Louis, once and for all. Accept that he is the weaker, that he will never rule as a king of his own country. He must be very fearful indeed since he is behaving in this cowardly fashion.'

'Weak? It is not fear or weakness that drives him!' Margaret was stung. 'He is a brave man. You know that.' Edward had turned away from her and she addressed his back. 'He is *not* a coward. He is just trying to understand what is best for his people. And best for you.'

That nettled Edward. He swung back and glared at Margaret. 'No man may think on what is best for the King of England but the king himself!'

The Plantagenet temper was in both of them, brother and sister; fighting, as children, each had been accustomed to battle without grant or expectation of quarter. The gathering storm was tangible as thunder in the room. Anne stood abruptly, her physical presence holding brother and sister apart.

'Please, Your Majesty, listen to your sister, the duchess. She loves you dearly.'

Edward snorted.

Anne turned to Margaret. 'Duchess, your brother is exhausted and if he is not fearful of the future, I am. There will be a way through this, and we'll find it, but let us please break bread together now. I'm hungry, and it will help us all to eat something.' Her voice rose from nerves at the end of this little speech. It took courage to stand between warring Plantagenets.

Unexpectedly, Margaret dissolved into giggles.

'What do you say, brother? Will you eat? It may help your temper!'

This last was said defiantly, but it was a sister talking to her brother, not a duchess to a king.

'Amen to that, sister. And may these preserves sweeten your mood also.'

When Edward grinned, it was still possible to see the boy he'd been, the spirit of mischief incarnate, blond hair flopping over his forehead, hands and feet too big for a soon to be massive frame, all lopsided grin and scraped knees. Now, standing beside his formidable sibling, Anne was moved almost to tears. The Plantagenets might be descendants of the Devil or his wife, Melusine, but their ancestor must have been most handsome. And then she remembered. If Edward and his sister were descended from the Devil, then she was too. She was a Plantagenet also.

A certain light kindled in the eye of Lady Anne de Bohun as she heaped white curd cheese onto a heel of bread, then licked her fingers, unladylike. 'Therefore, how do we convince the duke that he must meet with Your Majesty?'

Edward's eyebrows rose. Anne had always been deferential to him whenever they were with others; now she was not exactly impertinent, but she was confident. Margaret noticed it too and flashed a quizzical glance at her brother.

The king made a mild enquiry. 'Does the duke still hunt?'

The duchess was trying not to dip the edges of her veil into the syrup of the preserved quince as she leaned over the table laden with food. She answered, abstracted, 'Certainly he does, when

208

he has time,' and licked her fingers also – with a smile to Anne – since the juice was so delicious.

Anne sat on the settle, gazing steadily first at the king and then at the duchess. She smiled. 'This is cheering news, Duchess. To hunt well is a noble pursuit.'

Edward cracked a walnut in one powerful hand and scrupulously divided the meat between Margaret and Anne.

'And I have always liked the chase,' he said, grinning.

The duchess spoke slowly, 'Hunting is well known to be dangerous, brother. Very dangerous, sometimes.'

Edward nodded. 'I agree, sweet sister. But that's the challenge, isn't it?'

A hunting party? No stags, no boar; Edward Plantagenet was hunting the throne of England.

## Chapter Twenty-Nine

'Plague-monger! Poisoner! Aaaaaaaaaargh!' The spurred hunting boot flew through the air and found its mark, painfully: the bowed head of Louis's terrified chief valet, Alaunce Levaux. 'I trusted you and this is how you serve me!'

Poor Alaunce: damned if he tried to explain, and condemned, assuredly, if he did not. 'Your Majesty is always most just, however–' That was as far as he got.

'Don't you dare "however" me!' The other boot

followed its partner. This time the spur sliced Levaux's ear and blood dripped onto the neckband of his shirt.

'They've been poisoned! Look! See here, there must be noxious matter on the leather.'

Some orders a man obeyed; some he did not. Alaunce knew that if he raised his head even a little, something else would be thrown at him. Unfortunately the king, so unhandy at most physical things, had a very strong throwing arm. An *accurate*, strong throwing arm.

Alaunce contrived to wriggle towards the chair in which the king sat, agitatedly waving his lower legs for his valet's inspection. Louis's face was slick with sweat and there was a hot and violent look in his eyes which, when Levaux allowed himself to glance upwards, was profoundly disturbing. The man inched closer, close enough to peer forwards without raising his head very high, and indeed, once there, became aware of why the king was so agitated.

The calves and shins of Louis de Valois, Monarch of all the French, were a mass of weeping sores, the surface of the skin marked by huge purpled bruises and the toes of each foot swollen into fat, violet sausages. Whatever it was, the affliction looked most painful.

Alaunce was so surprised he forgot to be afraid. He sat up and inspected the nether limbs of the king with keen attention. 'Fleas, Your Majesty? Suppurating flea bites?' He knew it sounded weak, but it was all he could think of.

'Fleas? Fleas! These are not flea bites – unless fleas have turned to pigeons and grown teeth.

210

Look, man! These are *holes* in my legs. Holes! It's happened today; this morning. What could cause this so quickly but poisoned boots? AND YOU ARE THE KEEPER OF MY BOOTS!'

For a man of indifferent height and narrow chest, the king could roar like a bull when he chose to and, for a moment, the sheer volume of sound, delivered so close to the valet's ear, destroyed all chance of rational thought.

Louis was correct: Levaux *was* the keeper of the king's boots, amongst other things, and he slept across the doorway of the king's sleeping-room; no one entered or left without his knowledge. And during the day, the room was locked with the key – the *only* key – that he, personally, carried.

This was all so perplexing. The day had begun in normal fashion. After mass and the late morning dinner, Louis had gone hunting in his favourite boots; boots that had been placed on his legs, as was usual, by Levaux. The valet could swear to the irreproachable sanctity of those boots, yet, if the king was right, and they had been sabotaged, who could have done such a thing? And when?

'Winter is a difficult season, Your Majesty. Could it be distemper of the legs, or an ague which has infected the humours so causing the swellings?'

'How would I know? Am I a doctor?'

A doctor. Yes! That was the way through this mess. Someone else to blame. So thought Alaunce Levaux, cowering on the stone flags before the smelly, swollen feet of the king. 'Shall I summon your personal physician, Lord King?'

Terror struck Louis de Valois. A doctor? 'No!

I'll not have them near me with their cupping and potions and poisons! I've seen them. Perfectly well people sicken and die. But not me! Oh ho, not me. I want a herbalist. A good man who is not of my court. Find me such a one, but tell no one. I will not have it whispered about that the king has been poisoned. That would be a disaster for France. Go. NOW!'

'At once, Your Majesty. Immediately.'

On his belly, Levaux crept backwards from the king's presence, almost dribbling with relief.

'Stop!'

The valet froze. It had been too easy. His heart suddenly filled the entire cavity of his chest, desperate to pump enough blood to his legs so that he could run, when that was needed.

'Bar this door when you leave here. No one, no one at all, is to enter until you return. Hurry! I am racked and burning!'

The king groaned as he said the words and Levaux dared not reply; he did not trust himself to speak in case he pissed his breeches from fear. But outside the doors of the king's chambers, he scrambled to his feet and brushed the dust and filth off the front of his black jerkin. Hurriedly, after exhorting the guards to prevent all access, he barred the door himself – all the rooms in Louis's private domain could be barred or locked from the inside and the outside – and left the suite of royal rooms at a hobbling run.

He knew of just such a man for the king's needs: a Dominican monk who worked with the very poorest in the city of Paris, prescribing only simples and herbs to remedy their afflictions.

A holy man, it was said. A man to whom money meant nothing. He was English, and had a strange name; a Greek name. Brother Agonistes, was that it? Yes. Perhaps the monk would know if the boots had indeed been poisoned or if something else was troubling the king's humours. Please God, let the monk know what should be done, for what would happen if the king died of this new ailment? What would happen to France? Louis was not loved as a king, but he was powerful – and feared. If he died, it would convulse the kingdom; convulse all Europe.

Levaux shivered. He didn't pay much attention to politics in the broadest sense, however he did attend to gossip in the palace. And gossip said that Louis was close to overstretching the resources of France in his support of the English Earl of Warwick. Gossip also said that the Duke of Burgundy was pitiless, and poised to invade France if he did not get his way in the Low Countries.

The skin on Alaunce Levaux's back tingled and stung as he hobbled on through the busy palace, which was gearing up for the Christmas revels. Please God, let it not be a premonition of the whip. He did not like his master, naturally – how could one like a king? – but he did understand him. Louis's father had treated him badly as a boy, and constantly undermined his authority as Dauphin when he was older. The nobles, too, had all laughed at Louis, since he had been ill-favoured and weak as a child and had grown into an ugly young man. No one had expected the wizened runt to live, much less to rule. But he had, and he did, and that was the way of it.

Born to trouble, both of them: this king and his kingdom.

But the English and the Burgundians? They would be worse, far, far worse.

It was his duty: he, Alaunce Levaux, must save the king for France, or there would be anarchy and destruction.

## Chapter Thirty

'Damnation to him. Perdition. Destruction!' It was a measured chant, punctuated by the work of the little dagger. Once, twice, three times and once more the silver tip pierced the legs of the doll, joining the legion of little holes already there. But the last thrust was so deep, most of the wood-dust trickled out, leaving one of the legs a little empty, flopping bag.

'Daughter? What are you doing?'

Elizabeth wheeled around, the doll that was the representation of Louis de Valois clamped to her chest. 'Hush! Be quiet, mother. They will hear you.'

Hurriedly, the Duchess Jacquetta hauled the door of the Jerusalem chamber closed behind her. It was heavy and had warped in the wet, cold weather and would not obey her easily; a symptom of so much else in her life. 'We must be careful! If you were caught at this, if you were seen, then...'

Elizabeth's eyes glittered in the gloom; the watery green light from the thick glass in the windows lent her skin a corpse-like pallor. 'I will stop when he is dead, mother. It is all I can do. Or you, for that matter. You have taught me willingly enough.'

'No! This is too public. Thomas Milling will not shelter you, or me, if he thinks that we are–'

The queen's blue eyes narrowed as she locked glances with her mother. Sometimes the likeness between them was startling. 'What, Mother? Witches? Involved in the black arts?' Elizabeth Wydeville laughed, a genuine melodious peal from deep within her chest. 'The abbot is not so worldly to even *think* such a thing. Why should he? He says mass for us often enough. In his mind, we are two pious ladies in dire circumstances, in need of God's saving grace. And he's right. Besides, your little toy...' Elizabeth brandished the doll; its arms and legs were limp and lolled pathetically this way and that '...is just a plaything. It has no power. We just like to pretend it does.'

The queen sat down abruptly and covered her face with her hands. She had spoken the truth and it was too much to bear, too painful. How childlike to pretend that she could harm the mighty king of the French by pricking a doll stuffed with dust from a sawyer's pit. Pathetic! A game, a fantasy. And her mother was right: it was foolish to flaunt such a thing in the abbot's parlour.

Jacquetta dropped a hand to her daughter's shoulder, hesitantly; physical contact between mother and daughter was rare. Unexpectedly, Elizabeth covered her mother's hand with her own. That encouraged the duchess.

'It has served its purpose – give it to me, child.

Can't have them burning you before me.'

There was a certain grim humour in the exchange. In happier times, mother and daughter had laughed about Jacquetta's reputation at court. Persistent gossip whispered the duchess had taught Elizabeth how to bewitch the king, since there could be no other reasonable explanation for his behaviour in marrying a woman five years his senior *and* the widow of a Lancastrian knight burdened with two small sons.

Sighing, the queen held the half-stuffed facsimile of Louis de Valois close to her eyes and gazed into its painted face. 'Goodbye, Lord King. May you not fare well.'

'Daughter!' The queen's mother was sharp.

Without another word, Elizabeth handed the doll to the duchess and averted her eyes as Jacquetta bent to throw the crudely made thing into the flames.

'Oh!'

'What is it, mother?'

Jacquetta stared, white-faced, at her daughter. 'I'm bleeding. Look.' She held out one hand; there was a deep scratch at the base of her thumb, across the mount of Venus, from which fat beads of blood welled and dripped.

The queen snatched the doll back. 'Well, well. Not so powerless after all. See!' One of the little silver daggers was sticking, point out, from the doll's belly; it was this which had slashed the duchess. 'It is not ready to be burnt; it's telling us that. But I must wash your blood from it immediately, mother, or there will be confusion.'

Jacquetta spoke sharply. 'Give it back to me,

Elizabeth. For all our sakes, we must burn this thing now or I shall not sleep from fear.'

But Elizabeth was restored to energy and purpose. 'It doesn't *want* to burn; it must do its work first. But it cannot have your blood, I must see to that.'

And Elizabeth Wydeville, the deposed queen of England, hurried from the Jerusalem chamber in a swirl of night-black velvet – deliberately chosen, in mourning for her lost kingdom. The queen seemed clothed in a remnant of the night sky so dark that when she moved through the shadows she disappeared, all but her white face, her trailing white veil.

'Daughter, come back. Give me that thing!' But the queen was gone.

Unaccountably, the door of the Jerusalem chamber opened and closed as if on oiled hinges.

There was a legend within the kingdom of England that the king and queen of fairyland went hunting with their court on nights when the moon was full and the forest quiet. And when they did, the parents of mortal children had best beware; for the king and queen who lived under the hill might take the unwary or unguarded child and ride away with that innocent so they were never again seen by human eyes.

Little Edward's own eyes were huge as spoon bowls when Edward Plantagenet, erstwhile King of England, told him that story. 'No. Not me! Not me!' He burrowed down beneath the bedclothes.

'Come out, little one. It's only a story.' Edward tickled his son through the coverlet of the bed, laughing. 'The fairies bow to the real monarch of the land. They know you are under his protection.'

The small head popped out from beneath the mound of bedclothes, eyeing the man suspiciously. 'I am?'

'Yes. Because the king loves you. You are his firstborn son.'

Anne, who had just entered her son's room, stopped dead from shock as the little boy wriggled out of the bed and into the man's arms.

'You're funny. My daddy wasn't a king. But tell me another story.'

The king looked up as the small boy snuggled into his chest, peacefully sucking his thumb, and smiled. 'Another story? We must ask Wissy first.' Wissy was the child's name for Anne; it came from 'mistress'.

Anne de Bohun spoke to her son, but would not look at the king. 'It was "another story" fully an hour ago. Time for sleep.'

Little Edward pouted and opened his mouth to protest, but the king slid the child neatly beneath the covers, pinning his wriggling body tight in the bedclothes with a hand on either side.

'Plenty of time for more stories tomorrow. And the next day I think.'

Edward said it lightly, playfully, but Anne, her back to them both as she tidied the foot of the bed, grimaced. If they didn't hear from Charles tomorrow, perhaps it would indeed be days more.

'You'd better go to sleep now,' the king said. 'Sleep brings strength, and you will need that if I'm to teach you how to ride your big blue horse.'

'Not blue. Not really.' But the little boy's words

were swallowed in a yawn.

One bright eye opened and inspected both the adults. 'Kiss? Kiss for Edward? Please?' He said it so winningly that Anne and Edward Plantagenet laughed as freely as all parents do when their child says something charming.

But this boy was not acknowledged as his mother's son, or – until now – his father's.

Solemnly, Anne and the king each kissed one flushed cheek and smoothed the sheet back as the little boy turned over contentedly, eyes fluttering closed.

'Good night, Wissy. Good night, Big Sir.' It made Edward Plantagenet smile to hear the name he'd been given by his son.

Putting a finger to her lips, Anne picked up the candle beside the little boy's bed and moved quietly out of the room into her own, next door. With exaggerated care, Edward, the former King of England, pulled the door to behind them.

'You're very good with children, Edward. You understand them.'

Anne spoke quietly as she looked at him standing in the doorway of her bedroom. Soon it would be supper time and, with so many to feed, she would be needed in the kitchen.

Edward sauntered towards her, smiling. 'No real wonder in that. When I was little, we all tumbled over each other in the nursery. And now, of course, with my girls–'

He stopped. Yes, it was true, he loved his daughters. And there would be another child to get to know soon – when he returned to London.

'I'm sure you're a very good father.' Anne tried

219

to smile. It was a brave attempt and he saw it. Compassion flooded Edward's chest.

'And I want to be. For our own son as well.'

Gently, he pulled her to him. 'I must tell you something my darling. You will need to be very strong.'

She nodded. 'Edward, I know. I know about the new prince. Kitchen gossip.'

He could feel how rigid she was; she could not allow herself to weaken, to break.

'And you did not think to speak to me, when you heard?'

Anne shook her head. 'I did not want to start that conversation. This conversation...' It was hard for her to say the words. He heard the strain in her voice.

'But this is good news, sweet child. It frees us both. England will be safe for him now.' He meant the little boy, so peacefully asleep behind the connecting door into his mother's room.

'How can you say that?'

She was angry and he understood. And admired her. Better a strong response than a bitter one.

'Elizabeth has her own son. She does not need yours now.'

It was a dark thing to say, a dark acknowledgment of the truth. Elizabeth Wydeville, Edward's wife, was Anne's enemy. The Queen of England had wanted mother and child dead, especially since she'd had no son of her own.

Edward smiled tenderly. 'When I have the kingdom back, I want you to come home. I want our son to come home too. I want to see him growing up in his own country. I want to know him, enjoy his company, watch over him as he grows to be a man. I want him to know his sisters. And his brother. And I want you there at court also. By my side. My acknowledged lady. The mother of my acknowledged son. He, and you, will always be safe in my realm.'

Realm. Kingdom. King – and queen. Anne, if she closed her eyes, could see it all as if she were a bird flying the breadth of England, from London over to the West Country...

From Westminster – the great hall where she'd seen them together first, Edward Plantagenet and Elizabeth Wydeville, truly the fairy king and queen – from the walls of the city of London, over the green fields and the woods, the grey castles, the neat villages, away to a home she'd never seen. Herrard Great Hall. Her mother's estate – hers now, if she wished to claim it. If she was allowed to claim it.

Anne sighed into Edward's chest, hiding her eyes so that he would not see the hope in them. 'Ah, the pictures are pretty ones, my liege. But we've travelled this road before...'

He lifted her face with a finger under her chin and kissed her gently. 'You give me strength. You always have. I need that strength.'

He placed both hands around her waist, the long fingers close to spanning the distance.

'You have not answered me, Anne.'

The girl was suddenly breathless; her back was against the casement and she felt the lead between the glass panes give slightly as he pressed forward.

'Anne, we have fenced enough.'

There was no escape now. 'Fenced?'

'The seaman. The man who said he was your husband. Are you his wife?'

She expelled her breath in a sigh, and would have told him the truth except that they both heard voices outside her door.

'Stop, Edward. Please?' she whispered urgently to the king. Frustrated, he kept her there, pinioned. 'No. Tell me.'

Urgent knocking at the door was followed by Richard of Gloucester's voice. 'Lady Anne? Are you there? Have you seen the king?'

'One moment, Lord Richard.'

Anne was wriggling, trying to squirm out of Edward's arms, but he would not let her go. They were both half laughing because it was so absurd.

'Edward, please let me go. This is embarrassing.'

'Tell me. Now!' It was a mock-fierce whisper; he was enjoying the fight. Anne was stronger than she looked as she twisted and pushed at his chest.

'Lady Anne?' Richard could hear the scuffles and was embarrassed, but he needed to speak with his brother.

'I shall call Richard in to witness your disobedience if you don't tell me!'

'My disobedience! Oh!'

She really was angry now, infuriated by the king's obvious enjoyment of the situation. Thoroughly riled, she spoke without thought. 'No, I am not married to him. There!'

She used that moment when her answer caught the king off guard: one determined push and she was free. Edward sprawled on the floor in a long heap of arms and legs as she marched to the door.

Hauling it open, she found the bewildered Duke of Gloucester staring at her. Lady Anne de Bohun tossed her head and stamped past, throwing over her shoulder some very disrespectful words from a subject to a king.

'He. That man. He is IMPOSSIBLE!'

Richard was bemused. And looked it. On the floor, his brother rolled onto his back, convulsed with laughter.

'One to me. One to me, Anne!'

That was too much. Anne ran back up the stairs and into her room, confronting both of them with her hands on her hips and the light of battle in her eye.

'The game is not over yet! Just you wait and see, Edward Plantagenet – not everyone does your bidding just because you are who you are!'

Edward scrambled to his feet and made her a deep bow. 'Of course not, dear lady. But one thing I would ask.'

Anne was icy. 'And what is that?'

'Please to keep your voice down or you'll wake the child.'

'Oh!'

Both men heard the fury as Anne turned her back and clattered back down the stairs towards the kitchen. Edward wiped the tears from his eyes as the suppressed laughter from both men erupted into guffaws.

'Got a bit of a temper that one, hasn't she?'

The king nodded, and sighed happily. 'Yes, she has. But a warm one.'

'Unlike–' Richard had been going to say 'the queen', but thought better of it. Elizabeth Wydeville was famous for her icy rages.

Edward glanced at his brother as he brushed the knees of his hose and the sleeves of his jacket for imaginary dust. Anne's was a very clean house, but the gesture bought him a pause. 'Still, it was worth chancing the storm for what I know now.'

Richard waited for enlightenment but, as none was forthcoming from his suddenly fastidious brother, remembered what he'd come to say.

'Despatches. From Charles. At last!'

# Part Two

# The Turning

## Chapter Thirty-One

The line of charcoal braziers placed at the bottom of the steps leading towards the throne sent pungent smoke into the stale air of the Presence chamber. So much smoke that the courtiers could hardly see the king through the veil of burning wormwood, rue, spikenard and myrrh.

Louis himself, irascible because of pain from two sources – his pustulent legs and his griping belly – was hung about with so many tiny reliquaries and crosses for protection that he rustled and faintly rattled when he moved. He held a rosary in his hands too, an especially valuable one of chalcedony, amber and gold, and he allowed the beads to slip through his fingers one by one as he spoke. They clicked like crickets, punctuating the king's words. It set the teeth of his courtiers on edge, as Louis knew it would.

'Brother (*click*) Agonistes (*click*), we (*click*) hear (*click*) much (*click*) of (*click*) your (*click*) skill (*click*) with (*click*) herbs (*click*)?'

The gaunt man dressed in shabby robes so old and patched that they were green-grey rather than black, bowed silently, his hands hidden within wide sleeves.

Silence without fear always surprised the king. He stopped clicking. 'But yet you are not a leech, a doctor?' Louis de Valois was suspicious. Why did the man not answer him? 'I want no doctors about my person, be certain of that.'

The monk raised his head and looked into the eyes of the king; his own were calm and clear. He sketched a cross in the air before he spoke. Was he trying to protect himself or bless the king?

'It is true that, once, I was a doctor at the court of the English king, Your Majesty, but I renounced that place, and my worldly past, some years ago. Now I do not give myself that title for it was the source of my undoing. I study herblore and use it in the service of all poor men who need my help. Herbs are simple things and, being created by God,' he crossed himself and all in the Presence chamber, including the king, followed suit, 'cannot be evil since they were set upon this Earth by Him to do His good purposes. Unlike the work of a man's hands, which can be turned to evil.'

Louis looked at the man measuringly. Perhaps this monk was touched by the Holy Spirit since he spoke with such passion. Possibly he was traitorous also, though to his former master. The king frowned. He might despise many of his fellow monarchs, but disrespect for the office itself was close to blasphemy.

'Which English king did you serve?'

The monk bowed deeply. 'I prefer, Your Majesty, to dwell in the present. I belong to God now, not Satan, and I bless the Father's gracious Son, our Lord, each and every one of my days that I am removed here to Paris from that evil place and its temptations.'

There, it had happened again: this man was refusing to answer him, and he was not afraid. The French king was truly intrigued.

228

'Evil, you say? How was the English court evil?'

Brother Agonistes dropped to his knees, then lay full length on his face in front of Louis, an ungainly lump on the floor. The heavy smoke from the braziers seemed to flow over him, forming a filmy cloak so that he was almost hidden from sight. Beneath the blanket of smoke, the monk began to cough, tears sprouting from his eyes, though he managed to speak, between the spasms.

'Do not, I beg you, ask me to recount the pits and snares of that place. My soul was made foul by sin and should I live to be three score years and ten, as the Bible says, I will never lose the taint of it. My only salvation lies amongst my brothers and the poor, of whom I am the last and the least, and whom it is my honour and penance to serve.'

The king turned and raised his eyebrows at his valet, Levaux, standing behind the Presence chair. It was a very long time since he'd been amazed, or indeed amused, by human behaviour, but this display was as good as an entertainment by any of the mummers at court.

However, the king let the monk lie there, gasping, as he thought about his words, but when he scratched his unbearably hot and itchy shins, his fingers came away bloody. Agony arced from his legs up into his groin, where it formed a burning knot with the ache in his belly. He closed his eyes, breathing deeply, fighting the nausea brought on by the pain. Unconsciously, he groaned.

The courtiers shuffled and glanced at each other. The king looked shocking, from what they could see of him through the smoke. Grey and sweating. But then, he always looked like that.

Louis's valet, no less amazed by the strange behaviour of the monk, was aware that time was passing. Brother Agonistes was no closer to performing his duty – the duty that was the key to advancement for the patron who had brought him to the king: himself, Alaunce Levaux. And to the salvation of France.

'Brother Agonistes, as you know, the king has particular need of your counsel in regard to his health–'

Louis held up one bony hand. The itch on his legs burned so much it ached, but he dared not scratch again. 'Certainly, that is the case, but I wish to consult with this holy brother privately.'

On the floor, the monk had covered his face with his two hands and, seemingly oblivious to his surroundings, was loudly chanting a prayer into the flags of the Presence chamber, much to the bemusement of the courtiers.

Levaux, who spoke no Latin, did not understand what the man was saying, but the king did. *'The Lord is my Shepherd, I shall not want...'*

Louis raised his voice so that all in the Presence chamber could hear him.

'Brother, we thank you for your care of the poor of our kingdom, and we are grateful that you have consented to give us the benefit of your wisdom. God, it is said,' all those present crossed themselves, even the man on the floor, 'moves in mysterious ways to accomplish His purposes. It may be that you have been sent here, to the court of France, as a test of your courage and your faith.'

The monk ceased to pray, but he did not remove his hands from his face. He was listening.

'Clear the chamber!' Louis clapped his hands decisively and ignored the pleading looks from his advisors. This would be a private conversation.

The reluctant courtiers shuffled from the room, leaving only the king, his valet and the monk.

'Come, Brother, I shall not hurt you.'

The monk spoke in a monotone from his place on the floor. 'I have only one king, Your Majesty, and He is in heaven. My earthly fate lies in your hands, but my soul,' the man shuddered, as if taken by a rigor, 'my soul lies at the feet of the Lord, sinner that I am.'

The king was conscious of growing annoyance. His foot began tapping, striking terror into the heart of Levaux. If this wretched monk could not be brought to speak with the king about his ailments, he would be blamed. And that would be the end of everything for him, and for his family. And, possibly, for the country.

Suddenly inspired, the valet caught Louis's eye. 'Your Majesty, may I speak?'

The king nodded, impatient and bewildered. Soon he'd become angry – he could feel the burning as it began in his chest, always a clear sign of what would come. He quite enjoyed his rages, but poor Levaux gulped when he saw the king's expression darken. He rushed to where the monk lay and knelt down beside him. Clasping his hands, as if to pray, he spoke softly into the monk's ear.

'Brother Agonistes, we are all brothers in Christ, are we not?'

'That is so. Bereft and alone we are born, bereft we die and all is turned to dust.' The monk sounded quite pleased at the thought, but the valet hurried on.

'Your brother, the king,' it was a bold thought, but so surprising that Louis said nothing, confused by the unusual notion, 'needs your help. He suffers for his kingdom, as Christ did for His.'

The monk looked up, startled. Levaux pressed on, suppressing the fear that was a cold hand fingering his liver and his tripes.

'And if Christ bore five wounds for His people, my Lord the King bears five times five. His suffering is very great. And God,' they all crossed themselves, 'has brought you here so that His servant, your brother, the king, may be healed by your special knowledge. You are a lucky man indeed this day to be about God's purposes.'

Brother Agonistes looked bewildered but then nodded. 'Yes. That must be so. Yes! This must be a test of my faith and my devotion, as my dear brother in Christ, the king, has said. I must face what I fear. I must welcome it.'

The monk was on his feet now, eyes to heaven – or in this case, the high vaulted ceiling of the chilly Presence chamber. 'I am here to serve my brother!'

Louis rolled his eyes. If he hadn't been in so much pain, he would have laughed at the idiotic solemnity of the man. Plainly, this monk *was* mad, but did that matter if he could stop the burning, gripping pain in his legs and staunch the agony in his belly?

The monk's eyes were lamps lit by zeal as he advanced up the steps towards the Presence chair, telling the beads from his rosary as he came.

Louis shrank back into the throne, suddenly

frightened by the look in the man's eyes. He had willingly committed himself into the hands of this lunatic. What if the monk had a knife?

But then Brother Agonistes was by his side and his eyes were gentle as a mother's with her tiny child. 'Where is the pain, brother? Let me heal you, for that is the Lord's wish, I feel sure.'

Wonderingly, Louis found himself raising the hem of his robe as if the action were the most natural thing in the world. He and the monk were wreathed in the smoke from the braziers as the monk gently probed his shins. And then the king remembered: myrrh. Was it not used for laying out the dead? Louis was deeply superstitious. The smoke from the fire of his own making was an omen – he was suddenly convinced of it. 'Am I dying?'

The monk sighed, dropping the hem of the king's robe and wiping his fingers, which were dabbled with blood and pus, on the skirt of his habit.

'No, brother King. You have an imbalance of the humours, that is clear, but such a one as can be healed. Your body is weakened and I can make it strong again. I will help your earthly pain and, God willing, that of your soul also.'

'You will?' Louis was suddenly limp with relief. And conviction. This monk might be a holy fool, but perhaps God *had* sent him. God, his fellow monarch on another plane.

The monk nodded and sketched a cross over the king's head. 'Please, open your mouth, Your Majesty.'

Obediently, like a child the king strained to

open his mouth as widely as he could.

'Ah, yes, I see what it is.'

'You do? Truly?'

'It is the sickness that comes from too much meat in winter and no green herbs. And not enough correctly directed prayer. First, the teeth become loose and then these' – the monk gestured to the sores and bruising beneath the king's robes – 'erupt. In your case, too, there is greater danger. Do dogs sleep on your bed, my brother?'

The king looked at the man, astonished by his question. 'Of course. Why?'

'Fleas, sire. With your blood in such a weakened state, the fleas from your animals have bitten you with great relish – corrupted blood is their greatest joy; they like its taste – and the bites have suppurated because of the weakness of your body.'

'Not poisoned boots?'

The valet avoided the eye of the king; his own legs were weak with fear.

The monk shook his head solemnly. 'No, my brother, your boots were not poisoned.'

Instant sweat soaked Levaux like a gush of clear water.

'What must I do, Brother?'

'Obey me, oh King, for I am the voice of the Lord. He will guide me, for you are His deputy on Earth, set over His earthly subjects to rule them in His name.'

The king crossed himself and, catching up the rosary that swung from the monk's girdle, kissed the little ivory body of the Christ figure that hung from its end.

Later, as Louis prayed beside Brother Agonistes for the restoration of his health, kneeling like his 'brother', the monk, on the bare stone before the high altar of his own private chapel, one small corner of the king's brain remembered. The monk had spoken of the evil at the English court. All the prayers in the world would not banish the curiosity of that thought from his mind.

At dinner, obediently eating an unusually meagre supper of pickled cabbage and bitter green herbs sourced from the monk's own physic garden, Louis gave words to the question.

'Brother, what was the evil you escaped from at the English court?'

Brother Agonistes trembled and sank to his knees, closing his eyes as he crossed himself repeatedly.

'Come, Brother, I have done what you asked. Now it is your turn. Does this evil have a name?'

'Yes. Its name was woman. The paramour of the king.' The monk spat the words and seemed about to vomit with revulsion.

Louis was thrilled. Gossip! He *loved* gossip, though he crossed himself in apparently pious concern.

'His paramour, you say? Who?'

The monk looked up and his eyes were dark holes. He whispered the name so faintly that Louis de Valois had to lean down to hear it – much to the disappointment of Alaunce Levaux, who was too far away to catch the monk's words.

'Anne. Anne de Bohun. King Edward's slut, the creature of the Evil One and the cause of my undoing.'

Louis shook his head, a suitably horrified expression on his face. But he stored away the name. He had a talent for such things. Unexpected information was often so very useful.


## Chapter Thirty-Two

'Where are we going, Captain?'

'To Delft, de Plassy.'

'Is it far, do you think?'

'Far enough.'

'Ah well, it is pleasant enough tonight. We shall enjoy our stroll.' Julian de Plassy looked at his companion and laughed, for the rain was relentless, driving full in their faces and bitterly cold.

Shrugging when he received no response, the Frenchman furled his cloak around his body and settled his raffish hat more firmly as he hurried on beside Leif Molnar. Prison quarters in the Binnenhof had done nothing for the quality of either adornment but de Plassy was philosophical. They were free, all of them, with the promise of a sea passage south if they could just beat any pursuit on this God-dark night.

'Your boat, Captain...?'

'My *ship* – yes, what of it?'

'You are sure, my friend, that she will have been mended by this time?'

'Monsieur de Plassy, I am certain of nothing. But if God is good, we have a chance. We will need that chance.'

Unconsciously Leif Molnar's fingers strayed to the sign of Thor around his neck. All these long weary days whilst he'd paced his prison cell alone, beneath the gate of the Binnenhof – three paces up, three paces across, three paces down – he'd kept up an unspoken prayer to Thor, Lord of Thunder, God of War. 'Hear me, Hammer-God, hear your servant. Help me, and the first black goat I see when I am out of this place I shall sacrifice to you. Hear me, help me!'

He had blamed Edward Plantagenet for his captivity. They would not let him go whilst the English king remained the 'guest' of Louis de Gruuthuse; the Dane knew he was too much of a threat to be allowed liberty. But then came the night when he was hauled from his prison. He had expected death; instead, without explanation, he'd been pushed into a much larger room with three barred windows high up in its walls. A room filled with Frenchmen – Julian de Plassy's wolvesheads. He found out later that Edward Plantagenet had escaped some days since.

His new companions stank, but so did he. More importantly, the Frenchmen were still strong; none of them was sick. Leif was grateful: sharing close quarters in a prison was often a death sentence, but the reason for the French-men's continuing health was quickly clear – better food than he'd been getting and clean air from the open windows, day and night. Cold air, certainly, but sweet.

Leif recovered his strength and found common cause with his new companions. Together, they began to plot a way out of the Binnenhof. Free-

237

dom and the *Lady Margaret* beckoned. Hopefully she was now repaired and sitting in the pool of Delft, and, no doubt, by now had built up formidable fees for wharfage. They'd deal with that when they got there.

'We have been lucky thus far, have we not, my Danish friend?' said Julian de Plassy.

Head down to keep as much rain as possible out of his eyes, Leif nodded in agreement. 'Some would describe it as such. Not me, though. I believe in planning.'

The bantam Frenchman looked back at his men, plodding behind them like subdued but faithful dogs. The euphoria of sudden freedom had washed away in the freezing rain.

'Ah yes, but who could have planned for this?' He waved the good sword he'd captured. 'Or that?' and pointed to the long dagger stuck through the rope Leif now called a belt. The knife was handsomely worked, with a jewel-set pommel, and therefore valuable. 'Or, indeed, for the unprepared foolishness of those we met. And this weather – this witch-black night to hide us? Surely, surely, that is luck?'

Leif nodded and actually smiled at the man who had become a friend. 'Your men fought well. Perhaps, in the end, I agree. We were favoured with luck.'

His fingers strayed to Thor's hammer again. After all his prayers, the God of War had finally sent the storm – and such a storm – and the mist that had providentially covered them once they had escaped the Binnenhof. That was after their guard had been foolish enough to stray too close

238

to the door of their cell; more foolish still to *open* that door in response to the yells, howls and cries from the men inside.

A desperate night on all counts – fighting, shouting, confusion, blood flying through the air like paint in a cathedral workshop – but they had broken out from s'Gravenhague with only two men of their own dead, and many wounded and dying Hollanders left behind to tell the tale of the escape of the men forgotten by the Sieur de Gruuthuse. And now they were marching, in reasonable order, to Delft. And the *Lady Margaret*.

But was Anne alive or dead? Leif did not know.

After the rain stopped there was moonlight to guide them. The Bible spoke of the power of the moon to 'smite'. An active word, a threatening word, but how could such an elusive glimmer be dangerous? Unless there was otherworldly magic in it and *that* was where the danger lay.

Anne and the king rode through the woods of the Duke of Burgundy's hunting park outside Brugge. They were alone together and silent, each focused on what must be done, and yet they now shared knowledge that could dictate the future. Knowledge that had an almost magical power to transform both their lives.

Edward knew that Anne was not married. The king tingled when he thought of it. No excuses now.

'There. Do you see?' Anne reined in her horse and pointed ahead to where light, warm and yellow, gleamed for a moment amongst dark trees.

'Where?' Edward stopped his horse beside

hers; he could see nothing.

'There. There it is!'

This time the uncovered lantern described an arc in the night. And then blinked out.

'Come.' Edward took the lead, nudging his horse to a trot along the faint bridle path. Anne had led this far, since she had ridden this forest countless times, hunting with the duke and duchess. But it was the king's turn now; he'd not let a woman ride first into possible danger.

The memory of light burns behind the eyelids even when it's gone, and this light, this humble lantern glowing in the dark, stayed with Edward all the rest of his life. It was the turning point – a light lit by fate to show the way into the future.

'Your Majesty?'

The accent was French and Edward's hands clenched on the reins. His horse threw up its head, startled, as the mounted man appeared on the path. But then the lantern shone on the stranger's face and Edward recognised who it was. When he spoke his voice was calmer than he felt.

'Monsieur de Commynes. You are well?'

'Exceedingly so, sire.'

Philippe de Commynes bowed low over his horse's neck, first to the king and then to his companion. Beneath the deep hood of her cloak, Anne's face was veiled so he had no clue to her identity.

'My master is close. If you would follow me?'

The king gestured for the man to precede them, but insisted that Anne ride behind the messenger while he, himself, brought up the rear.

Anne sat straighter in the saddle. She fixed her

attention on the pale horse ahead – the swaying cream tail was an easy marker to follow. It was comforting that Edward was guarding her back on this strange, glimmering night. The rising full moon cast the trees into stark shapes as they rode deeper and deeper into the woods towards – what?

The small hunting lodge showed few lights when the party of riders entered the clearing. It was not a noble building, more a homely, convenient hideaway for Charles of Burgundy when he wished to escape the ceremonial weight of his days at court. A place where he could retire with a few well-favoured friends and relax, free from prying eyes.

Edward reined in his horse. He understood entirely why Charles would wish to meet him in this obscure place, but he was dismayed. Such discretion was not optimistic to his cause.

Anne glanced back at the king and smiled; white teeth gleamed through the sarcenet veil as they caught the light. She leaned over to speak to him. 'All will be well, Your Majesty. I feel it.'

Edward dismounted and turned to assist Anne from her saddle. 'Are you a witch then, that you can see the future?'

It was meant as a harmless joke but Philippe de Commynes turned and stared at them, startled. He had heard the word 'witch'; it made him fearful. One did not laugh about such things.

Anne saw the man's uneasy glance in the light that spilled from the opening door, but her sudden fear was extinguished as she looked down at the king. Edward Plantagenet had opened his arms wide – a blatant invitation. His smile was heart-

241

stopping and he was focused, intently, on her.

'Come to me.' So few words, but there was such promise in them that, suddenly, she could not breathe.

Anne allowed herself to ease down into Edward's arms and, for one moment, stood close against his body; but then the muscles in his arms tensed around her.

'Brother. You are welcome.'

Startled, Anne stepped back and the sudden movement dislodged the hood of her cloak.

'And you also, Lady Anne.'

It was said with a certain irony and Anne blushed, dropping her head as she curtsied to the duke. Charles bowed ceremoniously to Edward before reaching down to raise Anne to her feet.

'Lady, my house is yours. The pleasure is greater for being unexpected.'

Edward laughed a little. 'Well, without Lady Anne, I'd still be riding around in circles, I suspect, since it took some time to find your messenger. All forest looks alike at night.'

Charles chuckled. 'As is also said of cats and—'

He stopped himself, but Anne knew what he had meant: 'women'. She raised her chin and smiled brilliantly at the duke as he conducted her into his hunting lodge. The moment of disrespect hurt, however, and Edward's frown told her that he, too, was offended on her behalf. It was unlike Charles to be coarse in front of a woman, especially since he understood so well the sensitivity of Anne's relationship to the king. Perhaps it was the first move in this complicated game they must all now play – a subtle signal that Edward could take nothing, nothing at all, for granted from his own, dear brother-in-law. The contest had changed: Charles was no longer the less-powerful partner in the game.

It was a still, cold night; the temperature was dropping outside the lodge. Soon, the air would freeze into fog and that would become a deep frost. Yet inside, the heat was intense – for more reasons than the enormous fire lit for their welcome.

Charles and Edward were now alone, seated on either side of the central fire pit in the hall. Compared to the Ridderzaal, the room was small and simply furnished with long benches and a few joint stools. A rough-made cupboard held pewter dishes and beakers and there was a single hanging on the lime-washed walls – a simple woollen curtain in muddy reds and deep blues slung from hooks near the ceiling. It billowed as a delinquent draught skirled sparks from the fire.

'Why?'

Those who knew Edward Plantagenet well would have left the room, if they could, when he spoke thus. His voice was controlled but the hint was in his eyes; they were half closed and, under the lids, a frightening light burned. He was very angry.

But so was Charles. From guilt and – if he allowed himself to face it – from fear.

'Edward, it grieves me but I ask you to understand. To support you now, with the French massing in Picardy just waiting to invade, is to invite war. And I am too stretched; Burgundy's resources are too stretched. I cannot support you until I know more of the situation in England *and* what Louis is doing. I cannot!'

'And yet, whilst I was immured at s'Graven-hague with de Gruuthuse – on your instructions, I think – I heard plentiful, well-sourced rumours that you were actually helping Warwick subdue my kingdom?' Edward was politely icy but now it was said, out in the open.

Charles got to his feet and threw the lees of his wine into the fire, where they hissed like a cat. He did not immediately answer, refilling his beaker from a jug that was warming by the open hearth.

'Well?' Edward was implacable and Charles turned to face those merciless eyes.

'A blind, brother. Merely a ruse. I did not give them much by way of aid, and it was only to buy myself time.'

Edward snorted. 'Some might give it another name than "blind", *brother.*'

Charles was caught by his own uncertainty. It was true: for some months he *had* been playing both ends against the middle, but, in the end, he'd been honest. What he wanted and needed was time; time to see the real shape of the situation as it developed – now that Warwick held England for the Lancastrians – and time to rebuild his own armies against the certainty that, eventually, he would have to declare his hand and fight for his domains. Against whichever enemy declared itself first – France or England. Or, indeed, both together.

'You ask much, Edward. Too much. I must think of my own country first.'

'Your country? What country? You're not a king

yet, Charles, and you never will be unless I can take back England and help you against Louis. You are a fool to place any faith in Warwick. How long do you think he'll last once Margaret of Anjou actually gets back into London? She'll sack the place and buy his destruction with what she loots there. Then Louis will turn on you, with her help, and the full weight of England will be behind them both. You are wilfully blind!'

The two men were on their feet and dangerously close to the fire as they stared at each other, unblinking. Two mastiffs looking for the first opening, the first weakening, of their opponent.

Charles's voice shook with rage. 'By God's entrails, Edward Plantagenet, I have but to call and men would take you from here for all your brave words. You cannot fight from a prison cell.'

The hair on Edward's nape was stiff and he could feel his scalp move as, wheat blond in the light from the fire, the hair on his head stood up. Suddenly he looked even more massive, more bulky, than before and the room was filled with the ozone of danger. Primeval fear shook Charles to his bowels, though he would not acknowledge it, even to himself.

Edward's voice was level, but only just, as he spoke, eyes boring into the duke's. 'Do not think to do this, Charles. God will punish you. I am an anointed king. You are not.'

Charles blinked and dropped his glance. He did not mean to – he was a brave man, many, many times proved in battle – but the roiling fire in Edward's eyes filled him with superstitious dread. Edward Plantagenet might be the deposed king of

245

his country – and a usurper at that – yet, yes, he was still an anointed king. And he was filled with utter certainty. Perhaps kings understood their holy office better than did mere dukes.

Annoyed and humiliated by his confusion, Charles wiped a hand across his eyes, as if to physically brush truth away like an annoying insect.

'It remains, however, that you are, officially, without support. And whatever happens in the future, for now Louis must go on thinking that. I cannot be seen to give you aid. Not now, not at this moment. It is not the right time to make best advantage.'

'Time has all but run its course in this matter, Charles.'

The duke was drained, unutterably weary. He had been dreading this interview, had even thought of riding away, out of Brugge, to join his troops massing on the southern borders where Burgundy marched with France, anything to avoid meeting Edward. But, in the end, curiosity and the last torn fragments of compassion had made him agree to this meeting. These things, and his marriage. Margaret was dear to him, and Edward had been his friend; was, strangely, his friend yet.

The duke sighed and leaned over to pour red wine into Edward's empty beaker before refilling his own. 'I cannot agree, my friend. It is hard to see the future, very hard. What my heart says and what my head says are two different things. And we must hold our nerve in this. Together.'

Edward said nothing, but held out his full beaker and the duke, reluctantly, touched it with his own.

'The future? I can help you with that, brother. I always have, I always will.' Edward smiled and it was unexpectedly sweet.

Charles could not help himself, he smiled in return. He'd known Edward since he was a boy, and that counted for something even in these fraught times.

The talk continued as long as the night lasted; the king and the duke wrangling and arguing back and forth, seeking a solution to their opposing needs. They spoke freely, believing themselves alone. But they were not.

Philippe de Commynes heard each word that was spoken as he sat in a spy-perch, high up in the shadows amongst the beams supporting the pitch of the roof. He alone knew of its existence and it had proved most useful – especially lately. Especially tonight.

After hunting, when men sat drinking, Philippe would sometimes excuse himself for bed, only to climb up beneath the tiles of the roof and crawl on his belly along the narrow plankway amongst the roof timbers, created so that the structure could be inspected from time to time. There he would lie and listen to what was said far below him by the duke and his closest companions as they fell deeper and deeper into their cups. Later, he would write down all that he had heard.

It was here that he'd understood the contempt in which the duke held him – his own cousin – and heard the laughter that erupted every time they called him Boothead; an experience that had curdled his heart, and his loyalty.

Tonight, as he looked down coldly upon a deposed king and an aspirant king, Philippe de Commynes knew that the wheel of fortune had turned and he was riding up. Yes, tonight was most fortunate for him, and even more so for Louis de Valois. For if he had saved the French king's life once, how much more grateful would Louis be when Philippe saved his kingdom?

## Chapter Thirty-Three

'How much is the kingdom worth to you, Edward?'

Anne had spent the night in the kitchen of the hunting lodge. At first she'd waited for the men to finish talking so that she and Edward could return to her farm, but in the end she'd gone to sleep, head on her arms on the trestle table, and awoken stiff and cold when Edward roused her at dawn. She and the silent king were riding back towards Riverstead Farm in the first light, and she could see Edward was brooding on his thoughts.

'Any price I have to pay. Except you.' He glimmered a smile, making an effort to be cheerful for her sake.

'Why?'

'Why what? Or why you?'

Now she too laughed, and reined in her horse so that the pretty mare snuffled a protest at such contrary directions, hands and heels, from her mistress.

'Do you never think of refusing to pay what is asked of you?'

Their horses were side by side on the bridle path beside the river, and human and animal breath joined, smoking, in the cold morning as a winter sun struggled up from the east.

Edward leaned over and rearranged a tendril of Anne's hair that had escaped onto her cheek. His touch lingered. He traced the shape of her cheek, her nose, the outline of her mouth, with one gloved finger.

She closed her eyes. She couldn't help it.

The king's voice was husky when he spoke.

'I'd take the glove off, but the cold is savage.'

That made them both laugh, giddily: two sillies caught up in the nearness of each other. The horses stamped and tried to circle, impatient with the chill and being made to stand there.

'I was serious, Edward.' She caught one of his hands and held it to her face, cradling it.

He sighed and leaned towards her, kissing her softly on the lips; a cold kiss, but heat ignited them both.

'I know. But I cannot answer you. I am fearful of the question.'

They were lost together, alone in the world as it came awake and, as he gazed at her and she at him, fear ebbed away. All that was left was the sound of their breathing and the restless stamping and snuffling of the horses.

'We should return to the farm.' Anne's mouth was dry as she spoke. Could words be a shield? Or a rope to tow the drowning to the safety of the shore?

'The world is full of should and would, my darling. Do you love me? Do you love me enough?'

It was an unfair question. He knew that.

'How do I answer? I do not think in terms of measure or dimension, Edward.'

The king slipped one hand out of its riding gauntlet and around her waist under her cloak as their horses stood side by side. Her body was warm, he could feel the heat through her clothes, and she smelled, faintly, of roses.

'Enough, for me, means following your heart without thought, without restraint.'

Anne shook her head to clear it, to resist the siren song, but she was torn; she could feel reason loosing its grip as he leaned towards her from the height of his horse and kissed the beating hollow at the base of her throat.

Suddenly, he wheeled his stallion, spurred it, and was off at a canter then a furious gallop, racing down the bridle path towards the boundary stone of the farm just up ahead. But instead of turning towards the farm buildings, he rode on until a curve in the river bank took him from her sight.

Anne, shaken by Edward's touch, by his smell, gathered her horse by instinct, tightened the reins and settled herself in the saddle. Her mare, fresh from a night of rest, needed no other signal. She danced for a moment, then sprang away with such force that Anne was nearly unseated.

It was a wild, wild ride. The rushing air whipped bright blood into Anne's face and exhilaration made her giddy as with wine. She could see the king up ahead, his cloak flying out behind him as his horse ate the distance with its stride. But then, as she turned her head to avoid the naked branch of a tree, and looked back – he was gone.

Gone where?

She hauled the mare to a quivering, dancing stop and swivelled in the saddle, this way and that. There was no sign of the king or his horse.

She'd come some distance past the entrance to her farm and had pulled up beside the river flats; the same river flats Deborah had acquired from the Landers family whilst Anne had been away. This was the land on which she would plant crocus bulbs, if fate allowed her.

She guided her horse through a gap in the hedge into the field that was resting, unploughed, over winter. She remembered a barn had been part of the purchase from the Landers and, yes, there it was – and there, also, was Edward's tethered horse, peaceably cropping forage beside the small building with its red-tiled roof.

'Edward? We must get back.' She called the words strongly but they sounded silly as soon as they were out of her mouth. She didn't want to return to her real life. Not yet.

'Come and see what I've found?'

The king's voice was muffled; he was inside the barn.

There was a moment to decide, a moment in which she could have ridden away. Two pictures formed in her mind. In one, she was riding towards the barn, dismounting, tying the mare beside the stallion and walking inside towards the sound of his voice. In the other, she turned the mare for home, riding away, riding away from him...

'Anne? Come and look.'

The king's stallion raised his head and nickered to the mare, welcoming companionship. Anne's horse, skittish, danced forward as if the woman's hands on the reins meant nothing. And then Edward was there, reaching for her, and Anne slipped down into his welcoming arms. She leaned against his chest, her head finding its natural resting place against his shoulder, as if she had no strength of her own to stand. Her body had made the choice.

With an unsteady laugh he gathered her and held her so tightly, so hungrily, that she moulded her body to his, the cradle of her hips a gift, an offering.

'Come with me. See...'

Holding her close, Edward brought Anne inside the barn. For a moment it was dark and then the girl's eyes adjusted. Silver light, moving with motes of dust, flowed through ventilation holes high up beneath the eaves and it was as cold inside as out. Now Anne remembered why she'd been so glad to have the barn included on the river-land title – it was sound and excellent for storage: in this case, summer hay for the few cows they were keeping over the winter. River land always cropped well, and the sheaves of hay were deep, stacked high and sweet-smelling even in the cold air.

Gently, Edward turned Anne by the shoulders to face him.

'I doubt that any man or any woman ever had a deeper, sweeter bed...' he kissed her softly, '...if this is what you want?'

She could feel the tension through his hands. His whole body was locked tight with discipline;

he would not permit himself to do what he most wanted until he was sure she felt as he did. Anne closed her eyes. All that remained was smell and touch. And taste.

As he kissed her again, her mouth opened. She did not resist any more. Her hunger was great as his – and he knew it.

'Ah, thank God. This has not changed.'

The dam broke, all restraint was gone, drowned.

Hay beneath them, his cloak to cover them, passion to keep them warm, this man and this woman found each other again and it was familiar and strange and joyous.

'I cannot see you! This is torture!'

'But we can see with our fingers,' she said huskily. 'Close your eyes.'

He understood and did what she asked, savouring the warmth of her skin as he pulled the skirt of her riding dress away. Velvet hose were held up with garters of ribbon but, above them, her thighs were naked, butter soft and smooth. Edward's hands were rough from riding; it almost felt like violation to touch her but the need was urgent.

'Oh, but I've missed you.' There was hardly breath to speak as his senses rioted.

'I saw you, all the time. In my dreams.'

'And I you. Oh yes, I have seen you, and wanted you.' He was kissing her eyes, mouth, neck, breasts, his words muffled and frenzied, hands roaming, remembering.

Their breath, warm and quick, smoked in the cold air of the barn, for theirs was an island of heat. Anne pushed Edward away for a moment. Her eyes searched his face, her hands held his away from her. He was strong, arms muscled by years of riding and fighting, but in her hands, for that moment, he had no strength at all.

'I do not know what this means, Edward.'

She didn't have to say more, didn't want to, but he understood. If they were lovers again, it might only be for now.

'We do not have to know. The fates will decide. But you and I? Oh, my beloved, we shall be lovers all our lives. Even if we live apart.'

Their minds were so close, they always had been. And now their bodies thought for them. No more words.

With shaking fingers, Anne helped Edward unlace the points of his hose, and he, clumsy with need, fumbled the lacing of her riding habit, impatient to free her breasts.

She was ivory and rose, the uncertain light silvering her skin; gently, caressingly, it touched the sculpture of her throat and her shoulders, the perfect answering curve of breast and hip, and suddenly this woman was sweeter to Edward Plantagenet than unclaimed land; this living girl whose breath and scent, whose texture and eyes and mouth, comprised the whole world, lifted him away from the appetites of his body and into another realm. An uncomplicated place that had no end and no beginning and was only now.

This – he and she together – was his home and his kingdom: a place of real substance, the one he'd always instinctively sought. He had never understood what its absence meant until this moment, but with Anne cradled in his arms, skin to skin, he claimed that knowledge. Her loss had been a long-suppurating wound. It had nearly poisoned him. But now, that loss was remedied and it was glorious to be held again, to melt, to shiver, to surrender. And to heal.

His torso was naked against her breasts – his body so hard, hers so tender – and Anne was wild within his arms. She could not hold him tightly enough, fiercely enough, her nails rending his back and shoulders as they lay deep within the straw and she pulled his body down to hers.

How easy it was. How easy to surrender. His thighs were between hers and the flesh and the bone of their bodies did not exist.

'We've lit this fire, you and I.' She spoke between panting as he slid into her body, slow and hard. 'And I want to burn, to be burned up.'

He caught her lip between his teeth then speared his tongue into her sweet mouth so that all words were stopped. She moaned and moved beneath him, catching his rhythm, meeting it, bracing her hips against his to drive him deeper into her body.

He was spread like a crucifix upon her, arms wide, holding her wrists apart, pressing her down into the yielding straw so that the smell of the long past summer grass was released to the air by the heat of their bodies.

'You are mine.' Primordial need, man to woman, spoke those words.

'I am, Gods help us.'

It was a prayer, an invocation, with its own power as the splintering wave took them both; a wave that was heat and light and obliterating dark as two souls who had been lost found peace. And each other. Once again.

255

# Chapter Thirty-Four

'Where has the duke deployed his forces?'

Philippe de Commynes was uncomfortable and tried to hide it. Adopting the bland face of the successful courtier, he bowed deeply, mentally wriggling on this hook of his own making.

'Your Majesty, my master the duke has given me no knowledge beyond what is contained within the despatches you hold.'

'Come, monsieur. Your master the duke, if he is a loyal subject of mine,' Louis fixed Philippe with a flesh-stripping glance, 'cannot object to this innocent enquiry?'

Pointedly, he handed the velvet despatch satchel embroidered with the arms of Burgundy to le Dain, the barber, who was standing beside the Presence chair.

Philippe cleared his throat nervously. 'My master fears aggression from the English – from Earl Warwick, Your Majesty – that is well known.'

Louis said nothing, but his foot began to tap. That tapping filled all who witnessed it with dread. Philippe hurried on.

'Recently, English privateers have harassed Flushing and Sluys, sinking many of the merchant fleet waiting for spring, and raided the coastal towns also, for trade goods. My master feels he must protect his people.'

'Yet His Majesty, King Louis, understands that

the greatest concentration of the Burgundian troops is within Picardy. At a considerable distance from the sea and the ports you name.'

The barber had spoken, oily smooth, on behalf of *his* master.

The neckband of Philippe de Commynes' delicate undershirt was soaked; shortly the sweat seeping from his armpits would also stain the expensive silk of his jacket irrevocably – he could feel it running down his sides. Again he bowed, arms clamped tight to his sides to minimise the stink. The king raised his eyebrows; the man before him now resembled a water fowl, ducking for weed.

'Your Majesty, these are matters that...' Unhappily, de Commynes found words deserting him. Whatever he said, however he said it, would be seized upon greedily and torn apart by the ravening gossips of the French court – and the Burgundian court also, when they were reported back to the duke. He tried again. 'Great King, perhaps I could beg an opportunity to speak privately? An indulgence, I know, but–'

'I am not a priest, Monsieur de Commynes, that I should hear confession in silence and darkness.'

The Burgundian envoy gulped; the king was abrupt and his tone freezing. But then Louis allowed his gaze to dwell on the supplicant for a moment and a curious expression softened his face.

The barber, watching, narrowed his eyes. Gratitude? Could that be it?

'However, on this occasion...' The king gestured irritably for the Presence room to be cleared. 'And you as well!' The king waved at le

257

Dain. The barber was annoyed, and suspicious. What could this effete courtier have to say to Louis that was not suitable for him, the king's chief advisor, to hear?

'Go, le Dain. This tries my patience!' The king half stood to enforce his will, then winced; his legs were still painful, though they were healing, slowly. 'And send for the monk. I need him.'

Grudgingly, the barber backed out of the Presence chamber, furious that he'd been sent on an errand like an anonymous flunky. Nevertheless, his face wore the polite, cheerful mask of all those who served the king. In whatever capacity.

Once outside the door, the barber scowled. Philippe de Commynes might think he had the king's ear just because of the incident of the poison, but he, Olivier le Dain, would make sure he met with the Burgundian envoy before he was sent on his way home. Oh yes, he would see to that!

The Presence chamber settled into silence as the doors were closed on the courtiers, twittering and fluttering like a noisy pack of starlings. Now Philippe de Commynes had his wish: he was alone with the king. Would that this moment proved a blessing, not a curse.

'And so, Philippe, what is so secret that you could not say it before my advisors?'

'The English king, Your Majesty...' De Commynes saw an odd look pass over Louis's face and interpreted it as anger. He was wrong. It was fear. 'That is, the Earl of March, the usurper of the English throne. He has met with my master.'

Louis swallowed the sudden rush of acid in his

throat. And instantly regretted it. It burned all the way down to his gut; but that moment of pain distracted him from dread, rising like damp through his body.

'When? And where?'

'A hunting lodge in the duke's chase outside Brugge. About a week ago.'

'Were others there?'

'Only me, Your Majesty. And a lady. A friend of the earl's.'

The king snorted. 'A friend of the earl's? Nonsense. Men and women are not friends. Why was she there?'

Philippe was uncomfortable. He was playing for high stakes and in asking for this audience, he knew he had crossed the line. The duke would hear of it, of course – but having come this far, how could he retreat?

'I do not know, Lord King. I did not see her face, but I heard my master...' – why was that word so difficult to say, now? Perhaps because the duke was his master no longer – 'I heard the duke...' Philippe looked Louis square in the eye and the king smiled at him, almost kindly, 'I heard the duke refer to her as Lady Anne.'

Louis de Valois sat up straighter in his Presence chair. 'Lady Anne de Bohun?'

Philippe was astonished, then humbled. Of course a king would know all there might be to know about his enemies, even the names of their companions. 'I do not know her patronymic, sire. But she waited for the ki– the earl all night. And left with him in the morning, just at dawn.'

Louis grunted. They would return to the topic

of this mysterious lady, but for now other information was more pressing.

'I suppose it is too much to ask what your master, the duke,' – an ironic smile directed at Philippe caused the young man to blush and drop his gaze – 'and the Earl of March spoke of?'

This was the moment. The moment when both men in that room knew that Louis de Valois had a new retainer as surely as if Philippe de Commynes had knelt and sworn fealty to this king of the French.

'They spoke alone, Your Majesty.' Slowly the young man raised his eyes and looked searchingly at the king. 'But I heard what was said.'

Louis smiled. Of course, he would not trust de Commynes in the time to come – why would he trust a man who was prepared to betray his own master? – yet he would encourage him. Assuredly, he would encourage Boothead well.

'Intriguing, Philippe. What did they say?'

The young man knelt humbly at the foot of the dais and clasped his hands, almost as if praying. 'The earl was seeking aid, Your Majesty. His brother-in-law, the duke, was reluctant to give it for fear of offending you, Lord King, and bringing ruin upon the dukedom. My mas– the duke is very torn, sire. Quite frankly, he cannot make up his mind where his allegiance should lie.'

The king had earlier swallowed his surprise that Edward Plantagenet had arrived at Brugge. The latest despatches he'd had from the Low Countries had told him that the deposed English king was still loose but in the wilds of the region, a fugitive from Louis de Gruuthuse. But he believed what de Commynes told him; simply, the man had too much to lose by lying.

'Yet Charles has been trumpeting his support of Warwick for some time. He has even sent coin to support his cause – or so I'd understood.'

De Commynes shook his head confidently. 'No, Your Majesty. He does not support the Earl Warwick, not truly. He's buying time, that is all. Time to truly understand the situation in England; particularly, whether the magnates will give support to the Earl of March should he return. When the duke sees the wind setting clearly, he will make up his mind. If Warwick succeeds in holding England, you have a powerful new ally – and naturally that will be the end of the duke's ambitions to crush the might of France and create his own kingdom.'

The king said nothing, but sat thinking. Then he sighed. 'Ah, who to trust. If kings – and dukes – knew the answer to that little question, we would all sleep so much better. My poor cousin Charles...' A gusty sigh followed, but the lipless smile gave the lie to the conventional words of compassion. 'Yet, he must gamble one day soon or he'll lose it all. All his territories, and such power as he currently has. I shall see to that myself. With great pleasure.'

Louis was talking to himself and, wisely, Philippe de Commynes kept still and silent, though his knees were aching on the unforgiving stone flags.

The king closed his eyes, the better to concentrate. 'I wonder if he has the resources?' The words were out before the king could call them back.

'For what, Your Majesty?'

Louis's eyes snapped open and bored into those of the younger man. 'To give Edward what he needs to take back England. What is your opinion, monsieur?'

Philippe de Commynes swallowed hard before he answered. 'The duke is stretched on several fronts, Your Majesty. And this winter has been hard. There is unrest within Burgundy. Food shortages, you understand.'

Each man knew what that meant. The French, when they took territory, inevitably burned it out and took all that was edible back to their own lines. The Burgundians replied in kind. And all the while, the people suffered cruelly.

'Well then, we must stretch him further.'

The king stood with a vigour he had not felt for weeks, even months. Perhaps the monk was right. Perhaps this medicine *was* agreeable to the humours of his body. It was unlike Louis to feel so optimistic, so – what was it? – so cheerful.

'Here, my friend.' In passing, the king bent down and patted the head of his new vassal. 'This is a very small token of what is to come if you serve me faithfully; as faithfully as you have today.' Into the nerveless fingers of Philippe de Commynes' right hand the king pressed a ring of gilded silver in which was mounted a sapphire. It was small but the stone was unflawed and of a very pure blue and therefore valuable.

Overcome, Philippe bowed, snatched the hand of the king and kissed it.

Louis smiled almost paternally and allowed the intimacy, then he strode towards the door of the Presence chamber, filled with new purpose.

At the door he paused and turned. 'By the way, Philippe, what made you do it?'

The young man blushed like a girl and felt like a fool, yet he spoke clearly. 'My cousin, the duke, has not used me as a kinsman should.'

The king thought and then smiled. 'Boothead! It's the name, isn't it? You hated the name!'

Tears of fury and humiliation stung the eyes of Philippe de Commynes but he managed a certain dignity in reply. 'Sire, nothing will please me more than that I be permitted to serve your house. My own, plainly, does not require my loyalty or I would not be treated as I am. I am yours until death.'

Strange, thought Louis as he hauled open the doors of the chamber himself – to the great scandal of the door-wards – he almost sounds sincere.

And then he forgot Philippe de Commynes, his wounded pride, and even his own duel with the Duke of Burgundy, in the delighted certainty that he, Louis de Valois, had found Edward Plantagenet's weakness. If a woman could be the embodiment of Nemesis, it was she. And he knew just the man who would bring her down on her own ground. And Edward's ambitions with her – since she so plainly distracted him from his duty.

Brother Agonistes had said the woman was a witch. Louis smiled his lipless smile. Witches didn't exist, but the credulous believed in them. Well then, let them have one to play with.

'The monk! Where is the monk?'

'Here I am, brother King, what do you ask of me?'

Louis de Valois, King of France, strode forward and clapped the filthy monk on his back. 'Brother, I have holy work for you to do. Work that God will give you strength to perform, though it may destroy your soul if you fail. Come with me, let us pray for strength. You will need it.'

Louis smiled tenderly at the confused monk and graciously took the man's hand in his own, dirty as it was, leading the holy fool towards the chapel where, normally, the king, and the king alone, worshipped.

'It concerns the Devil, my brother; the Devil and the flesh. The Devil *in* the flesh, indeed. And I believe you are God's chosen instrument in this duel between the two.'

The monk found his tongue. 'In what way, Your Majesty? How can that be so?'

The king stopped and turned to the monk, solemnly sketching a cross over the man's head.

'Many years ago, a woman, an evil woman, destroyed your life with the lure of her corrupted body. Is that not so?'

Brother Agonistes paled visibly beneath the encrusted grime on his face. 'Yes. I was cursed. Her beauty dragged me into a pit of despair; it became a dagger in the Devil's hands.'

The king closed his eyes and nodded. It was as if he were listening to a voice far, far away. 'And yet this woman lived on, unscathed, whilst you became a lost and wandering soul?'

Brother Agonistes nodded. It was true: the woman had lived and he had been damned, all these years, to a life of poverty and penance in expiation of his own tormented lust.

The king's eyes opened very wide; they were unsettling coals in a skull-like head. 'And if I told you that I know where this woman lives? That she wallows, even now, in her bed of sin with that adulterous usurper, the Earl of March? He who was formerly called the King of England.'

Brother Agonistes felt dizzy. True, he had fasted for the last three days in preparation for the holy feast-day that would mark the birth of the Saviour, but that did not explain the ringing in his ears, or the breathlessness that suddenly collapsed his chest.

'Brother, let us pray, you and I. For, as I said, I believe you to be God's chosen instrument to smite these sinners down, both of them.' The king smiled, as cold as lakewater. 'Come, let us seek His guidance. He has called us to execute His will here on Earth, and so that is what we shall do, Brother, together, as loving sons of a compassionate and all-seeing Father should.'

Before Brother Agonistes could reply, the king's bony fingers had clamped around his fragile wrist and he was being towed along, unresisting, in Louis's wake.

Was that sulphur he could smell? Yes, most assuredly it was. Sulphur, stronger than incense. Stronger than fear. But only just.

# Chapter Thirty-Five

This close to the Christ-mass, the Prinsenhof in Brugge blazed with reckless brilliance. Branches of candles stood on every surface, ornate candelabra hung in the rafters, flambeaux and great fires were everywhere, as the court of Burgundy prepared to celebrate the season of the Saviour's birth. Beyond the city walls was darkness, metaphorical as well as physical; but the court and the town ignored the fear that darkness brought – best to enjoy all the fun that could be had, and think about the rest tomorrow.

The duke, determined to show the world and his followers a confident face, had planned a Christ-mass feast. No part of his winter-starved lands would be spared an additional tithe to feed the court and its seasonal guests. If his people must suffer to confuse his enemy, so be it.

Charles sighed, rubbing his temples.

'You are distracted, my dear.' The duchess put down her embroidery frame and reached across, catching up one of the duke's hands.

The duke and the duchess were experiencing a rare moment to themselves – if one did not count the cluster of waiting women grouped together in a window embrasure playing at knucklebones.

'Tell me, Charles. The trouble may lessen if you speak of it.'

The duke smiled at his wife, though she could

sense his tension still.

'There are some things that are proper for me to carry alone, dearest girl. That is my duty.'

Margaret patted her husband on the knee, laughing brightly, though her eyes were anxious.

'Now, Charles, we are married. I am here to share your burdens. I promised to, in the cathedral at Damme. This is my duty also.'

Now it was his turn to pick up her hands and look into her eyes. He kissed each of her fingers, one by one, so it was several moments before he spoke. Then: 'Louis has declared war on us. He has rejected the Treaty of Peronne.'

Margaret said nothing for a moment as she gazed at her husband; there was no point expostulating. She kissed Charles gently on his slightly whiskery cheek. 'Well then, this is what we have been expecting. And now it has arrived.'

Margaret sat back calmly and picked up her work. 'Charles?'

'Yes, my dear?'

'Did your man not shave you this morning?'

The duke laughed out loud. How typical it was of his wife to be practical, even when she was frightened. He prized her for that quality. She was the sane centre of a spinning, dizzy world.

'Perhaps not. I do not remember.'

Of course he didn't remember – he'd been awoken in the hour before dawn and had hurried, half dressed, to receive the despatches from the hand of his emissary to the French, Philippe de Commynes. Since then, he'd been issuing a stream of orders – to his troops in the field and for the raising of more levies – and had barely had time to eat, let alone restore his appearance to something his wife might approve.

'What will you do?'

Charles shrugged. 'Well, much has been done already. The call has gone out for the levies to join the men we already have in the field. If Louis insists, well then, we will fight him.'

Margaret said nothing, but he knew her well. He chuckled to lighten the atmosphere. 'We shall still make our feast, lady. I will not allow Louis to think his foolishness has interrupted our wassail.'

Margaret's industrious fingers flew as the needle pierced the backcloth of the embroidery again and again. 'Where will Louis strike, do you think? And when?'

Watching Charles of Burgundy at this moment, a stranger might have thought he did not care, was not treating this threat to his dukedom with any seriousness. But that was his way – it was a grace he had and he knew it inspired confidence. A priceless attribute.

'Picardy. He's massing against us there, on the border. He's called in the English also. Warwick will send men.'

'And what will you do, Charles?' Margaret spoke sharply and her needle stopped, poised over the cloth.

The duke rose, restless, and paced over to a window. He stood there, his back to the room. Then he swung around to look at his wife.

'Louis has shown his hand. By God's bones, so will I.'

The knock was thunderous in the sleeping house.

Anne woke instantly from a deep dream, a happy dream of homecoming and laughter. Now, as the wisps of fantasy were blown away like mist, she sat up in a huddle of bedclothes, reaching for Edward.

The imprint where his body had lain, beside hers, was still warm, but he was gone. Then, distantly, she heard men talking.

Naked, Anne threw the bedclothes back and ran shivering to the pegs on the wall where, every night, her clothes were hung. It was dark, so she had to feel along the surface until she found them, first a linen shift and then the house kirtle she'd worn yesterday. Fumbling, unaccustomed after all this time to dressing herself, she dropped each garment over her head and pushed her feet into the felt house shoes neatly placed on the floor beneath them.

Her hands flew to her hair. It had been braided the night before, ready for bed, but when Edward had crept into her room after the household had gone to sleep, it had become disarranged.

She would not think of that now.

She could no longer hear men's voices – they must have gone somewhere. The kitchen?

There. She was ready now to face whatever was needed, having bundled her hair up into a kerchief and tied it severely tight. Groping her way across the room, she found the door and lifted the latch. Little Edward had slept through the noise and so, it seemed, had Deborah – though Anne did not believe that.

She stepped down the treads of the spiral stone stair in the corner of her house, placing her feet gently to make as little noise as possible. For some reason, each of her senses said 'caution'.

'...you are certain of this?'

'Yes, Your Majesty. The duke asked me to ride to you immediately.'

One lone candle had been lit in Anne's brick-floored kitchen, the wavering light making odd shadows on the men's faces. Richard was there, William Hastings and Lord Rivers. And so was Edward. Somehow he'd found enough of his clothes from where he'd dropped them on the floor of her room to look entirely respectable. Anne marvelled at that fact. Battle readiness, was that it? She turned to see a messenger too, wearing the Duke of Burgundy's livery.

'Gentlemen, is anything wrong?'

Each of the men bowed to her, Edward most deeply of all.

'Lady Anne, the duke has finally decided. He will help the cause of the king.'

Richard of Gloucester suddenly looked fully as young as he was, a boy not even twenty years old. Anne was surprised. He'd been a responsible lieutenant for so long in his brother's service that she'd come to think of him as mature. But now the lilt in his voice, the way he jigged from foot to foot, betrayed the youth he still was.

'Money?' Anne found she was sitting on the settle by the banked embers of the kitchen fire.

'Better than that. Ships and men, as well. There's to be a meeting, an official one this time, tomorrow, after the Christ-mass feast, and then we shall see.'

Edward spoke carefully, his tone composed, but

Anne knew him, body and bone. She saw the light in his eyes. He was looking at her so eagerly, so happily, and she knew that if the others had not been there, he would have scooped her up in his arms, wanting her to be a part of it, a part of the future that was being born.

A slow shiver made its way up her spine until it reached her scalp. This, then, was the tipping point, the time when all would change. When her life, too, would change – again. For this man.

Did she want that?

'Lady Anne, you should go back to bed. We are sorry to have wakened you.' William Hastings spoke from the shadows. It was a courteous dismissal from Edward's chamberlain: *this is the world of men, lady*, he seemed to say, *you have no part to play here.*

Anne lifted her chin and her eyes sought William's. 'I am grateful for your care of me, sir, but I'm awake now and eager to hear more. This is a lucky day for all of us.'

*Be careful, Chamberlain,* was Anne's response to Hastings, *the king needs me, I am important to him; you should understand that.*

Anne rose and curtsied to the man who had only so lately been in her bed. 'I am so happy for you, Your Majesty. The wait is over. At last.'

Edward bowed in response and waved Anne back to her seat: an honour, since the men crowded into her small kitchen were standing.

'There is still a way to travel, Lady Anne, but this is the end of the beginning, I am certain of that.'

'Do you have a plan, sire, as yet?'

There was an embarrassed silence. Anne looked

271

from face to face. None would meet her eyes. And, suddenly, she understood. They would not speak in front of her nor share anything they'd been discussing, not even Edward. Anne was more than shocked. She was hurt, and beginning to be angry. Did he not trust her? Was that possible?

'Lady Anne, we have much to ponder on and it is very late – or, rather, very early. We are so grateful for all that you have given us, the valuable and tireless assistance you have rendered to our house.' Anne sat mute, staring up into the bright eyes of the king. He was using the royal plural, speaking at her, not with her. 'The courage you have shown will ever be dear to us. And it will be rewarded.'

Anne would not let herself cry. Good enough to be his lover, but not good enough to be his trusted friend?

'Reward?' Anne stood and faced Edward, not even an arm's length from where he stood. She spoke over the king, interrupting him, her anger just greater than her hurt. He was silent from surprise.

'I want nothing from you, sire. Your greatest gift to me is your presence in my house. I need, or desire, nothing more.'

Head high, Anne turned to Hastings. 'You were right, Lord Hastings. It seems I am more tired than I knew.' Anne managed it well, even smiled, but the chamberlain would not meet her glance.

Turning back to the king, she bent her head and curtsied, low. 'Your Majesty.' Edward was pale, staring at her. 'I should be grateful for permission to withdraw.' Anne kept her tone neutral, light, and steadfastly gazed at the second pearl button on the king's jerkin. Above it his throat worked.

'Certainly, Lady Anne. We are sorry your rest was disturbed.'

It was hard to swallow what she burned to say, and Anne took a deep breath before the words could escape her mouth. But one glance from her and the king knew.

*It was never rest I wanted from you. I thought I had your love and trust.*

He heard her in his heart, and knew Anne knew it as she walked from her kitchen, leaving it silent behind her.

Great damage had been done and he, Edward Plantagenet, had done it. But he had a kingdom to think of, not his own personal happiness. He was right to confine the discussion to his men, and his men alone.

Yet what had he lost in that one moment?

He would not think about that now. It frightened him.

## Chapter Thirty-Six

Brother Agonistes was exhausted by the journey from Paris. On Louis's instructions, he'd been given a litter for part of the distance – such a jolting ride, his very joints had shaken loose, not to mention the teeth in his head – but the remaining days had been a blur of cold and pain in muscles unaccustomed to such exercise as he and his escort rode north until they came to the walls of Brugge.

Lodged now at a Dominican priory near the Prinsenhof, Brother Agonistes had slept very little for when Philippe de Commynes knocked at the outer door on the following morning, he was advised to seek the visitor in the order's chapel. Entering the opulent little building quietly, de Commynes could not see the monk at first, but then what he had taken for a dark rug lying before the altar twitched.

Face down upon the cold tiles, arms outstretched in imitation of Christ's last suffering, Brother Agonistes heard nothing of worldly sounds and saw nothing. Privation, pain and exhaustion had brought him to the emptiness and silence of perfect peace. He was preparing himself for the trial to come.

'Brother? Can you hear me?'

A faint voice was calling. God, at last?

'Brother?' Philippe de Commynes shook the monk gently by the shoulder. 'Brother Agonistes? We have very little time.'

The human world claimed him. In despair, Agonistes fell down, down from the Light, into candle-flickering, incense-woven dark. He returned convulsing, curling in on his own body like a foetus, for to re-enter the world of men brought back the agony of locked muscles and lungs bruised by the freezing air of the recent journey.

Philippe de Commynes gazed at the writhing heap with distaste. If this fit killed the monk, what would he tell Louis? He nudged the man with his foot, unwilling to dirty his hands.

The monk opened his eyes; they were clouded as those of a newborn child. A moment later he coughed, hawked and spat green phlegm onto the pristine tiles of the chapel floor. The contempt was deliberate. This was a worldly place, far too close to the court for Holiness to dwell here naturally.

'Brother?'

'I hear you, monsieur.' The monk was hoarse; it felt unnatural to speak and he was too weak to stand. He gave up the effort, closing his eyes once more.

'Brother, give me your hand. I will help you.'

Philippe de Commynes was sweating with anxiety as, overcoming revulsion for the man's dirty flesh, he reached out his hand to Agonistes. The monk ignored him as he recited a novena.

Time was passing. Already they were late. 'Come, dear Brother. The duke will be most offended by our absence. King Louis expects you to obey him, also.'

Agonistes heard de Commynes, but unwillingly. He sighed. 'Very well then, messire. But tell me again, what must I do? I am so fuddled...'

Turning his head away from the stench, Philippe leaned down to help the monk stand. 'You must tell the duke and his court all that you know. Much depends on what you say today. More than you can possibly understand.'

As he hurried the weak and stumbling monk from the chapel, Philippe de Commynes gloried in the mission bestowed on him by Louis de Valois, his *true* master under God. This stinking monk would today accomplish a noble purpose; his words would be a weapon in the hand of God.

Like a stag in the forest, Edward Plantagenet would first be wounded in his most tender part – the heart – then he would weaken, falter and fall as he was hunted, and *then* he would be torn to pieces by the dogs of his fate.

A deluded monk and a slut – fit tools indeed to serve his master's ends. Between them today, these two would turn the key, the key that would unlock the greater destiny of France: dominance of *all* Europe.

## Chapter Thirty-Seven

'Brother Duke, hear me on the anniversary of Christ's birth-day. Hear the word of God, of which I am the humble conduit.' His voice shook but Agonistes had power now; the words carried well throughout the huge space beneath his feet.

The great hall of the Prinsenhof was a restless mass of moving colour as Duke Charles, Duchess Margaret and their court settled before boards bending under chargers, dishes and great bowls of rapidly cooling food. The duke's stomach rumbled; the monk would need to be quick in his homily, or all heat would depart entirely from the feast.

'If you fail to destroy the abomination and embodiment of sin and earthly lust that walks amongst you, even on this most Holy Day, all your works will turn to ash and dust as God strikes you down in your pride.'

Charles was not concentrating on what the monk was saying; he had so much to do that sitting here, at the feast, was to be racked on the bed of lost time. Around him, however, the fidgeting court slowly settled and grew still, listening. The monk's intensity was compelling.

'...I am here, wretched, unworthy sinner that I am, to guide you to the truths offered by Our Lord and Saviour, and to give you, Duke Charles, the courage to act so that your soul and the souls of all here present in this great hall today may be saved.'

Margaret, Duchess of Burgundy, was immune to the heightened rhetoric of Brother Agonistes. Having been brought up in the courts of England, she was a connoisseur of sermons. She gazed with detachment at the filthy, emaciated monk in his temporary pulpit, the gallery above their heads, but she was beginning to be irked by the direction his words were taking. He was altogether too grim, too fervent, for the season.

The duchess frowned as she thought back to the meeting earlier today with Philippe de Commynes. In the end, Charles had agreed that the monk would be permitted to deliver the homily since Philippe had assured them he was a most holy mystic and seer, well known in Paris. There was the added interest, too, that Agonistes had lately been the personally appointed healer to the body of the King of France. The duke had decided he would speak with the man after the feast; in war, too much information was never enough.

The duchess, however, did not favour smelly mystics, whatever their credentials. Her nose wrinkled – the aroma of the monk's unwashed flesh, even at this distance, competed powerfully with the food in front of them. Perhaps the man was merely mad? In her experience, such ascetics often were and this one bore all the signs. Ranting, spitting, skinny arms flailing as he mouthed dire warnings and promises of damnation – of what, and against what, it was hard to grasp – into the air above their heads.

'...you must know that the Whore of Babylon exists in your midst and pollutes this place with her lusts and her sorcery, for she is a witch! And does not the Bible say, "Thou shalt not suffer a witch to live"? Seek her out, brother duke, burn her! Cleanse this place of her evil or you shall be lost and all your people with you.'

Margaret frowned. Homily or no, the monk was stepping over the line in accusing the duke of personally harbouring a witch. How ridiculous. How primitive!

'Husband, perhaps we have heard enough? The food grows cold.'

Charles shot Margaret a glance and raised his eyebrows as if to say, *And what would you have me do?* He patted her hand and whispered back, 'It will be over soon.'

This time, the duchess distinctly heard her husband's stomach growl and suppressed the urge to giggle. She returned her attention to the monk. Something about him – was it the voice? – tweaked a distant memory, which unsettled her. She had seen this man before. Where?

Margaret scanned the hall for Philippe de Commynes; she wanted more information, for the monk's accent was decidedly odd for a

Frenchman. Was that an English cast she heard in his rantings? How could that be?

As she glanced around, Margaret saw that the courtiers were riveted; the reference to sorcery had sent a buzz around the hall. It was said that sinners were easy prey for devils and witches, for they could *see* your sin, just as if you wore a bright red dress. More than one guilty conscience in the hall listened with mounting dread.

'Hear me!' the monk ranted. 'Absorb my words most carefully! You are all damned and these end-times prove it. Hear also the precious words of John, the Divine. God is coming, arrayed for battle, and this mighty city will be cast down – cast down! – because you, you who are all alike in this great hall, are smeared by the sins of lust and pride. Only repentance, today, here and now on the anniversary of our Saviour's birth, will snatch you – yes, you pretty lady, and you, handsome sir – from Satan's terrible jaws.'

One of Margaret's youngest waiting women, taking it all to heart, burst into tears. The monk swept on.

'But there is one here today who is worse than any of you. It is she, in all her loathsomeness, *she* who has brought war to your door. Yes! And I will name her, I will name this witch, for, oh, she is cunning, and oh, she is powerful. She has corrupted you with a false glamour so that you cannot see her scaly claws, her bloody fangs. She is Satan's lure and many men has she ruined, many more will she yet destroy if you will not hear my words.'

Neighbour was peering fearfully at neighbour

now, and a rising babble of sound grew so that the monk had to shout over the hubbub, his spittle flying through the light of the torches.

'Act to root her out from her rancid bed of destruction, her bed of infamy, so that you may be saved in doing God's work, here, today! Adulteress, whore of kings, chalice of evil, to drink from that cup is to drink Hell's fire and think it the most sweet wine...'

The duchess had had enough. In the last weeks, fear had unsettled Brugge as constant rumours of destruction and war swept the city. At times such as these, people would believe anything and here, at this feast, it was as if this fool was speaking of a real person, a real woman, as a Jonah, the cause of all their problems.

Unwillingly, Margaret fastened her eyes on those of the monk – he was scanning the hall like a hawk seeking prey; he was searching for someone. Then he paused, theatrically. And smiled, exposing rotted teeth.

Raising a stick-like arm, he pointed.

The hall was instantly, breathlessly, silent.

Brother Agonistes leaned forward, eyes burning, and spoke again, in a reedy whisper. 'I see you, woman. I know you. God knows you. But I am his instrument and your days of power are ended. Ended NOW!' His words finished in a scream.

There was a horrified buzz and, one by one, the courtiers swivelled their heads towards where the monk was pointing. His bony finger stabbed the air like a dagger, beckoning all to look, to see.

'There! There she sits in all her scarlet, loathsome pride. Witch! Adulterous whore of Edward

Plantagenet! Succubus! Anne de Bohun, Anne de Bohun. ANNE DE BOHUN!'

The monk locked his gaze on Anne's as she rose from her bench to face him. And the entire hall saw that she wore red velvet.

'No! This is nonsense.' Margaret, Duchess of Burgundy, spoke in a clear voice as she stood to defend her friend.

There was a collective gasp. Then utter silence.

Frowning, the duke stood also and waved his hand. The monk was to be removed.

Brother Agonistes smiled as he saw the guards approach him, pikes held ready should they be challenged. Calmly gazing down from his perch, the monk made the sign of the cross in two great sweeping movements, and, bowing his head, made no resistance as the duke's servants shepherded him away. His work was done.

## Chapter Thirty-Eight

The town of Brugge was a heated mass of rumour after the feast. Was Anne de Bohun indeed the Jonah who had brought war to their gates? Was it all her fault? *Was she a witch?*

The extravagant strangeness of the accusations – so bizarre, so unexpected – gave them a substance it was difficult to counter. Gossip became authority.

*Consider the facts, only consider what is known!*

Item: Brother Agonistes was a stranger to

Brugge and said to be the personal healer to the body of the King of France.

Item: he was also known to be a holy man who had selflessly tended to the very poorest in the slums of Paris.

Item: this same monk had been introduced to the court by Philippe de Commynes, cousin of Duke Charles; a sponsor with the very highest connections.

Item: this humble brother *knew* Anne de Bohun's name; how could that be so, if God had not put knowledge of the facts into his mouth?

Some shook their heads doubtfully, but others nodded. It seemed compelling, put that way. Perhaps it *was* true then, that she, Anne de Bohun, *had* personally brought disaster for the city because of her evil ways.

Anne's friends rallied.

*Nonsense! Superstition! Everyone likes the Lady Anne and she is popular with the town, the court and the merchants of Brugge. Jealousy of her good fortune and her beauty, mean-spirited rivals putting about malicious gossip – that's the key to this sorry story!*

But many were not convinced. When the people of the town discussed these strange events, discussed her, they saw that Anne de Bohun *was* mysterious, had always been mysterious, ever since she'd come to live amongst them with her little nephew, more than three or four years ago.

Many remembered how rapidly and how, yes, even scandalously, she'd prospered once she set up to trade. She'd succeeded by her own efforts, even though the powerful English Merchant Adventurers in Brugge had opposed her. Had not rumours swirled around her even then? Rumours that her unnatural, unwomanlike success had been caused by sorcery?

Nodding heads recalled *that* scandal well.

*Wasn't it whispered then that Charles – their charming duke who liked women so very much – had protected the beautiful Lady Anne for reasons of his own?*

The word 'lust' floated, musk-like, on the air.

But others, wishing to be fair to Anne de Bohun, said, *Time has given the lie to that shameful rumour. Our duke has married our duchess, and fallen deeply in love with his wife.*

*Ah*, said some, *but our duchess was formerly the Lady Margaret of England. And now Louis, the King of France, desires to crush Burgundy because of our duchess's brother, the former King of England, Edward Plantagenet. And he was mentioned by the monk as well, did you hear that? Named as Lady Anne's lover...*

A wise head in an alehouse piped up. 'Someone tried to murder Anne de Bohun, didn't they, in the weeks before the wedding of the duke and duchess? That was very strange.'

And another said, 'Stranger still that she nearly died, was sure to die, but survived. William Caxton's wife, for one, named Lady Anne for a whore. And a witch. And *she* was a most respectable lady, God rest her soul.'

Yet many who knew them both acknowledged that Maud Caxton had never liked Anne de Bohun, had always disapproved of the English girl because, some said, her husband William, the man who led the English Merchants, also lusted after the girl.

There it was, though: smoke from a barely acknowledged fire. Had Anne de Bohun been, in
truth, an adulterous whore? With Caxton? With
the duke?

All through the anniversary of Christ's birth,
whilst the emotional temperature of the town
rose and rose with this astonishing and develop-
ing scandal, the girl herself, this named 'witch'
and 'whore', said nothing, did nothing. She
allowed her friend, the duchess, to defend her.

'This *is* ridiculous, Charles. You must see that?'

Margaret of Burgundy strove for calm as she
watched the duke pace up and down. His face
was impassive but she knew that masked confusion – and doubt.

'The man is mad. *Insane*. What mystic or
prophet – if he is truly God's creature – speaks
with such venom? God is love. Especially at the
season of his birth, when He came to us as a little
child.' Margaret was convinced of the truth, but
she knew the monk's words had caused sensational damage to her friend, bursting, as they
had, like a dam of filth over Anne's head. 'My
Lord, what has passed today *is* astonishing, and we
all saw it and we all heard it. But we all know it to
be *nonsense*. Lady Anne de Bohun is my friend, as
she is yours. As she is the friend of Burgundy and
Brugge. She has proved that to me, and to you.
That man, that spitting fool, has called her a witch
and ... other things. Yet you and I both know our
friend. We know her for what she is. A kind lady
who lives quietly and has the good of all at heart.'

Charles nodded as if he accepted every word.
But Anne, mute, understood. Charles, Duke of

284

Burgundy, was mired in a terrible game of politics. What would he do, what could he say? Especially since Edward's name had been dragged into this sorry mess just before they were to meet, officially, for the first time on the following day.

The duke looked at them both. 'Lady Anne, can you explain any of these accusations?'

Anne raised her head. Her eyes were huge and shadowed.

'I think I know who he is. Brother Agonistes, I mean.'

Margaret sat down beside her friend, taking one unresponsive hand in her own.

'Once, he called himself Doctor Moss.'

The duchess jumped. 'Yes, you're right! I knew there was something—'

'Margaret, let Lady Anne speak.'

'He came to my then master's house after I fainted in the abbey when Aveline ... when my sister was churched. After the birth of her boy.'

Margaret and the duke looked at each other. 'Your sister's son? Little Edward?'

Anne looked down at her hands and nodded. Partial truth was dangerous, but better some than none. Aveline's baby had indeed been called Edward, but he wasn't *her* Edward – not the little boy Anne called her nephew. She had always called Aveline her sister and passed off her own child, her own son, as that of her dear, dead friend. They had been sisters under the skin, and Anne had closed Aveline's eyes with pennies. She'd earned the right to call her such.

The duke turned to his wife. 'Doctor Moss was a physician at your brother's court, madame?'

285

'Yes, Charles, he was. And a friend of the king's as well.'

Anne looked up. She would tell the truth now. 'Yes, he was in favour at court. But he was more than the king's friend. He was a pander – oh, a very good one. Discreet, elegant and worldly but–'

Margaret was astonished. 'He supplied women to my brother?'

Anne nodded. And her eyes filled with tears of shame. 'Me, he supplied me; though I did not know, at the time, that such was his intention. Moss made sure I came to court and was noticed by ... by the king.' She had nearly called him 'Edward'. 'Moss thought to advance himself, using my body. But, in the end, he wanted me for himself.' She flushed with remembered anger. 'He nearly destroyed me. Because – God help me – in the end, I fell in love with your brother, Duchess, even though I knew it was wrong. And I nearly lost my soul because, by then, I knew...'

The duke was intrigued. An extraordinary story was emerging, wrenched out of this girl sentence by sentence. 'What did you know, Lady Anne?'

Should she tell them? She no longer held the proof of her birth. Perhaps the duke and duchess would not believe her. But she had little defence against the monk's accusations, and family helped each other. Didn't they?

Anne's voice was a whisper. 'I knew who I was. Who I am. I am your cousin, duchess.' She stumbled on, not daring to look up. 'I am the natural daughter of Henry VI, that poor distracted man, whom I have never met. And, Duke Charles, I must tell you the truth now.'

The duke's eyebrows rose and the duchess gazed, astonished and speechless, at her friend.

'The child I call my nephew is Edward's child, the child of a king of England, and the grandson of another.'

The duke was direct. 'Does the king know all this?'

Anne laughed, an odd sound in that charged atmosphere. 'Oh yes, he knows. He knows everything. It's the reason I chose exile from England and came to Brugge.' She raised her eyes to the duke. 'He wanted to kill me when I told him about my father, gave him the proof, and yet ... we fell so deeply in love. I love him still. And I had thought...'

The words trailed off. She would not voice her hurt and confusion, the uncertainty she felt now about Edward's true feelings for her.

'But the monk called you a witch. Why would he do that?' The duke's tone, as he digested all these surprises and asked this final question, was entirely neutral.

The duchess spoke firmly. 'Thwarted lust. Perhaps self-righteousness. Then again, he may be truly mad.'

Anne said nothing. When she had fallen in love with the king, the doctor's downfall had begun. Today, at the feast on the anniversary of Christ's birth, he'd been revenged on her, and on Edward.

And though the duke saw the honesty in Anne's eyes, he noted the fact and noted it well: she had not answered the question. Perhaps, after all, the accusation was true. Perhaps Anne de Bohun really was a witch.

# Chapter Thirty-Nine

News of the fiasco at the Christ-mass feast had reached the farm late in the day from a bargeman who'd tied up at Anne's river gate to buy butter. And as the English ate their supper, fact and rumour became more and more lurid in the retelling.

Earl Rivers was drunk. 'I'm telling you the truth. The bargeman said the monk called her a whore. *And* a witch. God save us, William – we eat in the house of a sorceress! He named the king as an adulterer, too. No surprises there, eh?'

He guffawed, punching Richard's shoulder and, in his glee, choked and dribbled ale freely from his nose. Hastings frowned at the extravagant fool, even now banging his beaker on Anne's board as he called for more to drink. The earl might be the brother of Elizabeth Wydeville, the queen, but he was also a rowdy idiot at times.

'Rivers, you're repeating gossip. This monk – he sounds touched.' Hastings put one finger to his temple and tapped it. 'Too much incense if you ask me.'

That got a big laugh.

Edward, who was talking with his archers, encouraging them to eat well for the days ahead, looked around. 'What? What's so funny?'

He sauntered over to his friends and inserted himself between them on the bench. 'Move up,

Richard. I swear, *you're* getting fat at least with all this lying around!'

Richard grinned. 'Well, brother, if I am, the remedy is close, with all the fighting that's to come. Long life in paradise to Stephen, saint and martyr. May he guide us tomorrow, on his day, with good counsel.'

They all crossed themselves and laughed with great good humour, joining Lord Rivers in the call for 'More ale, more ale!'

Lisotte and Vania, harried with the serving of so many extra mouths and stomachs, hurried back to the house to drain the last of the Christ-mass brew. Good-humoured catcalls followed them from the men in the barn. 'What sort of inn is this place? Too slow! Too slow!'

Edward frowned and William Hastings took the hint, rising to his feet and calling out, 'Hush now! You are discourteous, my friends, even humorously. Lady Anne's women work very hard.'

'So does Lady Anne. On her back at least!'

Earl Rivers was convinced it was the best joke in the world and, unsuspecting, the archers guffawed along with everyone else. Then each man in the barn saw the look on the king's face. It was murderous. There was instant silence.

'*What* did you say?'

Edward rose and the unfortunate earl had a sudden urgent desire to piss himself. He wriggled off his bench and knelt before the king, head bent as if for execution. 'Nothing, liege. Nothing at all.'

Eagle-like, the king glared down on his brother-in-law; the earl could almost hear the beating of great wings. Quavering, Rivers uttered the fatal words: 'Sire, I was just repeating what the monk said.'

Edward, closeted for the day with William and Richard, planning for tomorrow's meeting with the duke, had heard nothing about the Christmass feast. 'Monk? What monk?'

The silence settled thick as snow. Earl Rivers swallowed to control his shaking jaw. 'The Dominican. At the duke's feast. He accused Lady Anne of witchcraft and ... and a number of other things.' Earl Rivers gulped and breath fled him; he could say nothing more. That saved him.

Edward's glance swept the faces of the men in the hall. He could see that each one of his companions knew what he did not.

He swung back to the earl. 'Get up,' he ordered.

Earl Rivers squared his shoulders as he stood, face scarlet from embarrassment. But the king turned away from his queen's brother.

'William, Richard, come with me.'

A blast of freezing air rushed through the barn as Edward strode outside. Hastings and Gloucester scrambled from their bench in pursuit.

They found Edward saddling a horse at speed; he was white with rage and fear. Brutally wrenching the saddle girth tight – a surprise to his chosen mount, which had blamelessly been eating its evening mash – Edward rounded on his friends.

'Who is this monk?'

William shrugged uneasily and cleared his throat, glancing at Richard for support. Bravely, the duke spoke first.

'Brother, he's a madman. We've had reports–'

'Reports? Reports! Why was I not told of these *reports?*'

William added his voice. 'You have far too much else to concern you, sire. This monk is a momentary wonder. His claims were entirely ridiculous. It will come to nothing.'

'I am most relieved, William. And grateful. You must have great confidence in this *intelligence* to limit my need for knowing it.' His glance at his old friend was cutting. 'What did this *madman* say?'

The king was in the saddle now, wrapped in his riding cloak, sword at his belt.

'Well? I must know whom and what I fight. What did he *say*, brother?'

Richard hurried to throw a saddle across another horse, fumbling with the girth. 'He called Anne a witch. And accused her of adultery. With...' Even he baulked at the final words, turning into the horse's belly as he hauled on the buckles of the girth.

Edward's brows went up at his brother's embarrassment. 'With me, perhaps?' Richard's busy silence gave the answer. The king wheeled his horse on a shortened rein. 'And witchcraft too? I hope this monk is well shrived!'

And he was gone, spurring in the direction of Brugge.

'Edward, wait!' Richard rode away from Anne's farm a moment later in pursuit of the king, his cloak flying out behind like great, dark wings.

Hastings was later by a minute, lashing his horse to catch the brothers on the path that led to Brugge. Witch or not, Anne de Bohun had some explaining to do, but William doubted very much that Edward would listen to sense where Anne was concerned. This morning the king had chosen duty before his passion for this girl. Now that decision was undone with light words and gossip. God curse Rivers! How had she come this far? A servant at court, nothing more, just a maid to the queen. Now Anne de Bohun was danger incarnate – danger for Edward, danger for England. He must diffuse that danger, if he could. It was his duty.

'Wait up, my lords, wait up!'

Lisotte, Deborah and Vania dodged the men's horses – one, two, three – as they flew past, trying not to spill the ale in their leather buckets. They stared fearfully after the riders as they disappeared, shouting, into the cold dark.

The Devil himself rode out across the night world just as these men did, gathering the souls of sinners. Something was wrong. Very wrong.

The other women crossed themselves, but Deborah did not. As Vania and Lisotte knocked on the doors of the barn, shouting for them to be opened, Deborah gazed into the black distance and prayed.

But she prayed to another, older god for help. The Sword Mother.

In these uncertain times, the watch on the Kruispoort, one of the great gates of the walled city of Brugge, performed its duty faithfully. Every night, the gate was closed at sunset and locked and bolted. All the gates of Brugge were closed and locked and bolted, and none was opened for any living thing – no man, no woman, no child – until the morning.

'There's an English Angel in it for each man if you will open the gate! Come, let us in, our business is most urgent. My master, the king...' Hastings shouted the words into the wind, but the gusting night air snatched them away.

'What? A king? Hah! If he's really a king, tell him to come back in daylight so we can see him properly. Now leave! Your noise disturbs the rest of the people here.'

Hastings turned to Edward, utterly frustrated. 'Unless there's another way into the city, sire...?'

Edward rode forward, tugging at the hood of his cloak and pulling it back so the men on the gate could see his face. 'I am Edward Plantagenet, King of England.'

The torches of the watch fought the same wind that snatched away his words; it was impossible to see who was yelling at them from the shadows of the city wall.

Edward bellowed louder. 'I have business with your duke, my brother-in-law. Open this gate!'

'You could be French Louis himself for all we care.'

A volley of arrows came from the ramparts of the gate – aimed to frighten, not kill. One sliced a trough in William Hasting's hair and another startled his horse, whizzing past its ear.

'Leave now. Or believe that worse will follow.'

Edward wheeled his horse abruptly and kicked it to a canter then a gallop, shouting as he rode, 'How many gates are there, Richard?'

Booting his horse to keep up, Richard yelled

back, 'Not sure. Eight? Nine?'

'One of them will open for us.'

William Hastings glanced at Richard of Gloucester, shaking his head. The duke shrugged helplessly. *This is madness!* his look said.

William nodded, grim-faced. No one woman on Earth was worth this. Somehow, he would make the king understand that. But not tonight; plainly, not tonight.

## Chapter Forty

It was close to the end of the Christ-mass night and Bishop Odo of Brugge had already been interrogating Anne – there was no other word for it – for some hours. He had hurried to the Prinsenhof immediately he'd been summoned, as news of Brother Agonistes' sensational accusations spread.

A public accusation of witchcraft was a most serious matter – a matter for the doctrinal arm of the Church, a *burning* matter. And though Duke Charles was not a superstitious man – he thought talk of witchcraft was nonsense in a modern state – he was a politician. Bishop Odo had influence in Brugge, and Charles needed his people united in support of the war that would come to their doors very soon. Under these circumstances, the fate of one woman was much less important than the survival of the Duchy of Burgundy.

He needed unity, good government and the trust of the people. For that, he must have calm in his city. And so, over the protests of his duchess, Charles ordered that, in the first instance, a 'meeting' between Anne and Bishop Odo would take place. In the interests of public stability, he would permit the Church to test the accusations of witchcraft against Anne in an informal way. To formalise the proceedings would be to sanction torture.

The bishop was delighted to oblige his duke with expert advice in this matter. He sensed that this woman – this named and branded servant of venery and the Devil – might be his path to a long-overdue archbishopric and, after that, a cardinal's hat.

Anne de Bohun would be his final test of worthiness for high office, and he would not fail. He would be her salvation also, of course – he would burn her body to save her soul if he had to, because it was his professional duty to find and drive demons out from her sinful woman's body.

And so, with the agreement, if not the unequivocal support, of the duke, tonight, he, Christ's servant in Brugge, would hunt for the truth. He would search out the signs of Satan manifest within this girl.

'Lady Anne, let us revisit the recent past once again. Formerly, you lived at the house of Sir Mathew Cuttifer here in Brugge. At that time, I believe you had a servant called Jenna?'

Anne rearranged the folds of her dress over her knees to gain a moment's thinking time. She'd been permitted to sit at last – if only on a small joint stool – and was exhausted after the long hours of questioning, though she would not let the bishop see that.

'Come, lady, dissembling is of no use. Did you once have a servant named Jenna? Yes or no?'

The bishop loomed over Anne, but the sconces in the room were behind his head and his face was in shadow. Anne could not see her interrogator's eyes, deep in his cowl, but she could hear the bray of triumph when he spoke.

'Yes. She ran away on the same day I was kidnapped by slave traders, just after the wedding of the duke and duchess. I have not seen the girl since.'

'But I have.' The bishop was breathing hard, sensing that Anne was weakening. 'Oh, indeed, *I* have seen her. She is a postulant now, in my care. She forgives you for all that you did and prays for you daily.' He signed a sweeping cross over Anne's bent head.

She looked up at Odo, bemused. 'Forgives me? For what?'

The bishop forced a hearty laugh, long and loud, and made a business of wiping his eyes. Lowering his ample arse into a cathedra placed opposite Anne's stool he brought his face down to her level; God's servant, sitting in judgment.

'You pretend bewilderment, Lady Anne, and that is most amusing. I do not believe Our Saviour ever laughed – never gave way to such animal passion – yet perhaps he might join with me here, tonight, the joke is so very good!'

The bow of his belly wobbled as he gleefully slapped his knees.

Anne forced herself to smile, her heart pounding. This man was a great, fat, lazy cat. She would not be his mouse.

'It is hard for me to share your enjoyment, Bishop, since I have no knowledge of what you mean.'

The bishop leaned forward. He wasn't laughing now and Anne could see his eyes – pale blue, the glitter of a cold sun on frost, light on icicles – no warmth in them at all.

'Your servant Jenna made her confession to me personally, eighteen months ago. She confessed that she had heard you raise spirits and have congress with them. She confessed that she observed your flagrant and adulterous relationship with Edward, the then King of England. She saw and heard you instruct a harmless child, your own nephew, in pagan ways, to the peril of his immortal soul. Do you deny these allegations, lady?'

Anne was mute, rigid. Her silence was a weapon in the bishop's hand and he did not mask his savage pleasure. He stood over the white-faced girl, thrusting his face close, whispering the words.

'Your silence condemns you, Lady Anne. Witch, whore, adulteress. Brother Agonistes named you as all three. How could he know these manifold sins if God himself had not made the truth a tool in his hand for smiting the ungodly? For smiting you, woman!'

That brought Anne's head up. 'God? No! It was that man's own sin that brought him to this place, dressed in those stinking rags. His betrayal of me and the king he served brought him here; his own lust and bitterness brought him here. He is not God's servant!'

But the bishop had snatched up his crucifix and

thrust it towards Anne like a weapon.

'Confess to me now, here, woman, and your blackened soul may be saved. Fail to confess, refuse this gift, and you *will* be damned. Further, the Church will hand you to the secular authorities in this city and your body will be burned to a puddle of black grease in the Markt Square, whilst your soul, your immortal soul, roasts in a lake of fire for all eternity.'

'Stop!'

The bishop slewed around, enraged. But he was not as angry as Margaret, Duchess of Burgundy, standing in the doorway of the cell.

The duchess moved forward with the gliding gait of a court lady and, reaching out her hand, helped Anne stand. She turned her dispassionate gaze on the bishop.

'I caution you, priest. Lady Anne de Bohun is English and, as such, is protected by the authority of my brother, the king.'

The bishop avoided sneering, but only just. 'Your brother has been deposed, madame. And in any case, he has no authority here. But *your* lord and husband has, and I expect that he, as a true son of the Church, will shortly punish your disobedience in this matter by giving you over to *God's* authority in this city; authority which I embody, as you well know. This woman's soul, and yours, are my domain. Take her now and I shall excommunicate you both.'

Anne detached her fingers from Margaret's and turned to face the bishop. 'Foolish man. Do not think to threaten your duchess, or me, with empty words.'

Anne's eyes were marble cold. Margaret moved closer to her friend. Together, they were of a height and, suddenly, similarly formidable. Their resistance confused and then frightened the bishop.

He held up his crucifix in a hand that shook. Christ's body was his weapon against the glamour and spells of the witch – of the *two* witches – before him now. He was a consecrated bishop: God's power, vested in him and ranged against sorcery, would prevail.

'Duchess, I am your pastor, set in authority over this city and all its inhabitants, of which you are one.'

Margaret's eyes sharpened on his. Hearing the quaver in Odo's voice, she spoke over him.

'Bishop, you have tried to frighten an important guest in my husband's domains. But this lady is defenceless no more. Be clear on that. She will come with me now and you will return to your brothers in Christ. There the matter will end. Soon this scandal will pass away and be seen for what it is. Sensational, meaningless nonsense.'

For a moment Odo almost believed Margaret of England, especially when she smiled at him. But then he rallied. It was his duty to stand against this foul manifestation of the glamour of women's enchantment.

'Be careful, lady. Very careful. A pleasing face and body are the foul road by which men are led to Hell, but you cannot sway *me* with these Devil's tools. I am a man of God and, though you may be married to our duke, understand this. Duchesses and even queens have burned for sorcery. Perhaps you protect your *friend* so staunchly because you too are a witch? Your husband must be told of this. By me. And he will put you away, out of your marriage, for the sake of his immortal soul and those of all his people. And even if he does not give your body over to be burned, be sure you will end your life immured within a convent, a silent penitent until the day of your death.'

But the Lady of England now stood before the Bishop of Brugge, not just his duke's wife. One piercing glance from Margaret and a sudden, hammer-hard certainty of misjudgment weakened Odo. Pain pierced the wall of his chest, squeezing his heart like a walnut in a vice. The crucifix dropped from his hand and he slumped backwards into the cathedra, heart jolting, breathing hard; his legs had the strength of empty sausage skins and they would not hold him up.

Behind the bishop, an arras rippled gently. It might have been a breeze, but Anne alone caught the movement. Something was forming in the shadows, an outline, the glimmer of a body shape. It was growing from something darker, denser than cold night air. The glint of gold shone there and, for a moment, a woman's profile turned and found definition. Margaret was focused on the bishop and did not see. Did not see the arm as it was raised; a woman's naked arm whose hand held a sword. Did not see as the arm dropped, the sword flashing downwards, carving the air…

Margaret tore at the bishop's neckband to loosen it but Anne was calm, speaking from somewhere far, far away.

'Leave him, Duchess. Let the Devil take his own.'

Odo was outraged by the sacrilege, the disrespect, of the girl's words. Trapped within his dying body, he rallied briefly, determined to speak, but the words drowned in spittle. He smelled something. With his last breath, he snuffled and sucked the air. Sulphur. It was sulphur! The bishop made a gobbling sound and his eyes rolled white in his scarlet face; then the tide of blood receded, leaving it bloated and waxy grey.

But consciousness was not immediately gone. Looking down with more than mortal eyes, Odo observed his naked feet dangling in vertiginous space over a black hole, the bottom of which was filled with a moving lake of fire. Desperate, he looked up, hoping for a glimpse of another, kinder place, but there, staring down at him, was a dark-eyed woman, long hair flying in the sulphurous wind. Spiral tattoos covered her face and a band of thick gold encircled her throat. The last of his heart's beats was born from the terror of that sight.

'Who...?' He could not speak, but watched with creeping horror as the woman smiled and held up her arm. Muscles slid beneath the healthy skin as she whirled the sword above her head once more.

He understood now: he had served the wrong cause all his life and now that life was ended.

'What are you?' he tried to say, but there was nothing left, no breath at all. His immortal eyes followed the movement for the last time as the woman pointed. Down.

## Chapter Forty-One

Margaret, Duchess of Burgundy, contemplated the corpse of her least favourite prelate in all the world. Anne and she had propped Bishop Odo's body upright in the cathedra. It hadn't been easy; in life he'd been a corpulent man. Butter, cream, eggs and much good goose fat had created this impressive bulk over many, many years. In death, the many chins, the bald head, gave him the look of a monstrous baby. The two women looked at the cooling corpse with horror. Their situation was desperate. Margaret had earlier sent her trusted maid to lure away the boy who was guarding Anne's cell, but he might return at any moment. How could they explain what had happened?

For Margaret, the clarity of an hour ago, the certainty that only she could save Anne, had evaporated and some of the bishop's words returned with dreadful force. Obedience. Duty. *Sorcery*. Could she *really* look her husband in the eye and lie about the events of tonight?

Anne sensed the duchess's growing fear.

'Margaret, listen to me. We can do this.' With one arm around her friend's waist, holding her steady, holding her up, Anne forced Margaret to look away from the corpse. 'How many people know that Bishop Odo is in the Prinsenhof tonight?'

Shock had filled Margaret's mind with mist. 'Um. Enough. The gatewards would have let him

302

into the palace. Charles's servants would know as well, of course – and the bishop's monks.' The duchess was feeling strange, very strange. She giggled. 'But why would they worry? Why should we worry either? Not going anywhere at the moment is he, our dear, dead bishop?'

Anne took her friend's hands and gripped them tight. 'We must make people think that Odo has left the palace. I will stay here. In this room. The guards must know I'm still here. And you have to go before you're seen.'

But the duchess did not move; the bishop's body was some dreadful anchor, holding her to the room. Round and round the words went, round and round. *What do we do? Sweet Mary, tell me what to do! He's dead. God in Heaven, we killed him. What do we do now...*

The smart crack as Anne's palm connected with Margaret's cheek was very loud.

Anne seized the Duchess of Burgundy by the shoulders. 'I'm sorry, Margaret, I'm sorry. I had to do it. Please, please forgive me.'

Margaret swallowed. After a moment she nodded shakily.

Anne grasped one of Margaret's hands again and, linking their fingers together in a web, took a deep breath. 'We need help. You must go and get it. Whom do you trust?'

Margaret closed her eyes, forcing herself to concentrate. 'Aseef. I will get Aseef.'

Anne nodded, her eyes darting around the room. 'Yes, of course! But first, Duchess, we must turn this chair.'

Margaret saw what Anne meant and hurried to

303

help her friend push the heavy cathedra with its ghastly contents around until its back was presented to the door. If the guard returned and looked in through the spyhole, he'd see the chair, and its contents, from the back and think that the interrogation was continuing.

Distantly, from the Markt Square, the great bell above the cloth hall tolled, once, twice. 'You must go now, Duchess.'

Margaret kissed her friend and blotted the tears from her eyes. She hauled open the heavy cell door and fled, leaving Anne alone with the corpse of her accuser.

The girl knelt reluctantly at the feet of the dead man, her eyes on the arras that now hung straight and undisturbed on the stone wall.

'Mother, help me now. Lift up the Sword of Justice and bring down the enemies of truth...'

And anyone passing would have heard the conventionally pious words and crossed themselves, perhaps even in sympathy. *Poor Lady Anne*, they might have thought, *she needs all the help she can gather, mortal and Divine. Hard to believe that such a pretty girl really is a witch...*

'If you won't say it, I must, Your Grace. This is futile. We must think about tomorrow.' Hastings turned in his stirrups to the king's brother.

Three gates later and the guards were no longer just abusive; very close calls with the watch at each gate had left one of the horses wounded and Richard with a graze on one hand. The duke nodded grimly. And spurred his horse so that it was racing beside the king's along the turfed bank of the Zwijn on the opposite bank from Brugge.

'Edward, stop. *Brother!* Hear me!'

Edward's horse was nearly blown and the king knew it, but he would not acknowledge that fact. Richard forced the issue: he was half a length ahead of the king when he slewed his animal around in front of Edward's, blocking his path.

'Christ's eyes! Richard!'

Only the king's strong wrists saved them both from disaster. He reined so savagely that blood ran from his horse's bit and it screamed in protest.

'I hope you're proud of that! You could have killed us both.' Edward jumped down to look at the horse's damaged mouth.

'No, I'm not proud. But neither should you be. We have to stop this, Edward. You have other things to do now. *Anne will have to wait.*'

Edward turned on his brother, eyes wild. 'Torture. Have you thought of that? She could die.'

William rode up, flecked white with foam from his exhausted horse. 'The duke is Lady Anne's friend, my liege. As is the duchess, your sister. No one will harm Lady de Bohun tonight...' He resisted the temptation to cross himself, because nothing *was* certain with such accusations. 'And we meet the duke tomorrow. We *must* think about tomorrow.'

William saw something die in Edward's eyes. The king gently wiped blood from his horse's muzzle with the trailing edge of his cloak, soothing the frightened animal. 'Tomorrow. Yes.' After a moment, he pulled himself back up into the saddle. 'What advice do you have, William?'

Hastings smothered relief and spoke carefully.

305

'Our greatest strength in this case is your sister, the duchess, sire. Tomorrow, during our audience with the duke, we should point out that Lady Anne is under the protection of England, since it is the country of her birth. And that she should be released to the duchess until such time as–'

Edward turned in his saddle to peer at his chamberlain. 'Until such time as I am restored and the Lady Anne can return to our court in London.' He gathered up his reins and patted the neck of his nervous horse. He was exhausted. And angry. Principally with himself.

Richard spoke with hearty encouragement. 'Exactly so, brother. A very good plan. Should we now return to the farm? There's little of the night left to us.'

Edward cast one long last glance towards the sleeping city of Brugge. Most was in darkness, yet, as he turned his gaze towards the Prinsenhof, there was a single light burning still. Was that where she was? Was that where Anne was waiting, in despair, to be rescued?

He turned his mount's head for home and kicked the horse into a gentle trot, mindful of its damaged mouth. His companions fell in behind him on the narrow track beside the rain-swollen river.

The decision had been taken.

# Chapter Forty-Two

The official visit of Edward Plantagenet, the deposed king of the English, to Charles, Duke of Burgundy, was to take place on the Feast day of St Stephen. Duke Charles profoundly hoped that Edward's presence would distract the people of Brugge from their fears – and now from the latest scandal: the strange disappearance of their bishop.

First light had brought the bishop's chaplain to the Prinsenhof, asking if his master wished to return to his palace to lead the household and his brothers in the feast-day mass.

The chaplain was conducted to the cell where Anne was being held, but the confused guard, watching at the door, said that the bishop had already left, hours earlier. It had been dark, but he'd personally seen him go, had even knelt to receive his blessing.

And, indeed, throwing open the door, the monk saw only Lady Anne de Bohun in the room, curled asleep in a vast cathedra. Of the bishop there was no sign except a certain aroma, discernible even now. The bishop, like Brother Agonistes, did not believe in water to cleanse the sinful body, except during the sacrament of baptism.

Shaken awake, the frightened girl had no more to add. Yes, she and the bishop had talked for many hours and he had counselled her; and, yes, when he'd left she'd presumed he was returning to his palace within the monastery. Where else would he go?

The chaplain did not look the woman in the face, fearful of sorcery. Out of charity, however, he sketched a cross over the anxious but very pretty penitent's head and expressed the pious hope that her 'conversation' with the bishop had brought her closer to God and therefore redemption. Then, frowning, he strode back to Odo's palace.

On his return, confusion lit the fire, and then uproar fanned the flames of uncertainty to furnace heat. The bishop could not be found! Clamour turned to panic, which travelled around the walls of the city, right back to the Prinsenhof, as the bishop's monks and servants scattered throughout Brugge, knocking on doors asking questions. Who had seen the bishop? Where could he have gone?

The crowds lining the narrow streets waiting for Edward Plantagenet to arrive with his party, became badly unsettled in the tumult. Accusations of witchcraft one day and evaporating bishops the next. Where would it all end? Signs and omens, frightening portents...

However, the visit of the deposed English king was a distraction the Bruggers appreciated. Edward Plantagenet remained popular in their city, not least because the citizens remembered the largesse from the king and his courtiers at the time of their duke and duchess's wedding. They were hoping for the same today. The crowd shuffled and shoved, each person intent on finding the best place from which to see the show. Men liked Edward Plantagenet because he looked like a proper king, and women sighed for him: his shoulders, his face, his long legs and his bright eyes. Yes, the people of Brugge wished him well and were happy to cheer him on in his quest to regain his throne – provided it didn't cost them too much.

Edward and his brother, surrounded by their few knights, archers and mercenaries, did their best to make an impressive show. They would not look like supplicants if they could help it! The brothers rode side by side into the city through its wide-opened gates; they were blessed with a brilliant blue day after weeks of cold and gloom. There was a certain irony in the respectful bows their party received from the men who manned the Kruispoort as they rode beneath its battlements. Of course, these men were the day watch...

Richard expelled a deep, relieved sigh. 'Promising so far, brother. The weather, I mean. The sun's back.'

The duke, apparelled in the most respectable of his good clothes, waved cheerfully to the curious citizens as they hung out of their windows to watch the Plantagenets and their party ride towards the Prinsenhof. He hoped the numerous pretty women amongst the spectators would be a distraction to Edward.

'A very good omen, Richard. Particularly the sun. Sol remains our friend it seems.' Edward, like his brother, nodded, smiled and waved at the women calling out from their doors and casements, but his eyes were bleak. Only the Lady Mary knew if Anne was alive or dead.

'It's clear that ours is a popular cause, my liege. Duke Charles will find comfort in the warmth of our reception.' William Hastings was riding directly behind the brothers and had to shout to be heard over the welcoming din.

'Amen to that, Your Majesty.' Richard was determined to keep Edward's spirits up, though none of them believed the crowd's adulation would guarantee anything from Charles of Burgundy.

Edward nodded and caught an orange thrown to him by a pretty girl in a casement window. Bowing his thanks as his horse carried him on beneath the tall gables of her house, the king handed the shrivelled little fruit to his brother.

'I have a plan. It has little to do with how his people feel about us. It's very simple. Ask for ships. Ships and money.'

'And men?'

They were passing now under the first of the great gates into the Prinsenhof, the horses' hooves clacking sharply on the cobbles. The sound bounced back from the massive walls around them. Edward shivered as he passed through the shadowed, echoing gate. Alive or dead, Anne was somewhere deep within this pile of buildings.

'What? I didn't hear you, Richard.'

Dismounting, the men in the English party gathered around Edward, adjusting cloaks, pulling tunics and jerkins straight, hauling up their hose to debag wrinkled knees after the ride.

'I said, what about men? Do you think he'll give us men?'

No time for a reply. The steward of the Prinsenhof advanced out of the shadowed interior of the building, bowed deeply, then more deeply again, until, finally, he sank down to kneel upon one knee, his gesture mimicked by a small fleet of palace functionaries in his wake.

In a resonant voice, the steward called out so that all within shouting range could hear: 'Your Majesty, my master the Duke of Burgundy, Lord of Peronne, Roye, Montdidier, Liege, Ghent, Flanders, the Lowlands and of Gorinchem; Governor of the most noble order of The Golden Fleece and Knight of the illustrious order of St George, bids you welcome on this most auspicious day.'

Edward bowed slightly from the waist to acknowledge the honour of the invitation and signalled that the steward should stand. As the man and his attendants rose to form themselves into a carefully graded procession of precedence, Edward raised his eyebrows and whispered from the side of his mouth. 'Very promising, Richard. Proper state, it seems.'

Richard of Gloucester grinned happily. 'Well, it's about time our dear brother-in-law acknowledged us, and you, properly!'

'I see our sister's hand at work in this, I think. Mustn't overreact...'

Charles, Duke of Burgundy was formally arrayed in his Presence chamber under a massively embroidered and gem-studded Cloth of Estate. As he waited for Edward and his men to appear, his face carefully schooled to calm dispassion, only those who knew him very well would sense his nervousness. Duchess Margaret was one such, and she yearned to touch her husband's hand or catch his eye and smile. But that would be incorrect at such a time. Still, she was grateful for the show the duke had chosen to make in welcoming her brother.

Today, Charles was dressed as grandly as any monarch in a black velvet doublet spangled with gold studs, teardrops of crystal and evenly matched pearls of great lustre. Beneath his left knee he wore the blue garter of the Knights of St George; he'd been made a member of that order by Edward Plantagenet himself, when he'd married Margaret of England. He had hesitated before agreeing with his wife that he should wear it today, but, in the end, he was at peace with the signal it sent to the court.

Louis de Valois would certainly hear of this gesture of support, but Charles had decided he had ceased to care what the king of the French thought. Louis, personally, had repudiated the Treaty of Peronne only so recently agreed between them. Let him now reap the whirlwind.

Charles had also chosen particularly provocative headgear today; it too would send a signal to Louis. As a duke, Charles was not entitled to a crown, but for this audience he was a wearing a tall hat fashioned from black velvet and glossy beaver skin. It was an impressive object, topped with ostrich feathers fixed to the crown by massive emeralds and encircled by a coronet of gold studded with diamonds. It was not a coronet in the conventional shape of that worn by a duke, however. No, this appeared much more like a royal diadem. Let Louis hear of that, as well, and make of it what he would. A warning? Certainly!

'Thank you, Charles, for doing this.' Beside him, his duchess, the former Lady Margaret of

312

England, contrived to whisper to him, almost without moving her lips.

Charles nodded gravely, but he was not certain his wife understood the real significance of this reception today. None of this ceremonial would have happened, no matter how much she'd wanted it, if the times had not changed.

Duke Charles allowed himself a small, fond smile. Margaret was looking particularly attractive today, if a little tense – which was to be expected. Dressed in a simple gown of pearl-white damask beneath a sideless blue velvet over-robe lined with white cloth of gold, the duchess had also covered her hair with a low-crowned cap of pure white silk on which was mounted an airy headdress of stiffened gauze, suggestive of butterflies' wings. Only one in a hundred women had the carriage and grace to carry off such an outrageous creation and not look foolish; his wife was one of them.

Suddenly, dramatically, the closed doors of the Presence chamber were flung open and the palace steward advanced into the room, striking his staff of ivory, lignum vitae and gold three times on the tiled floor. The servants of the palace fanned out to form an honour guard and the courtiers thronged, twittering, into place behind them, avid to observe every moment of the meeting between the two men at the centre of today's event.

'His most august and gracious Majesty, the Lord Edward, King of England, France, Ireland and Wales. Duke of Cornwall...'

As the endless titles were recited, Charles, Duke of Burgundy rose, as did his duchess, and stood waiting whilst Edward Plantagenet, his brother, Duke Richard of Gloucester, and their party of supporters entered the vast space that was the Presence chamber of the Prinsenhof.

His face devoid of expression, Edward paced towards the distant dais, his brother by his side. The king's doublet of silver-grey Flanders velvet was slashed in the sleeves and on the body to allow a cream silk undershirt to puff out pleasingly from beneath. A black velvet cloak lined with red cloth of gold flowed from his shoulders to his heels, and his hose also were smooth black velvet, plain and unadorned, except that he too wore the blue garter of St George below his left knee. Edward's hair – dark gold, since it was winter – lay curling on his shoulders, loose and thick, and his head was encircled by a massive but plain gold band, its only ornaments Plantagenet leopards and stylised lilies. It was the single key to who he was, and was being acknowledged as the Sovereign Lord of England, and of France.

Duke Charles narrowed his eyes for a moment at the graceful sight advancing towards him. Was it fair that one man should be given so much physical beauty? Perhaps this fact alone was the source of all of Edward's travails? The duke swallowed a sigh and shook himself slightly at the absurdity of the thought. So be it. Let them gamble with fate once more.

Bowing to Edward from the waist, Charles stepped forward and spoke first. 'Your Majesty, at last we meet.'

Edward bowed too, a little less low, in a rustle of expensive cloth and the scent of powdered

314

orris root. 'It has been too long, brother. How delightful it is to be here in your enchanting city once more. Truly, Brugge is most noble and this, your palace, one of its greatest adornments. How charmed we are to stand here in this place of such happy memories.'

Not even the shadow of irony entered Edward's tone as, smilingly, his sister gave him her hand to kiss.

'Dearest Duchess. We find you well?' It was effortless to switch back to the speech of a royal personage – that person he'd been for nearly ten years.

The duchess curtsied in reply. 'Very well. I thank Your Majesty for asking.'

Her eyes were cast down to the flagged floor, but Margaret glanced up quickly at her brother when Charles was momentarily distracted. *I have news*, said that look.

Edward raised his eyebrows, but could not reply for, at that moment, the steward of the Prinsenhof was bowing him towards a Chair of State. Heavily carved, richly gilded, the chair was placed on a small riser on the very top of the dais itself, thus ensuring Edward sat fractionally higher than his host and hostess.

Optimism wound a diamond-bright thread around Edward Plantagenet's heart. Perhaps all truly *would* be well? Charles's reception was that of a duke to a reigning monarch, but the king had eaten confusion and disappointment for more than two months. The richness of this feast today was still suspect until it was consumed and paid for.

315

And there was Anne to think of. Never forget Anne.

After a nod from her husband, the duchess spoke out clearly for all the court to hear. 'We have an old friend for you to meet, Your Majesty.'

'An old friend – how delightful that will be.' Airy court phrases, so long perfected amongst them all. But would former ways of speaking, and seeing, be sufficient now?

Edward turned towards the door of the Presence chamber as it opened again, and this time his smile was deeply amused, as was that of the man who advanced towards him up the length of the chamber.

'Louis! Or perhaps more properly in this city of yours, Lodewijk, my dear friend. Has it truly been an age since last we saw one another? Time moves so fast, I swear it only feels like days. I look forward to another hunt together, when there is more time?'

Louis de Gruuthuse smiled and bowed as he made his way up the hall. 'An age, Your Majesty? Surely not. But how delightful it would be to ride out with you once more. Under easier circumstances than hunts of the past, of course.'

Edward laughed, freely and loudly. 'Ah, my friend, how pleasing it is to see you. Again.' The last word was heavily ironic, its significance lost on all but a very few in the Presence chamber.

Charles turned to Edward. 'I asked my governor to return to us from the north. We have need of his advice since Louis de Valois is spreading his net to catch us all up.'

There, it was said. The time for pretty speeches

316

was past.

Edward nodded thoughtfully. 'Yes, there is much to be said and much to speak of. But we are all friends here, and comrades. Louis de Valois is nothing to us if we act. Together.'

Dread crawled over Margaret of Burgundy's body like a biting insect. The men were frowning and the room itself had become sombre as the brilliant day outside dimmed.

'Your Majesty? Your Grace?' Margaret rose, in clear breach of protocol since the king had not indicated that she should. 'I should be pleased to withdraw, sire. The palace has many unexpected guests at this time of the year...' Margaret flicked a glance at Edward '...and I can see that Your Majesty and the duke, my husband,' she curtsied formally to Charles, 'have much to discuss which cannot concern me or any other member of my sex.'

Charles was momentarily distracted by the intensity of the look that passed between sister and brother as the duchess spoke. However, Margaret was right: family reunions must play second fiddle today to much weightier concerns.

'Come, Duchess, allow a long absent brother to escort you.' Bowing to the duke, Edward rose and picked up his sister's hand. As they processed down the hall, their backs to the dais, there was a precious moment in which to speak to one another.

'Is she safe?'

Margaret nodded. 'Yes. The bishop was ... interrupted last night before he could do anything but terrify her. However, he died. The city is frantic looking for him.'

Margaret's voice was unemotional and Edward resisted glancing at her, but a wave of strangeness prickled his skin. Staring straight ahead, he spoke from the side of his mouth. 'Gossip as we arrived said he was missing.'

Margaret smiled, left and right. That took effort. 'He is. He was … removed. After he died.'

'Where is the body?'

Margaret laughed merrily and patted her brother's hand, as if he had said something witty. 'We will speak of this later. Meanwhile, tell me the truth. Is Anne the old king's natural daughter?'

They had reached the door and it was opened soundlessly by the door-wards. Edward slewed a glance at his sister, profoundly disconcerted. There was no time to ask how she knew, so he nodded. 'Yes. Tell Anne I love her. She has my protection – she is not to doubt that.'

Margaret swept down into a curtsy as the king bowed. 'And mine, brother. And mine.'

'Where is the monk who accused her? I want to question him myself.'

Margaret rose and smiled brilliantly at the king. 'And so do I, as does Charles. He will be brought to the Prinsenhof later in the day. Then we shall see.'

The duchess was engulfed by her suite of ladies. Many a discreet glance was cast towards the distractingly handsome king, her brother, as the party of women left the anteroom of the Presence chamber, but, for once in his life, Edward was completely oblivious of female admiration.

# Chapter Forty-Three

'Brother? I am so truly sorry to disturb you...'
The sharp rap on the door jamb was followed by
a creak as the cell door opened.

Agonistes could hear fear fluttering in the
abbot's voice and decided to ignore it. Prayer
would take him away from the earthly concerns
of this corrupted world and all its servants. He
bent his head lower, clasped his joined hands
tighter and raised his voice.

'Holy Lady Mary, stainless and uncorrupted
Mother of our Saviour, look down on your sinful
servant this day. Help me, I beseech you–'

'*Brother!*' A hand descended on his shoulder.
The hand was heavy and the shoulder frail. When
had he last eaten? Agonistes slumped beneath
that mortal weight. He was tired, so very tired.
He ceased to pray. Slowly, he opened his eyes,
though it took some time to focus on the anxious
face looming over his.

'I would not disturb you but there are matters
we must discuss. Urgent matters.' The abbot
could not help himself; his breathing was shallow
and his tone at least an octave higher than it
might normally be.

Agonistes understood. Years as a courtier had
taught him much, even if he avoided remembering. He, in the grip of doing the Lord's work,
had slandered a good friend of the duchess and

she, the former Lady Margaret of England, was powerful.

The monk smiled. 'Brother, why fear for the future of the mortal body when the eternal soul is all that matters?'

Was it that lipless smile or the fatalistic tone that ramped the abbot's nervous state to panic? He breathed deeply through his nose, a curious whistling sound. He hoped he sounded firm. '*However*, dearest Brother, I must speak plainly. You are our guest, our cherished brother in the sight of the Lord.' The abbot swallowed; this was a little flowery, even for him. 'And I must care for your mortal state, even if you do not.'

Agonistes heaved himself up from his knees and stood, swaying, beside the narrow plank cot. His interest in playing this game was nonexistent.

'By which you mean, Brother Abbot, you fear for the mortal future of *your house* if I remain beneath its roof?'

The abbot was offended and, yes, resentful. Their lady duchess had always been a most generous patron – witness the new painted-window paid for by Margaret and dedicated to St George, the premier saint of England – but he very much hoped the close relationship between his order and the court of Burgundy was of lesser importance than his duty.

'Brother, I have prayed most ardently through this last night and God has brought me his precious guidance on this ... matter. He has told me that I must think of the welfare of *all* in this house. Souls and bodies, both. But my care begins with you.'

Fine and gilded lies. Agonistes shrugged. 'I am ready to return to Paris, Brother, if that is what you are trying to ask of me. Do not distress yourself. We all have our duty.'

In truth, the monk would be relieved to leave Brugge, especially as during his earlier prayers he'd heard the tumult surrounding the triumphant entry of Edward Plantagenet into the city. Agonistes closed his eyes and ears at even the memory of that sound. And his heart. He would not willingly allow that adulterer, the cause of so much suffering in his life, into his mind in any form.

Surreptitiously the abbot wiped the sweat from his upper lip. It was now a little before tierce, the third canonical hour of the day, and, if he moved fast, he could have this 'dear brother in Christ' out of the priory by the time the bell tolled for prayers.

'Since you have chosen your path, Brother, I support your decision. Here. These are for your journey to Paris, to help you on your way.' Like a magician, the abbot presented the monk with a saddlebag. 'Food, coin money – not much, of course. Ours is a poor house.' He coughed; it had not been easy to decide how much to give – too much, and Agonistes might see the money as a bribe and, being mad, refuse to leave. Only a madman would have said what he did at the feast yesterday. 'And there is a donkey also. Come with me, Brother, you must meet him, your new friend and faithful companion-to-be. He is a charming animal. And sturdy also.'

Relief made the abbot chatter, giddy as a society lady, as he swept the monk from his cell, yet Brother Agonistes strove not to judge the man's venality. Perhaps, after all, it *was* on behalf of his brothers that the abbot cast his own 'very dear brother, through our Saviour' onto the pitiless road. The monk also knew that if he declined to leave, if he remained in Brugge, he would be forced to explain his accusations to the duchess.

Agonistes yearned for peace, but his head ached and his vision clouded when he tried to understand what God truly wanted from him now. Surely, his usefulness to his brother, the King of France, would cease if Duchess Margaret recognised in him the wizened remains of the sinful Doctor Moss? That could not be within God's plan, could it?

Louis de Valois was a holy spear within the hand of the Lord, but perhaps *he*, sinner that he was, formed the tip of that spear – however unworthy his metal might be? No, on balance, it felt right to leave this pestilential city, this haunt of vice and sin, behind him. He had accomplished the task he'd been given; the monks here had told him that Anne de Bohun was even now in the hands of the Church's justice. And though he was puzzled by the enthusiastic welcome the ex-king of England had received, at least he was now named and shamed as an adulterer. Yes, he had done his work.

Thus, even though the Feast of St Stephen had turned bitter with dark sleet and a cutting wind, Brother Agonistes set out patiently enough just as the midday bell chimed out from the belfry above the cloth hall in the Markt Square. Despite the cold, he was dressed in nothing but his own filthy robes and a patched winter cloak wound tight around his emaciated body. He had refused the last-minute offer of a fur-lined mantle from the abbot. His feet were blue-white in the same holed sandals he had made for himself, long ago. Because of his manifold sins, he was certain that new boots could not be in God's plan for him, now or ever.

Therefore, he would rejoice in the certainty that the journey to Paris would take many weary days and, during that time, be grateful for the opportunity to consider, and reconsider, all his faults and failings. Perhaps his current sufferings could be offered up to God in further expiation of all that he'd done in that other, worldly time at Westminster.

Almost immediately on setting out there was evidence that his surrender to the will of God was pleasing to the Saviour: the donkey between his knees seemed suddenly certain of its mission in life. Where before it had ambled through the streets of Brugge, now it trotted busily out from beneath the battlements of the Kruispoort and onto the echoing wooden drawbridge that linked the city gate to the river bank of the Zwijn, despite the fact that Agonistes had not given the animal a direction of any kind. Reverently, the monk crossed himself. Surely God was good, He had sent him a donkey that knew the way to Paris.

Once free of the city, Brother Agonistes closed his eyes with confidence; prayer might warm his freezing fingers as he told off the beads on his rosary. As if to reassure him, the little donkey moved tirelessly ahead, along the road beside the river, its neat hooves clicking on the last stretch of cobbled roadway before the path reverted to winter-frozen mud.

They had a long, long way to go together.

At last they could see the battlements and towers in the distance and each man in the cold and hungry party allowed anticipation to create the mirage of a good meal and a warm bed. Perhaps there was even a willing woman in that bed as well? They picked up pace as fresh energy flowed into weary, freezing feet.

'So, Brugge it is for all of us, master mariner. Perhaps you'll find news there of your wife.'

Leif paused for a moment, leaning on his long staff. Could he face this? What if there was no news of Anne?

'I hope so, de Plassy. My wife has many friends in the city. As do I.'

The Frenchman turned to his companions and winked. 'My friend, I am certain you do, married or not. And now, my boys, if we hurry, we'll be within those walls long before last light. Plenty of time to find new friends and playmates. Brugge has always been kind to such as us.'

It was the best thing the men had heard since the scrape of the key in their prison-cell door, and they were all for it. Whoops and cheering swept the group on around a long bend on the road where they saw the great gate of the Kruispoort visible in the distance.

Leif let them stride ahead for a moment as he pulled his hood down over his eyes; the mercenaries had become his friends and companions and were chattering happily as girls, despite the sleet driving into their faces. He trudged on to catch the party up, falling in beside Julian de Plassy. The Frenchman pointed into the distance.

'Here's an encouraging prospect to put a little coin money in our pockets, captain. Just what we need.'

Coming towards them on the path was a skinny monk riding a donkey. He was wrapped to the eyes in a stained cloak and his head nodded in time with the short gait of his little mount.

Leif laughed. 'Ever the optimist, de Plassy. Why would you bother to rob a monk?'

The Frenchman narrowed his eyes. 'Ah well, they all lie, you know, clergy. They're rich, every single one of them. They pretend to be the opposite just to fool us. See, this one has a saddlebag. A nice, fat new one.'

At that moment, distantly, the noise of drums banged out from the city, and many voices rose together, cheering.

De Plassy raised his eyebrows at the Dane. 'So ... a little conversation-starter for our new friend.'

The Frenchman strode ahead of the group and planted himself in the path of the donkey. Haltingly, he spoke with the little Flemish he had. 'Your blessing, Brother. Today's festivities – what do they honour?'

The donkey baulked and stopped. The monk's eyes opened as he stopped telling his beads. He scowled at the sight of the men crowding the path in front of him. 'I do not speak your language, sir.' Unwittingly, he replied in English. Brother Agonistes' frown deepened; it was an odd thing to do after speaking and thinking in French for so many years.

Leif was also perplexed that this emaciated and filthy man – no doubt extra holy because of such privations – spoke English. He called out, 'I speak English, Father. Can you tell us what festival is taking place today in Brugge?'

The monk crossed himself before hawking phlegm and spitting. He just missed the seaman's boots. 'No honest celebration, certainly, though it is St Stephen's day. The former king of the English has come to Brugge to see the duke. That is all I know. Let me pass.'

Julian de Plassy smiled. 'Edward Plantagenet? Is that who you mean?' He exchanged a delighted glance with Leif.

The monk sniffed contemptuously. 'Yes. His evil deeds are his undoing, as all men will now soon see.'

The Frenchman signalled for his men to back away from around the donkey. Brugge was suddenly as precious as Jerusalem – for what it contained – and far, far nearer. He could afford to be magnanimous. He would free the monk who had given them this good news.

Agonistes spoke up angrily, to mask fear. 'Yes! Clear my path. I am about God's work. For the salvation of your blackened souls, do not think to delay me.'

Julian bowed. 'Do not be fearful, honoured father. We respect men of the cloth as we do our own mothers.'

He uttered the airy lie without shame and Leif coughed to avoid laughing. De Plassy's men stepped back smartly from the crown of the road to allow the monk on his way. Agonistes kicked the donkey in its flanks and the bony little animal lurched into its customary trot.

Leif Molnar and Julian de Plassy wasted few moments watching the monk on his way. They strode out together towards the distant city, setting a brisk pace for their followers.

'Our luck is turning, my friend, I am certain of it. I must remind the English king of the service my men performed for him. He will be grateful – if one can ever count on the gratitude of kings.'

He glanced at Leif. The Dane was gazing at the city also, but his face was sombre. 'Do not despair, Leif. Have courage. I feel your wife waits for you, somewhere very close. Believe me, when these feelings come to me, they are never wrong.'

Leif smiled but said nothing, and swung on down the road at a steady pace.

His 'wife'. If Edward was in the city, was she with him ... or was she dead?

## Chapter Forty-Four

Anne needed a wash and to sleep, but she needed information even more.

By the light through one high window, she could tell that a night and a day and some of another night had passed, but with the exception of food she'd been given nothing else. Certainly no news, though she'd tried hard to get the guard to talk to her.

He was young, her guard, little more than a

boy, but his fear was plain when he brought Anne her food – coarse bread and a porridge of barley and flaked stock-fish. He'd never met with a witch before and terror made his eyes enormous in his face. And when Anne had tried to thank him, the youth backed away, silently crossing himself as if the Devil himself had opened his mouth and addressed him personally.

Anne would have laughed at the memory, except it made her anxious. How could anyone look at her, a girl with tangled hair and, no doubt, a dirty face, wearing a slept-in dress, and think she was a servant of darkness? Surely selling your soul to the Devil should guarantee cleaner clothes for a start!

Anne paced up and down, skirts swishing. It was time she took a hand in her own fate, instead of waiting for help that might not come. That thought squeezed her heart, but she banished it. She would not allow panic to cloud her judgment. It was just a matter of time.

To calm herself she recited, almost like a prayer, the things she knew.

Margaret and Charles of Burgundy were her friends, and she was in their castle. Margaret had gone to get help. Margaret would not desert her – she was *certain* of that fact. It was just taking a little longer than they'd both thought.

Also, Edward was somewhere in the city even now; she'd heard the clamour of the bells this morning at his entry. She'd tried to climb up to the one high window to see the procession, but even by putting the stool onto the seat of the cathedra and balancing on the very ends of her toes, it had been impossible to see out. But Edward would know of her situation by now. And Edward loved her. Yes, certainly, he would know where she was and was just waiting for the right time to...

She might be an optimist, but there was another voice in Anne's head also, a companion born of fear and lack of sleep that she tried to ignore, tried not to hear.

*He won't come*, said that voice. *He's had what he needs of you. Once he's with Charles, and making plans, why would he bother what happens to you or your son? He's forgotten you already. Why wouldn't he? He's got a proper, legitimate boy of his own now, a real prince...*

'No!'

The guard outside heard the girl shouting in the empty room. It gave him the creeps. Was she raising spirits in there, yelling like that? Unwillingly, he stepped a little closer to listen, but her voice had sunk to a whisper. What was she saying now?

'He'll come. He'll come. You'll see.' Tears choked Anne's throat. 'And I'll see you soon, too, my baby. Very soon...'

*Women are such foolish creatures. Hoping, believing, where a man would have courage enough to face the truth. You have been deserted and will die here, Anne de Bohun. Alone. Duke Charles knows everything; he has prevented Margaret from coming back to you because she's told him about the death of the bishop. He's sent her away, to a convent, just as Odo said he would. And Agonistes is, even now, dropping poison for all to hear. Listen carefully. Can you hear? They are building your pyre in the Markt Square. The King of*

329

*England and the Duke of Burgundy must support the burning of witches. That is their duty.*

'No! Get away from me. I will not hear you. I will not die here. They will never burn my body!'

The guard clapped his hands over his ears and marched away to the end of the passage, the furthest point of his post. He would not listen to the witch's ravings any further. He was too frightened of who she was talking to.

Anne, in her cell, ran to the door and pounded upon the bare, unyielding wood. She had to have news!

'Guard! I must speak with the duchess.'

But the guard was reciting the Pater Noster, fingers stuffed in his ears.

'I know you're still there. I can hear you!' Anne shouted the words, but then she broke. 'Answer me! Oh, please answer me. Have pity.'

Anne slid down to the floor of her cell. Her prison was in an old and remote part of the palace, high up beneath the battlements. Did they mean to keep her here until she went mad, or died? Was that what the future held? Was that better than burning?

Tears fell before she could stop them. 'Deborah. Can you see me? I can see you. And my baby. My little boy. Mummy's watching over you, my darling. I'll be home soon...'

*You'll never go home... Your cause is lost and you are abandoned. You'll never ever see them again in this life...*

And there, on the floor of her cell, terrified and alone, Anne cried herself to sleep like a child lost in the night.

## Chapter Forty-Five

The feast of welcome in the Prinsenhof finished very late and it was long after midnight before the king, Richard and William Hastings returned to their opulent lodgings: the town palace of the Sieur de Gruuthuse. Tomorrow would bring another long day of meetings, discussions and wrangling, but at least real negotiations between Duke Charles and the English had begun.

It was there, in a luxurious suite of rooms on the second floor of Louis's mansion beside the substantial Onze-Lieve-Vrouwekerk – such a handsome church with its recently completed Gate of Paradise portal – that Edward Plantagenet and his brother closed the door upon the world.

Their host had supplied his guests with fashionable new clothes to wear to the evening's entertainment, however the brothers had rejected the offer of servants to help them undress on their return. Now was the first moment they'd had to themselves since their ceremonial entrance to the city that morning.

'Thanks be to all the gods that are, brother. We're alone!' Richard tore at the many tiny gold buttons of his tight court jerkin. His belly was distended from rich food and too much wine after many Spartan weeks. He felt bilious, but welcomed that unfamiliar feeling back into his life; it was a positive sign.

331

'Hush!' Edward flashed a glance at his brother. Kicking off his soft dress boots he strode, barefoot, to the door and listened, even dropped his eye to the large keyhole. Richard giggled at the sight. The giggles ended in hiccups.

'What do you ... *hic* ... want to do now? *Hic*. Sorry.'

He looked so penitent that Edward strode back across the room, smiling, and ruffled Richard's hair. It was easy to forget just how young the duke actually was. 'Do? Nothing, until this house is properly asleep. I can still hear movement on the other side of the door.'

Richard shifted from foot to foot, uneasy. 'You're planning ... *hic* ... something, *hic*, aren't you? *Hic*. Tell me. *Hic*. Sorry. Edward?'

The king ignored his brother as he stripped down to his undershirt and britches. Gone was the magnificent and heavily embroidered blue velvet jerkin with the trailing sleeves lined and cuffed in ermine – tossed onto the bed as if it were a thing without value. Gone too was the massive gold chain of interlinked 'S's, which had lain around his shoulders; it landed on the fur-edged counterpane. The massive diadem that marked him as a king followed the collar in short order – slung through the air in a nicely judged arc, which pitched it onto the pillow where his head would later lie.

'Margaret tells me that Anne is locked up and guarded, but otherwise well.' Edward grimaced as he said it; *well* was an inadequate term, under the circumstances.

Hurrying, he pulled a close-woven riding tunic

over his head. Cut from a double layer of finest English broadcloth and dyed a deep forest green, it had been in his saddlebags when he'd ridden into Brugge this morning. It had survived much, having taken him warmly enough across half of England and Europe in these last long weeks. It would be his companion in further adventures, he was sure of that.

Richard caught something of Edward's urgency. He shrugged out of the constricting jerkin at last and, shivering, looked around the vast room for the things they'd brought from Anne's farm. 'But Lady de Bohun is not being blamed for the bishop's "disappearance", is she?'

Edward flung him a look as he pulled on long, supple riding boots. 'No. Not as yet. Margaret has managed it well. She's even fooled Charles.'

The king frowned. Had she? More than once during the feast tonight, as talk turned to the missing Bishop Odo, Edward had caught Charles of Burgundy gazing at his wife with a certain detached calculation. *Never forget the politics of pragmatism.* The king shivered at the thought. His sister had the nerve of a seasoned gambler – and he hoped he did also – but each of them was just a piece on the chessboard of politics. Charles was very good at chess.

'What will happen to Anne, brother?'

Edward said nothing as he hauled on his boots until they moulded to his calves. He had no certain answer.

'She cannot stay in Brugge,' the duke continued. 'Things need to become a little calmer before she'll be safe behind these walls again.'

333

A little calmer? A masterly understatement. During the preceding day, as Edward, Duke Charles, Richard, Louis de Gruuthuse and Hastings had gone over the intelligence regarding the placement of French troops, the current situation with Warwick and Clarence in England and the amounts of men, money and material Edward needed to retake his realm, even they could not entirely escape the rising babble of conjecture that the bishop's continuing absence had caused at court.

'Did you hear that the monk has fled?' Edward bared his teeth in a very unpleasant smile. 'He can't be completely mad, after all.'

Richard twitched a grin at his brother, but remained troubled. 'Do you think they'll find where Margaret has... I mean, say they find the body, do you believe that a corpse bleeds in the presence of its murderer? Do you think that's possible, brother?'

Edward was searching for his sword, but he swung around and laughed. 'Richard, I'm constantly surprised at you, I really am. Margaret didn't murder the bishop and neither did Anne. Our sister has been very clear on that. The man had a fit and died. That happens sometimes to the gross in body, as well you know. By the way...'

Richard, like his brother, was now dressed for riding. 'Yes?'

'Your hiccups have gone.'

Anne awoke swollen-eyed, aching and cold. The reeking tallow candle she'd been left with had long since flickered out and the floor of the stone room was cold and hard as lake ice.

She sat up, shivering. Frigid air burned her throat and her lungs as she breathed. The shock of it had a bracing effect and she found she was angry. Furious, in fact. Rage propelled her to her feet and she ran to the door, kicking it and hitting it with all her force.

'You! Open the door. Now!'

She would not allow herself to think, her mind focused on making something, anything, happen.

There was a click as a key entered the lock; the latch was moving. Anne gasped and stepped back.

'I thank you. My friend, the duchess, will be most pleased.' She heard the quaver in her voice and tried to suppress it, tried to sound proud and confident, but then it was too much – her eyes filled with tears, blurring the small stone world that had become her compass.

'And my sister will be most grateful you are safe. As, indeed, am I. Very glad.'

Edward.

In two strides he had her scooped up hard against his body and she felt, as he did, each of their hearts beating against their prison of bone.

'I'm sorry, I'm sorry. I could not come before this. Hush, hush now.'

Anne's sobs came from deep within her chest. Edward held her, soothed her, rocked her. She clung to him like a vine.

'There, oh, there...' He was kissing the tears as they ran down her face, kissing the side of her mouth, her mouth itself as she tried to speak.

'I was so afraid. And I had such dreams, Edward. Such dreams of fire and death and...'

Her terror was so palpable that the king felt it

pass from her body to his like a physical thing. 'But I'm here now. We're together.'

Anne was suddenly stricken. Was this a dream too?

She looked down at their joined hands, felt the warmth in his fingers. Looking up into his eyes, she smiled with relief. 'Yes. We are together.' And then she took his face between her hands and kissed him softly.

He tightened his arms around her but she shook her head. 'I must go home, Edward. As soon as I can.'

But she allowed him to hold her, encompassed; just a little longer. It comforted them both to stand like this, no thoughts, no words. They were each made stronger in that dreamlike warmth.

But then Anne stepped back, breaking the circle of Edward's arms, and looked up into the face of the man she loved so dearly.

'I need a horse – and an escort.'

Edward nodded. 'They're waiting for you. Margaret has arranged it. I will take you to your home and my dear brother-in-law will be none the wiser.'

His hand touched her face and one finger traced the outline of cheek and mouth and chin, resting on the pulse that beat in the hollow of her throat.

'But you cannot stay at your farm, my darling. You must pack lightly and be ready to leave. Margaret will see that the place is looked after.'

Anne frowned. 'And if that is not my choice?'

Patiently, Edward took one of Anne's hands and led her towards the door. He peered out into the passage beyond – it was empty, apart from Richard.

'I need to know you are safe. I can arrange that. And then, once I am in London and all is secured, we can be together. Properly.'

The beating of Anne's blood was like a drum, a distant fluttering drum.

'No.'

Edward Plantagenet turned back to the woman he loved so very much and his eyes were bleak.

'Anne, please do not be foolish in this. You are subject to my will as your sovereign. I command this. Our son must be safe, and if you will not–'

He had gone too far. Anne was a proud being and the feelings between them were very tangled.

'Command? Command is not a word for lovers. It is a word for followers. And slaves.'

The temperature of the room dropped and the candle that Edward now held flickered in his hand, as if in a violent wind. The light steadied, but the king found a very different woman staring at him. Anne was taller, suddenly, and the flame of the candle found an answer in her eyes.

'In this last night, when I thought I'd been abandoned, I came to understand many things. I go willingly with you, Edward, or I do not go at all. You do not have the means to force me. I am not a serf to be picked up, used and put away when it suits your whim.'

The king was astonished. And then angry. Did Anne not understand just how much he had to deal with, how desperately he needed a clear mind if he was to accomplish what must be done? She and the boy must be made safe, then he could focus, fight, and come back for her later.

'Anne, this is foolish. Please do as I say?'

He had not intended to plead with her, but, astonishingly, his voice broke. And the marble statue in front of him turned back into the woman he loved.

'Once I am home again, I shall consider what is best. No!' She held up her hand to stop him as he reached for her – she would change her mind if he held her; they both knew that. 'This is *my* choice now, Edward. Not yours. And I will ride home alone with the escort tonight.'

She had dismissed him, declined his help, and would say nothing more. Sad, furious and silent, Edward Plantagenet bundled Anne de Bohun into one of the duchess's riding cloaks and hurried the girl through the palace down to the duke's stables. Richard, who'd been guarding the door of the cell, loped beside them as they ran.

There was a palfrey waiting in the yard, a small spirited mare, and four men dressed in Burgundian livery. The moment had come. And still Anne said nothing.

Standing with her at the shoulder of the horse, Edward spoke first. 'Anne, can you not see–'

'Shush.' Anne placed a finger on Edward Plantagenet's mouth. She was staring up at him and they were close, so close. But she shook her head.

Edward was proud also. He would not beg again. The former King of England placed his hands around Anne de Bohun's waist and swung her up into the saddle. With his own fingers he tied the riding cloak at her throat and insisted she wear the red riding gloves lined with catskin so thoughtfully provided by his sister for her friend.

Because others were watching, they did not kiss, but the last look between them was a long one.

Then Anne turned the little horse's head towards the stable gates and tightened the reins. The mare was a well-fed animal, impatient to be off, and, being given the signal by its rider, sprang forward so that the men accompanying Anne had to scramble to form up behind her as she led them out of the Prinsenhof.

Edward's last sight of Anne as she disappeared into the deep surrounding night was the wave of one scarlet hand, then the great gates groaned closed behind her and the portcullis came down.

Dread seized him. How long would it be before they met again?

## Chapter Forty-Six

'I can hear you thinking, Margaret.'

The duchess held her breath; she thought she'd successfully pretended sleep. She sighed and turned over to face her husband. The lighted candle beside the bed was a small star in the vast dark room.

'I cannot sleep, Charles.'

The duke smiled faintly. 'Conscience, perhaps?'

For a moment Margaret couldn't find words and her heart filled her mouth.

'Conscience? No. Too much of the last march-pane subtlety. You know how greedy I am for sweet things. Perhaps it's a sign I'm breeding?'

The duke sat up against the bolster and looked at his wife.

'You're shameless, Margaret. I know she's gone. And I also know what you did with Bishop Odo.'

There was a moment's charged silence before the duchess forced her tongue to move, forced herself to find words. 'But ... Aseef cannot talk or...'

The duke nodded and his amused expression became severe. 'Or hear. You are correct, my dear. But Aseef was my servant before you were ever my wife. True, he has no speech and he *is* deaf, but he can write quite well; I had him taught. It is one of the reasons his loyalty to me is so strong. I gave him the means to communicate. Ah, you didn't know that?'

Margaret closed her eyes. 'What will you do, Charles?'

The duke got out of bed, pulling a fur coverlet around his naked body, and hurried over to the chimney breast, cursing under his breath at the cold. The fire was nearly out. Energetically, he set about rebuilding a blaze.

'Charles? Don't play with me.' The duchess sat up, fear sharpening her voice.

'Do? I shall do nothing, wife. You have done what I could not be seen to do. And saved me a very difficult decision, on two counts.'

The relief was astonishing. It washed through Margaret's body as if her blood had been replaced by sherbert. Tingling, shivering, she joined her husband by the fire, wrapped in a heavy blanket hauled from the gigantic bed. The blanket trailed behind her over the rushes on the floor, whispering, as if it had a secret to tell.

'Two counts?'

'Yes.' The duke smiled at his wife. 'Come closer to the fire. Warm yourself.'

Margaret held up her palms to the flames; her hands glowed from the flickering light behind them. Her husband measured his fingers against hers: both their hands shone blood scarlet now.

'Aseef told me that Odo died from a fit. Is that true?'

Margaret nodded. 'Yes.' Her voice was barely a whisper.

'And you made Aseef take the body away. How did he avoid being seen?'

Margaret shook her head. That night – only a day since – was a blurred nightmare. 'It was very late and the palace was asleep. We stripped the body, Anne and I.' She shuddered as she remembered the filthy, lice-ridden undergarments; the fat-larded body; the weight of him, and the stench of flesh unwashed for years and years, as they moved the corpse to undress it, then clothe it again...

'I dressed him in some of your clothes. They were all I could find quickly. Old ones, I promise you,' – she added the detail defensively –'but they were far too small. We had to rip them up the back. We wrapped him up in a cloak. Then Aseef carried him out, over his shoulder, as if he were too drunk to stand.'

'Where did you put the body? Aseef has not told me. But then, I haven't asked him.'

The duchess shrugged guiltily. 'I remembered

the crypt beneath the great chapel.'

The duke nodded. 'A judicious choice. Who would think to disturb the sleep of my ancestors looking for a missing bishop?'

The duchess was close to tears. 'I didn't know which tomb to choose. It was very dark, but one had a damaged lid and we put him inside that. It made a terrible noise when we moved the top aside. The loudest sound I've ever heard in my life and the worst – I can hear it now.'

The duke picked up Margaret's free hand. 'What happened then?'

In the semi-dark of the bed chamber it was impossible to read the expression in the duke's eyes. The duchess shrugged unhappily. She was ashamed and frightened.

'It was necessary to make the guard think he'd seen the bishop leave. My body maid, Estella–'

'Ah yes. It seems her loyalty to you is very great. She entertained the guard?'

The duchess nodded. No point lying now. 'Yes. He's very young, Charles, and gullible. And I don't want him punished. She kept him as long as she could. In the end, Aseef returned to Anne only a moment before the guard himself came back.'

She swallowed. 'Anne dressed Aseef in Odo's clothes. He put the cowl up and ... walked out of there.'

The duke guffawed until tears streaked his face. 'But ... he's ... *black*. He's a *blackamoor!* Ah, this is too much.' That set him laughing again.

The duchess was defensive. 'Well, it was very dark in the passage so the guard couldn't see properly. Estella had taken the torch.'

'Estella took the torch, did she? Of course.' The duke sighed happily. 'You really don't understand the concept of obedience, do you? I must see what I can do about that, wife.'

Margaret truly relaxed for the first time in this long day. She leaned against her husband's broad chest. 'Well, you shouldn't have married a Plantagenet, should you, if you'd wanted obedience?'

He laughed again and kissed her, held her close. They stood together, watching the flames.

'What did you mean, Charles, that I saved you two difficult decisions?'

Charles was caressing Margaret's naked waist.

'I had to let Odo see Anne. We couldn't have an accused witch in the city without the Church having its say on the matter. But I couldn't work out what to do next. How to get him away from her. How to get *her* out of the city. You solved that for me. But now...'

The fire was raging, sending out real heat. Margaret looked up into her husband's eyes. 'Yes, Charles?'

The duke dropped the fur coverlet from his shoulders and stood naked in front of her. 'Now, I want to forget all about Anne de Bohun, the bishop and how we're going to deal with all of this. Until tomorrow.'

In one swift moment, he pulled the blanket from around his wife's shoulders and she was in his arms, nothing between his skin and hers. 'And you're going to help me do that. It's your first lesson in obedience.'

'And shall I need many, many more if I'm to subdue my rebellious nature, husband?'

343

'You shall indeed. And I shall enjoy teaching you your proper place. Beneath me, here and now...'


## Chapter Forty-Seven

The farm was in darkness. The man stood at the kitchen door and knocked gently. 'Mistress?'

A shutter scraped open above the man's head. He stepped back and looked up. There was just enough light to see her face.

'Leif?' The terror of a strange voice in the night ebbed, to be replaced by guilt. This was normal, however; she was dreaming again – she saw Leif's face often in dreams – and would wake soon. Wake into the nightmare her life had become.

Below her, the big man smiled. 'Yes, lady. No need to be afraid. Will you let me in?'

Anne shook her head to clear it and, as if for the first time, felt the cold iron of the latch on her window, saw her breath as it floated in the still night. This was no dream. She was awake. Leif was *real*.

'Yes. Of course. Stay there!'

Leif gazed up at the woman whose face had haunted him all these long months in the north. Faint light glimmered. It caught the lines of her face, the curve of one shoulder as she leaned forward to throw the shutter back – being careful to crouch a little behind the window's sill so that he would not see she was naked. Her hair was unbound, like a child's.

Leif swallowed hard. Anne was alive. And seemingly unhurt. The tiny hammer at his throat was warm as he touched it in silent thanks to the God of War for this unexpected kindness.

'Yes, lady. I'll wait.' He spoke softly. He would always wait for her.

Anne nodded and ducked back inside the room, pulling the shutter closed as gently as she could so as not to wake Deborah or little Edward. She padded back to her bed, shivering. Groping along the wall in the dark, she found her kirtle, an undershift and her shawl. They would have to do. Her feet were cold, but bare feet would be silent in the sleeping house and that was good...

A moment later, Anne slid the three stout bolts on the kitchen door from their keepers and lifted the latch.

'Lady Anne.' Leif bowed to her and ducked beneath the lintel. She didn't catch the expression on his face, but her voice quavered when she replied.

'You are welcome in my house, Leif. So welcome. I'll make a light so we can see each other.'

Leif watched Anne as she tried to apply flint to the wick of a pottery oil lamp. After three attempts he took it from her and coaxed a small bright star from the wick. 'Sit, lady. On the settle. I'll restart the fire. It's cold in here.'

Anne nodded and sat while Leif took the great poker to the ashes of the fire, stirring them vigorously and blowing hard until he found live coals buried deep. He fed the small flames with twigs and a little straw. Warmth bloomed and rosy light transformed the kitchen, winking on copper pans and gilding the edges of the pewter chargers on the cupboard. It was a cosy, homely place – beautiful in its simple usefulness.

Anne saw nothing of this, however, as shame, joy and confusion pulled at her like a trinity of wolves. She had no right to this kindness and she would not take advantage of what he felt for her. How could she do that when the substantial shadow of Edward Plantagenet was still such a huge part of her life?

Leif turned and smiled at her.

'Room on the settle for me?'

Anne found words for simple things. 'Yes, yes, of course. It's late, and I'm sure you're hungry. Are you hungry, Leif?' She could hear herself prattling; she sounded like a loon! Action was a remedy for such foolishness.

She jumped up as he sat down and hurried over to the three-legged pot sitting in the fireplace. It was half full of good winter stock simmered from bones and scraps of meat and the last of the stored root vegetables. The soup was one of the staples of Anne's kitchen, and each evening barley was added, along with wild garlic, and then the ashes banked high so the broth would cook overnight, ready for break-fast in the morning.

Anne lifted the iron lid and dipped in a ladle, then poured the thick, savoury liquid into a wooden bowl. She carried the soup to Leif, realising again, with something of a shock, how very big he was. The work of hauling ropes and straining at the tiller of his cog had given Leif a broad chest and massive arms and shoulders; even seated, he dwarfed Anne's standing height. And she could smell him: healthy, warm, male – musk and spice. He was the captain of a trading vessel, and when he moved there came the scent of cloves and quills of cinnamon – the ghosts of previous cargoes. His scent sharpened her sense of loss.

'I have bread, also. Yesterday's, but still good.'

'Bread would be excellent. If it's Deborah's?'

They both smiled. Try as she might, Anne had no skill at kneading bread and her loaves were always heavier than her foster-mother's.

'Don't worry, I've not had my hands anywhere near it.'

A flour-dusted round loaf and a little pot of rendered goose fat were quickly found. Anne hesitated for a moment, then sat down beside her guest and watched, without speaking, as Leif tore a thick piece off the loaf and dipped it in the goose fat. That task accomplished, he spooned soup into his mouth, glancing quickly at Anne. She was tired and the circles beneath her eyes spoke of trouble. Or fear. He didn't like to see that.

'This is very good.'

The praise was sincere, but Anne would not look at Leif as she fed more wood, unnecessarily, into the flames.

The Dane ate steadily for a little longer, then, sighing, put the bowl down and turned to her. 'I don't blame you, lady. You had to go with the king. I was told you had no choice.'

Anne ducked her head to hide sudden tears. When she tried to speak it was in a choking whisper. 'I'm sorry, Leif. So sorry. I deserted you.'

He shook his head, a smile glimmering. 'No,

347

you didn't. He did, though.' Anne rushed to defend the king, but Leif laughed. Actually laughed. 'When I got over it, I understood. It's what I would have done too, if I'd been him.'

At that moment, little Edward ran into the kitchen in his nightgown. 'Leif!' he shouted and hurled himself at the big man. The sailor pushed his bowl away and gathered the child into his arms and up against his massive chest.

'Well now, Boy, I thought you'd have forgotten me.' Boy was Leif's nickname for Anne's son.

Edward wriggled his way up the giant's torso until his arms were locked around the seaman's neck. The little boy shook his head solemnly. 'No. Not ever or ever. I love you. Good to have you home, Leif.' He patted the big man's face and they both laughed.

Deborah entered the kitchen in time to hear the last of this little speech and saw the wistful expression on Anne's face as she gazed at the man and the child. She clapped her hands quite sharply. The trio looked up, three startled faces.

'What *are* you doing out of bed, young man?'

'I heard them talking, Deborah. Don't be angry.'

'I'm not angry, but you really should be in your bed, child.'

Edward started to protest vigorously then changed his tack. 'Read me a story, Leif? Then I'll go back to bed.' Such shining innocence; such emotional cunning!

Leif laughed, and so did Anne. 'I'd like that, Boy, except I can't read. I can tell you one, though.'

Anne interrupted. 'Let Edward stay here, Deborah. You too. Isn't it nice that Leif's back and we're all together again?'

The old woman smiled at her foster-daughter but said nothing. In truth, it was good that this kind and dependable man had returned, but perhaps it would make things more complicated for Anne. Was that a good thing?

Anne kissed her son. 'Come, Edward, you can sit here next to Leif for just a moment. Would you like some soup?'

Anne put a small bowl of soup in front of her son as Deborah searched for something in the shadows of the kitchen.

'What's lost, Deborah?'

'The warming pan. I just want to heat the child's bed before he goes back up. It's very cold. Ah ... here it is.'

Deborah shovelled hot ash into the hinged metal pan, talking over her shoulder as she worked. 'You be quick, Edward, because you'll need a big sleep. Long day for all of us tomorrow.'

The sailor cut off a lump of bread for the little boy and showed him how to dip it neatly in the liquid and convey it to his mouth without dripping.

'Well done. Now, another bite...'

The child yawned hugely, exposing the half-chewed food in his mouth. His mother did her best to sound severe. 'Edward, I've told you before. Hand over your mouth.'

The little boy giggled and exhibited the contents of his mouth again with a big grin. That set them all off and soon the three adults were laughing so hard, tears streaked their faces. Then Edward yawned again, his eyes fluttering as he rubbed them with his fists.

'Come, sweet babe,' said Deborah. 'Enough of this. We'll warm the sheets together. Then Wissy will come.'

'Leif too?'

'Yes, I'll come. Now, tuck up warm, Boy.'

The big man leaned down and placed the small boy carefully on his feet again, kissing him warmly. A visitor at that moment would have thought them a family – mother, father, child and grandmother. Anne caught Leif's eye and seemed about to say something, but then turned to her son. 'Don't I get a kiss?'

Briefly she hugged her son hard, and then, hand in hand, Deborah and the child left the kitchen, singing as they went. 'Up the stairs, up the stairs to Bedlingford...'

There was silence in the kitchen now, except for the crackle of the fire. Anne added more wood and poked hard at the ash bed, avoiding the man's eyes.

'He's grown. He'll be a tall man.' Leif did not add, 'Like his father.'

'What's all this?' He gestured around the kitchen; there were roped coffers and piles of possessions stacked in the shadows. 'You're leaving the farm?'

Anne half turned away, nodding.

'Why?'

'It is my choice.'

Leif got up and took the poker from Anne's hands. It was the same one that had killed Edward Plantagenet's messenger.

'You don't want to tell me?'

350

Anne shook her head, tears close to the surface. 'We must leave Brugge as soon as possible.'

Leif digested that statement without comment. Then, throwing another log from the autumn trimmings of the orchard onto the fire, he gently turned Anne's head towards his. She could not escape.

'I heard the story in town. That's why I came here. Where will you go?'

Anne dropped her eyes from his. 'South. Italy, perhaps. We will start again, Deborah and Edward and me.'

The words were brave, but the loneliness in Anne's voice touched Leif's heart. He said nothing and it was Anne who broke the moment, taking the empty bowls from the hearth. A moment later, she returned and sat down beside him on the settle, her eyes far away. Defeated.

He reached over and gently covered both her hands with one of his own. 'You don't have to do this alone, Anne.'

She looked up at the giant man with the kind eyes and it was too much. Deep, wrenching sobs tore from her chest. Instinctively, Leif reached for the girl and this time Anne did not resist; she allowed herself to rest against him as he rubbed her back gently, rhythmically. After a time, she gulped herself into silence and leaned against his shoulder, numb.

'Lady, I'm here to take you home. If you'll let me.'

Anne's swollen eyes flew open. 'Home?'

Leif nodded. 'England. I reclaimed the *Lady Margaret* from the pool of Delft and she's

351

moored at Sluys. The tradesmen who repaired her were honest. You were right.'

He smiled gently. There was silence for a moment. Then Anne sat up, worry creasing her brow.

'But how can we sail to England? The war is–'

'About to begin in earnest, I'd say. Talk in Brugge was that Duke Charles will help the king at last. But that won't happen quickly, so we can beat him back. If you'll trust me to take you there.'

Leif made it all sound so easy. The heartache and confusion were blown away on the fresh wind of common sense. Tears spiked Anne's lashes again.

'I told the king that I must choose what was best for us all – little Edward and Deborah and me – and choose I will.' She blinked hard and shook the tears away. 'Can you really take us to London?'

The Dane stood up so abruptly he hit his head on the low brass candelabra. 'Ow! Never mind! Why do you think Sir Mathew hasn't seen the *Lady Margaret* before now? Yes, of course I can take you home.'

Deborah had re-entered the kitchen unnoticed and stood now in the shadows. She heard the unspoken end to the sentence: *and take you for mine, as well*.

Thor's servant, the servant of war, had returned in another guise to Anne. Her daughter had better be careful or she would unleash a mighty force in her life. No fight between nations, no difference in class, could ever be as strong as overwhelming love. The love this man held for Anne de Bohun.

# Part Three

# The Return

# Chapter Forty-Eight

As the darkest part of winter settled over France there was a monster born in Paris. A two-headed child with three arms, one attached to its chest, and hands which, it was said, resembled the claws of a lobster. It was a bad omen, a very bad omen, and the priests, monks and bishops all called for national repentance if this work of the Devil was not to be the portent of more horrors to come.

Dread crept through the exhausted, starving kingdom of France – a pale, slow disease compounded of unreason and gathering panic. Louis de Valois could smell it, could almost see the miasma, as even his court became infected.

'I must see this creature. You must see it too, Brother, and tell me what it means.'

Brother Agonistes raised a tortured face. Not long returned from Brugge, he was kneeling at the foot of the dais in the Presence chamber, three shallow steps beneath the Chair of Estate in which the king sat. After his long journey south through the iron-cold land, he was thinner than ever, dirtier than ever and his stench was even worse; *Truly*, thought Louis, *he smells like a nine-day corpse.*

Agonistes breathed like an old, abused mule and his hand shook as it sketched a cross in the air between Louis and himself. 'Brother King, I have no special knowledge of what this thing might mean. It is a living creature. They say it sucks well from its mother's paps and is strong. Perhaps it is God who has sent it to us, rather than Satan.'

Louis clucked his tongue impatiently. 'That cannot be. Our Creator does not make monstrous children, for we are made in *His* sacred image. No, this is a sign. I am certain of it.'

Brother Agonistes shrugged wearily. 'The king, my brother, knows more than I can possibly understand, since he is anointed by God.' The man's fingers crept to the rosary slung through his rope belt. He closed his eyes and silently began to tell the beads, oblivious, it seemed, of the presence of the king.

Louis felt no affront, for the behaviour of this monk was always extraordinary. For a moment the king forgot his fear of the monster in wondering what the monk saw when he prayed so intensely.

'You are as devout as ever, Brother Agonistes. But also greatly changed. Are you ill?'

Without speaking, the monk shook his head, the rosary beads clicking through his fingers with relentless rhythm.

'Well then, do you fear death perhaps, that you mortify yourself so greatly?'

The monk's eyes flew open and he glared at the king. 'Yes, I fear death. As you should also. Sin is the stinking, loathsome burden we both carry. Lust has been my downfall in the past and now, with the sight of that woman in Brugge, the memory of it has reared up once more to besmirch me. That woman *you* sent me to, brother.' Agonistes sounded almost reproachful.

Louis was so astonished by the monk's presumption that he forgot to speak.

The monk's face split with a pained smile. 'And yet, brother, it pleased you and the Lord to bestow this task upon me, therefore I am grateful for the privations given to me in this matter. I hope they are pleasing in the Lord's sight, and yours also, brother king. And the woman may be burned by now – if that has been God's will.' He crossed himself solemnly.

Automatically, Louis mimicked the action.

'And you, brother,' the monk continued, 'you too must put away the sins of this Earth if you are to govern your kingdom for God, and in his name. Pride in this war will bring you down, for it is the vice of kings and the greatest sin of all. Pray with me now that we may both be cleansed.'

Opened to their widest extent, the monk's eyes were bleak pools of emptiness. Louis felt consumed by the horror of eternity they contained. Suddenly, Agonistes collapsed onto his belly, hauling himself towards the king, as if he were a worm or a slug, or some other loathsome crawling thing. Louis reared back, panicked, as Agonistes arrived at the dais, where he tugged insistently at the hem of the king's gown and seemed about to climb up his legs, hand over filthy hand.

'Grant me the solace of joint prayer on the matter of the monster, I beseech you. Only then may I be of greater use to you, and the kingdom of France, in uncovering the Lord's intentions for this creature.'

Stifled by the stench wafting upwards, Louis covered his mouth and nose with one hand and waved urgently for the guard to escort Agonistes from his presence. Instantly, the monk was engulfed by a tide of armed men and half dragged, half shoved from the king's sight. Louis shuddered with relief and sucked clean, untainted air deep into his lungs.

The king was convinced that the monk conveyed God's thoughts directly to him, the Lord's own mortal deputy on Earth, but sometimes the stench of the man encouraged a certain confusion in his mind. Why must holiness equate with dirt? The Bible did not speak of the Lord being filthy. What if Agonistes were not a sanctified messenger at all, merely a madman?

The king's musings were interrupted by the arrival of more guards, with a gaunt black crow in their midst: Olivier le Dain. The escort surged away and the Presence chamber doors swung closed. Bowing, le Dain advanced cautiously towards the king until he stood at the foot of the dais.

'Well?' The king sounded dangerously testy.

Le Dain gulped. 'We have found it, Your Majesty.' Unnerved by a basilisk glare, le Dain sank quickly to his knees.

'And?'

'It has been brought here, to the palace. Its mother also.'

'Very well.' Louis waved a hand and le Dain took this for an instruction. On his feet again, he backed the entire length of the room at speed, bowing so deeply from time to time that the crown of his head touched the floor. An amused smile stretched the wizened muscles of the king's face as he watched le Dain scuttle away. He rarely smiled, certainly not at le Dain.

The barber gagged back the vomit of fear. That terrible smile! Hastily he jerked one of the great doors open as if it weighed no more than a gauze curtain. 'Bring them!' The barber bellowed the order and was comforted by the fear on the faces of the courtiers in the anteroom. Reflected power, like reflected light, could still sear the eyes of the unwary.

A muttering began deep within the crowd and the clotted mass of court functionaries parted in one smooth movement to allow passage to a small frightened girl carrying a large basket.

The courtiers closed in again behind her as she walked forward amongst a guard of men much taller than herself. Decently clad in a woollen high-waisted gown the girl's head was covered in the white linen coif of a married woman. As she was brought closer to le Dain, he saw she was not quite as young as she had seemed at a distance; rather she was sixteen or seventeen, though very small for her age. This was the mother of the monster.

'Let me see it.' Le Dain sounded as remote as the king – slavish imitation of his master was a learned knack from his early days at court – and the girl visibly paled. With trembling hands she placed the basket on the floor and gently drew back the small blanket covering its contents.

For a moment, le Dain was confused. These were two healthy babies that he saw, lying side by side, still somehow asleep amongst the racket, and breathing peacefully. But then the young mother drew the covering down and the full horror was exposed.

Eager courtiers pressed forward to see for themselves what lay in the basket. 'Keep them back!' the barber shouted to the guards, who instantly responded, lowering their pikes.

Was it le Dain's harsh tone, or the outraged protests from some of the greatest grandees in the kingdom, that woke the thing in the basket? It began to wail like any other hungry child, and those who caught a glimpse of the basket's contents told how, miraculously, each of its two faces was as beautiful as an angel's, with curling black hair and eyes bluer than a summer lake.

'Enough,' le Dain ordered. 'Cover this ... thing. The king is waiting.'

The mother bent to the basket and tenderly replaced the covering, whispering half words, as every mother did to her child, as she raised it from the floor. Le Dain noticed dark patches had spread across the bodice of her dress. The child's crying had caused the girl's milk to let down. Unwanted, unexpected, le Dain experienced a rush of pity.

'Here.' He held out his hand, indicating he would carry the basket. For a moment defiance flared in the girl's blue eyes – these, at least, she had successfully bequeathed to her child – but then fear chased hopelessness across her face. Bowing her head she surrendered the basket as her child – or children – screamed inside.

Strangely, as he took the basket from her and rocked it in his arms, the crying stopped and le Dain found himself gazed upon by four blue eyes. Were they – was it – really watching him? Perhaps this was proof of devil-born powers, or was it just the accidental focus of the newborn? Le Dain, himself a father, was unsure. If this was a demonic creature, perhaps it was the former. But having held his own newborn children in his hands, he felt some certainty it was the latter.

Nodding to the door-wards, he motioned for the girl to follow him into the Presence chamber. 'Come. The king is most interested in your monster.'

The girl winced and blushed with shame. She was not used to it yet – being the mother of a minion of darkness.

Joining her hands together protectively over her breasts, an unconsciously touching gesture, the girl hurried after the great official. She longed to cross herself, but was confused. If she was the Devil's creature, perhaps she would be turned to ash by the power of a disgusted God if she sought His comfort and protection?

The king watched the odd party approach with dread and fascination. If this girl was Satan's own infernal Madonna, why did she not look more impressive? She was humble and small and terrified. But perhaps this was a cunning disguise, a glamour?

'Show me.'

Le Dain put the now-silent monster's basket on the lowest step of the dais and signalled for the girl to come forward. She was so frightened it seemed entirely right that she should crawl towards the Presence throne on her knees, the rustle of her dress the loudest noise in that chilly room.

Reaching into the basket, she lifted out her child, wrapping it tenderly in its woollen covering. Once the baby was in her arms, she cuddled it against her chest, without thinking, and the smell of the leaking milk started the two little mouths mewling. Both small heads turned towards her, desperately seeking to suckle. Helpless tears dripped down the mother's face, as, ignoring the cries, she held her child away from her body so the king could inspect what she carried.

'Sit. Show me how you feed it.'

The young woman scrambled to do as she was ordered. Daring to whisper comfort to her baby, she plumped down onto the step and unlaced the front of her dress as fast as she could while both little heads wailed vigorously.

'There now, there now, not long. Here, here it is...'

Modestly, she turned slightly away from Louis de Valois and the crying subsided into urgent snuffles when she placed the body of the baby across her lap and directed one bud-like mouth to one nipple. Then with greater difficulty, she succeeded in offering the other breast to the second head at the same time. Like most healthy babies, this one settled in to nurse vigorously, gulping the milk from the marble white breasts, both heads suckling in rhythmic unison.

It was a sweet sight, despite the poignant oddness of the little pink 'lobster claws' that crept up to rest near the mother's nipples and the added surprise of the third arm, its claw now resting in the valley between the girl's breasts, opening and closing in unison with each suck the two-headed child took.

Peace stole over the face of the harried girl as she watched her baby feed with all the tenderness any new mother feels. Gently, she rearranged the child's covering, making certain the strange little thing was warm.

The king beckoned le Dain forward until the man stood beside the Presence chair. He found himself whispering when he spoke.

'What is it, do you think?'

Le Dain, as fascinated as the king, replied without thinking, 'God alone knows.'

Louis looked at his advisor sharply. 'God, you think? Not...?' He would not say the name, instead crossing himself and fervently kissing a little silk bag of holy bones hanging around his neck.

'Should it be killed?' the king continued.

The girl heard him and her eyes were sudden terrified saucers, the pupils so huge the blue was drowned. Simultaneously, the child opened both mouths and screamed. Had it heard the king also?

The two men looked at each other fearfully as, with shaking fingers, the girl persuaded first one head, and then the other, to reattach itself to her nipples. Four small eyes closed as the mouths suckled once more, and the mother rocked back and forth, back and forth. To comfort her baby. Or herself.

'Perhaps, Your Majesty, this ... child is a symbol?' Le Dain heard his own words with surprise. He'd called it a child.

The king nodded thoughtfully as he gazed at the domestic scene in front of him. 'The war. God has sent us a sign about the English war. I see that now.'

Le Dain smiled with relief at his master. 'I am certain you are right, Your Majesty.' Nodding vigorously, always the courtier, he bowed deeply. 'I, of course, do not have the power to see. But Your Majesty, anointed by God, knows well those things that are mysteries to the common people.'

The king inclined his head with magisterial gravity, acknowledging the compliment. 'It is very clear, le Dain. See, two heads: this signifies the two kings. Myself and Edward Plantagenet. Three arms: these are the armies that lie between us – the joint army of France and England; the army of Burgundy; and *his* army, the army of York. Two are mighty and one is smaller.' Louis waved to each of the little limbs in turn; the third, attached at the chest, was certainly smaller. 'The army of York – see how powerless it is, trapped between the two others. Also these arms symbolise the three states that are at war: France, England and Burgundy. Burgundy is the smallest arm, of course.'

Le Dain allowed a certain breathless rapture into his voice. 'Of course! And the ... hands?' He had nearly said 'claws'.

The king frowned. This was more testing.

'They are not as mortal hands, it is true...' Each man contemplated the odd little flippers. 'And yet, there is a message here also.'

Unbidden, le Dain dropped to his knees and bowed his head reverently, as if about to receive the host at mass.

Gently, the girl detached one little mouth from her breast. The head's eyes were closed; it was asleep, like any normal baby after a feed. Strangely, the other little head still suckled, its eyes glancing around the room whilst its mouth was busy.

'Yes. The hands are as mighty weapons. See, they have the shape of claws. Claws can snap shut and crush their prey. Now see, also – one head sleeps and the other does not. It is very strange, but this is what God has told me. Behold, the true king anointed by God must never sleep, must never be lulled, or destruction awaits. I am the true King of France. Edward Plantagenet is a usurper! I must be unsleeping. And I will crush my prey, the false king, whilst he sleeps!'

Le Dain had never heard Louis so elated and had certainly never heard him happy before. He was awed. This was a miraculous day. He forbore to point out that the likelihood of Edward Plantagenet actually sleeping at this time of national danger to his realm was unlikely.

Louis de Valois stood and pointed at the girl below him. Instinctively, she huddled herself over her child, shielding its tiny body from the gaze of the king.

'Do not fear, girl. Your child is a sign from God! It will be protected by your king, for it has much to teach us.'

Louis waved his hand over the girl's head, which le Dain took to mean dismissal of them both. He clapped his hands and suppressed a spasm of irritation as the girl looked up at him fearfully, like a sheep about to be slaughtered but accepting of its fate. Bowing, he backed down the steps of the dais as quickly as he could and hissed, 'Be quick.'

Trying to oblige, the girl handed him the child as she fumbled with the lacings of her dress. This informal, human moment was an affront to the dignity of the advisor, but the palpable gratitude of the girl salved his dignity. She was really very pretty, and quite plainly she saw him as her saviour and the saviour of her child. That might be useful. A symbol always had value and he would control access to this particular symbol. And its mother.

Le Dain meditated on this fact as he, the girl and the child approached the door of the Presence chamber, both walking backwards as fast at they could.

The king's voice stopped them. 'What is the sex?'

The girl looked at the chamberlain in mute terror. He smiled as kindly as a parent, which confused her, though hope sparked in her eyes.

'It is a girl, Your Majesty,' she whispered.

The king looked puzzled. 'A girl? A girl...' Then enlightenment brightened his eyes. 'Ah, I see. A girl: the weaker sex. Yes! The army of God will subdue that which is weaker. An excellent omen for our cousin, Queen Margaret of England. This is very clear!'

'But, this is marvellous, Lord King. A wonder!' cried le Dain. 'Perhaps I may repeat these revelations – to comfort the court, and the country?'

The king nodded in gracious assent. 'Yes. Comfort my people. Let it be published throughout the realm. And guard this child and her mother well. There is much for us to ponder upon. God wishes this child to flourish as a marvel for us all. She shall be called Louisa. That is our command.'

Overwhelmed, the girl, previously Satan's minion, fell to her knees and knocked her head on the floor with gratitude. When she finally looked up, dazed, she saw a speculative light in the advisor's eye as he gazed down upon her swollen breasts. Tentatively, she smiled at her new protector as he picked up the basket that contained her daughter. Slow certainty replaced fear. She would live. And so would her child. And her husband would just have to get used to the situation.

Their two-headed monster might prove a blessing after all.

## Chapter Forty-Nine

'But how much aid and support will Duke Charles give the king?'

It was late and at Blessing House in London – Mathew Cuttifer's home in the capital – the fire in the solar was burning low. Mathew, Lady Margaret and Anne had spent the night discussing the situation in Burgundy but Anne was so weary it was hard to focus on the conversation. She blinked and rubbed her eyes; it felt as if there were sand beneath her lids.

'I'm sorry, Sir Mathew, but all I know is that the duke met with the king on the day after the Christ-mass. And Ed – the king was hopeful that he would get what he needed. We left in a hurry you see and...' The girl vainly tried to stifle a yawn.

Lady Margaret stood up decisively. 'Mathew, we can continue this conversation in the morning. Anne is exhausted. She's been on that boat for days, what with the contrary winds.'

'Ship, my dear. Your ship.' Mathew liked people to get their facts right.

Margaret flashed him a glance. 'Anne needs sleep more than correct terminology, Mathew. We can talk again tomorrow. At least she's safe and so is little Edward. Everything else is of secondary concern.'

'And Leif.' Anne stood slowly, yearning to stretch the ache from her bones but feeling she must suppress the urge. It was odd. Automatic respect for her former master and mistress took her back to the constrained role of servant; the body-maid she'd once been in this very room. She must be tired to be haunted by such thoughts.

'Leif?' Mathew looked confused.

'Leif's safe also. As is the *Lady Margaret*. Thank God.'

Margaret put her arm around Anne's waist. 'Leif served you well, my dear. And he has served the house of Cuttifer most faithfully also.'

'About time he did some actual work!' Mathew muttered, but he caught his wife's eye and closed his mouth with an audible snap. He had a somewhat different view of Leif's service to Anne.

'Do not be angry with Leif, Sir Mathew. He was very torn between his duty to you and getting little Edward, Deborah and me back to London alive.' There was much else Anne could have said, but did not.

'And we're very glad he did, but now it's time for bed. I'll find Jassy – she's given you our newest chamber. You'll like it: it's big and it's even got a fireplace. No more smoky braziers in this house! Deborah and the child are there now, I think. Stay here, Anne. I'll return in a moment.'

Lady Margaret hurried out of the solar but not before casting one more glance at her husband. *Be nice* said that look. *Be kind.*

Mathew cleared his throat. 'Leif did well, in the end. And I'm glad to have him back. There is much to do with our ships and not much time. I want them taken out of the pool and around to Bristol. If the rebels get as far as London, they'll loot and burn everything as they come – on land and on water.'

Anne said nothing. Leif had said a hasty goodbye earlier this evening and hurried away to do Sir Mathew's bidding. He'd caught Anne's glance just once before he left, but she'd lowered her eyes from his, shaken by the intensity of his gaze. Now he was gone and she felt hollow.

Mathew interrupted her brooding thoughts. 'Aren't you hungry at all, Lady Anne? You must eat.' There was food placed on a coffer but Anne had eaten almost nothing throughout the evening. 'It's not good to go to bed on an empty stomach. Let me give you a little of the egg cream at least? You'll sleep well on that.'

He was as anxious as an old hen; Anne did that to him, even now. He well remembered when she'd come as a servant to this house all those years ago; just an ordinary girl – but with an extraordinary smile and something different about her manner. Different, alright. To think they'd harboured a princess – baseborn, but still the daughter of a king – under their roof and not known it. And she'd once been their servant!

'Lady Anne?'

She was staring into the fire, remembering, just as he had, when first she'd come to this place. If she looked at the door, it seemed it would open at any moment and there would be Piers, Mathew's son. She shivered as the pictures forced themselves behind her eyes. He'd tried to rape her, tried to... She shook her head. She would not allow that dark night back into her mind.

Anne looked at her former master and smiled warmly. 'After all this time, I'd so much rather you called me by my name. It was good enough for all in this house once...'

Mathew picked up one of Anne's hands and kissed it in the gallant French manner. 'Each wish of yours is my pleasure and command.'

'Bravely said, master. Bravely said.'

Mathew smiled at Anne a little ruefully. 'Do you know, child, I think it most unlikely that any man will be your master ever again. Not even the king.'

Anne was silent for a moment as she gazed at her good and kind friend. Then she kissed him gently on the cheek. Her breath was sweet. Mathew resisted the urge to touch the spot where her lips had been.

'I am so grateful to you, and to Lady Margaret, Master Mathew. You're my real family, with Deborah and little Edward. I owe you much; so much it will be very hard to repay even a fraction of what you are due. And now this. Sanctuary.'

The old man felt the unexpected prick of tears and was astonished by the rush of feeling. He cleared his throat noisily.

'I am due nothing. And this is certainly your sanctuary until you choose to go elsewhere. It has pleased Our Saviour to give some part of your welfare into my keeping. I am honoured by His trust in me. You are important to our king. You will always be important to me and mine.'

'Amen to that, husband. And now it is time for rest. Come, Anne, your bed has been warmed.' Lady Margaret had returned with Mathew's last words and was holding out her hand to Anne, as a mother to a daughter, happy her child was warm and safe.

Now it was Anne's turn to swallow tears as Mathew and Margaret smiled at her together.

'Goodnight, child. Tomorrow we will speak of the future. For now you are safe with us. Sleep without dreams.'

And as Anne lay warm in her lavender-smelling bed and listened to the wind hunt around the buttresses and battlements of the old house, in the moments before velvet oblivion took her, she said a prayer.

*Keep him safe also, Mother Keep him safe...*

But she saw two men in her dreams that night. Edward.

And Leif.

'But where is he now?'

Elizabeth Wydeville was pacing the Jerusalem

chamber, up and back, up and back, as the rain beat hard against the black windows. It was the coldest hour of the night but she could not sleep. Sometimes, she felt as if she would never sleep again.

'Calm yourself, daughter. This will not be good for the milk, or the child when you feed him.'

The queen rounded on her mother. 'Calm? How should I be calm? My son does not need me calm, he needs me to be *Queen of England* so that *he* can be acknowledged as who he is, the rightful Prince of Wales instead of that Anjou woman's bastard. We've heard nothing for days and days, mother. *I must know where the king is!*'

Jacquetta winced; it was remarkable that such a volume of sound had its source in such a slender woman. She sat back from her embroidery frame with a smothered sigh and rubbed her temples, forcing herself to speak softly. One of them had to remain calm.

'Very well, let us review what we *do* know, shall we?'

Elizabeth made a sound between a bark and sob and sat abruptly in one of the two chairs the vast chamber contained. It was a decidedly old-fashioned piece of furniture and unforgiving, made of sturdy oak with a very straight back. She wriggled to get comfortable and waved her hand. Perhaps that was agreement. Of sorts.

Her mother held up a finger. 'One. We know that Charles has given the king money.'

'Yes, but how much – and what about the ships and–'

'Do not interrupt! I repeat. One. Edward has

money. A substantial sum: enough to bring men to him and buy armaments. Two. Charles is fitting out ships for him at Veere. Three. The English merchants in Brugge are supporting him. That much is certain – your brother Rivers has told us so. And, four. Well, it is clear the tide is turning with the barons here at home. *And* Clarence.'

'Clarence! I swear, if I should meet that man again I'll have him flayed and–'

Jacquetta was implacable. 'That would be very foolish. Edward needs Clarence. If the duke returns to your husband, he'll bring many of Warwick's supporters with him and the rest of the waverers will begin to turn again in our favour. For all his foolishness, Clarence can see what's happening. His chance at the throne has gone.'

Elizabeth stared mutinously into the fire, biting at the edge of one finger. Jacquetta sighed.

'Ah, daughter, daughter, we need them all. Each one of them. Even Clarence. When Edward lands–'

'*If* Edward lands,' the queen muttered.

'*When* the king returns, he must pull the country together again, unify the lords and the warring factions. He's the only one who can. The barons are uneasy; they know this truce between Warwick and Margaret can't last. Enmity that deep doesn't just disappear. No, they're just waiting now, you'll see. They'll follow Edward, not Warwick and Margaret, once he's back in the country because of your son; the dynasty is safe now. And no one truly wants the French queen back; they're all too frightened of what she'll do.'

Elizabeth shuddered at the word 'queen'. 'But

Warwick's married *his* daughter to *her* son! You know that's true. Anne Neville could reign in this country one day. *Anne Neville!*'

Jacquetta shook her head. 'Really, Elizabeth, you were not brought up to be so poor-spirited. This is a marriage of convenience only. It will mean nothing at all when Edward returns; it won't be worth even this.' The duchess held up a hank of red embroidery silk. 'Expensive, decorative but, in the end, only embroidery, nothing of substance. You'll see. Have faith.'

Elizabeth leaned forward and poked savagely at the fire. The logs collapsed and threatened to roll out onto the flagged hearth. The queen kicked at them just in time. Flushed from her exertions she plumped back into the chair, staring moodily into the flames. Then her expression lightened.

'I wonder if they burned Anne de Bohun, in the end? At least *that* was a bit of good news: the monk denouncing her on Christ-mass day. Just what she deserved. It must have been so very embarrassing. Rivers was quite naughty about it all when he wrote.' She giggled and flashed a glance at her mother. 'I always *thought* she was a witch, you know.'

Jacquetta's tone was caustic. 'Unlike you, you mean? Or me.'

Elizabeth was shocked. 'Mother, how can you say such things? It's dangerous.'

And then she laughed, long and loud. 'Gone. She's really, truly gone. At *last*. Gone for good!'

# Chapter Fifty

Herrard Great Hall. It had only been a name, something she'd seen written on parchment, but now, at last, as the battlements rose up from behind the trees, she understood. Anne de Bohun had come home, truly home. To her mother's house. The house she had never seen.

It was late February of the year of our Lord 1471 and it was fiercely cold, yet in this afternoon, as the sun began its slide to the west, long, pale light silvered the black trees and the surface of the road sparkled. It was ice, but it looked like diamonds.

She'd not known, not understood, how much she missed the wooded depths of England since she'd been away, but as Anne sat in the body of the cart behind the yoked oxen, the clean smell of the winter forest restored her soul to childhood.

'Edward! Wake up. Look. We're home. We've truly come home.'

Anne de Bohun's son, worn out by the excitement of their long journey from London, was cuddled up asleep in a nest of rugs behind Anne's plank seat. He'd hated to miss even a moment because each turn in the track brought places and sights and sounds he'd never experienced before, but, this late in the day, the wayfaring had finally made him drowsy. Now he was awake in an instant. 'What?' He sat upright, flushed from sleep, as the wagon lurched to a stop.

Anne climbed down and stood on the hard roadway beside the bullocks' heads. She turned back to look at little Edward.

'Come with me. We should see this together. Just the three of us. Deborah?'

During the long miles that Anne and her party had covered since first light, Deborah too had fallen asleep, slumped against and between piled-up coffers in the second cart. She startled awake, finding her low-crowned henin askew over one eye with its sarcenet veil nearly blinding the other.

The little boy, scrambling down into his mother's arms, laughed. 'Deborah looks funny!'

'It's very rude to laugh at old ladies. There'll be terrible, terrible trouble and you'll have seven years' bad luck. Tell him, mistress.'

Deborah's smile belayed the severity of her words as Anne helped her down from the dray. The three men that Mathew Cuttifer had supplied to guard the women, the boy and the carts relaxed in their saddles.

Edward giggled; he'd heard such threats before. 'Seven? Bah! I'll be big when I'm seven and I'll chase all the bad luck away!'

The triumphant flourish of a wooden sword by the small but doughty warrior left them in no doubt of his determination in the contest to come. Even the phlegmatic bullock drivers, Wat and Crispin, joined in with the laughter of the Londoners from Blessing House. The men watched the little boy prancing happily between the women as they walked on down the track towards the gap in the trees.

Wat Anderson shifted his aching buttocks on the seatboard of his cart and stretched his arms and shoulders. He yawned and got down into the roadway, scratching.

Crispin too got down from the second dray to stand beside his lead bullock, Davey. Perhaps he should hobble the animals if they were to wait for a while? He patted the placid creature between the ears. 'Hungry, Davey-boy? So am I. Anything to eat, Ned?'

Ned was one of Mathew Cuttifer's town servants. He sighed as he slung a leg over the pommel of his saddle and jumped down to the roadway, joining his mates. 'There's ale, but we finished the bannock a while back.'

He unhooked a leather bottle from his saddle-bow and turned to the others, waving the flask. Ale, even one small flask amongst several, was a powerful pleasure at the end of a hard, cold journey. A good swallow each was all they got, but in winter men are opportunists. The big old house at the end of the road would have more, much more – cauldrons of it, surely? Home-brewed ale. And, perhaps if they were lucky, a pretty alewife?

Good ale, a pretty face to look at and clean hands to serve it up in a nice warm kitchen – these four made up for much. The men stamped their feet, hoping to shock some blood into their frozen toes. What was keeping their mistress?

'There's no one here. The place is empty. And it's huge.'

The two women and the boy were staring up at the walls of the house in front of them, intimidated. It was mellow stone, to be sure, but the walls were very high. And with castellated tops. There was a dry moat – now a wide, puddled ditch – and the front of the house presented a blank face except for arrow loops and a pair of massive gates.

'I thought it was a hunting lodge?'

Anne nodded slowly. Deborah was right: the king had told her that Herrard Great Hall was a former royal hunting lodge with its own chase. 'Yes. It was. But I think it must have been a fortress once.'

Deborah held out her hand to the little boy. 'Stout walls are no bad thing in these times. Come, Edward, let's explore.'

Chatting loudly to subdue the silence, the two women each held one of Edward's hands and, picking up their skirts, marched across the drawbridge that spanned the moat. Creeper twining through gaps in the boards beneath their feet said it was a long time since anyone had raised or lowered this particular form of defence. Their footsteps echoed beneath them.

Anne felt a sharp tug on her skirt. She looked down at her son.

'How do we get in, Wissy?' he asked.

Anne laughed from nerves, and the oddness of this homecoming. 'Well, we have a key, my darling.'

She thrust a hand into the pocket-bag at her waist and withdrew it holding the biggest key that Edward had ever seen. His eyes widened with astonishment. 'Let me see?'

When she placed it in his hands, the length of the key shaft spanned both the child's palms. It was old and black and cold.

'Let's see if it fits.'

It was hard to find the keyhole in the outer gates – they were massively bound and studded with black iron boltheads in an intricate pattern. Then Anne smiled, relieved. Within the shape of one of the two great gates there was the faint outline of a smaller door: the long slant of the late afternoon light allowed her to see it.

'Ah. See here – there's a little door within the big one. And there's the hole for the key. See?'

It was cleverly disguised, for the hole itself seemed at first glance merely a part of the pattern – the pointed end of a long curling leaf of iron. Once found, the key, massive and cold, slid home easily, but Anne could not engage the mechanism of the lock. She jiggled the key, withdrew it, put it in again and tried once more. Finally, she was rewarded. A satisfying click told her the teeth of the key had married with the workings. It was nearly seized from long disuse and lack of oil, however, turn it did.

'Let's see what's on the other side of our gate, shall we?' Anne spoke loudly. She wanted her voice to be heard by this old house.

Using the key like a handle, pushing and then pulling hard, she found that the door opened outwards, after protesting on its hinges. The new lady of Herrard Great Hall nodded approvingly. It made sense for a door to open outwards, rather than inwards. Harder for invaders to force their way in... *Now, why did I think of that?* Anne shook her head. The watchful atmosphere of this place was getting to her. Ducking her head, she stepped through the opening.

'What can you see, Wissy?' Little Edward had a penetrating whisper and it made Anne laugh as she popped her head back out through the open door.

'Come and see for yourself!'

She disappeared through the door and the child looked doubtful, but then caught Deborah's encouraging smile. He smiled too. 'Here I come!' he shouted, and jumped over the small step at the bottom of the little door, ready to run into this new world. But then he stopped, his mouth a perfect O of astonishment.

Anne was standing beneath a naked oak in the middle of a huge paved space, open to the sky. So ancient, so enormous, its branches reached out like old and comfortable arms to welcome the weary traveller.

'Have you ever seen a better tree for climbing?'

Whooping, the small boy hurtled across to Anne. 'Help me, Wissy. Help me up!'

As Deborah joined them, Anne cupped her hands to boost Edward up to a large burl that stuck out from the massive trunk. From there, Edward could scramble into a natural place for a small boy to sit and survey his kingdom: the junction of two thick branches as they left the central bole of the tree.

'You can sit there for a little while if you like. But don't climb higher, please.'

Edward pouted. 'But it's easy. Very safe, really.' He nodded earnestly.

Anne smiled as he wheedled. 'It's safe to climb while I'm here with you, or Deborah. When you're bigger you can climb by yourself, as much as you like, but not just yet. But from today on, this can be your own tree. We'll make sure our friends all know its name: Edward's tree.'

'Mine? Just for me?' Edward was nearly glowing with happiness.

'Yes, just for you.'

'What do you think of this place, Anne?'

Anne switched her attention from the boy to her foster-mother. 'I'm not sure. It's very quiet. Perhaps, after the life we've had, silence is no bad thing. It's odd that there's no one here, though.'

Deborah shivered. The sun was westering, casting long cold shadows into the central courtyard as it dipped down behind the castellated walls.

'It's long indeed since any soul has lived here. Or that's what I'm thinking.'

Anne cast a speculative glance around her new domain; there was much to see. The forbidding exterior presented a blank face to the world outside, but inside, all around them, on all four sides of the interior central ward, Herrard Great Hall showed itself to be an ancient, well-fortified house. In its own massive way, it was even beautiful in the last light from the red winter sun. It would take time to explore, however, for clearly there were many rooms piled up three and four storeys high on all sides.

'Hello? Is anybody there?' Anne's voice was caught and thrown back at her from the ancient walls of her home.

No one answered.

Anne and Deborah looked at each other. Each repressed what she really wanted to say.

'Very well. There is much to do if we're to sleep warm tonight. We can explore properly in the morning. Deborah, would you go back to the men, please, and ask Wat and Crispin to bring the bullock drays? Meanwhile, I'll open the great doors to let them all through. Edward, come down now, please. We have work to do.'

For once, there was no dispute from Edward. He slid down the trunk, hand over hand, and allowed himself to drop into Anne's arms, before running after Deborah, calling excitedly, 'Wait, Deborah, wait for me!'

Anne hurried back to the great gates after them. Seen from the inside of the courtyard, the house-side, there was no portcullis and the doors themselves – her gates – were easily unbolted. It was just a matter of levering the long iron bar – the width and thickness of a man's forearm, it spanned both doors – up and out of the keepers, and then turning the giant iron ring that lifted the actual latch. She'd expected the doors themselves to be hard to haul open, but when she braced herself to pull the first one back she was surprised that it swung so easily. Deserted as the place seemed to be, someone had kept the hinges of the great doors to Herrard Great Hall well greased. What did that mean?

And then Anne de Bohun surprised herself. She was happy, really consciously happy, and that was something she'd not felt in a long, long time. Questions and uncertainty were for tomorrow; for now she was standing inside the opened doors of her mother's house – her house – and waving their escort and the bullock carts past, into the inner ward. The men were cold and exhausted, as she was also, but it wasn't hard to be cheerful when the world felt so pregnant with possibilities.

'Take the drays over there, Wat. I think there are stables. We'll only unload what we need tonight. You'll see, we'll have everyone settled in no time.'

There were a number of doors, big and little, in each face of the buildings. Anne waved towards the one that was closest as she hurried in front of the men.

This door was not locked and it too swung open easily. Behind it was a range of rooms, each opening out into the next and all mostly empty, though one or two contained wooden racks on which were placed bulging sacks that had been neatly sewn closed.

'Storerooms. Excellent. Produce from our own lands? Wat, Ned, can you help the men and Deborah stack everything we need from the drays here for the moment? I'm going to look for the kitchens.'

Leaving Deborah to supervise the men, noisily seconded by her small, excited son, Anne passed through one empty room and into another. This one had a large stone sink. *The scullery*, thought Anne. *The kitchen must be close.*

A flagged passageway led her to another door, over-wide and studded with iron nailheads. Lifting the latch, Anne pushed it open and found what she was looking for.

The kitchen was vast – far larger than that of her farmhouse in Brugge and nearly as big as Mathew Cuttifer's kitchen at Blessing House in London. Three fire mouths lined one wall – the smallest closed in to make an oven, the others big enough to roast an ox.

Anne shivered. The kitchen was cold and smelled of old smoke. Time to bring life and human noise back to these empty rooms.

'It's nearly dark. Here, take this. I thought moving in deserved it.' Deborah had brought light – a precious wax candle for Anne and an oil lamp for herself.

'Deborah, I think we should all be in here tonight. We can sleep by the fire. We can feed everyone here, and it will be warm.'

Her foster-mother nodded and bustled back the way she'd come, calling out, 'Wat, Crispin, Ned, my mistress wants the trestle board here, in the kitchen. And whilst you're about it, I'd like the greatest of the coffers also. It has our pans in it and my big three-legged pot. The black one...'

Grumbling from the men – no alewife, it seemed, and no house ale either in this deserted place – and the excited yells of one small boy came distantly to Anne. She had questions, so many of them, chaotic questions bred by exhaustion.

She closed her eyes for a moment and found herself praying. 'Those who were here, those who are here now, help me. This is my mother's house, but it's my home too, and the home of my son. Bless us. Keep us safe. Watch over us and give us rest in this night to come. I ask this in the name of the Mother of us all.'

Opening her eyes, she held her candle high. There was a small window pierced through the thickness of the wall and Anne set the light down on its ledge. The flame was doubled by the panes of rare green glass and she felt better. She lit straw from the candle and thrust the burning wisps into a quickly assembled nest of oak twigs on the hearth. They caught satisfyingly and light bloomed from the fireplace, banishing shadows into the corners of the room as Deborah and the men brought more of their goods into the kitchen.

'Things could be worse, mistress. At least this place has been swept regularly and I think the roof's sound. I can't smell damp either.' Deborah was loudly cheerful for the men's benefit.

'Yes, it does seem sound, this house. Food, warmth and sleep is all we need now and then we will see...'

'See what, Wissy?'

Anne smiled at the small boy proudly staggering into the kitchen under the weight of his own possessions.

'Why, we shall see where all the people are, Edward. They can't be very far away.'

Anne's eyes met Deborah's over little Edward's head.

Let it be that their neighbours were friends.

## Chapter Fifty-One

A cold coming and a wild landfall at Ravenspur was all that Edward Plantagenet had when he landed on the Yorkshire coast in the howling midst of the storm that had scattered his ships.

It was mid-March and in this bleak part of the

world – the estuary behind the hook at the mouth of the Humber – there was little habitation to observe the return of the previous king. The nuns at the small, prosperous convent of Our Lady of the Sands heard the news of the arrival first, and that was only because Beck, their idiot carter, whipped his one poor horse through the gate of the convent, gobbling, 'Men! Horses and men! And boats. Run, sisters, run. The Norsemen, the Norsemen! They've come back!'

Beck upset the geese with all his shouting and so frightened the sister sacrist that she rang the bell with all her strength for over an hour after matins, vainly hoping to warn the countryside around.

Terror, inflamed by the bell, propelled the other sisters of Our Lady of the Sands in a flapping huddle to their Mother Superior as she prayed in the chapel, disturbing the air of that holy place with a rising and scandalous babble.

'Mother, Mother, what shall we do? Can it really be the Norsemen?'

Mother Elinor, abbess of the convent, was as alarmed as her sisters, yet, for their sakes, would not permit them to see her panic.

'Do? We must pray, of course. But first, bar the gates with all we have that's heavy!'

Edward heard the wild clamour of the distant bell and saw where the sound came from – a cluster of grey buildings surrounded by a stout wall. He was being rowed ashore, with William Hastings, from the *Anthony*, his borrowed flagship now moored inside the wide mouth of the river. The high wind was dropping and the ship rode easily at anchor, in contrast to the bucking, gut-churning ride they'd had when she'd crossed the treacherous bar beneath Spurn Point.

'Home, William. We're home.'

Edward Plantagenet jumped out of the skiff into the freezing shallows before their little boat touched land; wading to shore, he dropped to his knees and kissed the kelp-strewn tidal mud. It could have been an absurd gesture, but Hastings, a court-raised cynic, was unexpectedly moved as he joined his master.

'Yes, Your Majesty. Home.'

'What now, Hastings? Do we wait?'

Hastings, regretting his wet boots – they'd take more than a day to dry in this God-cursed weather – managed a cheerful nod. 'I think we do, liege. The wind is turning. It will bring most of the others to us in time.'

Both men turned to survey the turbulent sea beyond the estuary mouth. They could see a straggle of sails in the far distance – a good number of them, though many of their ships had been beaten up the coast, away from the river's entrance.

'Richard's there, I think. And Rivers. The tallest ones, with the pennants?'

Hastings counted out loud. 'Three, four, five, six … ten. Fifteen, sixteen…' He turned to the king and crossed himself. 'More than twenty here, Your Majesty. Most of the others will make it as well, I think, if the wind and tide stay our friends.'

Edward knelt again and held up the pommel of his sword; it made a cross against the low, dark sky. The wind, whipping off the sea, almost took his words but Hastings heard enough as he knelt beside his friend and master.

'We swear on this, our father's sword, that we will take back the kingdom and restore order and prosperity to our people. And this time, with your favour, King of Heaven, none shall ever unseat us again. We thank you also, Lord Jesus, for the help and support of Charles, Duke of Burgundy and of our sister, the duchess his wife, and also for the aid of the English merchants in Brugge. We salute the courage of the English captains, John Lyster and Stephen Driver, who brought their ships to us in Flushynge. And may you bless Henry of Borselle, Lord of Vere, who provided his great ship, the *Anthony*, so that we might return to our kingdom. And for all who have befriended our cause in these last months, not least Lady Anne de Bohun, we give thanks to you. These, my friends, will have cause to be grateful when we have been restored to our own as your anointed servant. So help us, Lord God and Father.'

'Amen.' William Hastings raised his brows at the mention of Anne de Bohun, but nevertheless crossed himself with complete conviction. God was with them now, he was certain of it.

Standing in the bell loft of the chapel, the highest vantage point the convent possessed, Mother Elinor strained her eyes looking into the distance. She could just make out the two kneeling figures and saw the flash as the sword was held up.

'Sister Bertha?'

'Yes, Mother?' The smaller sister sacrist was halfway up the ladder, holding onto the abbess's ankles to steady her.

'They're not heathens! Blessed Mary, we thank you for this at least. Yet they have a fleet at their back. This is certainly invasion! We must keep the bell tolling, Sister.'

The two nuns swapped places on the ladder with difficulty and Sister Bertha took up her stance beside the bell once more. The first mighty clang filled both their heads with so much noise that it hurt. Bertha knew she'd be dizzy and deaf for days to come but offered up her suffering to God with a glad heart. *For you, and for my sisters, Lord, I perform this task. For you and for my sisters...*

Mother Elinor, too, understood her duty. She hurried out into the muddy yard surrounding the chapel. Her nuns were milling around helplessly as if they had, in truth, become sheep and she the shepherd.

'Sisters, sisters, into the chapel now. And on your knees before God in His mercy.'

Hastings frowned as he brushed river sand from his knees. The sound of the distant bell came and went on the wind; whomever was ringing the peal was determined to give good service. 'Well, if there are souls to hear in this deserted place, they've certainly been warned of our arrival now. Should we silence the bell, lord?'

Edward shook his head. 'Let the word of our return spread. It has to start somewhere. But I will not have my men sack even one barn, one byre, let alone a church. We return in peace. For the moment.'

The king slid his sword back into its scabbard,

the cold shiver of steel against steel contradicting his pious hope. He shaded his eyes, looking into the distance. 'The north first. And then London. We have much to do.'

Edward opened his arms to the wind from the sea. Energy flushed through his body like potent wine. Striding back to the water's edge, he waved his hat back and forth in welcome as ship after ship ran the bar and the rip at the river's mouth to enter the calmer waters of the estuary.

His brother's ship was the first to anchor and he could see Richard in the sterncastle, surrounded by a compact knot of men. One of them was waving his hat in a wide arc, determined to attract the king's attention. Edward's lips quirked. Julian de Plassy! The man was indestructible. How ironic that a French outlaw and his band of enthusiastic cut-throats would play a part taking the English throne back from a French queen.

In the distance, the bell ceased. A moment later, women's voices came to them faintly; they were singing the Miserere. Edward listened attentively. The women behind those high walls would be terrified by his arrival and that of the ships behind him.

'Hastings, I want that convent left alone. If any man attempts an outrage against that place, you will hang him immediately, so that all can see. Let that word go out to the men as they land. We come with God's support, and all his servants are safe in this country, under my rule.'

They were a long way from London, but they would begin here, today. He'd left with twenty men at his back. He was returning with two thousand, and half of those were Flemings – plus a handful of French desperadoes.

But they would be enough. They would certainly be enough.

## Chapter Fifty-Two

'We have a cow.'

Anne sat up in her great bed, one of the few pieces of furniture she'd retained from her farm, which, for the moment, she shared with Edward and Deborah. She rubbed her eyes briskly, banishing the rags of dreams. 'How wonderful! Where did it come from?'

Deborah wiped her hands on a sacking apron and sat down. She'd been up since before dawn and her face was flushed from cold air and hard work.

'Wandering in the old orchard. I heard her calling. Very distressed; udders this big, poor thing.' Deborah held her hands wide, shaking her head. 'But I've milked her now. And do you want the good news?'

Anne laughed happily. 'Yes, please!'

'She's yielded buckets and buckets. It's all settling in the creamery. We'll have enough to make butter!'

Anne closed her eyes dreamily. Butter! How long since she'd tasted real, home-made butter? But then she frowned. 'I don't understand. She should have been dried off long ago, shouldn't she? And where did she come from?'

Deborah got up briskly. 'I, for one, am not questioning God's bounty. She's certainly not wild – she followed me when I called, very eager to be milked. And, best of all, I suspect our fine new friend is pregnant; either that or she has the greatest case of bloat *I've* ever seen. I think her calf will be born very soon, to our good fortune. And that's what I've called her: Fortuna. She is an omen. We are meant to stay here.'

Anne threw the covers back and jumped down, shivering as she searched for her working clothes. 'I do not doubt that, dear mother. But there is so much to do. We must send the men back to Sir Mathew very soon, I think. They've done well in helping us set this place to rights, but we must have our own assistance now. It's time to visit our village.'

Deborah helped her daughter lace the back of her kirtle. Normally Anne was fastidious about washing in the morning, but there was so much to do, that would come later today.

'I'll just see how the food's going in the kitchen. I'm famished and I should think the men are also.'

Anne slipped stockinged feet into willow-wood clogs. 'I'm grateful that Fortuna has arrived in our lives, but perhaps we can ask for information in the village? Someone must own her...'

Wincanton the Less was a very small place. A hamlet rather than a village, and even that description flattered reality.

*But it's* my *hamlet.*

392

The thought came to Anne unbidden as she and Deborah walked, unannounced, down the one broad street towards the common land, the focus around which most of the neglected little houses were clustered. Edward was running ahead of the two women, a stick in his hand, which he whirled and threw and ran after, shouting. At least he was carefree.

Anne was not. She'd been expecting more: this looked a grindingly poor place and it was now her responsibility. She owned this collection of buildings and, for all she knew, perhaps the people as well.

'Wissy, Wissy, look! Ducks. Come here!'

Edward had reached the common land and the pond that lay near one end of it and was lying on the bank beside it, trying to coax a duckling to come closer to his outstretched hand.

'Be careful, child!' Deborah hurried ahead of Anne as she saw Edward wriggle ever closer to the water. She reached him at the last moment; a large handful of the cloth of his shirt just prevented Anne's son meeting the duckling at very close quarters indeed.

'You scared him away!' Edward was indignant. 'Not fair!'

'Hush now, child. We don't want folk here thinking Lady Anne has a rude boy for a nephew.'

'Not rude. Just. Not. HAPPY!'

The decoration of pond weed on his face was a keenly felt assault to Edward's dignity, but his mutinous expression was somehow so charming that Anne couldn't help herself. She laughed out loud.

Deborah tried not to join in, but laughter spread faster than any disease and soon even Edward was giggling, pond weed and injured dignity no match for fun.

It was good to laugh after all the tension of the last days, the last months. Anne closed her eyes for a moment. She'd fled Brugge and now run far from London – with Mathew Cuttifer's help – and here she was in this world-deserted spot. Would it be far enough? Could she build a life here?

Anne sensed another presence and opened her eyes. In front of her was a girl. She was tiny and dressed in a much-patched short kirtle, so old and faded it had lost all colour and was now mealy earth-brown. Bare feet, white with cold, an apron made from sacking and stick-thin legs told the story of this place.

'Who are you, child?' Anne asked, but was met with silence.

'Well, if you will not tell me your name, you shall know mine. Anne. My name is Anne de Bohun.'

The child's mouth fell open from shock and she whirled away, running and yelling, 'Mam, Mam, she's here! Mam! *MAM!*'

The child had reached the nearest cottage and was heaving open the door as Anne stood up. 'They know about us?'

Deborah joined her, dusting down her dress. 'It's a little place and we've been here for a few days now.'

The two women glanced at each other and Anne reached down to help Edward to his feet. 'Let's make you respectable, Edward. Have to look tidy to meet our neighbours.' Automatically she brushed Edward's shirt free of grass seeds and twigs and hauled up his britches, retying a couple of the points that had come loose. She felt oddly calm, no trace of the nervousness that had sat on her chest this morning when she woke.

Anxiety. She was always anxious before a big change in her life. Old men with arthritis ached with a coming storm. She ached with a sense of the future. She'd learned to trust that, though often it frightened her. But she felt no fear now. That was a comfort.

As she smoothed her own skirts, out of the corner of her eye Anne could see a small crowd of people gathering in front of the cottage the child had run to. She turned to face them and smiled confidently.

'Shall we go to them?' Deborah's voice was a murmur.

Anne shook her head and held more tightly onto the hand of her now silent son. 'Let them come to us.'

In her heart, Anne de Bohun understood the importance of these first few moments. This was her village, these were her people. Without forcing an appearance of authority, it was her task to give them faith in her. That meant playing a role, the role of chatelaine. It was why she had dressed so carefully this morning in her third best dress: light wool dyed a dense, expensive blue. Sober, discreet. The clothes of a lady, despite the fact she'd walked into the village, not ridden.

For a moment it seemed there was an uncertain stand-off and it took all Anne's nerve to stand there, waiting patiently, before, in a straggle, the small group – women and children and two old men – at last ventured closer. She was reminded of half-tame birds who took some time to hop to the outstretched hand once it was offered.

'Mistress?' One of the old men had made his way to the front of the group and pulled a greasy leather cap off his head as he spoke.

Anne bowed her head graciously, smiling. 'I am Anne de Bohun. And yes, I am living at Herrard Great Hall now. I am happy to be home.'

A sigh passed through the little group. Up the back, a child cried; the whimper of a very young baby. Anne smiled more broadly. 'May I see the little one?'

Heads turned towards the girl who stood at the back of the small crowd. She blushed and half turned her body away so that Anne would be spared the sight of the baby now attached to her breast and tugging fretfully at the nipple.

'Show her, go on.'

'Yes, let her see. Let the lady see the boy.'

A movement, a turning of each of the bodies, and the girl was propelled forward until she stood within Anne's touching distance. Anne was moved by the fear on her face as, tremulously, the girl held out her tiny baby for inspection. Somehow, Anne kept smiling, holding sudden tears in check at the sight of the starving baby.

'He's a handsome boy, your son.'

Huge eyes inspected Anne from that wizened little face. It was true. He might grow to be a good-looking man, if he survived. His child-like mother blushed and bobbed her head down to her baby, embarrassed but pleased. She was barely as tall as Anne's shoulder and so thin the line of her ribs could be seen beneath her ragged dress. Her tiny stature spoke of long, hard times.

'Will you be here long, mistress?'

This time, the voice came from the middle of the group. Anne located the speaker – a thin woman with few teeth and a hard face. The tone was insolent, almost sneering.

Anne responded calmly, 'I don't know your name, dame?'

'Meggan is my name. But names, yours and mine, don't answer my question.'

The crowd drew breath audibly and shuffled. The old man looked embarrassed.

'Now, Meggan, it's no business of yours what the lady does.'

Anne smiled. 'I am happy to answer, Master...?' Offering the honorific, she nodded encouragingly and he responded.

'Will. Used to be Long Will once.' He drew himself up as he said it and Anne could see he'd been a tall man but was now shrunken. Bad seasons and old age had robbed him of much, including his teeth.

'Master Will, and you, Dame Meggan – all of you – please let your families know that I have returned to my mother's house. She never lived here but I think of it as her home. It is our home now.' Anne put her arm around Edward and nodded towards Deborah. 'This is my nephew, Edward. And Dame Deborah, my housekeeper. We are getting ourselves settled but I will need help. Help from all of you, I think.'

'Oh yes?' Again, that truculent tone from Meggan but this time she was shooshed by the crowd, bending towards Anne to hear each word she spoke. 'And will you pay us then?'

Long Will frowned at Meggan's truculence. 'I'm sorry, lady, but it's been very hard here for two seasons. The harvest failed last year and, well ... we've need of coin money in this place.'

Anne nodded as she considered what the man had said. Then she smiled. 'This Sunday I should like there to be a mass of thanksgiving for our safe arrival here. Do we have our own priest here in the village?'

There was silence until the little girl who'd been the first to see them spoke. She, like the others, had heard 'our own priest' – Anne including herself amongst them in that way made her brave. 'Priest died. Last summer.'

'Well then, perhaps someone can tell me where the nearest priest lives? Perhaps he might consider giving us a blessing at the Hall? And if he does, please come. I should like to know you all because–'

Meggan shouted out angrily, 'You own us! That's why. We're just beasts to you and your kind. Ox! Horse! Donkey! That's all we are. All we've ever been.'

The rage crumpled into sobs and a woman put her arm around Meggan's bony shoulder, patting and whispering. Meggan's hand went to her mouth, as if to close it up and stop the sobs. A thin hand, a thin face. This was a woman beyond exhaustion. A woman who was starving. Without thought, Anne went to Meggan and grasped her other hand. The skin of the palm and fingers was very rough and dirt was ingrained in every crease.

'Things will change, Dame Meggan. I will see to that. Beginning today.'

She meant it. For a moment only she and Meggan existed in the world, so intense was the focus between them.

Holding the older woman's hand in both of her own, Anne turned to her people and spoke from the heart.

'There is to be a feast tonight for all the village at Herrard Great Hall. Will you spread the word amongst your people? Come this evening, before the light goes from the sky. There will be plenty for all.'

Anne looked into Meggan's eyes. 'Plenty for all, Meggan. That is my pledge to you.'

Deborah caught Anne's glance and shrugged. There *would* be food enough, just, with the supplies they'd brought with them from London and what they'd found stored at the hall. And the two of them would cook it.

Deborah crossed herself, blessing providence for the unexpected gift of the cow. Fortuna, and they, would have a very busy time today if all these mouths were to be fed. All very well being lady of this manor; rather than the people of Wincanton the Less helping their lady, it seemed she must help them to survive first.

Deborah welcomed the thought, and the task. Less time for Anne to brood on the past. Less time to brood on the king.

Now, if only Anne would avoid asking whom the cow belonged to...

# Chapter Fifty-Three

'Can you see him, Edward?'

Edward shaded his eyes against the rising sun with one mailed hand, the light dancing in shards off the polished steel. The morning was dazzling, a hopeful sign after long, dark days.

'Not yet. Yes! There!' Edward stood in his stirrups and waved. Richard scowled.

The brothers were on the Banbury road, surrounded by a good number of their men. Today it was particularly important to appear well-supported; the rest of the Yorkist army had been left outside the walls of Coventry, behind which Warwick was lodged, refusing to come out. It was barely two weeks since they'd landed and, after a slow and difficult start with the northern barons, thousands of men had joined the brothers as they rode south, and more arrived every day.

'Many with him?'

Edward turned to his younger brother. 'A reasonable number. He wants to impress us.'

Richard shrugged and said nothing, his face thunderous.

Edward smiled. 'He's our brother, Richard. He's been stupid. He knows that now.'

'Stupid? Stupid!'

'We need him if we're to–'

'To overcome Warwick. I know, I know. That's all very well, but still...'

In the distance, the party of men with their backs to the light reined in their horses.

'This is important, Richard. Be nice.'

'Nice? He betrayed us. Betrayed *you*. Have you *forgotten* the last six months, Edward?'

The king turned to his younger brother and spoke softly. 'Don't be bitter, Richard. I forget nothing.'

Smiling, Edward Plantagenet settled himself comfortably in his saddle and waited. The king would not be the first to ride forward. This was a moment that would be talked of amongst both sides in the conflict for many days to come. Signs and signals were important.

A moment's impasse, then one man from the other party rode out from the close knot of his companions. He crossed the space between the two groups until he was less than three horse lengths away. He stopped and pushed up his visor.

'Brother! And Richard! How good it is to see you both. Welcome home.' He waved to show he had nothing in his hands.

Richard nearly choked at the cheery tone. 'Edward! You're not going to...'

But the king was, and he did. After handing his sword to the simmering Richard, he nudged his destrier forward until the animal stood shoulder to shoulder with that of his younger brother.

'George. You're looking well. Marriage suits you.' Edward smiled and reached out to clasp his brother's arm; and, doing so, pulled the horses even closer together. The brothers were a hand-span apart. Clarence did not blink. It was a game they'd all played as children: who had the nerve

401

to stare the other down.

'And never better, brother, now that you've returned. I've missed you. Both of you.'

Breathtaking! Edward began to laugh, long and loud. He laughed until he choked and Clarence had to slap him hard on the back. That started Edward off again, and Clarence. And the men around them. But not Richard. He was red with fury.

'Richard, come and say hello to your brother.' The king turned and waved Gloucester forward affectionately.

Richard was never very good at hiding his feelings. His rigid back and dropped visor told the tale.

'Richard, come and give your brother the kiss of peace, as we used to do. I command it.'

Suddenly there was steel in the king's voice and Richard, sulky, did as he was told. He flipped the steel veil up and leaned forward, planting two hasty kisses on his brother's cheeks, then turned away, seeming as if he wanted to spit. Clarence smiled at Richard, lips quirked over exposed teeth; the smile of a dog, or a wolf. Edward slapped both of his brothers hard on their mailed shoulders.

'Family. United again. The way it should be, eh, George?'

'Yes, it's good to be friends again. Welcome home, Richard, as I have already said to our brother, the king.'

There. It was said. Clarence had acknowledged the changing world order. Edward covered a long, deep sigh with a brilliant smile.

'And so, brother, tell me about Warwick. Will

we get him out from behind those walls? Supplies are running very low with my men, perhaps we're best to strike for London. What do you think?'

'Well, Edward, I have the beginnings of a plan, if you'll bear with me whilst I give you some background...'

Richard listened, glowering, as Edward spoke cheerfully with Clarence. Looking at them, one would think this discussion had no more importance than the way the French were tying jesses this year...

'Richard?'

'Yes, Your Majesty?' His youngest brother leaned heavily on the honorific and Edward's lips twitched with amusement.

'This is an excellent meeting between us all, but I swear my belly's rumbling. What say we have a fire lit, here beside the road, and share a cup of hot wine, as brothers should? For old times' sake.'

And shortly many beheld a sight they had never thought to see again. The three sons of the old Duke of York making camp beside the road like companions who'd never been apart.

'What happened at Honfleur, le Dain?'

'Winds, Your Majesty. Contrary winds. The queen left there well provisioned, with all her ships and her son, the Prince of Wales. But a great storm beat them back again and again, and, finally, they returned to port in some disarray. They are there now, waiting for the weather to turn.'

Le Dain shifted from foot to foot. The king was silent. That worried him.

'And the child. The monster. How is it?'

'The baby Louisa is very well, Your Majesty,' le Dain lied stoutly. 'Thriving, in fact.'

This cheered the king. 'Very well. Nothing but a small setback, it seems. Send a despatch to Queen Margaret and let her know that the child lives and is doing well. It will comfort her to know that the Lord is with us still, as she waits. Spring is ever a changeable season.'

Le Dain bowed as deeply as he was able. He had done all he could to make sure that the only news Louis ever heard about his little protégée, Louisa, came from him and was entirely hopeful. In truth, the little monster was sickening. It was feeding less and crying more and its poor mother was distraught. That affected le Dain unaccountably. He'd become fond of them all; more than fond of the girl. Which was strange: he rarely felt affection for anything but dogs.

He dreaded what would happen to France – and to him – if the child died.

'Le Dain!' The barber jerked out of his anxious thoughts. Gallantly, he knelt. 'Your Majesty?'

'What other news? The Earl of March, for instance. Have the English turned him out of the kingdom yet?'

Le Dain swallowed. This was going to be difficult.

'Well, Your Majesty, not exactly...'

## Chapter Fifty-Four

The news from the north was not good for Margaret of Anjou and her champion, the Earl of Warwick. Desperate, those of Warwick's supporters who remained paraded the old king, Henry VI, through the streets of London to show him to the people. It was supposed to be a mighty display of power and confidence by Warwick's adherents, but it didn't work because they got it wrong, seriously wrong.

George Neville, Archbishop of York and brother to Earl Warwick, could feel the city turning against the cause of Lancaster in an almost physical way as he rode through the city's streets beside Henry. It was there in the sullen, closed faces of the Londoners as they hung out of their windows, watching the court party process along beneath them. None called the old king's name or shouted, 'God Bless King Henry'.

Instead, they looked down, almost silent, as the strange old man, who'd been England's king since he was a baby, rode past St Paul's and on towards the Chepe beneath the clustered, leaning houses. George Neville rode alongside the king, holding the old man's hand – a touching, loyal gesture, he thought. It was noted well by sharp, unfriendly eyes. Eyes that did not see it as loyalty but for what it was: the only way to keep Henry reliably in his saddle, so fuddled was his state.

The people gossiped quietly to each other as they watched Henry pass. Their former king was pale as milk and wisps of his white hair flew fine as thistledown in the fresh breeze off the river. *Someone's been keeping him locked up and out of the light*, they said. *Look at his colour – just like a ghost!*

But Henry smiled sweetly at his people, even waved to them as a kindly grandfather might, and that counted for something – some small reminder of the old days. But his eyes wandered this way and that, as restless and vacant as a baby's, and he was poorly dressed in a long stained gown of shabby blue velvet, with not even a decent bit of fur to keep his thin neck warm. That too was noted. The Londoners hated a poor display.

George Neville tried not to wince as he looked at Henry. Haste had undone the purpose of this procession and it could not end too soon for him. They should have taken the time to find the old king something better to wear, they should have brought out more jewels from the Chapel of the Pyx to dazzle the crowd. They should have made poor Henry look more like a king. Should have ... would have ... too late now. Neville could see in their eyes that the Londoners were disappointed and shamed. Henry of Lancaster didn't look like their sovereign lord, no matter how many men rode in front of him shouting out his name and titles and blowing their silver trumpets. 'Make way for Henry, by the Grace of God, King of England and France and Ireland, Lord of...'

This old man's time would shortly be over and all in the streets today knew it; even George

Neville, though he pretended otherwise, fooling none.

The people of London also knew that Edward Plantagenet was close and that fact alone made this sad parading of the past even more upsetting. They'd all heard how Edward had ridden down the country from York, gathering the support of thousands. At this rate there was great hope he'd be in London well ahead of the old queen, Margaret of Anjou, who was still stuck in port on the other side of the Channel.

Londoners had something to look forward to at last, for Edward, their *young* king, would protect them from the old queen and all her fearsome hordes. They were certain of few things in these topsy-turvy days, but they were modestly certain of that.

Then came the moment that most frightened George Neville. One by one the Londoners turned away and closed their windows and their doors; soon the streets were nearly clear of people. The old king didn't seem to notice, but the Archbishop did and his heart squeezed tight in his chest. The Great Wheel was turning once again; he could hear its iron rim grinding...

The mud-flurried herald came through the door of the Jerusalem chamber so fast he skidded on the tiles. Heedless of the damage his filthy boots and spurs were doing to the floor, he knelt at Elizabeth Wydeville's feet, dripping onto the hem of her skirts. For once, she didn't care.

'What word is there? Where is the king now?'

The man was dazed but triumphant. 'Not even

ten leagues from the walls, madame, and he has a great company with him. Many, many supporters.'

'Clarence?'

'Clarence also.'

'Thank you, Lord Jesus. Praise to you, sweet Lord!'

It was a piercing cry of gleeful triumph and Elizabeth Wydeville, once a queen and close to that state again, joined the herald on her knees, mud and all. She crossed herself and crossed herself with such intensity that the happiness on her face could be mistaken for pain. That upset her baby son, Edward, who, wailing from fear in his grandmother's arms, had to be taken from the room to find comfort elsewhere.

'Lady Mary, Mother of sorrows, Mother of the Lord Jesus, hear me. Support the king, I beg, in this journey. Bring him here, safe to me, at last, so that he may see our son, the prince.'

'Amen,' intoned Elizabeth's newly arrived confessor, the oily Dominican, Brother Peter. Brother Duckshit they called him – well behind his back, however – so smooth was he. He'd not been seen since last October – 'on retreat' as he'd styled it – but in recent days he'd popped up at the abbey again, declaring God had called him 'back from the wilderness to minister to the queen'.

Elizabeth said nothing, welcomed him back as if his absence had been days, not months. The wind was changing its quarter and this migratory bird was testament to that fact. Loathe him as she did, resent his opportunism as she might, his presence filled her heart with fierce joy. She would deal with Brother Peter later.

Piously, the queen crossed herself for one last time and then a storm of activity was let loose in the holy surrounds of Sanctuary at Westminster Abbey.

'I must dress! Mother! Where are you?'

It seemed to the suave confessor that women erupted as mushrooms might and filled the abbot's noble parlour in a twittering, chattering flurry as Elizabeth Wydeville, heedless of the presence of the priest, began tearing at the plain gown of tawny velvet she'd been wearing whilst praying the morning away with her few women.

Brother Peter, a seasoned courtier, discerned that his presence was no longer required. There would be no more prayers from the ladies today; now Mammon must be served and, with him, primpings of the hair and the person that no righteous priest should witness or condone. Therefore, rather than offend the sight of God with worldly opulence, the retreat of his servant was to be preferred. Silently, the Dominican bowed to the queen and began to back away from the Presence. Elizabeth Wydeville barely noticed.

Poor lady, thought the monk as he left the chaos of the Jerusalem chamber behind him, poor faithful wife! Penelope to Ulysses. Surely the Lord was merciful to reunite this virtuous woman with her noble husband, the anointed king. And yet, as Brother Peter strode on through the abbey, bowing gravely to acquaintances amongst the brothers as they paced together in pairs, contemplating 'Heaven' in the centre of the cloisters, were there not shortly to be *two* anointed kings within London? Could God – would God – allow that?

Brother Peter shook his head. This must be part of the Lord's greater plan, or it would not take place. And it was not for him, a lowly monk, to ponder or question the doings and the will of the Lord God.

'The gold, Your Majesty, or the red?'

Elizabeth Wydeville was stripped to her silk undershift. Her women clustered around, brushing out her hair, swabbing beneath her arms with a sea sponge soaked in rosewater, adding colour to her lips with red geranium petals ground to pulp and mixed with sheep's lanolin and almond oil.

'The white. I want the white damask! Pure, holy, that is how he must see me first.'

Elizabeth Wydeville had worked hard to restore her figure after the birth of this, her sixth child. She had starved herself, resisting even her favourite violet comfits, since there was little else she could control in her life. Blessed by nature, she was one of those women whose body seemed made for children, since it was still supple and pleasing to the eye – supernaturally so, it was whispered.

Elizabeth was now seriously distraught, however, for when the delicate dress of glistening white damask was dropped over her head, it was too tight in the bust and the waist. She'd put on weight. Despair! Catastrophe! How would the king ever reignite his lust for her if she was fat!

'I knew it. I should never have allowed that child suck! What will I do?' The queen began to drive herself into a tantrum, convinced she had become old and ugly in an instant.

Jacquetta attempted, unwisely, to calm her. 'Now, daughter, it is well known that feeding a child strips fat *from* the body. Perhaps you might consider–'

'No! I am the queen, not a cow! I only let the baby have my paps because he will be the king one day, and it seemed right to me that he should know his mother's milk, if only for a time. But now, what shall I do? Oh...'

Tears and rage, in Elizabeth Wydeville's case, were potent and frightening twins. Once begun, the tempest was best left to run its course, which this one did in an unusually short time because Jacquetta, seeking inspiration, saved them all an hour or two of further anguish with a remarkable statement.

'I believe it has shrunk, Your Majesty. See, here and here? Yes, it is *much* shorter from the waist to the floor. And that explains the tightness in the waist and bosom.' It was a wild leap of logic, but a comforting one. 'Those foolish laundresses – in cleaning this dress they have allowed it to shrink! They shall be found out and removed from your service! This cannot be tolerated.'

Elizabeth Wydeville raised a tear-streaked face made brick red with passion – an unbecoming shade even on skin as beautiful as hers.

'Yes. Yes! I see you are right, mother.' Surreptitiously, all the women in the room turned away and crossed themselves. 'But the problem remains. I cannot allow the king to see me as anyone but his queen. What do I have, after all these weary months, that is good enough, and clean enough?'

'Your Majesty?' An insignificant girl stepped forward from behind the other women. Plain and drab as a sparrow, the expression on her narrow face, in her dark brown eyes, was disconcertingly direct.

'Yes, Lady Leonora?' The queen found the Earl of Shafton's daughter set her teeth on edge, since she was generally silent, even dour; however, she'd been a faithful companion in Sanctuary and deserved civility, not least on account of her powerful father, an important Yorkist supporter in the north.

'Does this please the queen?'

Lady Leonora was displaying a dress of fine silk-velvet of a shade between amethyst and purple. Silver flushed through the material as it slid through the girl's hands for the queen's inspection. There was a deep sigh through the room.

'Oh. I'd forgotten that one. Where did you find it, Leonora?'

'It was hung in the anteroom of the abbot's private garde-robe, Your Majesty. Many of your dresses are there, where we left them first...' She meant when the party of women had fled into Sanctuary at the abbey with the heavily pregnant queen.

'The poor abbot. We really have taken up far too much of his space for far too long. How happy he will be to see us in our rightful domain once more!'

All the women laughed, heartily and freely, for the first time in a very long while. Yes, it would be good to leave Thomas Milling to his own concerns. He would be particularly pleased to have his parlour returned once more.

'But do you think it will fit me?' The queen was eyeing the lovely dress fearfully as Leonora held it up to the light from the casements.

Jacquetta nodded vigorously. 'Certainly, Your Majesty. Perhaps you would like to see for yourself? But first...' She made shooing movements with her hands. 'Leave. All of you. Go, now. And prepare for the return of our rightful king as his subjects should. With prayers. Go!'

Elizabeth breathed in happily and almost smiled, though at the last moment she stopped herself. It would not do for her mother to think she had found a way to influence her through understanding, in an uncanny manner, just what she, Elizabeth, most desired. In this case, she was grateful to try the dress on without her usual band of women. That way, if the fate of this lovely garment was the same as the white one, only she and her mother would know it.

Jacquetta advanced towards her daughter, a reverent expression on her face, the dress laid out across her upturned palms as if it were an offering to the Holy Virgin.

Regally, Elizabeth stood to receive her mother's gift. She would breathe in, and in, until the dress fitted her – with the assistance of tight lacing. And she would not eat until the king returned to her. That would help. She was the queen and, if she desired it, she would be thin.

Edward would still love her, their little princesses and now their son, his legitimate heir. All would soon be right with the world. She would be queen once more, her sanctified place in the bed of the king secure. And in his heart also. She would resume her place there because she had given him this precious boy.

Elizabeth Wydeville smiled as Jacquetta dropped the lustrous velvet over her shoulders, her breasts, her hips. It fitted like the skin of a snake. The queen rejoiced.

Where was Anne de Bohun now? Lost, long lost, and she, Elizabeth, had won.

## Chapter Fifty-Five

With the help of women from Wincanton the Less, Herrard Great Hall felt clean at last; or, rather, that part of the building Anne wished to inhabit had been well scrubbed with ashes and river sand and all the walls whitewashed with lime they had made themselves from crushed and burned shells (the sea was not far distant) and powdered white clay, a seam of which ran in the bank of their own river. New rushes too had been cut and their fragrant smell flowed through the building like a sweet green tide.

Slowly, slowly, order was appearing out of chaos in Anne's domain: her house, her lands.

The first thing she had done, after feasting those who lived in Wincanton the Less, was to consult the head man of the village, Long Will, to find out who needed food. And as the recent history of the hamlet was recited to her in answering that question, Anne had become more and more angry.

When she had gone into exile, Edward Plantagenet had promised that her lands would be well run by agents of the Crown. It seemed that promise had been kept for the first two years, but increasingly, as the country had fallen into the chaos of war, men had abandoned their long unpaid posts and gone home. The Westminster-appointed reeve who had managed Anne's lands vanished one day. The rumour was he'd gone back to his family in London when the fighting became desperate before the king's flight.

That was all the people of Wincanton the Less heard – that, and rumours of war. And though the villagers saw no actual fighting, the occasional noise of battle and the screams of dying men and horses muttered like thunder in the distance. Even the travelling tinkers, reliable seasonal distributors of news, had failed to return with the swallows. The village was left alone by the world.

This last year had been disastrous. The weather had turned cold and wet with late and early frosts at each end of the growing season. A murrain had passed through the cattle and even the precious house pigs had died of the pest before they could be slaughtered, so there'd been little laid away ahead of an unusually hard winter – not even the usual bit of salt pork or sacks of root vegetables. Then sweating sickness had visited the village. Babies and the old had died, and now a spring drought had withered the fragile wheat planted before winter clamped the land.

The hamlet was barely surviving.

Anne made up her mind. She had coin money

hoarded from Brugge and some of her store, quickly spent in Taunton, bought wheat and twenty-five meat sheep, some with precious lambs afoot. There were also two cows, alarmingly shaggy, with wide horns. They were in milk and heavily pregnant. Anne bought a saddle horse for herself in Taunton also. A real horse, a big, strong, spirited mare with a deep chest and straight legs, not a lady's palfrey. She called her Morganne.

Wat, the last of the men who'd accompanied Anne from Blessing House, delayed going back to his master in London and it was he who drove the sheep to the village and delivered the sacks of wheat as well. The cows would be walked there the next morning by their previous owner.

'Your lady says to kill what sheep you need now and keep the rest to breed from. The cows, when they come, are for you all, and for the children especially. And if someone will show me where the mill is, we can get this corn ground. I'm to take some back to the Hall, but again the rest is for you.'

There was utter silence. Then the cottars, Meggan included, danced and shouted and screamed. Tonight there would be another feast – the first in the village itself for many, many years. Eat? They would eat until the fat ran down their chins and their bellies hurt from overstuffing.

And that was what they did.

Anne smiled. The wind brought her the smell of roasting meat. And, standing on the battlements of the Hall, she saw the smoke from the fires rising up from amongst the huddle of buildings in

416

the valley below. If she strained to listen, she could hear them shouting too. Her people.

Happiness, ecstasy and terror all found the same voice in extremis.

Anne furled her cloak about her body as she turned away. She was glad to feed her people, it was her duty. She was happy for their happiness, too. In the end, it took little enough to change the life of a man or a woman. Or a child.

She shivered. The joy on the valley floor below was poignant and she was surprised how deeply she was affected by it. When had she herself last felt such joy? She closed her eyes and tried to block the knowledge, the truth, but what was the point of lying to herself. Edward Plantagenet: for all the suffering he had brought into her life, he was her joy.

Would she ever see him again? And, if she had the choice, what would she do?

Darkness had settled on the valley and she could no longer see the shapes of the village houses. The shadows crept up around Herrard Great Hall. Soon she would go down to her lighted kitchen and sit companionably with her child, her mother and Wat. Perhaps she would embroider by the fire, or spin.

Deborah, with Wat's help, had set up a weaving frame and both women were determined that, by the time the next winter came, the walls of the Hall would be brightened by hangings and the beds would have new covers and blankets. Work was good, it kept her from thinking too much, but, sometimes, Anne despaired.

Was this how her days and nights would play

417

out, now and into the future?

Perhaps it was, and perhaps, in the end, that was for the best. A quiet life, lived amongst her own people, bringing up the boy in her mother's house and away, far away, from the dangerous, noisy world. The world of courts and intrigue and war. And kings...

## Chapter Fifty-Six

For Edward Plantagenet, Easter Sunday began with silent prayers in a freezing fog and ended with armour turned black from dried blood.

Only three days ago, the streets of London had seethed with those welcoming him home. They'd brought him into his city with a blizzard of flowers and sweet herbs – jonquils, snowdrops, rosemary and sage falling beneath his horse's feet, tender petals and leaves crushed to pulp in the mire of the roadway – and the sap-green smell had almost overcome the stench of streets starting to stink in the spring thaw.

Three days since the gates had been thrown open for him and he'd entered London with his men streaming out behind him, screaming like eagles for revenge. That fearsome, city-wide roar, echoed by the people of the capital, had sent George Neville and his supporters at a run from the city – abandoning the old king in the Tower as they fled.

And on that wild day, the people of London had

recrowned their summer king, reconsecrated Edward Plantagenet at the high altar of the abbey; Edward still in mailed half-armour, his father's sword at his hip, the hands of the Archbishop of Canterbury shaking as he brought the crown down so carefully, so firmly, on Edward's waiting head.

Three days since he'd met his wife once more, and his new son, in Sanctuary in the abbey. Yes, three days after six months gone.

He'd forgotten how beautiful Elizabeth Wydeville was. She looked imperial that day too, in her purple robes. She'd curtsied to him, tears in her eyes, and he'd taken the sleeping baby from her hands and kissed him, holding him high for all his men to see, and claimed him as his own acknowledged, legitimate son, the heir to his kingdom. And the bells of the abbey had pealed and boomed out across London, waking the child, who'd screamed with fright. But the king, his father, held him against his armour and soothed him, smiled at him, until the baby ceased to cry. He'd always been good with children.

And now, on the fourth day, he'd come to Barnet. It was only a little place, but it was here that he would truly earn his kingdom back, paying the price in the bodies of his men and Warwick's men as well. All English, all his subjects. Around him, he could hear the cheering and the screams; the screams of battle.

The fog did not lift on that long fourth day. In the chaos of the battle, Edward fought on, a machine equipped with an axe and a sword, surrounded by men he knew, men who had come to him at last and who, amongst the screams, would kill or die with him, united at last.

*Wump!* He felt the impact in his shoulder as the axe in his hand sliced the helmet, and the head, of an attacker. Blood and brains. He wiped the muck off his face, out of his eyes, pushed the corpse away as the man fell towards him; and again, again the axe bit down, this time a horse caught the blow and it screamed like a man...

He heard himself bellow, knew it was his own voice joining those of his men as they gathered and pushed hard into the blood-flying chaos of the mêlée, seeking the Earl of Oxford's men and the earl himself in the middle of a plomp of spears.

But then the miracle. When he had no breath, no strength, left – his axe the weight of an anvil in his hand – Edward heard it and saw it for himself. Warwick's troops were firing upon their own men, Oxford's men, before the earl's soldiers could stop them. The badge! They'd mistaken Oxford's badge for Edward's. Killing their own?

The king threw down his blunted axe and drew his father's sword. Gathering his weary horse he charged over corpses and writhing, half-dead men. *'To me, St George! To me!'* he screamed. Cries of *'A Warwick! A Warwick!'* answered, but he had them now...

Thrust, and parry and thrust. And scream and kill and thrust again. And again. The terrible rhythm of battle, the music of death played on and on in that mist-plagued day.

And then, suddenly, a party of mounted men peeled away to chase a knight flying from the carnage. Edward saw them, saw who they chased – the shield with the ragged staff! Warwick!

Spurring his horse, Edward wheeled after his men, but they reached the earl before him.

Warwick was alone, surrounded: one sword against too many. 'NO!' Edward roared, but before the word left his mouth it was too late. The king spurred his horse, faster, faster, screaming orders, 'Leave him. LEAVE HIM!' but he saw the swords flash, heard Warwick bellow as he sold his life as dearly as he could.

Blood spurted through the earl's armour as an axe took his shoulder and sword arm from his body; then he fell as if he'd never been, making a hole in the air. Like hounds at a hunt, his pursuers howled victory, stabbing as they dropped from their horses, hacking, screaming...

'STOP!'

That roar cut through and the pack ceased its bloody work; confused faces spotted with blood slewed in the king's direction as the battle passion ebbed. The king jumped down from his saddle and the men who had killed the Earl of Warwick stumbled back. Already they had half despoiled the body of its costly armour and one man held the earl's sword in his hand, distinguishable by Warwick's badge worked into the pommel.

Edward Plantagenet twitched the sword from the man's fingers, glaring at him, then looked down on the broken body of the enemy who'd tried to take his throne. Slowly, stiffly, he knelt beside what was left of Warwick's head and, lifting it up, raised the visor and kissed the clean, white brow. He'd known this man all his life and, once, he'd been a second father after his own was killed.

From that day to the end of their lives, those men who had only thought they were carrying out the king's commands did not understand Edward Plantagenet's terrible anger at the slaughter of his enemy. They did not understand why he wept as he knelt there in the red mud beside the mutilated corpse of the man who had driven him from his kingdom.

Then dark closed in on the fourth day.

Louis, the king of all the French, was woken from his sleep by terrible news. Less than five days had passed from the end of Holy Week and now they dared to tell him, in the black middle of the night.

'Barnet? Where is this place? Is it certain?'

Le Dain stood, trembling from equal parts cold and fear, at the foot of the king's bed.

'Alas, Your Majesty, the reports are true. The Earl of Warwick has gone to our own good Lord. He was murdered in battle on Easter Sunday by the usurper, the Earl of March.'

'Personally murdered? Do you mean Edward killed him?' Louis sat up, shocked.

Le Dain shook his head. 'No, Lord King. His men killed the earl and despoiled the body also. Disgusting pigs, these English, to treat one of their own in this fashion. They say that the king ... ah, the Earl of March, has had Warwick's body and, sadly, that of Lord Montague' – le Dain coughed nervously; it was well known that Montague was the lover of Margaret of Anjou – 'displayed at St Paul's Cathedral in the city of London. Bar-

barians! The cathedral is hard by London Bridge, Your Majesty, and–'

'Idiot! What do I care for geography? Where is my cousin, the queen of the English, now?' Louis growled.

Le Dain dropped his eyes. He swallowed. There was more bad news to tell.

'Well?' The king's voice cut like a boner's knife.

Laboriously, the barber knelt and shuffled forward on his knees. He bent his head humbly on reaching the side of the king's bed.

'Queen Margaret has now landed in her kingdom, Your Majesty. She is in the southwest of the country, raising support. Those counties have always been loyal to the cause of Lancaster. There are still many who flock to her cause, even now that...' Le Dain coughed. He would not willingly say the words that must be said.

'Now that the earl is dead, you mean? But will they hold to her, le Dain, will they hold?'

The king leapt from his bed with unaccustomed energy, the flaccid bag of his belly shaking like a custard as he hobbled towards his working table, snatching le Dain's candle in passing. Naked, Louis was an unheroic sight, especially since the livid pockmarks on his legs appeared leprous in the uncertain light.

'Get me a pen. And a despatch rider. And a robe. NOW!'

Le Dain rushed to find a covering, any covering, for the king and then, having draped an ermine-lined dressing-robe over Louis's narrow shoulders, hurried to do the rest of the king's bidding. But as he rushed through the palace, shouting for

'Light! Heat! Guards!' he thought it was too late to be sending counsel, of any kind, to Margaret of Anjou.

The game was too deeply in play since the death of Earl Warwick. The former queen of England would need a miracle if she was to take back her kingdom without her warlord.

## Chapter Fifty-Seven

May Day was passed with much celebration in the village. The days were getting longer at last and there was a flush of warmth in the air. Branches of flowering hawthorn were twined around the gate and porch of the small Norman church, and bees droned noisily as they plunged into the wilting blossoms, emerging with legs burdened with pollen. Perhaps this year, after all, would be fruitful?

It was a good omen for the future that Anne had prevailed on the monks at Appleforth – the former owners of Wincanton the Less – to send them a priest each Sunday until a permanent occupant for their church could be arranged. Anne had discovered she held the living of the parish in her gift as lady of this manor, but it would take time to select the right person, and she made it clear to the monks she would not have someone imposed on the village without her agreement. Meanwhile, the brothers were deeply shocked by the realisation that the parish had been so neglected since the previous priest's death. There was much irregularity in need of correction: several couples were openly living together without benefit of churching, and there'd been children born outside marriage also.

So it was on this May morning that nearly all the villagers walked in procession to the porch of the sturdy, squat-towered church, led by three young couples, two carrying babies. And there, huddled beneath the low porch, the men amongst the three couples recited vows of marriage on behalf of their wives-to-be, carefully echoing the words of the priest as he intoned them. The babies were held close to the bodies of their mothers so that they could be made legitimate at the same time as their parents were declared legally married.

Anne smiled wistfully at their happiness. Would her son ever know his father, as these children would? She shook her head, trying to banish unwelcome thoughts, and her glance caught Deborah's. Her foster-mother leaned towards her daughter and, as the priest pronounced a final blessing, scattered May blossom petals into Anne's hair, just as the villagers were doing for the newly married couples.

'Your turn will come, sweet child. This will be a good year, for us and for all here. I feel it.'

Tears glinted for a moment amongst Anne's long lashes. Leaning down, she kissed her son and gave him the petals she'd so carefully hoarded. 'There, Edward, you can throw mine.' Her son hopped forward and joyfully threw the flowers with all the force in his small body, shouting,

'Bless you! Bless you!'

The villagers cast warm smiles in their direction as Edward ran back to Anne's side. 'And bless you too, child. And you, Lady Anne. Our May queen, you are.'

May queen? Anne was suddenly breathless with fear as a black fog descended and the church, the laughing people, the running children, disappeared.

Screaming, all she heard was screaming, and there was a red fog all about her. A fog in which she saw and heard the flash and clang of swords. Horrified, she looked down. Her dress was soaked with blood almost to the height of her knees. Men's faces loomed at her, black mouths screaming, eyes slashed from their heads. Soon she would be engulfed, soon she would be swallowed by this horror, this rolling cloud of death and terror and pain.

One word. There was only one word amongst the screaming. A name, a name she had never heard before in her life. *Tooksberry. Was that it? Turksbury? TEWKESBURY. That was the name.*

And then she saw him and gasped. Edward, surrounded by men nearly as tall as he was, and though his face was covered in blood, she recognised him: he wore a gold diadem around the steel of his helmet and he was braying like a stallion, screaming like an eagle, as his axe rose and fell, rose and fell, with a terrible, remorseless rhythm.

She would not look, she would not look as he bore down upon the boy, the stripling who screamed out in French, rallying his supporters,

'Did he kill the boy? Ah no, please God, no!' Anne swam towards consciousness, so deeply distressed that tears ran from her closed eyes. She smelled rosewater but that made it worse; rosewater and the wet-iron smell of blood were a nauseating combination.

She struggled to sit, but didn't have the strength. Cool hands soothed her, pressed her gently back against the bolster. With a sigh, Anne surrendered, her eyelids fluttering as Deborah held a wrung-out linen rag to her temples.

'It was the heat, Dame Meggan, after this long winter,' Deborah whispered to her companion. 'She'll be fine now.'

Meggan was not convinced. She whispered back, 'Looked more like a fit to me.'

Anne lay still, apparently asleep once more. Deborah put one finger to her lips. 'Come with me, Meggan. There are fresh curds you can take back to the marriage blessing – for the priest, from my mistress. We should let Lady Anne sleep.'

Anne, hearing their voices recede, struggled to sit up – and regretted it. The room swung and spun around as if she'd drunk too much new beer.

*Tewkesbury.* That was the name she'd heard. A real name. What did it mean?

Death, that's what it meant. Assuredly. Death.

# Chapter Fifty-Eight

As the king's army approached the walls of London, a large party of joyful citizens, all shouting, came running towards them across the green May meadows outside the walls. The surging roar from many throats was as powerful as the sound of the sea and they made a vivid sight, this dancing mass of colour – red, green, blue, gold – every face pink in the heat, every mouth open as they sang and shouted, waved banners, scared the cows out of their way and set the sheep running through the pasture.

William Hastings knew the king's treasury would have to bear the cost, eventually, of all those missing animals, these trampled swathes of standing corn. But the money would be found; it would be his pleasure to find it.

Edward, dusty and sore after the fighting of the days and weeks before, was lifted by the sight of his joyous people. Energy streamed into him from the love they offered him. He forgot how mortally tired he was; now was the moment, the real moment to savour. He had truly come home at last and the country was his, was with him once more.

He'd returned with an army at his back – his men stretched out behind him, bag and baggage, for some miles – and amongst that army were most of the important baronage and magnates of

England. They'd been clever, they'd seen the change of the wind. One by one, like weather-cocks, they'd swung around and many had abandoned Warwick even before Barnet.

Then more had come, until at Tewkesbury – the final battle, when he'd met the threat of Margaret of Anjou and her son, Edward, the so-called Prince of Wales, and destroyed their army – they'd queued up to fight by his side.

In the end, he was sorry that the boy had had to die, but then, once mighty forces were in play, who could control one man's fate amongst the carnage? Edward crossed himself as he saw an image of the youth's broken body when it was brought to him after the battle, a body still not quite grown, but with the promise of a large man in his long legs and strong back.

The king sat straighter in his saddle and closed his eyes. He forced himself to summon up the death of his own brother, Edmund, when not much older than Margaret's son. And the death of his father, Richard of York. He crossed himself. God would understand. Some deaths were neces-sary for the greater good. And as reparation.

Another image troubled him before he could banish it. The old man in the Tower who had looked at him so trustingly, called him 'dear cousin' and held out his hand in greeting ... he'd not think of that now. The country's stability was paramount; personal squeamishness was just that – personal. It would not be permitted to interfere with his duty.

Throwing his cloak aside, Edward drew his father's sword and held it up by the blade so that the sapphire set in the hilt caught and flashed light as he waved it.

Those who saw him do it – saw the cross formed by the hand guard and the pommel, saw the leopards of England and the lilies of France embroidered on the tabard over the king's ringmail, the red-gold circlet in his sweaty hair – began to shout, 'The king, the king'. And they kept shouting it, until the chant spread across the entire host, like wind across the sea, spreading from the army to the citizens of London: 'The king, the KING!'

And Edward, smiling, waving his sword, saw Clarence, his formerly treacherous brother, now as joyous as all the rest, shouting 'The KING, the KING!' as if he too had been the most loyal supporter Edward had ever had. Edward nodded graciously, even bowed, never allowing the irony of the moment to register on his face. Clarence, beaming, bowed ever lower in his saddle whilst bellowing again, with all the force of his lungs, 'The KING! The KING!'

Edward caught the eye of his other brother, his true loyalist, Richard, Duke of Gloucester, and raised his eyebrows. Richard grinned back and waved his sword in the air. He too was shouting 'THE KING! THE KING', as was Hastings, faithful Hastings.

Edward found he had tears in his eyes, but he was not ashamed. He would think about Clarence later. And Anne.

Now here was the mayor, John Stockton, and his aldermen, plus the valiant recorder of the city of London, Thomas Urswick, who, the king had told, had led the levies of Londoners he'd personally raised and paid to help see off the Warwick-backed Bastard of Fauconberg, only lately besieging the city having sunk all the English merchant shipping in the pool of London. Edward hated seeing his merchants upset. He'd claim a price for that from the Bastard later.

The king twisted in his saddle and looked back along the columns of men behind him, shading his eyes in the brilliant light. He shouted to Hastings, over the noise, 'Where is Margaret? I want her brought forward.'

Hastings nodded and wheeled his mount out of the slow-moving press of men and horses around the king. This was something he would see to personally. Ever the pragmatist, he cantered back down the line on a wave of male voices, 'THE KING, THE KING', at peace with his task. If Edward chose to behave like a conquering Caesar returning to Rome, parading his captives before him, it would be done. He had earned the right. But then, he hoped too that his master would remember to be merciful. It would help to heal the kingdom.

Hastings could see the former queen of England, Margaret of Anjou, now. She was sitting on the floor of a wagon that had high sides made from wattle – a fragile cage to hold such a woman. But all that was left of her former state and power was a filthy gown of jewel-embroidered velvet; no crown, no sign of rank. The old queen's hair was loose around her shoulders. From this distance she was still a handsome woman, but she had aged in these last days after Tewkesbury and, as

431

Hastings rode closer, ready to give the order to bring her cart towards the front, he could see rips in the material of her dress. One sleeve had even torn away from its lacings, exposing her upper arm upon which there were long, bloody scratches.

Edward would be furious if any of his men had offered her violence, or worse. Margaret of Anjou had been an anointed queen, even if she was Edward Plantagenet's enemy.

But, closer yet, Hastings could see the truth. The queen had slashed her own clothes; was doing it still, worrying at the skirt of her dress, trying to rip one of the seams open. Now he could see the blood on her nails and hands – she had mortified her own flesh. There were bloody marks on her face too, deep gashes. And crowning her head, amongst the still dark hair, there was white powder. Ashes?

This woman was deep in biblical grief. She mourned her son as she saw fit, and she did not care how she was judged, what she looked like. It was all she had left of her queen's pride: indifference to the opinions of others.

'Bring the queen's wagon up to the king. He has commanded it.'

As Hastings shouted the order he bowed to Margaret from his horse. She ignored him, but stood up, no easy feat in a lurching wagon that was picking up speed on the deeply rutted track.

'Madame, are you thirsty?' Hastings addressed the ex-queen directly as he rode beside the wagon, the easier to clear a path around and through the slow-moving mass of men.

'THE KING! THE KING!' The soldiers were

432

shouting it, yelling it, bellowing it. Not to insult this woman – they weren't frightened of her any more, she was just a woman – but to express the relief of coming home as winners. It might so easily not have been the case.

Margaret of Anjou, straight-backed, swayed as she balanced herself against the movement of the wagon. She looked, unseeing, at Hastings. 'I shall never be thirsty again.'

'THE KING! THE KING!'

She could not stop the sound. It wrapped her like a cloak, binding her, stifling her, filling her throat and head.

She had played to win, and she had lost. She would hear them screaming those words in her dreams for the remaining days of her life.

Please God that life was short.


## Chapter Fifty-Nine

Elizabeth Wydeville had returned to her rightful place and station in life. She was, once again, the acknowledged queen of England and co-ruler with her husband, Edward Plantagenet, the fourth of that name. As she processed down the nave of St Peter's Abbey, it was hard, very hard, to keep from smiling.

It was a hot and glorious day in early June and the bells of the great church were ringing, ringing for her, ringing for her much-delayed churching after the birth of her child, the most noble, the most high Prince Edward. The king's precious son.

The queen felt herself smile, widely, blissfully, as she turned the words over inside her mouth and tasted their sweet strength. The king's son. Delicious; they were the most delicious words she'd ever heard. Words with the power to transform her life. The mother of the king's most undoubtedly legitimate son, the first lady in the kingdom, smiled like a living saint. And those who did not know her were awed. Beauty incarnate walked before them. Their queen.

As was fitting, after living in Sanctuary in the most straitened way, Elizabeth Wydeville was now brilliantly dressed. Hers was the stiffest, the heaviest gown in the abbey today. Cloth of gold made up her dress, along with purple velvet and white silk; winter miniver lined her enormously long train, carries by the daughters of four dukes and six earls. The queen gloried in the handsome weight of her clothing, welcomed the heat the layers of fabric brought to her body, welcomed too the burden of her crown. Never before had her graceful neck carried that grave mass more gladly, not even at her coronation, years ago. The rich gems, the gold of its construction, flashed and glimmered as she bowed, left and right, acknowledging friends, ignoring enemies.

She shone and she knew it. Brighter than candle flame and more glorious than the icons of the saints adorning the high altar beyond the rood screen, she drew and magnified light in a way that challenged even the tomb of St Edward, confessor and king. She was only an earthly woman and yet, when she passed the entrance of the Lady Chapel, she bowed as one monarch to another. Today, she was the equal of that other reigning deity, Mary, Empress of Heaven, and those who were in the abbey knew it well.

And here they all were, her witnesses, for the church itself was full, stuffed full, with all the barons, the lords, the earls, the dukes in England and their wives and daughters. Dressed as richly as idols, slung around with ropes of pearls, ropes of jewels, they waited, row behind shimmering row, for Elizabeth Wydeville to pass; hopeful that she would nod, would acknowledge them, as she paced her measured way out of the abbey and towards the rest of her glorious, beckoning destiny.

But the queen had not forgotten, even if Edward pretended to. She had not forgotten the treachery of so many of them standing here today.

There was Clarence – traitor, jealous brother, ally of Warwick and that other woman who had dared call herself queen, Margaret of Anjou – and yet he presumed to smile at Elizabeth Wydeville so radiantly, to bow so deeply, that none might suspect the rage in his heart. But she knew his malice, and her fury matched his when she saw him. As she drew level to where the duke now knelt, very deliberately she turned her head away, almost turned her back on him, ostentatiously directing her tender glance towards Richard of Gloucester, kneeling beside George of Clarence. *There, that is what I really think of you, George,* the gesture said, *you are dust beneath my shoes.*

The insult hit home and instantly the veil of joy – so well counterfeited for this occasion – was ripped from the face of Edward's younger brother and something uglier was seen for just one moment. But then the smile returned to George of Clarence's face. Fixed, but certainly a smile.

Beside his elder brother, Richard of Gloucester dropped his head piously, hoping none had seen his own sardonic twitch of amusement at Elizabeth's treatment of Clarence. He'd never like Edward's wife but he was proud of her today. They felt alike about his brother George.

Whispers flew from mouth to mouth and rippled away to the altar, to the doors, to the galleries above as the queen processed down the nave of the abbey. Without even turning, Elizabeth Wydeville could see the courtiers muttering to one another as she walked on, head humbly bent. She did not care. Let Edward chastise her later for her treatment of Clarence; she would not allow this moment of triumph to be taken from her.

She had borne Edward Plantagenet a son. There would be others. She was fertile. She was the queen and she had reclaimed her kingdom.

Processing towards the banqueting hall at Westminster Palace for the churching feast, bowing right and left to the throngs of his newly reassembled court, the king nodded and smiled graciously as he carried on a very private conversation.

'Where is she, Hastings?'

Justly reinstated after his master's comprehensive victories at Barnet and Tewkesbury, the Lord High Chamberlain of England suppressed an irritated sigh. Today of all days, with Edward and Elizabeth worshipped like deities at the very centre of this triumph, and the king was still, only and always, thinking of the troublesome Anne de Bohun.

'Sire, I do not know. There's been no time to–'

The king said sharply, 'Now is that time, William. Sir Mathew Cuttifer – he'll know where she is, I'm certain of it. I want you to send a message to him. I will formally revoke Anne's exile tomorrow, he's to tell her that. Then, when order has been properly restored in London, I want her to join the court. Sir Mathew is to reassure the Lady Anne that I remain her loving friend.'

For a moment Hastings had a flash of the queen's radiant face in the abbey and it took all his self-control to present an untroubled expression as he nodded pleasantly to his master. Over Elizabeth Wydeville's dead body would Anne de Bohun ever come to court.

'But if Sir Mathew does not know where Lady Anne is, sire...?'

Edward frowned. 'Then we shall cast our net more widely. After the feast, we'll talk about what's best.'

'Your Majesty, does the queen know of your intentions?'

Only a long and close friendship with Edward Plantagenet could allow William Hastings such liberty. Sometimes the king preferred to ignore the emotionally difficult things in life, but it was the restored chamberlain's duty to be plain.

'No. And I do not intend to tell her.'

Sweat sprang from William at the thought; for a moment he felt dizzy.

'Sire, forgive me, but ... you will permit the queen to hear of this invitation *without telling her yourself?*'

Edward shrugged. He gazed into the middle distance and wiped the sweat from his own eyes, waving cheerfully at no one in particular. His cloak of scarlet velvet was very heavy on such a hot day and the stiff collar of the black damask jerkin chafed his neck. He'd forgotten the tedium and inconvenience of correct appearance.

'Sire, I would not ordinarily speak–'

'Then do not!' Suddenly Edward was truculent, his face dangerously flushed, whether from heat or anger it was hard to tell. June warmth did not sit well with velvet and both heated the blood.

William gazed at his master. Very well, he would say nothing more. Today.

'I can see what you're thinking, William. You might as well be lecturing me still!'

The king was laughing now and that was fortunate. There'd been too little laughter in all their lives in the last long months. Defeated, Hastings smiled and sighed. 'Well, lord, if we're to call up this storm perhaps we should enjoy the calm before it?'

The king was sunny as the day. 'Much better, William. Why would I seek to annoy the queen with my intentions today of all days? Let us all be peaceful and happy. As my father told me, the science is all in picking the ground. And not engaging in the fight, unless you are sure you can win. I have not yet selected where my ground should be in this matter. I will tell you when I know. Then, perhaps, I will speak with the queen.

But only perhaps.'

Hastings shrugged. 'I capitulate, sire. It is your business when, or if, you choose to tell the queen of Lady de Bohun's visit to your court. I shall say not one word more on the subject except...'

Edward was harder, tougher, since his exile. Hastings' playmate was long gone, lost in the fields of the Low Countries, and there was menace in his face as he glanced at his chamberlain. William gulped but struggled on; it was his job.

'...to ask where will the Lady Anne be lodged? Westminster is very full, and will be for some time as the numbers at court swell.'

The king waved to the crowds again. There was a jewel on the third finger of his left hand – a square-cut ruby so rich in colour it was almost black until he held it up into the light. Then it glowed, bright as heart's blood.

'You are right, William. As usual. Lodging must be thought of. But there is time to solve this problem for it may still take some days to convey my invitation to the Lady Anne. Once we have found her.' He touched the ruby to his lips. 'I believe we should make a bower. A very special bower that she will not want to leave. Ever.'

They were close to Westminster Hall now and the king increased his pace, striding out ahead of his friend, waving exuberantly to the pressing crowd of besotted Londoners. He flung his last words over his shoulder. 'See to it, will you, my friend? After all we've been through, this will be such a little task...' Edward's sardonic laughter floated back to his exasperated chamberlain.

A bower? Where and how would he conjure

439

such a thing into being? The chamberlain sighed. There would be a way, of course there would be a way, but he would not think about it until after the churching feast was finished. Right now, he was going to get good and drunk. Then he would think about his duty.

## Chapter Sixty

Blessing House was locked tight for the night and all the lights had been extinguished when the unexpected visitor knocked at the door. It was a huge door and a sharp knock, and because the sound echoed around the receiving hall, it was not long before the sleepy door-ward lifted the cover on the spyhole and spoke.

'What is your business? It's long past curfew. This house is asleep.'

'Open the door.'

Alone in the street outside, the tall cloaked man pushed back his hood. The door-ward's fingers were suddenly thumbs; he rushed to obey the muttered order but it took minutes, not seconds, to unlatch, unbolt and unbar. The sounds were explosions in the darkened building.

The door-ward could not speak from fear, instead he made a gobbling sound as he stumbled the door open, hanging on as if it were the only thing keeping him upright.

'Close it, man. Quietly.' The tone was patient; the stranger was used to the effect he had at close quarters. But in what light there was in the receiving hall – not much, just flickers from the banked embers in the fireplace – Edward Plantagenet was an impressive sight, something he didn't always fully grasp. The door-ward was a short man: strong, well muscled, but undeniably short.

To the dazzled servant the king seemed to soar up and away over his head like a dark angel come to visit. Night, and shock, did strange things to a person's sight.

'Your master?' The king understood, finally, what the man was trying to say. 'You will get your master?'

The door-ward nodded and finally found the words. 'Yes, sire, I will fetch my master.'

He managed a shambling bow as he ran towards the stairs that led to the upper part of the house. Only later did he recall he'd turned his back on his king. He didn't sleep for days afterwards when the shame of that hit home.

*'What?'* Mathew Cuttifer was exasperated. Someone was shaking him, making him return from a deep dream and a place where he was free from pain. No more sore knees, no more aching hands and...

'What do you WANT!'

He awoke, truly furious. Lady Margaret, his wife, his dear wife, was shocked. Sir Mathew was a temperate man, not given to sulks or displays of temper.

'Mathew, we must wake. And dress.'

Mathew's fury was dowsed by befuddlement. 'Dress? Why dress? It's dark.'

But his wife was already nimbly hopping out of their bed, naked as a babe, and skipping over to the pegs on the wall where her day kirtle hung. He must have misheard her reply. Surely he had?

'The king? Did you say the *king?*'

Some deep instinct got Mathew's legs going before his brain, and suddenly he too was out of the bed, also naked, and absurd without his clothes. Thin legs, a hard little paunch and soft arms – bookman's arms, not tanner's arms, as his family inheritance had been.

'Yes, Mathew. The king is downstairs, asking to see you. Walter has just informed me. We must think, carefully and quickly, of what we shall say to him.'

Mathew's heart leapt like a lamb in his chest. The messenger from the palace – they'd sent him away with lies earlier today.

Walter, the door-ward, was dithering from foot to foot outside the door. His heart, too, was racing but for different reasons. In just one night, he'd opened the door to the king and then run into his master's chamber unannounced and unasked and woken him. Where would this all end? Right now, he just wanted to be told what to do. He couldn't see himself going downstairs to chat blithely with the king all by himself. No, best to wait here, wait for his master.

'Walter? What are you doing here? Why aren't you downstairs with the king? Hurry, man!'

Half dressed, pulling on hose and trying to tie them off to the points of a half-donned jacket, Mathew Cuttifer was wild-eyed and looking for someone to blame. That was the logic of fear.

Lady Margaret, her kirtle decently laced – somehow – and a plain kerchief covering her nightplaited hair, was vainly trying to persuade her husband to stand still so she could help him dress.

'Mathew! Stop! Stand still. We will get through this. He's here by himself – that tells us much. Now let me help you or the king will see you half naked. Is that what you want?'

Sir Mathew was suddenly rigid. No, that was, most assuredly, just what he did *not* want. He called to the door-ward again.

'Go on, man. Downstairs, now! Raise the cook – we must give wine to our guest. And food! And tell the king we're coming.'

Walter shivered. Speak, uninvited, to the monarch who'd only so recently slaughtered his way to London? There was a comforting thought!

'Go. What are you waiting for? Go!'

Walter saw the look in his master's eye. He didn't know the king, but he did know Sir Mathew. In the end, he knew whom he'd rather face. He bowed quickly and hurried away.

'Stop! Torches! Light torches!'

Gulping with the pressure of the extra task, Walter bowed again and scurried from the bed chamber to the receiving hall in the span of two breaths. Was it a dream, was he flying? How could he have got down those stairs so fast?

But, there, suddenly, he was, bobbing bows in front of the king again, hopeful that this fearsome giant would not take it into his head to split him as he had countless others, including the old king, the one who'd been in the Tower. They said

443

he'd died from sheer displeasure only yesterday. Walter didn't believe that. Not one bit.

In the door-ward's absence Edward Plantagenet had, with his own hands, fed the banked embers in the great hall fireplace so that a bright glow now flickered across the vast space.

'My master and Lady Margaret are–'

'Here, Walter. Go now and do as Sir Mathew asked. Hot wine is needed, and refreshment for our sovereign.'

Lady Margaret, her hand lightly on her husband's arm, had a clear voice that carried, and the tone on this occasion was quite clear. *Pull yourself together, Walter. Think about one thing at a time. Go!*

Giddily relieved to relinquish the task of entertaining the king to those who were more used to it, Walter cantered to the kitchen, casting one startled glance at the feet of his mistress as he went. No, he wasn't hallucinating. They were naked. And she didn't know it. Should he tell her? No! Raise the cook, get the wine heated...

'A good man but I suspect Your Majesty made him nervous.'

Sir Mathew Cuttifer, mercer, had been an intimate at the courts of two kings in his lifetime, and this king, the man now standing so unexpectedly in his own hall, had knighted him personally. They had known each other for a long, long time but Anne de Bohun had caused a falling out between them that had never been completely mended. And now, only today, Sir Mathew had denied to one of the king's messengers that he knew where she was. Would he, could he, lie to the king if Edward asked the question himself?

444

Edward smiled at his wary host and his lady. He did not believe, for one moment, that Mathew Cuttifer was ignorant of Anne's whereabouts, however he honoured that faithfulness to a friend – he'd needed more of the same in the past, and not had enough. These people were important to the woman he loved and it was time to reknit old bonds between them; if only for Anne's sake.

'I must thank you for your many kindnesses in the past, Sir Mathew; and you, Lady Margaret.'

Margaret hardly dared to breathe. It had come, then, at last. Reconciliation. This was a good omen.

'And I came here tonight since I might not have another opportunity for some time...' Edward coughed, using the moment to think of the right words, '...as all our lives have changed so suddenly, and there is so much to do.'

During this little speech, Sir Mathew had guided the king to a noble cathedra standing to one side of the fireplace. There was another, a matching chair, but he would not sit unless instructed to. Meanwhile, Lady Margaret, to her horror, had realised why her feet were so cold.

'Yes, so many tasks to bring the country back to a reasonable state. I mean to do that as speedily as possible. And I will need trade to flourish if we are to accomplish all that must be done.'

Sir Mathew nodded. The king smiled at him encouragingly. An opinion was clearly called for. Sir Mathew cleared his throat, constricted by fear.

'Your Majesty is entirely right. Now that you

445

have returned to your throne,' he bowed deeply; Edward nodded graciously, 'to the great comfort and delight of all your people, it is needful that we all work together – commons, lords, all of us – to bring this country back to rights. The house of Cuttifer will play its part, Lord King. In whatever way, on whatever terms, that you shall instruct!' Mathew finished with a flourish, his voice a noble clarion in the great empty room.

Lady Margaret smiled discreetly at her husband. *That was well done, my dear. Now, if the wine would just be brought, we might avoid talking about...*

'Lady Margaret, will you not sit?'

The king gestured to the other cathedra and, with great grace, because there was no other choice, Margaret curtsied with a serene expression on her face and sat. The king did not allow Margaret to see that he had glimpsed her naked feet when assisting her to her place. But her husband had observed those slender toes and the mad desire to laugh nearly choked him. What was going on? Surely the king hadn't visited them to talk about trade reform in the middle of night?

'You may wonder, Sir Mathew, and you, Lady Margaret, why I have chosen to visit you tonight?'

Somehow the knight and his lady preserved expressions of polite indifference, as if that question had been the last thing they'd thought of.

'I believe you told Lord Hastings that you have no current knowledge of Lady Anne de Bohun?'

For one mad moment Mathew thought of lying, but that was where it had all begun before with the king; lying about Anne had nearly destroyed his English trade and his family. What to say now? His wife saved him.

'Lady Anne left this house in February, Your Majesty. Earlier today, when the messenger came, we were concerned to say as little as possible since that is our ward's wish. Her one desire now is to live a life of quiet retirement.'

The king smiled. 'Ah, Lady Margaret, you are a good friend to the Lady Anne, and therefore you are my friend also. I wish to invite Lady Anne and her nephew to the court that the queen and I shall shortly hold. Perhaps you can assist me? Lady Anne must know of this invitation, and that it is my intention that her exile be revoked. Formally. She has been my friend through countless trials and it is our wish to reward her for her faithful service to our person.' He smiled radiantly.

Lady Margaret smiled also but her face had lost all feeling, though the mask of courtesy remained in place. She dared not glance towards her husband, though she heard him gasp and then cough to cover the sound.

'An invitation to court? How kind Your Majesty is. And the exile. Most generous.' The blood hummed in Margaret's ears, so loud she could hardly hear the words that came out of her mouth. Some part of her brain was engaged, at least, and intent on saving the house of Cuttifer from disaster once more. How could they possibly persuade Anne to obey the king in this? And what would be the consequences if she refused his invitation?

Sir Mathew, knowing his wife so well, picked up the thread. 'But of course, sire, we would be

447

most pleased to find a way for your, um, invitation to be conveyed to the Lady Anne.' Invitation, in this context, was the polite disguise that *summons* wore.

The king bowed in acknowledgment and the Cuttifers held their breath. Would he ask them where Anne actually was? But Edward did not press the point; above all now, he wanted to build Anne's trust in him. He believed the Cuttifers; they would pass on his message, he was certain of it.

This was a night of shocks and surprises for, as the king nodded pleasantly to acknowledge the service they would render, he extracted a small roll of parchment from inside his jerkin. It was sealed with his own personal badge, the sun rayed in splendour. He held it out to Sir Mathew, who went down upon one knee to receive it, as he had when the king had knighted him.

'I thank you, sir knight. And you, lady. Please see that Lady Anne de Bohun receives this as soon as you can arrange for it to be delivered.'

His business over, the king rose and wrapped himself once more in his cloak. At that moment Walter returned, leading a stream of wide-eyed servants from the kitchen. Between them they carried enough food and wine – gently steaming in great jugs – to refresh twenty or thirty hungry men. The party made a creditable sight. Somehow each was properly and cleanly dressed in the Cuttifer livery, and the food smelled delicious.

The king smiled charmingly at his hostess and had the grace to look embarrassed. 'Alas, I fear I have detained you all from your beds for far too long. However, since this well-ordered house has been put to so much trouble' – the king strode over to the servants – 'this is for your pain.'

Quickly, he dipped long fingers into the pocket at his belt and extracted a gold coin for each man and woman who'd come to wait upon him. The gesture caused a little confusion as, one by one, each of the servers attempted to receive the gift whilst juggling substantial platters laden with delicate viands piled high and hot. But it was soon done and Sir Mathew waved the food and the servants back to the kitchen. They'd all enjoy an early and unexpectedly splendid break-fast today.

The king smiled as he turned back to the merchant and his wife. 'You have been most generous, Sir Mathew, and you, Lady Margaret. I am grateful for your help and for your great loyalty to Lady Anne. She and I will not forget. Now, it is more than time for sleep. For all of us.'

In the light from the fire, deep exhaustion was written on the king's face. He'd come tonight to accomplish something that was very important to him, and it had cost him great effort to ask for this favour.

Lady Margaret felt real pity for this man. He'd returned as a victor to London, that was certain, but he'd done it sailing in on a moontide of blood. And he would never, ever rest easy again as long as he lived. 'Sire, may we arrange an escort for you back to the palace?'

Edward Plantagenet shook his head. 'This is my city and my home. It holds no fears for me, lady.' One final smile to Margaret Cuttifer and the king was gone.

There was a moment's stricken silence after Walter had bolted, locked and barred the house once more. Husband and wife looked at each other searchingly.

'Well, wife, what do we do now?'

## Chapter Sixty-One

Now all had changed, changed again. Because of the letter. His letter; the parchment placed in her hands today by Mathew Cuttifer's messenger.

How the world had tipped and spun as she'd fingered the wax seal with its familiar device. But she had not opened it. Perhaps she would not ever open it.

Anne stood still, made herself as dense and strong as a stone pillar; as unassailable. She composed herself, half grateful that the contest had arrived. The contest between the past and the future.

She was in her favourite place in all the world – the castellated walk of her house from which she could see the valley below, and, if she looked hard enough on a clear day, the sea in the deep and changing distance.

Soon it would be suppertime and her son must be fed. Anne walked towards the door that opened onto the stairs leading down to the other floors of the Hall. But then the wind stirred and lifted her unbound hair until it streamed out around her head, around her shoulders. And she heard the voice.

*Anne. ANNE.*

The Sword Mother stood between her and the door. In the evening light her mole-dark cloak made her part of the shadows in this windy place. Anne's eyes locked to those of the cloaked woman and the wind died away. Utterly.

And then the cloaked figure moved, one graceful step, and the way to the stairs was clear.

There was only a moment and a low whistle, such as a bird might make, and then the shadows swallowed the woman whole and she was gone as if she had never been.

Anne blinked as if sun-blinded. But there was no sun.

Night had eaten up the day.

Anne's bed was in a room on the third level of the Hall. Not quite a solar – it was too large for that – and with doors opening from three of its four walls, yet it made a tolerable bed chamber with a high view of the countryside. The two women sat huddled behind the red curtains, talking quietly as the rest of the household slept. Lying on the counterpane was the king's letter.

*Edward, by the grace of God, King of England, France and Ireland ... commands that the Lady Anne de Bohun attend the king's court at Westminster...*

Anne stared at the parchment. The words had almost lost sense, she'd read them so many times. Deborah picked up the letter and scanned the bold black words

*...with all speed. It is the king's express pleasure*

451

*that the said Lady Anne de Bohun join with His Majesty's family in a mass of thanksgiving to be held…*

'This is official. An official summons. You must send an answer.'

Anne was surly. 'Let the messenger wait. Or go. I don't care.'

Deborah tried again. 'The Cuttifers will pay dearly for this if you do not go to court, Anne.'

'But this is not of my choosing.' Anne hunched the coverlet over her shoulders, an adult substitute for pulling it over her head. Deborah smiled tenderly and reached out to stroke her daughter's hair. Sometimes she could still see the wilful child beneath the woman's skin.

'Of course. Yet they have been kind to you.'

Anne covered her eyes with her fingers. The adult was in full flight. 'What can I do, Deborah? How can I choose?'

*Anger is the most useless of all emotions, daughter.*

How many voices spoke? One? Two?

*But how can I go to him?* It was an instinctive response as Anne's hand sought Deborah's, the words unspoken.

All was still within the tented bed as mother and daughter breathed together, deeper, slower, deeper once more.

*There is only one choice and anger must be put aside. You have an obligation and a duty.*

Herrard Great Hall was soundly asleep except for these two women. And the third who had joined them. The curtains of the great bed shivered. The voice was a breath, a soft wind that passed through the room like a swallow.

*One choice. You will choose, and then you will know.*

Outside, something barked: dog or fox? The sound was answered by a distant howling.

It was the mid-dark of the night, a time when even the restless dreamed most deeply.

*Are we dreaming, Mother?*

There was nothing further, no answer to this question. Why, then, did Anne see a door open and light stream through and the sound ... the sound of what? A waterfall? Water falling from a great height?

'Anne, can you hear me? Anne, wake.'

Deborah was shaking Anne by the shoulder. And that intensified the dream from the past, which had returned with full force. The dream of the wolf, tearing, ripping at her shoulder as she lay in the snow. There was a scream and an eagle dropped from the sky, driving the wolf away with its slashing talons, its beak. Cowed, running with blood, the wolf howled and fled as feathers brushed Anne's face. The eagle settled beside her in the snow. Its great pennons were raised, casting a shadow across her body.

*The eagle and the wolf... Why?*

'Wolf? Ah, sweet girl, wake now. Come back to me.' Deborah's throat was dry with fear. 'There are no wolves in England. They're gone. They're all gone to Scotland. Anne? Anne!'

Anne de Bohun opened her eyes and saw the silver tracks on the lined cheeks. Gently she reached out and wiped the tears from her mother's face.

'Yes. You are right: there are no wolves. Eagles rule us now.'

Anne rode into Wincanton the Less to speak with Long Will and Meggan about the planned rebuilding of the cottages in the hamlet; their tumbledown state was her personal reproach and she meant to make that good.

Guilt was a powerful force. If she stayed, or if she went to London, that decision would trouble her hour by hour, day by day. Anne shook her head, as if to distract a troublesome wasp. Step by step, step by step. All she could do was all she could do.

'Take timber from the spinney by the mill,' she told the two villagers. 'Work must be accomplished before autumn if you're to have a better winter in this place.'

Dame Meggan smiled at their lady. For the first time in long, long years, the village women had the possibility of fat on their ribs over winter, and if they did, it was Anne de Bohun who would put it there.

'Lady, the labour's not such a problem – we'll all work – but with so many men gone from the village to fight, a skilled builder to help us join and raise the house frames is what we sorely need.'

Anne nodded. 'Very well. We must find you a builder.'

Morganne, Anne's mare, nudged her mistress, impatient with standing whilst the people talked. Automatically Anne reached up to smooth her nose. 'Enough from you. You've had breakfast. Perhaps I should shake your legs out and you will not be so impertinent.'

A long ride – that would help to clear her thoughts, help her find the impetus to action.

'Will, you and Dame Meggan must decide what is most urgent and send me a message at the Hall. I can spare Wat for a day or two. He shall go to Taunton and get what is required.'

Holding Morganne firmly beside the bit, Anne walked the horse to a crumbling wall. Finding a large rock, she stepped up and swung herself neatly onto the horse's back, arranging her right knee around the pommel of the saddle so that her skirts hung down, decently covering her legs. No more riding astride for Anne de Bohun.

Gathering the reins in her gloved hands, Anne swallowed a shaky breath. To settle herself on the back of this good horse, to smell sweat from a well-worked animal, was to sweep back to that mad ride from s'Gravenhague to Brugge through a frozen world. It was just more than half a year since she'd huddled behind Edward Plantagenet in that frigid winter, riding across Europe as the world changed its balance around them. And now he wanted her to return to him. No, had *ordered* her to London.

'Mistress?' Meggan was smiling up at her.

It was good to be wanted, needed; to feel useful in the lives of these people. Should she leave this place? Could she?

'We heard. About London.'

The horse danced for a moment as Anne's fingers tightened on the reins. Meggan nodded and, though she smiled brightly again, anxiety made her voice rough. 'The summons from the king.'

'Who told you?'

Meggan looked down, embarrassed to meet Anne's eyes. She shrugged. 'People talk, lady.' Then she lifted her head. 'Will you stay long at the court?'

Anne patted the restless mare and when she spoke, in a clear, carrying voice, she chose her words carefully. 'You may tell them all, everyone here in Wincanton the Less, that the king is an old friend. An old friend of my family's and, therefore, of yours. And if I go to London, *if* I go, it will be for the good of us all. And I will hurry back.'

Dame Meggan too spoke loudly, for the benefit of the villagers who were standing in their doorways, watching the exchange curiously. 'We are all sure of it, lady. And no doubt the king will be pleased to consider your wishes when you ask to return?' Years of fear, years of hard winters and little food were behind Meggan's truculence.

Anne understood. Her reply was patient and kind; she hoped her words were true. 'Yes, Dame Meggan, he will consider my wishes. Good day to you all.'

Anne nodded confidently to the villagers as Meggan took a step back. The chatelaine of Herrard Great Hall settled herself more deeply into the saddle and straightened her back. Heeding the signal, the mare danced; she was eager to run, eager to stretch her stable-slackened muscles. At the edge of the hamlet, the broad, dusty road between the houses became a two-wheel track. It led straight: deep into a substantial wood of well-grown oaks and elms. Anne's trees. Anne's land.

Yes, she would let Morganne run and run, and perhaps she would find the answer. She leaned forward, whispering, 'Come, dear child. Fly for me.'

The horse needed no urging and instantly the handsome grey mare and the woman moved over the ground together like coupled birds. But Anne de Bohun knew the truth.

*Run all you like,* truth said. *You will have to face me at last. Pride contends with passion. The king has beckoned and he believes you will come to him gladly.*

'Ha! Gladly?' Anne shouted the word and startled Morganne, who stumbled mid-stride. Her mistress reined the confused animal to a standstill. Horse and rider were both breathing fast.

In the end, did she, Anne de Bohun, have strength enough to defy Edward Plantagenet should she decide to stay at the Hall, to ignore the summons?

Truth laughed heartily. *Defy? The proper question you must ask is, do you want to?*

## Chapter Sixty-Two

It was the feast day of John, the blessed and holy Baptist, and June was approaching the end of its proud season. This perfect summer had begun in late May, as if to bless the return of the king, and it had continued with blue skies and sharp stars, with soft winds and the greatest splendour of foliage in the lanes and byways that any could ever remember in the kingdom of England.

But still she did not come to him.

'And? What do you hear?'

'Lord King, I know that the Lady Anne declined the escort you sent to her recently, and they have returned to the palace. The message, given verbally, was that her people had need of her presence and she must tend to their needs first.'

The king paced the privy chamber, blood itching beneath hot, tight skin.

'First? What does this mean? Perhaps she means to come later in the year?'

William suppressed a shrug. 'I do not know, sire. Those whom you sent said the lady locked them out of her Hall and declined to tell them more. Short of besieging the place, they had no choice but to return.'

Edward Plantagenet was pacing, back and forth, back and forth. Hastings was reminded of the lions at the Tower before feeding time.

'Is the bower fit to receive the Lady Anne when she does come to court?'

The chamberlain nodded. The bower was prepared. He had created a wonder for the eyes of one woman and one man alone. An ancient tower within a wild garden had been found and, in less than two weeks, all had been refurbished within and without so that now it stood, empty and perfect, to receive this woman who so obsessed the king, to the great danger of the kingdom.

'Why, William? Why does she not come to me when I ask her?'

The words were out of William's mouth before he could stop them. 'Perhaps she is frightened, liege?'

'But I am her protector. How could she, or the

boy, come to harm if I make it clear Anne de Bohun is my chosen favourite?'

Denial lay behind the confident words and they both knew it. Hastings said nothing and Edward whirled around to face his oldest, closest friend. There was dread behind the fury.

'Elizabeth? Perhaps she makes Anne fearful? I understand my duty and so does the queen; she will always be honoured as my wife and I think we are closer, as we should be, since the birth of our son. But Anne ... I need her here!'

William Hastings was an unusually well-educated man for a soldier, and as the king roared, filling the small stone room with his rage, an image troubled him. An infant, held by the heel of one foot, plunged into a cauldron of shining water and emerging red-faced, screaming. But invincible. Godlike. Except for the one place on his body that had not been dipped into the water of the Gods ... Achilles. The great hero of Troy who died from a wound to the unprotected heel.

Anne de Bohun was Edward Plantagenet's fatal flaw. Now, when the king should be focused completely on rebuilding his dynasty and convincing the populace of its stability – and his right, therefore, to the throne – the spectre of this girl rose up once more; rose, as it had far too many times in the past, to distract the king from his duty. William understood sexual infatuation, that was tolerable since its power always waned with time, but this was different and he feared, as the Greeks had, the curse of love.

'No! I know that look, William. You think she is

459

bad for me. You do not understand. You cannot.'

Fury fled the king's face to be replaced by such sadness William was nonplussed.

'Your Majesty, she is just a girl. There are many girls.'

'In London? In my kingdom? Yes. And each one eager to boast of bedding the king. Each one hungry for the advantage that would bring. But don't you see? Anne doesn't want any of that. She wants me. Only me. I am her knight and I am the father of her son. And he is my eldest son.' Moodily, the king gazed off into the distance.

William suppressed irritation with a determined effort. In the end, when sentiment was set aside, Anne's son, enchanting as he was, was only a bastard and there was now a *legitimate* prince. Not for the first time did Hastings regret the court's fondness for reading books of chivalry. Otherwise rational men, such as the king, risked becoming distracted by a fatally emotional view of existence – a misty, changeable *female* vision of life – as a result of these ridiculous stories of knights and their unattainable ladies. Simple things – relationships between men and women, for instance – became muddied and confused where before there had been clear rules of engagement between the sexes. Still, he was wary of speaking that particular truth.

Edward was exhausted from having fought his way down the kingdom in the last three months. Speaking bluntly now would serve none of them well. Plantagenets were known to be highly strung, highly charged, and Edward was no different. It was the obverse face of the coin of greatness. On one side there was the image that was public, that of a pitiless man of war, the leader of his people, sword in his right hand, scales of justice in his left; but on the other side there was the private man, the father, the lover and, yes, the dreamer of courtly dreams. This man was in love with Anne de Bohun. And she was his unprotected, unblessed heel.

Like the girl as he did, admire her courage as he'd always done, William Hastings knew that Anne de Bohun had been dangerous to Edward's stability for the last six years, and never more so than now. Perhaps, in the end, she really was a witch, a malign force let loose in the king's life?

William resisted the urge to cross himself. What was he thinking? Witches were creatures of fantasy. Peasant superstition. Action was required, like fresh wind through a stuffy hall.

'Your Majesty, what would you like me to do?'

Edward turned and stared at William, his face tormented.

'Go to her yourself. Now. Bring her to London. Just ... do what is required. And I want you to tell Her Majesty the queen of my wishes in this matter. Later, you may give me her response to this command.'

William Hastings bowed low so that the king would not see what he felt. Never, in all the time they'd been together, in all the battles they'd fought back to back, had he smelled the rank breath of potential ruin so clearly, so potently. He dreaded talking to the queen.

'And William?'

461

The chamberlain paused in backing from the little room. 'Your Majesty?'

'Do not frighten Lady Anne. Make her understand...'

'Understand what, liege?'

'Why she is necessary to me. And that I love her.'

The door closed softly behind the Chamberlain of England and the door-ward dropped the latch into place as if it were bedded in velvet.

He'd heard the last part of the exchange. They were all in for it now, when the queen found out about the king's doxy.

## Chapter Sixty-Three

'When?' One word, but it contained much meaning. And a world of frozen menace.

Hastings, who had called upon the queen to give the message he'd been instructed to, stiffened his spine and squared his shoulders.

'His Gracious Majesty has instructed me to tell you that Lady Anne de Bohun must be called to court since she has returned to this country without his permission. And, as she has broken the terms of her exile, proper enquiries must be made of her for the preservation and maintenance of good order in the kingdom.'

He was mildly pleased by the sonorous nature of the speech he'd delivered – and its economy with the truth. That pleasure did not last long as the queen put down her embroidery and gazed up at her husband's best friend.

'I had thought she was dead, Hastings? Burned as an accused witch in Brugge not long after the king left that city?'

William cleared his throat nervously. 'The Lady Anne de Bohun was the subject of some rumour at that time, but it seems to have been just that, Your Majesty. Rumour.'

The queen's glance had the prick of a needle. 'Well then, witch or not, if this woman is illegally in this kingdom, I presume an armed guard will fetch her from wherever she currently hides and escort her to the place that awaits her in the Tower? So to perish, as must all traitors to my husband's cause.'

Lord Hastings tried to match the queen glance for glance. And failed. He bowed and spoke earnestly to Elizabeth Wydeville's embroidered velvet slippers.

'Arrangements are being made, Your Majesty. The king, your most noble husband, felt you would prefer to know of all that passes in his name.'

With glacial dignity, the queen crossed herself. 'You may thank the king, my lord, for this, his care of us, the very least of his subjects. He has chosen to enlighten his queen that a new threat exists to the restored stability in this kingdom and for that I am most grateful. You may tell my husband such. Now I must see to our son, his precious, legitimate heir.'

Though William Hastings did not like Elizabeth Wydeville, her calm was impressive. She too had grown steel inside her spine during these last tumultuous months.

Bowing more deeply still, he stood to one side as the queen rose and, clasping her hands at waist height, stepped down from the dais on which her Presence chair was placed. Leaving the room, her steps were so tiny she seemed to glide over the floor of the great day solar, robes whispering on the inlaid, brilliant tiles as her ladies trailed out behind her, talking quietly.

William Hastings had a moment to gather himself in the sweating quiet of the queen's absence. The king was waiting to hear how Elizabeth Wydeville had received the news and he, the king's highest officer, should not delay, yet he stayed for one moment, fingers restlessly tapping the stone window ledge as he gazed down on the river as it moved east and south towards the sea.

*Anne de Bohun curdles the king's judgment*, thought the High Chamberlain of England. *And the queen is right. There is much to do and the king's obsession could threaten this hard-won peace. For the good of this country, something must be done…*

'You have a rival.'

Elizabeth Wydeville hissed through closed teeth, as a cat does before it strikes. 'Tell me what I do not know. I begin to think you have no power at all.'

The queen sneered as she spoke but her voice shook. The woman she had summoned seemed not to hear; she was focused on her scrying bowl, nodding gently as if listening to voices from far,

far away. Elizabeth, against her inclinations, was fascinated. It was not often, in these days, that she met people who were unafraid of their queen.

'Why do you need that thing?'

The girl smiled sweetly and raised her face. She was blind and had been from birth; milk-white eyes turned towards the sound of the queen's voice. Elizabeth shivered in distaste.

'Perhaps I see differently, Lady Queen. The bowl is useful. I can smell the light it sends me.'

'Smell the light? Nonsense! Light has no smell.'

The girl, Lilliana, shook her head. 'To me it does. And when I do this, what I smell gives me answers to my questions...' The blind girl cupped her hands around the precious glass bowl. It was very old. The queen had never seen another like it. Delicate and pale blue-green, the surface of the glass was clouded as if it had lain in the sea, or a river, through aeons of time. As indeed it had. Miraculously, it was entirely whole.

Elizabeth Wydeville, superstitious as she was, had no patience for time-wasting blandishments. She needed information and she'd been told this woman was as good as a sibyl. 'Tell me more. Describe this woman.' The queen sat back in her cathedra. This would be a test. If the girl passed it, she might believe what else she said.

'Since these eyes of mine have never *seen* as yours do, my descriptions may be strange to you, Lady Queen. But I shall do what I can.'

Silence filled the little room. It was so quiet, the queen heard the whisper of her own blood. It was uncanny. Unsettling. Then...

'Do you hear that?'

Elizabeth jumped in her chair as the blind eyes settled on her own. The whispering grew louder; they could both hear it now. Water, not blood; rushing, falling from a height. There it was again: insistent, tumbling, a gathering roar.

The queen's mouth was dry. She forced her lips to form words. 'Water? Why do I hear water?'

Lilliana held up her hand, listening intently, and when she spoke she raised her voice against the sound. 'There is a waterfall. Bright, shining. And there is bronze ... something bronze, glinting in the sun. A kingfisher flies. An eagle flies beside it. There is another eagle ... it attacks the kingfisher; the eagles are fighting. And now there is a peregrine. She flies at the kingfisher whilst the eagles are distracted...'

The queen sat back with flint-hard eyes but one shaking hand held the other tight. 'You speak in riddles.'

The blind girl shook her head. 'No. It is clear to me and, I think, to you.' She cupped the glass bowl in her hands, clouded eyes gazing down on the clear water it contained. 'Hair the colour of bronze and eyes like bright feathers, like jewels. Blue jewels, green jewels. You are nothing alike, Queen. But her rights are as strong as yours.'

Elizabeth Wydeville was lost between rage and fear. 'You speak of rights, but she has none. None!'

'But if the truth was known, the people would feel differently. She has lost so much...'

'And what of my losses? My husband in exile and me fleeing to Sanctuary? Never knowing if he would return or if I, and my new son, my

466

daughters, would be murdered as we slept! Did I not suffer loss as she did?'

The girl glanced at the queen. 'All that is yours has been returned. You remain the queen. That is what you want most. She, your rival, has given that up, willingly, for the good of the child, and the man.' The blind girl shook her head. 'She lost everything that should have been given; now she has regained some of what was hers. Perhaps it will be enough. And yet, if she chooses to stretch out her hand...'

Elizabeth choked; hammering fury burned her chest.

'If you mean my husband would marry this whore...?'

Lilliana, unperturbed, shook her head. 'No whore, and not whilst you live. That tears at them both.'

The queen crossed herself with slashing movements. It never worked, this endless, restless search for answers to the questions that tormented her.

'Take your fee. I will not keep money that has been besmirched by such malicious lies.'

Cruelly she threw her coins onto the table top where they bounced and scattered across the wooden surface; several rolled to the floor where they skipped, spinning, into the corners of the room. The girl made no move to scrabble for them.

'Keep the money, lady. Give it to the poor at your gates. I accept no payment for this gift – it is not mine to make money from.'

The girl turned her head this way and that,

seeking to sense where the queen was. It was unnerving and eerie.

'I do not understand everything I say but I know that I speak the truth. I am sorry if this offends you but it is the only obligation I have for what has been given to me.'

Lilliana slumped back in her seat. She was exhausted, sweating and pale as the limed walls. White skin, white eyes, white headscarf. Perhaps she was an effigy made from snow? An effigy that would melt, leaving only a pool on the stone floor. The queen shook away the thought as she hurried to the door, turning her back without a further word. But as Elizabeth lifted the latch, Lilliana spoke once more.

'The king has a friend who is not his friend, not in all things. He should beware the man who comes out of the dark. The dark which he made.'

The queen paused for one moment more, questions clamouring to be answered, but as she turned back to demand information, she saw that the room was empty, even though there was just one way in and one way out: the doorway in which she was standing. Nothing else was there. No bowl, no table. No girl.

But there was a pool of still water on the floor. It shone white, reflecting the colour of the walls.

And then Elizabeth Wydeville, the Queen of England woke. Screaming.

# Chapter Sixty-Four

Two nights later and the weather changed. Herrard Great Hall was buffeted, suddenly, with wind. Shutters banged all over the building as the gusts built and built, until a storm broke with the sound of an invading army.

Little Edward woke in his truckle bed and shivered with terror; most frightening was an echoing crash that came and went. Storm giants!

The lightning flashed and flooded the room with white light. Outside, in the inner ward, his oak tree groaned and creaked. Thunder pealed directly above and the child screamed.

'Wissy! Where are you, Wissy?'

He yelled with all his strength, but no one came. For a moment, he huddled under the blankets, but then it happened again: a crashing noise in the distance. The giants were breaking in! He must save Wissy!

Edward tumbled from his bed and ran across a space that was instantly vast in the dark and the light and the dark. He stumbled towards one of the three doors and, heart hammering in his chest, sobbing, struggled to lift the iron latch that was nearly above his head, stretching his toes to reach it until the bones seemed to crack.

Twice more white light broke the darkness, twice more the hammers of the storm beat down on the roof, but then terror helped him trip the latch and he was through the door at a run, calling frantically.

'Where are you? Where *are* you, Wissy!'

This night, the familiar was suddenly strange. In the daylight it was easy to find the twisting stair that descended to the hall. Night was different and there were no torches to show him the way.

He ran, ran on, through the flashing darkness, through the rain gusting from the arrow slits and, at last, at last, his feet found the first tread of the stairs. But there was darkness in the stairwell and suddenly the certainty was overwhelming. They'd gone, they'd all gone to London and left him here. The crashing began again – the giants were coming closer. Edward screamed and covered his eyes with his fingers.

Below, there was chaos and noise in the great space of the hall as rain blew through the opened door, ripping the one piece of arras Anne still owned from its hooks. Struggling with its weight and the power of the storm, Anne felt her skirt lift and billow as she tried to close the door behind the cloaked and dripping man who'd been pounding on it.

'Leif!'

'Yes, lady. Here, I can do this.' It was a big door and a huge wind but Leif leaned into them both. The door closed on the howling night and there was almost silence.

'*Wissy? Where are you?*'

The cry of her child struck Anne's heart. Snatching a torch from one of the sconces, she ran towards the stone staircase. Questions could wait.

Taking the stairs two at a time, she soon found her son. He was slumped, a small shivering bundle, on one of the stair turnings, and though he was trying not to cry, his little pale face and terrified eyes told the story. Shoving her torch in a sconce, Anne stumbled on her skirts in her haste to gather the small body into her arms.

'I was trying to save you but I thought you'd gone. I thought you'd left me alone.'

Frantic, Edward hid his face in the bodice of Anne's gown when the thunder pealed again. 'Make it go! Make it go away!'

A massive shadow wavered up from below, the head a grotesque blob followed by a huge, dark shape. Edward looked up and screamed, *'The giant!'*

The turning of the stair had hidden Leif Molnar from sight; now the light he held preceded him. A flash from the storm captured the child's fixed, staring eyes. For one moment he looked like a corpse, dead from terror.

'Is the boy...?' Leif's heart lurched. He would not say the word.

'No! He just hates storms.'

Edward burrowed more tightly into Anne's shoulder. She chose to ignore what she saw in Leif's eyes as she rocked her son, speaking softly.

'There's nothing to fear, my darling, nothing to harm you.' Distantly, the sky muttered, the thunder moving away. 'See, it's nearly gone, and we have a visitor. Your friend, Leif.'

The little boy spoke, not daring to look up. 'Not a storm giant?'

The Norseman went down on one knee; his

head was level with the child's. 'Have you forgotten me, Edward? That would make me sad.'

Little Edward sat up slowly and looked at the man in awe. 'Are you a giant, Leif? You look like a giant.'

The Norseman shook his head, smiling, but his gaze was fixed on the woman. 'Give me this boy, woman. There are things we must speak of. It is time for him to understand the thunder, and his own fear.'

Leif handed his torch to Anne and opened his arms to the child. Edward allowed himself to be scooped up and Anne walked down behind them. The two torches she carried cast the shadows of the man and the boy into the hall before them.

And Deborah was there, waiting, as the fire climbed high in the chimney and the flames rushed up to meet the dark night sky.

It was late and little Edward was sleepy, resting against Leif's chest. There was a story, a long, long story, and he was at peace.

'Thor commands the thunder, Boy. And the storm. They are both his servants. You have nothing to fear because Thor watches over me, and since I watch over you, therefore he is your guardian also.'

That made Edward's heavy eyes flick open. 'But you said he was a war god?'

Leif shifted the child's weight slightly, settled him in the crook of one great arm and drew a fold of his cloak around the little body.

'That is true. But I am a fighter; so too are you.'

Edward chuckled. 'A fighter? Me?'

472

Leif nodded gravely. 'Certainly. You showed courage tonight. A coward would have stayed in bed, under the sheets, but you were brave. You faced the storm to help your aunt. As a fighter, all you need is technique. It will be my job to help with that. When you are grown, you will be taller and stronger than I am.'

Edward's eyes were wide open now. He laughed – a bright sound in the dark hall. 'But you are a storm giant!'

Leif laughed too. 'Even so. Now, I was telling you about the thunder. When you hear it sound and see the sky torn apart, well then, you know your guardian is close by. So that even if I am not here with you, you know you are protected. Storm and thunder are the God's preserve. Mortals cannot control that: not your mother, and not me.'

Edward's eyes fluttered closed, feathery lashes resting on his cheeks. 'My mother?' The little boy yawned hugely. 'I've never seen my mother. She died.'

Leif's glance crossed Anne's as she sat embroidering by candlelight. She saw him form the words, saw him say them, though no sound came from his mouth to disturb the drowsy child.

'No. Your mother lives.'

There was space between them, four paces at most; space they could cross, if they chose to.

But Anne dropped her gaze, attentive to her sewing, and he, after a moment, wrapped the boy more tightly and stood, ready to carry the sleeping child up to his bed again. And they said not one word more that night.

# Chapter Sixty-Five

'Why did you come?'

The Norseman shrugged. 'You needed me. You need someone to look out for your interests here.'

'But your work for Sir Mathew...?'

'You are his concern also. Sir Mathew wants me here.' Leif yearned to say, *do you?* But something stopped him. Confidence; he'd never been confident with women.

Anne, well aware of what he had *not* said, picked another quince. She and Leif were in the neglected orchard outside the walls of the Hall, gathering fruit into reed baskets. This hot, early summer had nearly broken the boughs with ripe fruit already, the season forced by more than a month. Apples, peaches, quince, medlars; Deborah and Anne would soon be busy preserving and drying – if Anne chose to stay.

Climbing down from the tree as Leif held the ladder steady, Anne loosened the straps that held the basket on her back. He lifted the weight from her and she sighed with relief, flexing cramped shoulders; she felt real satisfaction as she looked at their progress.

'One, two, three, four, five, six ... I believe we have near twenty baskets filled, Leif. And we've hardly touched the trees at the back. All those apples yet to be picked – what a thought.'

She was laughing; once she'd thought nothing

of such hard physical work, but her muscles were protesting today. And her throat was very dry. Leif smiled and held out a leather flask.

'Here. Drink.'

The deep green grass beneath the oldest of the pear trees was inviting, it was true, but there was so much to do. Fortuna and her bull calf would do well on such fodder – grass and windfalls; she must remember to mention it to Deborah.

'Anne?'

'Yes?'

'Stop thinking. Sit. The fruit won't go away. We've still got hours of light today.'

She smiled at Leif and sat down beside him. He was a kind companion and friend and, he was right, of course: she needed his help. In so many things.

Closing her eyes against the hot light, she swallowed heartily from the offered flask: their own ale, the first they'd brewed in this place. Thirst made it taste like nectar. Wiping her hand across her mouth, she handed him the bottle. 'Do you have advice for me, Leif?'

For a moment he too drank and she watched his strong, brown throat as it moved.

'This is good, lady. You have the touch. With ale at least.' He smiled and so did she, but he had not answered the question.

To cover the moment, Anne removed one of Deborah's pies from its linen wrapping. It was big enough for several men. 'Are you hungry?' She'd asked him the wrong question and blushed; what had possessed her? She knew what his answer, his true answer, would be.

With a wicked smile, Leif reached across her body for the large wedge she'd cut. 'Of course.' They were sitting very close, close enough for her to smell the fresh sweat of him. 'I'm always hungry.'

Anne dropped her eyes as she cut a piece of the pie for herself; she was confused by her feelings for this man and talking only made it worse.

She cleared her throat and spoke, unnecessarily loud, in the humming, buzzing warmth of the orchard. 'So, you will not give me guidance?'

Leif shook his head, chewing slowly, his eyes on her face.

'You wouldn't accept what I'd say, lady.'

She flashed him a glance. 'That's not fair. How can you know that?'

He smiled and took another bite of the pie. 'I know you, lady.'

Anne had no reply. She brushed the crumbs from her skirt and stood, untying her hair kerchief to mop her hot face. There was a small stream at the edge of the orchard, one of the reasons the trees had been placed where they were. Water close by meant good fruit.

'Give me the flask, if you've finished the ale. I'll fill it with water.'

Leif smiled lazily as he held the leather bottle up to Anne. She leaned down to grasp it but then, as her fingers touched it, he jerked it away. Trying to catch it, she unbalanced and tumbled down, across his lap.

'So, lady, would you like me to tell you the truth?'

Now she really was confused, and breathless,

her torso across his, her breasts against his body.

'That's *really* not fair, Leif.'

He caught her hands as she wriggled, trying to twist away from him. She was breathing fast, so was he.

'Let me go.'

'Only if you hear me out.'

She was fit and strong but he was much more than her match, holding her effortlessly, relentlessly tighter.

'Say yes, Anne.'

'To what?' Her heart was jolting now, but there was no fear.

'To the truth.' And then, just because he could, he kissed her.

She wasn't shocked, but she was rocked by the impact of him as his lips touched hers. He relaxed as he kissed her so, without thought, she freed one hand and hit him hard in the chest. 'No!'

He laughed. 'Yes!' And kissed her again, catching the errant hand easily. Her world buzzing, light colliding with dark, she kissed him back.

And in that moment, when all the certainties of her world were shaken to the core, Anne de Bohun made up her mind. She had to go to London. She had to *know*.

# Chapter Sixty-Six

'I need to say goodbye to him. I cannot leave it unresolved.'

Her foster-mother stirred the vat of quinces steadily, evenly, being careful not to break the fruit. 'Why? There's a peaceful life to be had in this place.' *Leif has returned to us. Stay for his sake and your own.* That was what Deborah wanted to say.

Anne turned away from Deborah's direct glance. She felt the heat rise to her face as she shook her head. 'I cannot have peace in this place. Not unless the king permits it. I returned without his permission and he could force us into exile again.'

Deborah turned back to the simmering fruit. 'He'd have done that by now, if he meant to do it at all.'

Anne scooped out the muslin bag of precious nutmegs, cloves and cinnamon quills with a long spoon, laying it carefully to one side for drying and reuse. 'He's still the king. I disobeyed him when I returned to England.'

The steam rising from the liquid was perfumed and rich. One last stir and Deborah tapped her own spoon on the rim of the three-legged pot. 'He wasn't on the throne then. He's king again now, but she's still the queen. New prince or not, there will be danger in London. From them both.'

'I will make an agreement with the king and try to reach an accommodation with Elizabeth, if I

can. It's the only way to secure our future here.'
Anne began sorting sound fruit from bruised in
the basket of unpeeled quinces as Deborah sat
down beside her and picked up her paring knife.

'Leif can help you do that, daughter. He can
help with a peaceful, secure future in this place.'

Anne swung around to face her foster-mother.
She knew the answer before she asked the
question. 'Why do you say that?'

Deborah lifted the first of the yellow fruit,
weighed it in her hand and carefully began to peel
it. 'If Leif and you were to marry, you would have
the protection you need. Here, on your own land.'

Anne began to speak, then changed her mind.
Deborah concentrated on her work as the long,
curling strand of yellow peel gathered and fell
from her knife.

'It would be a good match for you. You could
build something, together. He's a good man and
a hard worker. You're well suited and he loves you
dearly. And the boy would have a proper father.
You could give your son brothers, and sisters. For
you, Leif Molnar would leave the sea, and though
he brings nothing with him but a strong back and
a calm mind, you have goods enough to found a
family. And this man will never let you down.'

'By that you mean Edward has? And will?'
Anne's frustrations sharpened her voice.

Deborah nodded, implacable.

'He has no choice. You can never be more than
his mistress. He has a wife. Do you really think
you can become his leman, known and shamed
before the whole world. You? How will your son
feel, when he is older? He will hate you for it.'

Picking out one of the largest fruit to peel, Anne turned her back on Deborah. Nothing could hide the quaver in her voice. 'You are cruel.'

The old woman reached out to grasp Anne's hand in hers. 'Are you sure you have the strength to go to him and then to walk away, truly walk away, knowing that, this time, you will never, ever see him again? *Must* not see him again?'

Anne was angry. 'How can you doubt me? I have done this in the past. It was not my choice to go to s'Gravenhague.'

The old woman nodded but would not be deflected. 'But it's different now. It would be so easy to slip into court life once more. You'd even enjoy it, for a time; you'd accumulate power. And perhaps you'd be acknowledged as your father's child – yes, no doubt the king would want to do that, to give you increased status – and that would remove some of the pain you've endured. But only for a while. It would never be enough. I don't doubt your strength but I know what you feel for this man. You have surrendered. You have allowed the king to become the lodestone of your life. How can you choose, really choose, to walk away if you see him again?'

Anne was shaky but defiant. 'You speak of my father. The father I have never met. Perhaps it is time for that meeting, also.'

Lovingly, Deborah brushed Anne's cheek, wiping away a smut from the fire. 'We can change most of what comes to us; we truly can. But some things cannot be altered. Love is one of these things. You cannot love where you have no inclination. And you cannot will love away, either. This is not about your father. It is about your lover.'

Anne shook her head.

'I have to go, Deborah. I have to resolve this. And I must secure my place and that of my son in this country. To meet my father may help me in that. Afterwards ... well, we must wait on fate for an answer.'

It didn't take so very long to travel from Somerset to London if the weather was kind and the roads dry. But for Anne de Bohun, this journey felt like the longest she had ever taken, though the sun shone faithfully day after day as a glorious summer smiled on England.

Wanting her journey to be discreet, Anne had hired a closed wagon in Taunton instead of riding. It was a cumbersome thing, set on high wheels with small, shuttered windows and substantial cushions, yet not even a mile from the town walls, Anne knew she'd made a terrible mistake.

The hardness of the sun-baked track caused the body of the wagon to sway and lurch on its leather straps as the team of horses picked up speed. Soon Anne was as nauseated and dizzy as she'd ever been on board the *Lady Margaret* and the cushions were so unyielding she felt every hole and rut in the track. Yet, even in the strange, hallucinatory state brought on by heat and dehydration, she was still certain that her decision to ask Leif Molnar to stay with Deborah and little Edward at the Hall was the correct one. He'd wanted to come with her, of course, but protecting the boy was now Anne's greatest concern; somehow she'd convinced Leif of that.

She'd decided to take Wat with her, to ride beside the wagon. Ralph of Dunster, a large, nearly silent man whom Leif had found and personally approved of as a potential guard, was driving the wagon. Jane Alleswhite, Meggan's niece from the village, had been half trained by Deborah to attend Anne once she reached court; she made up the last member of this little party.

This same Jane was now sitting opposite Anne, faint and pale from having puked her recent dinner all over her new lindsey-woolsey dress, and was deeply shamed.

The smell in that closed, stuffy wagon was vile, yet Anne knew they could not stop each time either of them felt the urge to vomit. It would take days longer to arrive at the capital and that was time she could not afford.

'When it hits you the next time, girl, hang your head out of the window. Better to be sick outside, into the road, if you can.'

Poor Jane raised her sweating, green face and groaned. Anne spoke urgently. 'We must resist, Jane. Count with me until the feeling goes away. One, two, three...'

Jane wailed, 'I can't count,' and threw herself to the window, thrusting the shutters outwards just in time.

'Oy!' Wat was riding at the back wheels of the carriage and his outraged bellow startled the horses, which Ralph, cursing freely, fought to control.

And so the journey went on, and each day – there were three of them – became more and more hallucinogenic. Even at sea, sailors learned to cope with seasickness on a long voyage, but this journey was different. The women gave up eating since nausea had killed their appetite. Even liquid was rationed: empty stomachs had little enough to give back when retching set in, but even water made a difference. Then, on the afternoon of the third day, there was an old familiar smell on the gusting wind.

London's summer reek was back in Anne's nostrils and its voice was in her head once more. Iron-clad wheels on cobbles, the braying of animals on their way to slaughter, human voices calling, shouting, laughing, cursing...

And soon the wagon joined the flowing mass of animals and people as they streamed along the Strand.

How many years ago was it since Anne herself had stumbled along this very road, bereft, following Deborah to a new life? A peasant girl clad in homespun, leaving her uncomplicated life in the forest behind for ever and intimidated by the strangeness, the noise and the stench. And the men who'd looked at her so lustfully.

Now, Lady Anne de Bohun, dressed in clothes worth more than some of the houses lining this ancient roadway, rolled past, hidden from view.

And as Anne's wagon lurched by, shutters firmly latched – there was stench inside certainly, but that *outside* was worse – the common people on the roadway grudgingly stepped back, shoved each other out of the way beneath the overhang of the houses, just as she and Deborah had once done on London Bridge. And they shouted out as the closed vehicle passed, liberally scattering muck from its wheels as it went.

Anne heard their catcalls, their whistles; heard them calling out, 'Are you too proud or too ugly to show yourself, lady? Show us your face so's you can see what you've done!' Yet Anne did not open the shutters. Once she'd been a peasant; now she was not. The workings of fate were all far, far too complicated to understand.

An hour, then two, passed inside that stuffy wagon on the crowded streets of London before the journey ended and Anne de Bohun found herself, once more, at the doors of a great dark house. Blessing House.

And there, at last, she collapsed.

## Chapter Sixty-Seven

Louis de Valois woke in the dead of the night. The dream he'd been sent – certainly by God – was a clear inspiration. It seemed to him that he was flying and, when he looked down, he could see the whole of the kingdom of England spread out beneath him, beneath the tips of his wings. He was a bird. Not just a bird. An eagle.

And then, coming at him out of the sun, was another eagle – huge, fierce, screaming. But he had fought that eagle and, though he himself had been almost mortally wounded, in the end he had found his opponent's weakness. With a last slash of his beak he had ripped the enemy's breast until it dripped blood to the earth far, far below. With a last defiant scream, his adversary had plummeted away, falling, fluttering, its life so clearly ebbing as it fell...

'Light! Light!'

Alaunce Levaux scrambled up from his truckle bed, which lay across the door of the king's chamber. He'd taken a long time to get to sleep because the rushes were old, smelly and lousy with fleas from the king's dogs, and they were heaped up far too close to his face. And now, finally, just as he'd been visited by oblivion...

'I'm here, master; here I am.'

Levaux always slept fully dressed. He'd learned from long experience that his master woke from restless sleep very often and he was heartily sick of the embarrassment – and the cold – of waiting on the king night-naked. It was the work of a moment to strike flint and light the candle he kept ready in a silver dish beside the king's bed.

The king snorted; his impatience was caustic. Levaux was getting old. And slow. Just like his master.

'Get me the monk.'

Levaux was fuddled with the rags of sleep. 'The monk, Your Majesty? Which...?'

The king roared, 'THE MONK! Agonistes. I want Brother Agonistes. NOW!'

That tone of voice meant many things: death, destruction, bad digestion. Levaux fled the room like a wraith but Louis's words followed him.

'He's to go to the court of that usurper. Tell him that! I want information, do you hear? INFORMATION! There must be a way to wound that regicide, to hurt him where he least expects to be

485

hurt. The monk will find a way. He's to leave tonight. Immediately. Go! Do this or remember well the cage, Levaux. Remember the cage!'

Levaux scuttled away. He would do his master's bidding, certainly he would, but the king was clutching phantoms to his breast for comfort.

High summer in France but the world had turned dark for Louis, as everyone at court now knew. Certainly, a fragile three-month truce was in place with Burgundy – but that was only because Louis's dreams of influence over the destiny of England had disappeared with Warwick's death and the defeat of his cousin, Queen Margaret. Louis was nothing if not pragmatic.

But what could the monk do in the face of such events? What difference could he possibly make if he went to the court of King Edward in England? Levaux shook his head as he stumbled through the darkened palace. He hated nights like this. He would have to wake le Dain, and the barber loathed being woken in the night – it made him frightened. And fear made the king's chief confidant savage.

Omens. Very bad omens everywhere. Especially since he, and he alone, knew the secret that le Dain was hiding from the king. No doubt it would come out, in time, then ... Heaven protect them all. Meanwhile, he would keep his head down and do what he was told. Obedience might save him for a little while longer, God willing.

# Chapter Sixty-Eight

'She's gone. Some days since, my lord.'

William Hastings, the Chamberlain of England, had the craziest urge to laugh as he gazed on Deborah's bent head. He stretched out a hand and raised her from her curtsy.

'Do not be frightened, mistress. Just tell me *where* the Lady Anne has gone.'

Deborah composed herself. She had some liking for William Hastings but the sudden wash of fear was a warning she should heed. 'My lady's business is her own, sir.'

The king's chamberlain was one of the greatest magnates in England and he was in Anne's hall, supported by a considerable force of armed men all waiting outside in the inner ward. It was bravely said. William's lips twitched. He liked courage.

'Nonetheless, I am on the king's business and here by his command, Mistress Deborah. He expects obedience from his subjects. I ask you again: where is your lady?'

'She has gone to London.'

William slewed around towards the sound of a man's voice. The chamberlain's eyes narrowed. 'I know you.'

Leif Molnar strolled forward until he stood beside Deborah. He was almost twice the old woman's height but he leaned down and picked up one of her small hands, and patted it to comfort her, before he replied. 'Yes. You know me. I have you to thank for months without light last winter in the Binnenhof. I had not thought to give so many dark days to the king.'

Hastings glanced at the giant Norseman, eyebrows raised. He smiled, not unkindly, and said mildly, 'There are worse prisons than the dungeons of the Binnenhof, my friend. Why are you here at this house?'

Leif could have taken the words as provocation. He chose not to. 'Guarding my lady's interests. From all who would trouble her.'

'Ah. That is a good answer and, therefore, we can be friends for I, too, am here to help guard your lady. Her interests are the king's. And the king's are mine.'

Since Leif was not a fool he heard the double tone, the ambiguity around the word 'lady'. 'Lord Chamberlain, my *lady* will be grateful for your kind interest once she hears of it. Yet I fear, since you arrive too late to tell her of it yourself, she may never completely understand the support and comfort you wish to offer. However, I am certain she would wish me to offer thanks in her stead, as her faithful servant.' He bowed gracefully, from the waist.

Deborah was astonished. Normally, Leif spoke as little as possible. Now his speech and bearing were perfectly polished.

The chamberlain found himself bowing in reply. That confused him. He'd presumed that this man who'd once claimed to be Anne's husband was a common seaman.

'And may I know the name of Lady de Bohun's

most distinguished servant?'

'My name is Leif Molnar. I am the captain of Sir Mathew Cuttifer's cog, the *Lady Margaret*. My master has set me the task to guard his ward, Lady de Bohun. It is my duty, my honour and my pleasure to fulfil that task.'

'And yet she went to London without you?'

There was the slightest, the very slightest, sneer to the chamberlain's words. Deborah's eyes flicked to the Norseman – he could see her concern and smiled, gently holding out a chair so she could sit. Should she? The chamberlain had not indicated his permission.

'Mistress, will you sit? You seem tired to me.' Politics and power crackled in the air as Leif addressed Deborah directly.

William Hastings slapped one riding glove against the other as the woman sat in a simple chair. 'You did not answer me, Master Molnar.'

The Dane smiled placidly. 'My lady is always well guarded now, lord. I see to that.'

Hastings ground his teeth silently. He was tired and covered in dust and now he faced the lengthy ride back to London, unsatisfied. Three more days. God only knew what would have transpired by the time he returned to court.

'Very well. However, since the welfare of your mistress,' – again, it was an ambiguous word – 'is close to the heart of our king, I must ask you to tell me where she lodges.'

Just at that moment, a child's happy voice was heard. 'Deborah, Deborah, where are you?'

The old woman broke the tension between the two men by calling out, 'In here, child. In the hall.'

489

A small blur of energy hurtled into the room and resolved itself into Edward as he jumped onto Deborah's lap. 'Look, look! A green frog. Really green!'

'So it is. But see, Edward, we have visitors. Here is Lord Hastings. You must greet him on behalf of your aunt, child.'

Edward turned to see Hastings gazing at him with great interest.

'Hello. I remember you. You stayed at our old house. You are welcome to our new one. Do you like frogs, sir?'

It was said with perfect poise and William Hastings, the father of sons himself, was enchanted.

'I am pleased to be remembered. May I see your frog, small master?'

Leif Molnar moved closer to the woman and the child as the chamberlain sauntered towards them. Their eyes met. And locked.

'Ah yes. A very fine, and no doubt rare, large green frog. You are most fortunate, Edward.'

The child nodded vigorously. 'He'd be very happy living with us here, you know. Don't you agree, sir?'

All guileless charm, the chamberlain noted. Just like his father.

'No doubt Mistress Deborah will have her opinions on this; however, it's my experience that frogs like ponds and long grass more than living in houses.'

Edward shook his head. 'Oh no. Not all frogs. This one's an indoors frog. He *likes* it here. See?' He slipped off Deborah's knee and carefully put the animal down on the rushes. It sat there, gulping rapidly but unmoving.

'We like freedom, Edward. That is most precious to us all. Frogs and people alike.'

Leif Molnar was looking at William Hastings as he spoke. Edward was on his tummy on the floor, earnestly inspecting the frog at close quarters.

The chamberlain stooped down and held out his hand. After a moment, the frog hopped onto his palm. A strange thing to see. Edward sat up and held out his hand. 'No! He's mine!'

'It is a big and dangerous world, Edward. Some handle freedom better than others. This frog, for instance...'

Edward was on tiptoe, holding up his hands. 'Give him to me. Give him to me!'

Deborah was shocked. 'Edward!'

The little boy took no notice. 'Please, sir. I found him. He's mine!' His bottom lip was trembling and William Hastings smiled compassionately at the child.

'You may have him back but...' – Edward raised a tear-stained face – '...there is a price you must pay for him. Where is your aunt?'

The little boy smiled happily. 'Oh, that's easy. She's at Sir Mathew's house. Can I have my frog back now?'

It was late in the day as Edward Plantagenet held the small parchment scroll in his hands. He touched the seal with gentle fingers; it was one he had granted personally – three Angevin leopards surmounting two drops of blood. Anne's seal.

'Your Majesty, may I pour you another–'

'Go!' The king's glance at the pot-boy was unthinkingly severe. So much so, the child almost dropped the ale flask as he scrambled to back away.

A moment before, the king had been serene. He'd been strolling back from the great mews of the palace after inspecting his hunting birds with a party of friends. It was a late and balmy afternoon; even the midges had cleared in the gentle breeze as the sun declined to the west. There'd been happy laughter, even jokes, from the court party as the king stopped to take the horn of ale.

But then the messenger had arrived with the little scroll. Now the courtiers stood silently, frozen by indecision. Should they follow the boy?

The king looked up for a moment as he tore the scroll open. 'Yes! All of you. Leave.' He turned his back as he waved them away.

There was quiet debate amongst the men as they trailed off in twos and threes. Was the king angry, or sad? Or...?

'The French, do you think? Louis back in the game with some deep play?' Wise heads nodded.

'He looked shocked. Bad news?'

There was a sudden whoop of laughter behind them and one or two dared to look back. The king's face was joyous and he threw his velvet hat high into the air as he hurried away, not caring where it fell.

Courtiers turned to one another astonished, and one bent down to pick up the king's headgear from where it had fallen into a pile of horse droppings.

'Should we go...?'

'...with him? No. He hasn't asked us.'

The man holding the king's hat shook it hard to dislodge the stable's donation to high fashion. The padded velvet would need to be dried and carefully brushed. Perhaps the brown stain left on its rolled rim would be close enough to the natural red not to be noticed when dry? He held it to the light.

His friend shook his head. 'Too late.'

For the hat? Or to catch the fast disappearing king?

'Where do you think he's going in such a hurry?'

His friend shrugged. 'Somewhere he doesn't want us.'

## Chapter Sixty-Nine

She was sitting in Lady Margaret's solar, embroidering all alone, when she heard a distant commotion. Voices, men's voices, one in particular suddenly raised and then shouting. The thick walls muffled the sound. Moments later, a rapid tapping at the door gave way to the luckless Walter's flushed face.

'Lady, I can't find my master or my mistress, but the king...'

Anne stood as the blood rushed to her heart, leaving her breathless and dizzy. Poor Walter; he stepped forward and held out his hand, deeply concerned the lady would faint: she was milk-pale.

'I'm sorry, mistress, I mean, Lady Anne, but the ... he told me to fetch you.'

Anne put her embroidery frame down so carefully it might have been a holy relic.

'Go!' Walter slewed around at the sound of the man's voice behind him and gasped. Edward Plantagenet was through the solar door in one long stride. He'd closed the door and bolted it before Anne had time to draw another breath.

The man and the woman gazed at each other, barely registering the sound of Walter's feet as he hurried away.

'Well, lady?'

Anne said nothing. Edward Plantagenet crossed the small space between them. His voice shook. 'Half a year. A lifetime.'

He stood within touching distance but still she was silent, though her throat worked.

'Have you nothing to say to me?' His tone was agonised, pleading.

A shiver ran from the crown of Anne de Bohun's head down her spine and lodged behind her knees. She held out one hand, one finger, and traced the side of his face, haltingly. Deborah was right. She did not have the strength.

Edward closed his eyes. He tingled where she'd touched him.

'Six months. A lifetime indeed.' Anne dropped her hand and, when the king opened his eyes, drops of water glimmered on her cheeks. He caught one of her tears and touched it to his lips.

'No more of this.'

He opened his arms and she stepped into them. She sighed as she rested there, the base of his throat near enough to kiss. His smell was unlike any other. Behind the scent of orris root and sandalwood there was the skin of a man; warm, musky, alive. She knew that skin.

'Come away with me.' He raised her chin with his free hand and cupped it. Bending down, his mouth was on hers; her own half opened beneath his. 'Yes...' He breathed the word into her. 'Say yes, Anne.'

He was holding her against his body, one arm supporting, the other arm wrapping her tighter and tighter. Boneless; she felt as if the scaffolding of her body was gone; dissolved.

Suddenly, she saw her son: smiling, playing in the orchard of Herrard Great Hall. Behind him, running after him, laughing, was Leif.

'Wait! Let me think.' She struggled and he let her go; she stood with her back to him, hands to her face.

'Let me make amends, my darling. Help me to help us both.' He hadn't expected to sound like a small child begging for his heart's desire.

Anne's hands dropped to her sides and she turned to face him. 'Very well. Give me peace. I want nothing from you except freedom. Let me live in my own country, unmolested, with my son. No more prying eyes, no more questions. From anyone.'

Her voice was low; her tone carefully neutral. What was she feeling? Edward could not tell but he held out his hand to her, beseeching.

'That you shall have. I will give you an honourable life and perfect peace.' He was one step closer to her, and now another. 'But I have a gift for you, Anne. It's a secret, yours and mine. Just for us. Let me show it to you? You will understand when you see it, I promise.'

Anne de Bohun knew Edward Plantagenet and she could hear the truth, see it in his eyes.

Would she take what was offered?

'This time you must trust me, Anne. God has given us one more chance.' Edward leaned forward and caught Anne's hands in both of his. 'Come with me, my darling, or you will wonder all your life.'

Slowly, never taking his eyes off hers, accepting her silence for an answer, Edward drew Anne towards the solar door. Her skirts trailed behind her, whispering, over the flagged floor.

He lifted the latch and folded her arm through his, holding her firmly to his side. And then he looked down into her face.

'You are the great love of my life, Anne. We can have the future. If you want it.'

Edward pushed the door open; together, he and the silent girl stepped through.

Unexpectedly, in this dark house, light dazzled them both. A great lantern had been set on a stand to brighten the gloomy passage outside as night fell. The king caught a glimpse of Anne's face as they passed into the light. She was terrified; and joyous.

Together, they hurried down the stairs of Blessing House. And, finally, Anne's fingers crept through the king's. He tightened his grip as they fled.

Unobserved, Margaret Cuttifer watched them

go, standing with her husband in the gallery that looked down into the receiving hall. Every servant in the house had been banished to the kitchen so that the king might leave when he chose to. Alone, or accompanied.

'Did we do right to send her letter to the palace?' Anxiety bled from Mathew's words.

Margaret was helpless, just as he was. 'She asked us to send it. How could we refuse?'

Below them, the great door of Blessing House opened and then closed. Anne and the king were gone.

Mathew sighed and did an unusual thing. Normally the most reserved of men, he drew his wife towards him and kissed her full on the mouth. 'I am grateful for you. Grateful that you are my wife. May the king and Anne find the happiness I have experienced with you.'

Margaret Cuttifer tenderly kissed her husband in return. 'And I with you, husband. I with you.'

They both heard the hooves of an iron-shod horse on the cobbles outside Blessing House; heard the animal canter away.

'Lady Mary bless and keep them safe from harm; as God's mother has preserved us in our marriage, wife.'

Margaret leaned against her husband's shoulder, sombre eyes on the great, closed door below.

'Amen to that, husband. Amen to that.'

Twilight splashed rose and silver into the western sky as the last light began to fade. Soon they would close the bridge and chain the streets, but not yet, not yet.

Anne de Bohun clung to Edward's waist as they rode through the streets of the village of Westminster. She could smell the warm wind as it touched the face of the moving river, she could hear men and women's voices as they passed beneath houses, great and small; she saw people moving in the shadows of their upstairs rooms as lights were lit, but all of this meant nothing, had no meaning. The horse's hooves struck a rhythm from the cobbles and she was dreaming again, surely?

Perhaps, in a moment, the wolf would spring and blood would spill out over the snow.

'What did you say, my darling? Snow?' Edward laughed and her arms, clasped around him, felt the vibration deep in his chest. 'Too warm for snow. Unless...'

'Unless what?'

He shortened the reins and urged his horse faster. 'Unless William has done his work even better than I expect him to.'

A dog barked suddenly, quite close, and the king's horse shied; Anne tightened her grip, her body pressed against his back as she tried not to slip off the animal's rump.

'Nearly there, my darling, never fear. Hold hard.' The king placed one hand over hers, their fingers knotted together on his tight belly; his voice was suddenly husky. 'I remember this. Your breasts against my body as we rode.' Anne said nothing; she remembered too. He spoke quietly as the horse settled beneath them. 'I did not want that journey to end even though we were cold and hungry; I thought I'd lost everything but you.'

'And I wanted to ride on too, for ever.' Anne's words were so low they were lost in the clatter of hooves as the king reined the animal to a stop. Anne had an impression of iron gates and flambeaux flaring in the dying light.

'Close your eyes. Please? Just to humour me.'

She heard the excitement in his voice.

'Very well. I can't see anything, now. I promise.'

With eyes closed, Anne's other senses were enhanced, particularly hearing and smell. She heard the creak of the king's leather jerkin as he reached out to bang on the gate, felt the vibration of his voice through her body as he called out; heard the gate open in answer – a metallic, discordant, scraping sound – and felt, too, the vibration of the horse's hooves as they struck the ground.

They were in a garden now, she was certain of it: she could smell wild woodbine and roses, the clove scent of gillyflowers and the last sweetness of late jasmine; in this warm night, the perfumes had lingered long after the sun. And there was no longer a clatter from the horse's hooves – they were riding on something soft. Turf?

Edward spoke softly. 'Unclasp your hands, my darling, but keep your eyes closed. Can you do that?'

'What, and not fall off? Just because I can't see?' Anne was scornful. Of course she wouldn't fall!

The king gently disengaged Anne's hands from around his waist and stood in his stirrups. With some effort he leaned forward over the animal's neck and managed to dismount from the front. Anne experienced momentary panic; she was slipping sideways!

'Let go – I'll catch you.'

Remove something you take for granted and the world becomes an odd place. Yet Anne did not hesitate – she allowed herself to fall and he was there to catch her. She felt his arms – one under her knees, one around her back just beneath the shoulderblades. And then he had her against his chest, her head tucked into the space where neck meets shoulder.

'I will show you wonders...'

She could hear his boots as he strode. Soft at first, on turf, then hard, on stone. A door creaked open and scented air embraced them both. The door closed – she heard it – then he walked over something soft that rustled; the green scent of crushed, new-picked rushes came to her. He stopped. He put her down and one hand dropped to her waist, holding her close to his side.

'Open your eyes, sweet Anne. See what has been prepared for you...'

Anne blinked, her eyes adjusting to the low light, and then she gasped.

They were in a perfectly round room and in the centre stood a massive table made entirely from gold; it glimmered in a pool of mellow light. And there were candles the height of small children; they were fixed to sconces fashioned like giant cupped hands at intervals around the walls. On the table were platters and silver bowls of simple foods: white cheeses, good bread, fruit, marchpane comfits, whilst beside these was a massive red marble basin in which lay flasks of wine.

'Is that snow cooling the wine? In summer?' Anne was awed.

The king nodded. 'Yes. I must remember to congratulate my chamberlain.'

Edward held out his hand to Anne. 'Welcome, lady, to the enchanted bower that has been made for you.'

Anne gathered up the skirts of her dress in one hand and walked slowly around the room. Everything she saw, everything she smelled and touched – all was an equal delight. Simple, exquisite, harmonious.

Instead of arras, curtains of trembling silk graced the walls: alternate falls of silver, falls of gold, they moved and billowed gently, responding to the breeze from the garden. There was little furniture aside from the gold table: several backless stools made from black wood were clustered beneath its top – ebony? – and one great chest stood beside the door they had entered from. Massive, it was made from bronze and had a joyous frieze of tumbling cupids running around each one of its sides. They would chase each other for all eternity.

And everywhere she looked there were flowers: swags of white roses and woodbine and peonies, all woven together with ivy and late jasmine and hung in graceful garlands around the walls, beneath the rafters of the floor above.

Anne de Bohun felt profoundly humbled. With this room Edward said he knew her better than she knew herself.

'This is the most beautiful room that I have ever seen.'

Edward's joy was transparent. 'But see, there is more...'

He strode to the bronze coffer and hauled up the

lid with some difficulty; it was massively heavy, even for him. The king reached inside and withdrew something, something that glimmered in his hands. He shook it gently. Lustrous white cloth, fine as mist, slipped through his fingers; with a gasp, Anne saw the entire surface was embroidered with tiny pearls like so many drops of milk.

'I saw you wear a dress like this once, in Brugge. On the second night of my sister's marriage. Please me by wearing this tonight?'

Anne was dazzled. Silk was one thing, but a dress graced with hundreds and hundreds of pearls? It was a magnificent, a princely gift.

'Your Majesty, pearls are the gems that reward a chaste wife.' She tried not to sound sad.

Reverently, the King of England carried the dress to his beloved and held it up against her body. He nodded. 'You gave me pearls once. And you are chaste, I know that. Except with me.' He was looking into her eyes. 'Except with me, my darling.'

He bent and kissed her, and after a moment, the precious dress slid down amongst the rushes.

Neither of them noticed.

## Chapter Seventy

He had never thought to see this place again with his mortal eyes, but now, if he turned his head, the distant spires of the abbey reached towards the first stars and there, the unwieldy mass of the palace crouched close by. Was it smoke that rose into the still air from those numberless chimneys, or the presence of sin made visible in this wicked place?

The monk shuddered and closed his eyes as he whispered the words of the ancient psalm. 'I will lift up mine eyes to the hills from whence cometh my help...'

Help, strength, support. He would need them all if he was to avoid the mire of human transgression that awaited him at the palace *and* achieve the task he had been given by his brother, Louis – God's anointed servant.

The king had asked him for information about Edward's court, but Agonistes knew the truth: what Louis *really* wanted was justice and revenge on the regicide Earl of March. As a king, Louis had that right – God gave him the power to smite his enemies.

'Son of a blackamoor's whore!' A porter, with great heavy baskets of vegetables dangling from the yoke across his shoulders, yelled at the monk who, oblivious, had just cannoned into his back.

Before he could control himself, the courtier, nearly asleep inside the monk, bellowed, 'Hold your tongue or it shall be torn out!'

The surging, pressing mass of people in earshot paused in surprise. He might be filthy and scrawny in his patched robes, but this monk had the voice of authority. The porter, hearing the threat, tried to hurry past just as, weeping, Agonistes fell to his knees, desperate to atone.

'Ah, brother, brother, forgive me. It is this place ... this accursed place that speaks and not I, the least, the most miserable of God's servants.'

The porter, frightened by such strange behaviour, tried to back away but the weeping monk now had him by the legs and would not let go. He dragged himself along, attached like a limpet, sobbing and calling out, 'Penance, brother, give me penance to subdue such evil pride.'

Uproar grew as the crowd banked up behind the strange couple and then, in a further moment, scattered, screaming, as they snatched their children and their possessions back beneath the shelter of the house-jetties above their heads. A knot of soldiers was upon them out of the gathering gloom, with whips and curses, trying to clear a path for someone very important.

'Way! Way for the king's chamberlain. Get out of the way!'

The porter panicked. 'Let me go, sir. Get up!' But Agonistes, a drowning man, did not hear him and clung to the man's legs yet more fiercely, begging, wailing for forgiveness.

'No!' With a mighty shove, the porter swung his baskets, knocking Agonistes away from his knees.

'Halt!'

William Hastings gazed at the monk, face down in the filth-choked kennel on the crown of the road. As Agonistes raised his head to a dizzying vision of an armed and mounted man dressed in blue and red and gold, a last spear of light from the dying sun bounced off the metal helm, gracing the knight's head with a halo. It was a sign. The Lord had sent him a sign – and aid for the task at hand.

Scrambling to his feet, the ragged servant of

God and Louis de Valois pointed his finger; this chance meeting had removed all doubt. 'Lord William Hastings. I know you. The Lord knows you. And I have come to do his bidding. Sinner that I am, I can save the king from himself.'

In that moment, Agonistes truly understood the mission he'd been given, and who had given it to him. His soul had spoken the truth. Whatever Louis had asked of him, he had a higher purpose.

William's eyes narrowed. There was something about the man he recognised; take away the filth, take away the rags and something remained. The voice, it was distinctive. He had a good memory for voices. And faces.

'Moss? Is that you?'

The monk straightened his shoulders. 'The man who was once Moss is dead. I stand in his place. I am the hammer of witches and I have returned to cleanse the court and save the soul of the king from sorcery.'

William raised his eyebrows, almost inclined to laugh at the solemn absurdity of the ragged spectre in front of him. 'Oh? And how will you do that?'

Moss smiled, exposing unpleasantly ragged gums. 'A woman lives who should have burned for manifold sins. Her name is Anne de Bohun. Whilst she breathes, the king's soul is not safe. The Lord has sent me here to tell him this.'

William's hands convulsed on his horse's reins. Anne de Bohun?

'Sergeant!'

The sergeant of the guard fought his way

through the press of disgruntled people – fed up with being held up on their way home – to his master's side. 'Yes, Lord Chamberlain?'

'Bring this holy brother to the palace.'

William Hastings indicated the monk, then rode on without a backward glance as his servant gazed at the monk with distaste. Filthy, smelly – that didn't matter; it was the strange look in the man's eye that made the sergeant uneasy.

Holy? He looked more like a murderer than a saint.

## Chapter Seventy-One

It was a warm night also within the Palace of Westminster but, as the long dusk deepened and night came down, there was no rest for the queen. She'd last seen the king when, after coursing for hares in the grounds of the palace, he'd decided to visit his favourite hunting birds to see how they were faring in the heat of this summer.

Time slipped away and the hour for evening prayers and supper loomed ever closer, yet still the king did not return. So that she would not be shamed by Edward's absence from the public events to come, the queen instructed her ladies to tell the king's chamberlain, Hastings – newly returned from a mysterious six days' absence from court – that she was suddenly ill. The court could shift for itself tonight; she would not be present at its revels.

Behind the barred doors of the queen consort's opulent range of rooms in Westminster Palace, the queen's body-servants and her ladies of the bed chamber prepared Elizabeth Wydeville for sleep. First her silver-gilt hair was unpinned, let down and brushed, with ivory-backed horsehair brushes. Then her women sectioned the flowing mass and polished each hank with silk until it glowed. After which, braids were fashioned into a crown for the night. This ritual was conducted in silence since the queen had forbidden them to speak.

Reverently, the women removed the queen's day clothes and dressed her in a sleeping-gown. Ever fashionable, Elizabeth Wydeville had decided to adopt this new mode from Italy. She was in her thirties now and had had six children. Whilst she knew her body was still fair – she had the largest silver mirror in England to tell her so – she worried what the king thought when he saw her fully naked. Since Edward had returned and they had been reconciled – it seemed only she remembered the long months of brooding estrangement even before he'd fled the country – she'd been tempted to insist that all candle flames be first extinguished when he came to her bed. But that was tedious, and a passion killer. Edward did not enjoy coy women.

Therefore, the silk sleeping-gown, semi-diaphanous and artfully arranged to reveal just a glimpse of flesh. With it Elizabeth had regained confidence that she could still provoke her husband's lust. She believed she'd proved it to her own satisfaction, and his, several times since he'd returned to their kingdom. Now she was not so certain. Perhaps it had been duty alone that had brought him to her.

'Go!' Elizabeth Wydeville clapped her hands after the last of her rings was removed. A giant pearl nested amongst diamonds, it was a belated gift from the king rewarding her for the birth of their son. 'All of you, go. I will sleep alone.'

One by one her seven attendant ladies and each of the thirteen body-servants descended into curtsies, bending their heads and bodies before the queen. They would stay there, knees creaking, until Elizabeth gave them the signal to rise. A petty tyranny, this, but one she employed when feeling out of sorts – such as when the king chose to be absent without cause. Such as tonight.

In the early days of Edward's reign a clutch of lady companions and six or seven body-servants had sufficed to tend Elizabeth, sleeping and waking. Now that the queen's fortunes were restored, she considered thirteen body-servants to be the minimum number she could accept. Thirteen was the number of the blessed Apostles plus the Lord himself, she said; vanity incarnate, was the whisper about the court: an ageing body in need of special, extra services to keep her beauty unnaturally bright, *they* said.

'You may rise.'

It was profound relief to unlock shaking knees and stand again. Even the queen's mother, the Duchess Jacquetta, had not been spared since she'd been present in the queen's rooms tonight.

'Not you, mother. Stay with me until I sleep.'

The duchess felt her heart descend deeper in

her chest – a physical sensation brought on by the shining malice in her daughter's glance towards her.

'Come, sit with me.'

The newly restored Queen of England patted the coverlet of her bed companionably. This moment, observed by anyone outside the knowing circle of the court, might seem like the careless intimacy of any daughter, any mother. Jacquetta knew differently. Elizabeth wanted something.

The duchess sat gingerly on one corner of the great bed, some distance from the queen, her daughter.

'Closer. We can't speak properly if you're all that distance away. Here. Sit here.' The queen patted the surface of the embroidered counterpane again.

The duchess stood and swallowed a sigh. Smoothing the floating billows of her skirts – a rich, flattering black (not actual mourning, of course, just because it suited her) – she trailed to her daughter's side, all whispering silk, and sat where indicated. For a moment there was silence between them, then the queen beckoned Jacquetta even closer.

'What have you heard, mother? Tell me.'

The command was clear. Nervously, the duchess glanced around the vast and empty room. There was one open casement in the range of windows that looked down upon the river; the sluggish air around the bed was undisturbed, however, for it lay fully twelve cloth yards distant, much too far to be overheard, all supposing an athletic spy could have scaled the walls from the river terrace more than thirty feet below.

The queen saw where her mother was looking and narrowed her eyes. She nodded. 'Close it, certainly. We can't be too careful.'

The duchess dreaded being her daughter's confidante. Time was, when Elizabeth had first come to court, that Jacquetta had welcomed and fostered every evidence of intimacy she could persuade from her daughter, for they'd all risen together, all the Wydevilles, out of the queen's miraculous marriage to Edward Plantagenet. But as time passed, and especially after the recent upheavals, the queen's mother had become deeply anxious about Elizabeth's increasing reliance on her for personal support.

Ten months since Edward had lost his throne, nearly six since he'd regained it, and in that time Elizabeth had become utterly paranoid about the motives of those who surrounded her. She'd decided that the members of her family were her only true allies, but there was a danger in this too: to be close to the queen, part of the suite of courtiers who saw her every day, was to become trapped in a breathing, dark miasma of relentless suspicion, and no one was immune.

Elizabeth's paranoia had even grown greater since the longed-for return of the king to London. She'd become convinced, rightly, that most court women actively sought to seduce Edward Plantagenet. In response, Elizabeth had forced her mother to spy within the court, driving the duchess to secure information that she, the wife of the king, could not. But it was never enough. Elizabeth Wydeville never knew enough, never heard enough. Tonight's intimacies between mother and daughter were the marker of that.

Duchess Jacquetta struggled to pull the heavy casement closed and retraced her steps to the queen's bed. She looked dispassionately at her daughter's face. Perhaps the queen's anxiety was justified. Even by candlelight, fine lines were clear beside Elizabeth's eyes and there were the first faint creases on the upper lip, the dreaded 'purse strings'.

'What are you looking at?' The queen was sharp; she'd seen her mother's appraising glance.

For once, the duchess spoke unvarnished truth. 'I was thinking, daughter, that you must control your scowls. You should smile more. Though gently, of course. As it is, you use your face too much and in ways that are not flattering.'

Fear turned the queen's eyes black. 'What are you saying?'

'Lines, my daughter. On your face. I can see them clearly tonight. Relics of your bad temper, I fear. Soon they will not smooth away with the morning.'

'One has only to gaze on your face, mother, to understand my fate in time.' Soft as poisoned cream. Mother and daughter smiled at each other as tension crackled between them.

'But what have you heard? Where is the king?'

Jacquetta thought for a moment that she might avoid telling what she knew – if only for her daughter's peace of mind – but in the end there was little point postponing the inevitable. Elizabeth would force her to tell, one way or another.

'He's been followed since he left the palace this evening, though I'd thought to spare you this.'

511

The queen almost frowned, and then remembered to smile. She sat up straighter. 'And so?'

'He was alone; he took a horse from the stables in the late afternoon when he received a message.' The duchess held up one hand to her daughter's look of enquiry. 'No, I don't know what it said. He rode straight to that troublesome mercer's house.'

Nuns' fingers had worked for months to embroider the queen's new and delicate sheets, but her hands twisted the precious fabric into a bundle of creases. 'Mathew Cuttifer and his sanctimonious wife. And then?'

Duchess Jacquetta of Luxembourg took a very deep breath. 'He left there not long afterwards, when it was close to dark. He had a woman with him and they were riding together on his horse. They went down beside the river to a private house. That is all I know.'

The queen's face was chalk white in the gloom of her bed. Her voice struck like a whip. 'No. There is more, I can tell. What is it?'

Jacquetta grimaced. The queen was, after all, her own daughter. And she was suffering.

'Ah, my child...'

She would not say it if she could avoid it, but Elizabeth Wydeville fixed her mother with a cool eye.

'Go on, mother. Tell me. You must tell me if I command you to. I am the queen.'

'Very well. Since you desire to know. The king and that woman are both still there, at this house. The gates are locked and the lights have been put out.'

The queen repeated the words as if tasting

them. 'The lights have been put out.'

Suddenly, she turned on her side and began to sob. The duchess was struck with pity and fear both – if the queen fell, if she lost the king's favour, perhaps the house of Wydeville would fall as well. She leaned across and stroked her daughter's brow.

'There, daughter, there. It's not so bad. This woman is plainly just a doxy. When has he ever spared more than a day or two for a doxy? You are the queen. The mother of his son.'

Elizabeth turned to face her mother so fast she was a striking snake. They were tears of rage, not desolation.

'It's her; it has to be. Anne de Bohun; she's the mother of his *eldest* son. And he loves her, not me.'

It took a moment for Jacquetta to gather her wits. 'But, child, kings have had bastards before and they will again. You are Edward's legitimate wife. *Love* of the kind you fear does not last. Position does.'

The queen turned on her side once more.

'Go away, mother. You don't understand. You just don't understand.'

## Chapter Seventy-Two

'Wake, my darling. They've rung the bells for tierce. It's morning.'

And it was. Blissful morning. Anne stretched languorously in the disordered bed as light filtered through her closed lids. Then she sat up, shocked.

'The Cuttifers!'

The king stopped tying the points on his breeches. He laughed and leaned across the naked girl to kiss away the strand of hair that had fallen across one soft breast. Then he stood and stretched, his eyes roaming this beloved woman, tumbled and supple in the chaos of the sheets. It was a deeply satisfying sight. Unbidden, his belly contracted as images of the last, long night provoked his senses once more.

Would he put his shirt on? No. He sat on the edge of the bed, half dressed.

'All is well, my darling. They've received word.'

Anne was worried. She covered her body, determined to preserve modesty, belatedly. 'What word? What did you tell them?'

'That you were praying for your sins with the good sisters at Sion and would not be back for some days.'

Anne yelped. 'Some days? Edward, that is a terrible lie! I must dress.' She swung her legs out of the bed. But she wasn't quick enough.

Casually, the king leaned forward and pushed the girl down against the pillows, catching her wrists in his hands. He was not especially gentle. Anne protested and the sheet fell down most engagingly in the little tussle. Edward held her arms wide.

'Why dress? I like you like this.'

Morning sun poured honey-light through the opened casements. Already it was warm and Anne, exposed, was touched with gold. Both of them were breathing faster.

'I don't think you should wear clothes, Anne. Ever again.'

With tantalising slowness, he bent down to kiss her. She moaned as his tongue was in her mouth and in a moment he had her pinned, naked, beneath him. Anne struggled, attempting to speak, trying to stop his ever busier hands, but he muffled each of her words with his mouth.

'We are together, that is all that matters. You have come back to me.'

'Edward... Oh, let me speak!'

He wasn't listening; tearing at his clothes as quickly as he'd put them on, careless of strings and points, passionate to feel his own skin entirely naked and against her own.

'Say you love me. Now. Say it! Or...'

It was delicious for both of them. He had her astride his lap now, kneeling over him, her legs either side of his waist but not quite touching; it had happened in a moment. The smell of their bodies, of sex and rising desire, was intoxicating.

'Or what?' She was teasing him, gently squirming, moving her hips, sliding her hips, allowing her breasts to brush against his chest for a moment, skin to skin. But she would not allow her lower body to touch his except for brief, tantalising seconds.

'Jesu!' He was panting, almost groaning, as he cupped her buttocks and his knees moved, spreading her own wider apart. Now she was breathing into his mouth, moving her hips more slowly, back and forth, back and forth, lower, lower.

'So? What will you do, liege?'

'This!' He pulled her down, forced her hips down. Instantly he was deep inside her body – rocking, thrusting, timing his movements to hers. She gasped.

Each time, each time, it felt so different.

And now she was on her back, her body splayed and slick with sweat as he thrust, and waited, and thrust, and waited and thrust. Deeper and harder and faster, the pause shorter each time. His mouth demanded hers, his hands were everywhere, on her breasts, between her legs, stroking, questing.

'Say it.' It was a growl, not words.

'Yes! I love you, love you, *love you!*' It was a chant as she raised her hips and offered them to his body: a gift; she held, helpless, to the posts at the top of the bed as he plundered her thighs, her willing, opened body.

'Again! *How* do you love me?'

'With my breasts and with my mouth and with my...'

The words were lost as he ate them: two souls in a joined, delicious prison of flesh. All sense of herself as separate from him was gone. She was delirious, dizzy with a deepening frenzied heat that made her want to open every part of herself to him, this man, her lover. The fierceness of it, his strength, the muscles of his back, his arms and what he was doing to her, with her – and she to him, with him – all these things were precious. She was his. He was hers.

'There. And there. And *there!*' He sang the words and, godlike, the wave of ecstasy took him, open-eyed; his gaze burned Anne's face as if written there was the meaning of all that was, and all that had ever been. Then his intensity caught her up and they rode it down together, plunged from light into darkness and such joy as they dissolved into one another whilst their bodies slowly withdrew from the clamour, the tumult, of the senses.

Anne was silent as the king lay curled around and beside her, panting; her body cooled and the rose flush subsided, though her chest rose and fell like a runner's.

Edward suddenly chuckled.

'What?' Anne stifled a yawn as she said it. The temptation of sleep was immense.

'They wouldn't have you now.'

'Who?'

'The sisters. You pray for different things, it seems to me. And in very different ways!'

Anne opened one eye and giggled. 'So do you, oh most Catholic and holy king.'

'Wholly yours, my darling. This king is wholly yours...'

Softly, very gently, he kissed her. As softly she kissed him in return.

She had chosen.


'Are you there, mother?'

The queen remained in her bed behind closed curtains. This was most unusual for it was late morning, well past the time for mass. The small crowd of women ranged around the bed dared not speak and looked at Duchess Jacquetta in mute appeal.

Clearing her throat nervously, the duchess spoke up. 'I am, Your Majesty. Good morning.

Did you sleep well?'

'I did not. I'm ill. Very ill.'

The ladies looked downcast and the body-servants exchanged frightened glances. Once more they gazed beseechingly at Jacquetta. She sighed. Very well, she'd take responsibility.

'Shall we fetch you a doctor, daughter?'

'No! I want no doctors about me. They'll make it worse. I want you. Come here!'

Imperious, querulous. Two bad signs. Two *very* bad signs.

Duchess Jacquetta moved to the bed with tiny, graceful steps. Her face was calm but those amongst the ladies who knew her best saw the convulsive grip of one hand on the other.

Hesitantly, the queen's mother pulled one of the embroidered bed-curtains slightly aside; it was dark inside the cave they created.

'Daughter? I can't see you.'

'Am I a beast in a cage, to be peered at? A bear? A lion perhaps?'

The duchess ducked as a bolster sailed past her shoulder and landed on the floor. As one, the ladies and the servants gasped and backed away.

'Well?'

'Now, my dear child, calm yourself.'

The wrong thing to say. The duchess knew it as soon as she voiced the words.

'Calm? CALM myself!' Another bolster, followed by a pewter necessary pot; its contents flew everywhere. This time the queen's mother did not duck quite fast enough.

'OH!'

'What did you say?' The queen's white face appeared between the curtains. Dark circles beneath each eye, cracked lips and wild hair. Where was the beautiful Elizabeth Wydeville today?

'You stink! Go!'

Duchess Jacquetta had been bred in courts; descended from the greatest nobility of France she had seen much, and done much, in a comparatively long life. Little had the power to move or shock her. But this was uncontrolled savagery; and she had bred the monster in this bed, created it from her own body. Tears swelled and burst from her eyes as the queen's mother hurried from the room, leaving an appalled silence behind her.

'Well? What are you staring at? Clean up this mess. I have changed my mind.' Elizabeth Wydeville's voice was an ominous growl. Dread spread softly through the room.

'Yes, Your Majesty.' The Duchess of Portland spoke, a slight quaver in her voice. She was the lady of most senior rank left in the queen's rooms. It was her duty.

'Yes me no yeses. I will dress. Now. Ill as I am. Then you will bring William Hastings to me. Immediately. *Do you understand?*'

Mute, the terrified women curtsied and then scurried forward to the bed, hearts hammering, some to clean (the body-servants) and some to display clothing for the approval of the queen-consort (the ladies). *Dress the queen! Dress the queen! Hurry! Find the chamberlain, find the chamberlain! Quickly. Quickly! Quickly!*

At the heart of this storm of sudden, earnest activity the queen sat silent and brooding. Her rage was gone and in her heart was a stone.

The king had not returned; he had not returned all night.

Anne de Bohun was to blame.

## Chapter Seventy-Three

'Your Majesty?' William Hastings advanced two paces towards the Presence chair and flourished a bow to the queen. Another two paces, another bow.

'Stop!'

William looked up, startled.

'Stop this. You'll be all morning getting here.'

For one bright moment the chamberlain thought the queen had made a joke, but a quick glance at Elizabeth Wydeville's sombre face and he squashed that happy thought. The queen's eyes had a dangerous hot glitter. William knew the signs and knew what to do. He moved forward faster, as gracefully as he could, and knelt on one knee at the foot of the dais.

'Your Majesty is radiant this morning.' A gallant lie, but gallant lies were useful things. Would the queen acknowledge his sally? No. Elizabeth, now that he saw her face at close range, actually looked close to tears.

'Tell them to go. All of them.'

William stood and surveyed the crowded Presence chamber. From the queen's expression, the court could sense something was brewing and, almost without him seeing them do it, as a body they were creeping closer and closer to the Presence chair, just in case there was something juicy to pick up on as the chamberlain spoke with the queen.

William clapped his hands sharply and there was an audible mutter. Dismissed! And just as things were getting interesting.

The chamberlain ignored the mutters and the smothered sighs of disappointment. He waited patiently until it pleased the queen to speak.

The great doors closed on the last of the court; Elizabeth beckoned Hastings forward.

'Did you find her?'

Hastings had prepared himself for this conversation, had thought carefully of what he needed to say to gain the best advantage from this awkward situation.

'No, Your Majesty, I did not. The Lady Anne de Bohun had already left her home.'

The queen did not seem surprised. She nodded and slumped a little in her chair, which confused William momentarily. Could news have travelled this fast from Somerset?

'And? What else?'

The chamberlain smiled confidently. 'Your Majesty, I know where she is.'

The queen stared into William's eyes. She beckoned him again. He stood on the lower step of the dais; she waved him closer still. Now he stood beside her Presence chair.

'So do I,' she whispered in his ear, a tickling sensation. In suppressing the urge to scratch his ear, William was distracted and completely unprepared when Elizabeth screamed, *'He's with*

521

*her now. He's been with her all night!'*

The sheer volume of sound nearly made the chamberlain fall backwards. Automatically, he put out a hand to save himself and his fingers closed around one arm of the queen's chair; the arm on which the queen was leaning.

'Don't touch me. How dare you!'

Elizabeth was furious and William was bewildered and confused. And shamed. The queen's person was sacred, not to be touched by unconsecrated hands.

'Forgive me, Your Majesty!'

William stumbled to the floor and knelt, head bent, to hide his flaming face. There was silence, though Hastings was certain his heart had migrated to his mouth and, if he opened it, the queen would hear its agitated thud.

'What am I to do, William? The king loves that woman. He will abandon me. Send me to a convent.'

She never called him William. Cautiously, the chamberlain raised his eyes and saw something remarkable. The queen was actually crying in front of him, oblivious of appearances. He'd never seen her cry before; the tears fell in a minor torrent, dropping onto the fingers she'd twisted together in her satin lap, dripping from the ends of her nose and her chin. They were real tears, not decorative in the least.

William held his breath. This was, potentially, an opening to the first big realignment of power and influence since the king had returned. The High Chamberlain of England recognised his moment and seized it.

'Your Majesty, I agree that the Lady Anne is a problem: for the king and, potentially, for the country. But do not despair. Later today there is someone I believe you should meet. Someone with much to tell us about the Lady Anne de Bohun...'

## Chapter Seventy-Four

When Anne awoke, most of the morning had fled, but she decided she'd dispense with anxiety and fear; enchantment was the ruling force in her life now – enchantment conjured by the king, her lover. Edward Plantagenet had caused a bower to be created for her and she had become the lady of this place. For the moment she dwelt within a tower surrounded by a garden – just as the Romances described. Anne decided she would explore this new domain whilst the king was away.

First, however, she should dress. It would not be decent to remain naked and in bed for the whole day, though it was a tempting and luxurious thought. Anne sat up and wrapped one of the delicate sheets around her body. She was surrounded by beauty and opulence such as she'd never seen before; it was intoxicating. But luxury was a close companion to sin, was it not?

Stretching to banish the thought, Anne stood and walked to a latched casement, the sheet trailing over the rushes behind her. But the glass panes were thick and leaf green and the outside world was oddly distorted when she tried to look through them. What did the garden truly look like from this height? Pushing the casement open as widely as she could, Anne looked down on her secret realm, the sun shining full on her face like a blessing.

The garden beneath and around her tower was thickly wooded and contained within it a high wall though, on one side, it appeared to finish at a natural rockface half hidden in trees. It was a lavish amount of otherwise empty land this close to Westminster; almost a nobleman's park.

Directly below her window there was a small building with a sharply pointed roof, from the highest part of which a thread of smoke arose, wavering, into the still air. A kitchen?

Anne yawned. And laughed. If she was to be the lady in the tower for a day whilst she awaited the return of her lover with the sunset, surely she must wash and dress suitably? But she would need help. And clothes. What about clothes? All she had was the dress she'd worn yesterday, now lying abandoned on the floor.

The white dress, the dress embroidered with pearls. Where was that?

As she thought about it, and remembered what had happened when she'd arrived the previous night with the king, Anne blushed, though there was no one there to see her embarrassment. Ah yes, that dress also, that beautiful, *enchanting* garment – it too had been abandoned.

Then something caught Anne's eye: a delicate silver hand-bell was beside the bed she'd lately left. Curious, the girl stooped down and lifted it;

rang it experimentally…

It took only moments after the clear sound shivered through the air for light, hurrying steps to be heard outside the tower room: a woman or a child, perhaps? A hesitant hand knocked at the door.

'Enter.'

The door opened slowly and a woman's black-veiled head peered through. A moment, and the body of the owner of the head arrived behind it, bowing.

A *nun?* For one mad instant Anne thought a professed sister had been sent to her, but when the stranger raised her head, Anne saw the truth. A widow: that explained the black dress, the white wimple.

Swallowing her embarrassment, Anne smiled pleasantly. 'I should like to wash and then to dress. Can you help me?'

The woman nodded enthusiastically and smiled, though her eyes remained respectfully fixed on the floor.

'What is your name?'

The woman opened her mouth and pointed; there was only a wriggling red stump of flesh where her tongue should have been. She was mute.

'Oh. I am so sorry.' Anne was shocked, but the woman smiled at her readily enough. She pointed at the bell in Anne's hand and mimed washing and dressing.

'Yes. Yes, I should like that, if you can help me? I need to find a dress: it's white and…'

The woman nodded vigorously and hurried

from the room. A moment later, she returned with the lovely garment laid reverently over her outstretched arms. Carefully placing it on the disordered bed, she led Anne to a stool near the window and, leaving her there, mimed that she was going to fetch water.

Anne watched her go and shivered, though the sun streamed through the window, bathing her in warmth.

Was this woman's guaranteed discretion part of the price of her love for Edward Plantagenet, and his for her? Perhaps kings thought differently about the human cost of love. Perhaps they did not count the cost at all.

'I don't remember you. When were you at court?'

Elizabeth Wydeville was back in control. And not especially impressed by what she saw. Bone thin and pale, the monk standing before her Presence chair was dressed in the robes of a Dominican, but robes so elegantly made, from such fine wool dyed a deep and lustrous black, that Brother Duckshit himself would not have disdained to wear them. The man raised haunted eyes.

'I was your physician, sister-queen. I brought you the blessed Girdle of the Holy Mother of Christ when the pain was too great at the birth of your eldest daughter, the noble Lady Elizabeth. And when it seemed that you might die, I helped the princess out of your belly and watched you cry when you saw the baby was a girl-child.'

The queen, already astonished at being addressed as 'sister-queen', choked on an indignant breath. 'How dare you! Guard!'

'No, Your Majesty! Let him speak. Please. For the sake of the king. And your kingdom.'

That stopped Elizabeth Wydeville. She lowered herself into the chair once more, alert. Very alert.

'Well, Hastings? Why must I listen to this ... to this creature?'

'Because what he says is true. He was your physician. Moss was his name then. But now, Your Majesty, this man, our holy brother as he now is, can deliver the king from the sorceries of Anne de Bohun, with your help.'

'Thou shalt not suffer a witch to live.' The monk murmured the words softly, his eyes fixed on the queen's.

Acid rose high in the queen's throat. *How did he know?*

'These are pernicious rumours. The court is full of envy at the restoration of my husband. They slander me to wound him.' The queen's voice shook and her hands gripped the arms of her chair. If she had to stand now, she would fall; of that she was certain.

Hastings was aghast. 'No, Your Majesty. This man accuses the *Lady Anne* of witchcraft.'

The monk nodded and signed a cross in the air between himself and the queen. 'Foul enchantment has made the king blind to his mortal sin of lust. This woman, who calls herself Anne de Bohun...' His face twisted and he wiped his mouth as if he'd fouled it by saying the name. 'This *succubus* in a girl's shape has attached itself to your husband's soul. She will destroy him, as she destroyed me, and the kingdom also unless...'

He was ghost pale and so sincere the queen's terror bled away. Relief took its place. 'Unless what, Brother?'

Spittle had gathered at the sides of Brother Agonistes' mouth; unconscious of protocol, he wiped it onto the skirts of the fine new habit supplied by the chamberlain – the man who'd also insisted he wash before talking to the queen. Vanity. Vanity! But soon, all such things would pass away in these end times...

'Unless she is given over to the Church. With your help, and that of the chamberlain, I shall remove her from this kingdom. Remove her to France, where, this time, she will be burned, most assuredly. To save her soul.' He added the last with great certainty.

'Amen,' whispered the queen. A brilliant solution. If only she, herself, could be kept out of it.

'Amen,' echoed the chamberlain, without even a twinge of concern. In the end, he was a pragmatist.

'Let it be done, Lord Hastings. Let her be taken away. For the good of the kingdom and the salvation of its king. This woman has broken the terms of her exile.'

Impulsively, Elizabeth pulled from her finger a large, square-cut emerald ring set amongst pearls. 'Sell this. It will buy the help you require to escort this woman from our kingdom.'

And, thought William Hastings, it would buy an excellent set of false documents as well.

The queen stood as she gave the monk her ring. 'You are about God's work, good Brother. It is my duty to assist you by all means possible.'

Brother Agonistes bowed. Surely his master, Louis, his brother-king, would be glad when he presented the woman to him for judgment. At one stroke, his will would be accomplished on Earth as his master's was in Heaven. Edward Plantagenet would suffer greatly for his sins in the woman's absence. The English king would be mortified by grief – especially once he heard of the woman's fate – and yet his soul would be exalted in the eyes of the Lord by this suffering. Righteous punishment, righteously endured was the path to salvation. That was God's will for all his creatures.

On a signal from the chamberlain, the monk bowed with the remembered grace of a courtier and backed from the Presence chamber. But before Hastings could follow, the queen beckoned him closer.

'I'll not be associated with this, will I, Hastings? Not in any way?'

The chamberlain shook his head, his face carefully neutral. 'Associated with what, Your Majesty? As far as I know, we have been greatly edified by the prayers of a very holy man. A great sinner who has surrendered his will to God. To the very great profit of all our souls.'

The queen waved her hand, dismissing the king's high chamberlain. She sat in the empty Presence chamber, silent and, for that rare moment, entirely alone. Would it really be over? Could Anne de Bohun be dismissed from her life, and Edward's life, so very easily?

Quickly, she kissed the crucifix that dangled between her breasts, seeking reassurance. Her anxious breathing slowed. Yes. She was sure of it.

She was about God's work – saving a Christian marriage. Her own.

She was the reconsecrated Queen Consort of England. She had a right to defend what was hers. And God was on her side.

Why else would he have sent her the monk?

## Chapter Seventy-Five

The queen curtsied to Edward Plantagenet and spoke sweetly, her face a smooth, unreadable blank. 'Does my husband the king want for anything?'

Edward's response was airy. He could be as charming as she, when required.

'Nothing at all, wife. I am graced by your presence.'

Elizabeth Wydeville curtsied again, deeper, bending her elegant head engagingly. She had picked the ground for this contest – the king's own private working closet. A tiny room, seen by very few, it looked down on the river and was the king's special retreat from the court. No one entered it except by invitation from the king himself. By her unannounced arrival, the queen signalled she had serious things to say.

'Well then, that is excellent news. I have been so concerned for Your Majesty.'

It had to come, of course, the meeting he had dreaded; this was just preliminary fencing between well-matched opponents. 'Concerned?

There is no need, my dear.'

The king took the queen by the hand, conducting Elizabeth to a delicately gilded stool in the shape of an X, the only other seat in the room besides his own carved working chair.

Graciously, the queen sat as he indicated and bestowed the folds of her gown to maximum decorative advantage. She was wearing pale pink velvet and cloth of silver today, a ravishing combination with white blonde hair. Pink diamonds in a simple coronet and a skein of blush-pink pearls around her neck completed the picture.

Delicate innocence and delicious youth, said the colours of her clothing and her jewels. The king, however, whilst admiring the carefully composed picture as a connoisseur, was wary. The queen's eyes shone crystal blue and cold when he chanced to glance into them.

'Are you thirsty, Elizabeth? Or hungry?'

The queen laughed delightedly. She shook her head, smiling. 'I will not make the obvious reply, husband, though it might amuse you if I did.'

He smiled too, to show he remembered. It was a joke from the beginning of their marriage: they used to say that the only thirst, the only hunger they ever felt was for each other. But those were the early days.

'Well now, what is this concern you have for me, my dear?' He cast one discreet glance towards the papers, the scrolls, piled up on his desk. *I'm busy, of course,* that glance said, *though never too busy to talk to you...*

'I thank you for this time, husband. There is much to do, I know; so many wait on your command. As do I.'

The king raised his eyebrows. 'Command, Elizabeth? In what should I command you?'

In a startling, theatrical instant the queen tumbled to her knees, clasping her hands and raising tear-drowned eyes to his.

'I love you so much and I live only to serve you and our kingdom. You must tell me it isn't true, lord and husband.'

'Elizabeth!'

The queen shed enchanting tears: it was a gift to cry drops that fell like crystal beads. Still, tears of any kind terrified Edward; he was now seriously alarmed. Elizabeth, beneath lowered lids, saw his bemused discomfort; it was a precious advantage.

'I have heard it said you will lock me up in a convent of silent nuns until I die, because I have displeased you. Dear Lord and husband, do not send me away. Please God, not that. What would our children do, deprived of their mother? Our precious son...' She sobbed heartbrokenly.

Now the king was truly confused. The situation between him and Anne and the queen was complicated and difficult to be sure, but he hadn't thought of such a thing. The queen was now the mother of a legitimate prince. He couldn't send her away, even if he might like to. The country would not accept it.

'This is pure nonsense. Malicious tongues, that is all. You have not displeased me, Elizabeth. This is just court gossip of the worst kind by those who are disaffected to our cause. Come now, let me help you to stand.'

He bent to prise the queen's convulsed fingers away from his shins.

'No! Not until you swear that you will not send me away. Swear it!'

The skein of pink pearls around Elizabeth Wydeville's neck had a crucifix at its end, tucked away between the queen's pretty breasts. The body of the Saviour surmounting it was rendered in white enamel bound in gold. With shaking fingers, the queen held the cross up to the king, held it in front of his eyes. 'Look closely at the sacred body of our Lord, I beseech you.'

The king had no choice as Elizabeth waved it: the glittering crucifix seemed to fill his vision.

'As the crowned queen of this country, and mother of your son, I ask you to swear on this broken body that you will not send me away.'

'You are making yourself ridiculous, Elizabeth.'

She could hear the embarrassment in his voice; victory was close. More tears and heartfelt sobs.

'Oh, Edward, you loved me once. Have I not been loyal to you and your house? Have I not been a good wife to you, staying staunch when all deserted your cause, our cause? Swear, swear by God's Son and His Blessed Mother that you will not put me away. Please, for the sake of our love and our children.'

It was the broken little catch in her voice that caused the king's resolve to waver. That and the guards outside his door, most likely hearing every word of this deeply mortifying charade.

'If it will please you, Elizabeth, though there is no need.'

Never had he been more reluctant or felt so

helpless; he hated himself for that. 'Very well. I swear it.'

That was not enough for Elizabeth Wydeville. She stood and pressed the crucifix between the king's fingers. 'Look at our Lord's tortured body. He died for us; for our sins, yours and mine, Edward.' She didn't need to enumerate the unnamed transgressions; they both knew what she was referring to. 'Say, *By the precious body of the Christ, I will not put you, my wife consecrated by God, away, ever, until death shall part us.*'

He was trapped by her eyes and his guilt; somehow the words formed themselves in his mouth and, to his horror, he heard himself speak them. 'By the precious body of the Christ...'

Her eyes were huge now, so close to his own, the black drowning the blue, and she spoke in a low, humming monotone. *'I will not put you...'*

'I will not put you...'

'*...my wife, consecrated by God...*'

'My wife, consecrated by God...'

'*Away, ever, until death shall part us...*'

'Away, ever, until death shall part us...'

'*...on my oath as King of the Realm of England.*'

For a moment the rhythm was nearly broken by this last, unexpected phrase, but her eyes were locked on his and the words seemed to say themselves, though somewhere deep in his mind Edward tried to resist. It was useless. He heard himself, heard his own voice, as if it belonged to someone else.

'On my oath as King of the Realm of England.'

The queen slid to the floor at the king's feet, a gracefully tumbled heap of expensive fabric. She

534

spoke with a bowed head; Edward could not see her face.

'Thank you, my lord and husband. Your children have cause to be grateful for this day.'

Edward wiped the sudden sweat from his forehead, dazed. 'You're a very strange girl, Elizabeth. What was the need for this?'

The queen raised her face to his, petal-soft, petal-sweet. 'Oh, just the foolish whim of your loving wife, nothing more. And since it's done, it's done for all our lives.'

The last sentence was oddly said, and he was uncertain what she meant by it.

The queen was not. She knew what she'd just achieved.

## Chapter Seventy-Six

William Hastings held the dice of influence in his hand and, as a last throw, he decided to talk with Anne de Bohun.

Because he was a good servant of the crown, the interests of England drove his actions. In this it made sense that the marriage of the king should be strengthened and the position of the queen, mother of the king's legitimate heir, buttressed with the support he could provide at court. Yet Hastings was not without pity or compassion. Or personal feelings. The king was his friend and he truly seemed to love this girl. And William himself actually liked Anne, even admired her.

Perhaps it was possible that the king's mistress could be managed so that she provided the king with what he needed emotionally, whilst living in retirement so as not to offend the queen. To find out, he had sent a written summons to Anne de Bohun, conveyed by her servant, the mute. Lunch would be served in the garden of the tower by the waterfall and he would be delighted by her presence.

As he waited for the girl to arrive, William surveyed the work he had caused to be done with satisfaction, even pleasure. He was a busy man, with little time to waste, but he was pleased his orders had been well observed. This place had something unusual. Peace; was that it?

Yet to say that the garden of Anne's bower was a tame and ordered space was to exaggerate. Wisely, William had made a virtue of necessity in this regard, because after such long neglect, and with so little time, a formal garden could not have been created. Better to allow most of the trees to stand and better yet to clear a number of glades and paths between them here and there, as if the garden had grown up in this manner. But flowers could be, and were, brought and transplanted – roses, peonies, gillyflowers, flocks, wallflowers, hollyhocks, all in full bloom, most of them scented – and small ponds created to be filled with exotic fish and fed by the stream that flowed through the garden.

Marble benches were robbed from the gardens of Westminster Palace and artfully scattered at the turn of newly created paths and under some of the more noble trees where the vista of the garden was pleasing; anywhere that lovers might be tempted to sit and dally.

The waterfall, too, was a welcome surprise when he'd first found it in the depths of the garden.

William had been alone on that first visit and had been drawn by its distant thunder. On that still day, the rushing hurry of its water had a distinct voice, a voice that seemed to call him. Long neglect had made the place a natural-seeming grotto, yet when he'd half-closed his eyes, he'd seen that the stone around the waterfall's pool had been artfully cut and fitted together.

The water descended from a fissure halfway up the height of a rock wall, where the sun caught rainbows from the sparkling air, a pretty sight. The fissure had the shape of a mouth. Half squinting, William saw that the mouth belonged to an enormous head which bulged outwards from the wall. And there were also eyes – though ferns, like green eyelashes, distorted their shapes – and there, a nose. Carved or natural? That face had a strange look. Very ancient somehow and, perhaps, malevolent.

A blue butterfly – as brilliant as the sky – had drifted past his face that day, wings moving gently in the languid breeze. The light shifted and he'd seen that the 'face' was just a lump of rock, after all, with no particular expression.

To preserve the intriguing mystery of the place, the surrounds of the pool had been carefully and selectively cleared of overgrowth and two handsome benches placed where they would catch dappled sun for much of the day. Now, as he waited for Anne to join him, he saw that one had been draped with a fall of embroidered jewel-red velvet; a piquant note of courtly luxury in this wild place.

Also, displayed on the lawn-like moss beside the waterfall, a small feast had been laid. William's gut grumbled as he contemplated such extensive bounty. The food was covered by white napkins and silver covers, but tantalising aromas reminded him that he had not eaten since early this morning, after mass. Perhaps if he were just to sample one of the pike and saffron fritters...

'I did not know about the waterfall, Lord Hastings.'

The chamberlain, startled, snatched his hand back like a guilty child. Behind him, Anne giggled. 'Oh, please, do eat, sir. I have kept you long enough and you must be very hungry.'

'Alas, lady, animal nature is stronger even than reason.'

He was glib until he turned and saw her. Then the easy words died. She was dressed in glimmering, lustrous white with her tawny hair loosened and eyes like jewelled adornments in her face; and William Hastings understood Edward's obsession with Anne de Bohun all over again. The king stood between two women – one fair, one dark. Looking at Anne, William's decision to choose the queen's interests above Anne's wavered. Theirs would be an interesting, and a testing, conversation today.

'Whoever built this garden made the waterfall, I believe, though it looks natural at first sight.'

Anne moved towards him out of the shadows of the trees and the sun touched her head with a hazy corona. The dress she wore was simple and yet the embroidery of pearls made it as precious as that worn by an icon; and as her white skirts trailed over the emerald moss it was as if the material, though loomed by human hands, had become another form of light.

Enchanted. Enchanting. Anne de Bohun belonged in this place; she too was an amalgam of the wild and the sophisticated, and it was hard to say such banal words as 'Are you hungry?' or 'Would you like to sit here, lady?' to a woman who looked like a visitor from Faerie.

'Perhaps you would sit on this bench here, Lady Anne? And allow me to serve you?' William began the conversation, taking the initiative.

'Yes, I should like that. I can't remember when I had food last.'

Anne sat and the folds of her dress flowed over the embroidered velvet of the seat he had chosen for her. Around the pool, trees moved in the slight breeze, dappling her body with shadow and light, shadow and light.

Anne was nervous. William could hear it in her voice and, when she glanced at him, her eyes were wary.

He cleared his throat, a harsh sound. 'I thought it best if we spoke together, alone, Lady Anne. Without even the mute. I hope you understand?'

He proffered a silver plate as he spoke – on it was piled food of a variety of kinds: the saffroned pike fritters he so lusted for; minced guineafowl napped in a sauce of pounded currants, cream and cinnamon; and whole baked gulls eggs, shelled and rolled in salt, honey and so much parsley they seemed entirely green. There was also a heroically large slice of raised pie filled with oysters, choice beef, young lamb and larks' flesh bound with eggs, new ale and peppered onions.

'A spoon, lady?'

'Thank you.' Anne accepted the plate with a gracious nod. The Chamberlain of England himself was serving her with his own hands. The picture of a gallant knight. Anne knew better; she took a deep breath. The contest for the king – body and soul – was joined.

Hastings returned with his own food a moment later and sat opposite her. 'I forgot this.' The chamberlain held out a knife with a short, gilded blade; a pretty thing with no serious edge.

Anne accepted the knife with a slight smile. 'A little blunt, I see. Don't you trust me, Chamberlain?'

William coughed as a piece of fritter lodged in his windpipe. 'I always trust beauty, Lady Anne; therefore, of course I trust you.' He was inured to lying.

Anne smiled wistfully, gazing at the waterfall as if it held some special power.

'I don't think I'd be able to if I were you, Lord Chamberlain. Trust me, that is.'

William Hastings was discomforted. Something had shifted in this conversation and he'd lost the advantage. He began to reply through a mouthful of food, but Anne spoke quickly.

'But do not fear me either, Lord William. I want nothing that is in your gift.'

Hastings swallowed his pie, conscious of a certain resentment. He enjoyed having power again, but it was tempered by this girl where the king was concerned; that annoyed him. However, today, *he* had summoned *her*.

'But until I know what you seek, you can't be sure, can you, lady?'

Anne shook her head. 'Trust me in this if you trust me in nothing else, Lord William.' The witty little play on words had an edge.

'Ah, lady, you are deep in a very dangerous game and, like it or not, you need my help if you are to survive.' Hastings allowed Anne to hear compassion, even sorrow, in his reply.

Anne was blunt. 'This is not a game of my making and, as such, I have not yet chosen to take part. I exist to the side, not at the centre. I have come to London for two purposes only and will not stay long. Should I change my intention, enter the "game" as you put it, then it is for me and the king to decide my actions and requirements. Not you.'

Now William was offended.

'Are you refusing my help, lady?'

Anne put the plate of food down, untouched. 'No. But if I take what you offer I do not want to pay for your assistance, Lord William. Allegiance, freely given, freely chosen by friends, can advantage both of us. You, too, may need what I can give you one day, if we are friends.'

She'd called his bluff. Was she suicidally foolish or, perhaps, very clever? He swallowed a snort with his pie. Friends? Men and women were never friends, not in the way that men were friends with each other – how could they be?

'Lady, you speak of choice as if one existed. It

does not. I can assure you of that. The queen is–'

'Seeking ascendancy?' Anne nodded. 'Yes, I know that. I've been told by many people that her influence grows at court, now that her son is born. She will fight hard to keep that. Yet...'

Something hovered in the air between them. The scent of power?

'You must believe that I do have a choice. The king is my friend, as he is yours, but he is my protector also.' She did not say, *lover*. 'We are bound to each other. I know that I could, per-haps, become a countervailing force to the queen, if I chose to. No, don't sneer.' She spoke gently at William's disbelief. 'I am telling you the truth. Whatever the king has done in the past, what he and I have is real. And strong. Even stronger now. He loves me. He always will love me.' It was said simply, but Anne was very certain. She lifted her head. 'And you are asking me the wrong questions, Lord William.'

The chamberlain watched Anne de Bohun rise to pour more wine for each of them, and decided to be patient. She was brave, yes, but in the end, foolish. The king might love her now, might have loved her in the past, might go on loving her for a time; but the queen was the queen. Edward Plantagenet would never marry this girl, lovely as she was, not even if the current queen died. The king would not make a second foolish marriage just because of the flesh and its attractions; next time he would marry royalty. That left Anne de Bohun with nowhere to go, in the end, but the oblivion of all baseborn mistresses. And there were many forms of oblivion. Some more pleasant than others.

The chamberlain accepted his silver beaker from the girl's hands and sat back, smiling slightly. 'And so, what questions should I ask you, lady?'

Anne heard the patronising tone in his voice. She knew what he thought of her and of her prospects with the king, yet she smiled because she had certainties, and knowledge, he did not.

'Because I have a choice, you should ask me if I want the life he offers me, for I know its price. And you should ask me who I am.'

There was a tone in her voice that flicked doubt into William's mind. What did she mean, *who I am?*

Anne looked towards the waterfall and a shadow passed over her face. 'And I know this, Lord William. When it comes to decide my future, *I* will choose what I want. Not you. And not the king.'

William Hastings returned to his pie, chewing on what the girl had said. There was silence between them and he did not break it. He would not play her game; shortly he would leave Anne de Bohun here in the garden to await the king and he would return to the palace.

He had made up his mind.

Anne de Bohun had achieved the impossible: she had made him frightened. She was not just an inconvenient and distracting mistress of the king, she was much more than that. Lady de Bohun had faith in her power over Edward Plantagenet and he had seen that power at work in the king. And, if she came to court, she believed she could pick and choose her allies – and her 'friends'.

One day, the king might be forced to choose between *his* best friend and the woman he loved. He, the Chamberlain of England, could not allow the politics of the bed chamber to ruin England as they had before – or to ruin him.

'More wine, Lady Anne?'

The girl shook her head and picked up a little of the food, pretending to eat.

They finished the meal in silence and, after a time, William Hastings rose and kissed Anne's hand before he bowed and walked away. Perhaps the monk was right. Perhaps this girl was a witch, ridiculous as that seemed. Hastings stole one glance back. The enigmatic 'god' of the waterfall almost seemed to smile down upon that still white figure in the green glade; as if she belonged in his strange domain.

William Hastings shivered. All Christian men had a duty where witches were concerned; the Bible was very clear on that.

He would do his duty. She had given him no other choice.

## Chapter Seventy-Seven

The lamps were lit in the tower as the warm day declined into dusk. In the west, the last flaring glory splayed across the sky in colours a painter could never match: ember red, flowing gold, grape black. And in the depths of the garden, Anne, in her glimmering white dress, knelt beside the waterfall, praying.

What did she pray for?

Her eyes opened. 'Guide me, Mother. Help me. This is too hard. Deborah was right.'

'I will help you, my darling. Here I am.'

And he was, thinking to surprise her, but he'd heard the sadness in her voice. It chilled him. Anne turned towards Edward. The wind was rising and branches sighed above his head.

'It gives me pleasure to look at you, Anne. It's almost enough.' Almost.

She reached out her hands to this man she loved so much: *hold me.* The king gathered Anne de Bohun. 'What's wrong, my darling? Tell me.' The eternal question that a man asked a woman. And there were many answers, but none that could be given words.

'Don't be frightened. I have you safe.' Edward tightened his arms around Anne and she smiled, leaning against his chest as he rocked her, gently, to and fro, to and fro. The king looked down at the head resting at the base of his throat. 'What do you fear, Anne?'

'It's not what I fear, it's what I now know.'

Edward frowned and led her by the hand to one of the benches. 'You speak to me in riddles tonight, my sweet girl. What causes you so much pain?'

For a moment, Anne had a sense that they were being watched. She glanced up as the last light in the west glimmered on the mouth, the nose, the deep-set eyes of the god of the waterfall. Was his presence benevolent or...

'People oppose us, Edward. Powerful people.

They want me out of your life.' Anne felt the muscles in her lover's arms and shoulders shift and stiffen.

'My darling, politics always swirls around the throne. But *I* am the king. I've earned my throne back and the country is mine. I know of no one who can challenge me now, not even Louis.' He was suddenly passionate. 'I need you. I need the love and comfort you bring me. The joy we give each other is precious. And I want you here, at court. I want our son to grow up with his sisters, and his new brother; they are his family also. The queen will grow accustomed in time. Other kings are granted happiness in their lives, why not me?'

It was a cry direct from his soul.

Anne put her arms around Edward and kissed him, held his rigid body, soothed him until, at last, he kissed her gently in return. And for that moment, she believed it was all possible, *must* be possible; they would stand against the world, together. She would not think about William Hastings or Elizabeth Wydeville; would not think about the shame of being the king's mistress. She would trust in what she and Edward had between them. And live from day to day, snatching what happiness she could. One thing remained.

Anne sat, and the king sat down beside her, kissing her lovingly. She picked up one of his hands and, looking into his eyes, asked the question that would change her life.

'I would like to meet my father. We heard little news at home, but some said he was in the Tower? I would like to ask his blessing.'

Edward dropped his eyes from hers. The wistful

catch in her voice was the thrust of a knife.

'I know he's been very sick, Edward, but I would like him to know I'm alive. I've been told he loved my mother very much, and when he heard she'd died – that I'd died too – he was distraught.' Anne sighed. 'His wife, the old queen – Margaret – she was responsible for my mother's death. Did you know that?'

Edward brushed tears from Anne's eyes but he said nothing.

'I've lived all my life without my father. It's hard when you have no family. My foster-mother has loved me so much, and I am very grateful, but I should have liked a father to guide me. I long to see him. Please let me visit him, Edward.'

The king tried to speak, but then he looked at Anne and she saw what was in his eyes. A nightingale's call broke the silence between them.

'He's dead, isn't he?'

He turned his face away. 'Your father, Henry of Lancaster...' The words died. He began again. 'The old king...'

She could barely whisper the question. 'Did you kill him?'

Agony. It was agony to think of it, for so many reasons. 'No. Not I, but...'

Anne stood with difficulty. Her joints had seized. 'You had him murdered.' A flat statement; she was completely certain, yet she longed, *longed*, for him to deny it. Suddenly she was burning. Fury, agony, fear lit a fire beneath her ribs; she had no breath. 'Tell me. Did he suffer? *Did he suffer, Edward?*'

'No!' The king stood. He reached for Anne but

she stepped back. She would not allow him to touch her.

And then she saw the tall cloaked woman. The light from the rising moon touched her face, a face made hardly human by the patterns of swirling blue tattoos. Anne lifted her hand in acknowledgment; they were old friends, old companions. Slowly, she turned back to the king.

'And the boy. Margaret of Anjou's son. Did you kill my half-brother also?'

Edward Plantagenet was haggard as a spectre. The sound of the waterfall was suddenly very loud, the rushing water echoing the pulse of blood in their veins.

'It was necessary. Whilst either of them lived, the throne was in danger. I ... it had to be done.'

'You killed them both. My father and my brother. Now I'll never know if we could have loved each other. If they could have loved me.'

He could say nothing; there was nothing to say.

Anne closed her eyes. 'I understand. I understand why you had to do it.' It was true. She did understand. One person's life was nothing, meant nothing. 'But this is not the way that I can live my life. One day our son might become inconvenient in the same way. To you, or to Elizabeth. I will not take that risk. I cannot.'

Anne looked into Edward's eyes, searching for his soul. Reaching up, she touched the king's face for the last time, tracing the line of his jaw, allowing one finger to follow the curl of his mouth. And then she kissed him, trying to imprint the smell of him, the sense of him, into her heart. Tasting tears, tasting joy. Tasting ... the end.

And it was done.

Turning her back, Anne walked towards the shadows, walked towards the Sword Mother where she waited, holding out her hand, scarred fingers loaded with massive gold...

Edward Plantagenet felt like rock, like stone. Nothing in his life had prepared him for this moment.

It was over.

There was no white figure in the moon-touched glade. Anne had gone.

## Chapter Seventy-Eight

It was a long journey, returning to Herrard Great Hall, but this time Anne de Bohun hired horses for them all to ride. It was a blur: day to night, then sleep at an inn – if sleep it could be called – night to day, then ride again; and the next day the same, and the next...

And as with all things that rearranged the heart, reached the soul, there were no words for what she felt. Fate had to be met and dealt with in silence.

Failure and loss, failure and loss: the beat of Anne's horse's hooves sounded the words. And never again, never again, never again...

She would have cried, if she could. But she was empty and dry, a husk, all feeling burned away.

It was not her own pride that burned her, or shame that she'd been wrong. What destroyed

Anne was that she'd not had the strength, or the will, to turn away from Edward Plantagenet without a much greater force than she could find in herself.

But then there was pity. Pity for Elizabeth Wydeville and the king, trapped in a marriage that would last all their lives, and must be lived for duty. With pity came remorse and the most terrible sense of judgment. That was the truly humiliating, scalding thing – judgment tasted like boiling pitch, like molten iron and acid mixed together, and now it was tearing at her throat, seeking to find her heart and burn it from her chest.

Jane Alleswhite was frightened of her lady's profound silence as they rode, day after day. Anne seemed suddenly to have become another person: haunted, hollow-eyed, hardly eating, unable to rest or sleep at night; she was fading to a wraith in front of them. Even the phlegmatic Ralph of Dunster had commented to her, the previous night, that perhaps their lady had a touch of the colic?

Wat – who had Mathew Cuttifer's release to return with Anne to Herrard Great Hall permanently – thought himself more sensitive than both of Anne's other servants and announced the cause, though it gave him no more than gloomy satisfaction in being right. 'Her heart's been broken – that's what's happened.'

Jane shooshed the man but surreptitiously crossed herself just the same. Her own opinion was that Anne de Bohun had been cursed in London. She'd heard all sorts of strange rumours about her mistress in the Cuttifers' house, because there were one or two people there who claimed to remember Anne from a previous time, years ago – a time when she'd been Lady Margaret's own body-servant.

These same people said that Anne's fortunes had been transformed by sorcery or worse, since, rumour had it, she'd once raised their same Lady Margaret from the dead by her black arts. Corpus, the wizened old pigman who lived with his animals, swore to the truth of it. He was full of talk about Lady Anne and the king too, *and* the queen. Salacious talk, vicious talk, painting her mistress as an adulterous whore, fit only for burning.

Poor, confused Jane, she'd experienced nothing but kindness from Lady Anne and thought, wistfully, that her lady must be very evil indeed to have such a well-disguised black heart since her beauty and grace suggested goodness, not its opposite.

And now, on the afternoon of their third hot day on the roads, watching her mistress ride home towards Herrard Great Hall as if returning to her own execution, Jane couldn't help but wonder if any of the gossip was true, though she crossed herself to ward off such terrible thoughts.

Autumn had touched the countryside with the lightest of fingers and, though it was still warm, the foliage of the great oak in the inner ward of Herrard Great Hall was withering to dried bronze, telling of what was to come. The first skittish winds of the changing season skirled around the massive trunk as the leaves took flight – so many at one time they revealed the little boy who'd been roosting unseen amongst the massive branches.

He was the first to see the riders as they came, the westering sun behind them.

'Deborah, Deborah!'

Barking his knees and elbows, he slithered from branch to branch and then, with a deep breath, dropped the last six feet to the ground; the distance was more than double his height. Edward rolled as he hit the newly fallen leaves and bobbed up unhurt.

'Wissy, Wissy! You're home, you're home!'

He was a small speeding blur and he covered the distance between the tree and the opening gate like a yearling colt.

'Oh, we've waited and waited and *waited*. I thought you'd never come.'

Anne jumped down from her horse and was kneeling, arms wide, to receive the small body as he hurtled towards her.

'Yes, I'm here. Home for good.'

Her son was in her arms and she could feel the frantic energy of his heart against her own.

'For good? No more going away?'

Anne shook her head, brushing away his tears, her tears.

'No. Home to stay now. Wat?' Anne turned towards her servants. 'Take the horses to the stable with Ralph, please. They'll be hungry. And Jane, I'd like you to help.'

'Anne!' Deborah hurried across the inner ward, ignoring the pain that autumn brought to her knees. 'Oh, child, child. You're so thin!'

Anne de Bohun tried to embrace Deborah but

the older woman held the girl at arm's length, looking searchingly into her eyes. Anne smiled crookedly.

'Thin, mother? That's easily fixed. Your good food and country air is all I need to make me strong again.'

Shading her eyes, Anne watched her three companions leading the horses away and then she turned from Deborah and looked, really looked at her house. The battlements cut a stark pattern across the flaming sky as the mellow stone darkened. The great tree stood like a sentinel and a witness to this moment. Was this enough? Was this place truly enough?

Deborah could see the truth in her daughter's face. Anne was wounded and the pain of that wound was very deep and fierce. Peace and rest: these were the things her daughter needed. And time to heal.

Edward was impatient. He tugged Anne's skirt. 'We've been so busy while you've been gone. Come and see.' He was pulling her towards one of the great storerooms under the Hall's living quarters; through the open doors, rows of neatly sewn sacks were stacked deep and high.

Anne was suitably impressed. 'Did you do this, Edward? All by yourself?'

The little boy giggled. 'Not me. Leif did. It's for you. A surprise. You like surprises, don't you, Wissy?'

Anne glanced at Deborah, who nodded. 'He's been driving everyone hard, himself also. Leif wants to gather the harvest in ahead of the rains. Edward's been a great help – he's very good at gleaning. Meggan says he's the best she's ever seen.' Edward puffed out his chest and nodded proudly. Deborah ruffled his hair lovingly. 'This good summer has given us grain in abundance, and food for the animals we'll keep over winter. And you're back in time for Harvest Home.'

'Am I? That's good. London makes you forget things like Harvest Home. It makes you forget much that is simple and good.'

The two women strolled towards the living quarters of the Hall, Edward clinging to Anne like a whelk. She wouldn't ask about Leif. Not yet.

'They'll be very pleased you're back. The villagers. They've been anxious.'

Anne nodded. At least she'd kept faith with her people. That was something.

'Would you like to rest, Anne?'

Anne shook her head. 'I think that Edward and I will go out to the fields. They'll be packing up now. I'd like them to see I'm home.'

'Yes!' Overjoyed, her small son grabbed Anne's hand and tugged her towards the gate. 'Come on, come on. Let's go!'

When Anne laughed with little Edward, some of the dull pain that had lodged beneath her ribs shifted like a physical thing; and because he made her run to keep up as they set off towards their home meadows, she forgot, for that moment, the weight she carried. The weight of sorrow.

The last light lay long across the strips of meadow land and gilded the backs of the men as they scythed the standing corn. Women followed, gathering, stooking, binding, gleaning; timeless rhythm, timeless tasks.

'Look, look who's here!' Edward danced ahead of Anne, yelling. 'Leif. Meggan. Look! Wissy's back.'

The tallest of the men stood up and turned, shaded his eyes against the sun. For a moment it seemed he would drop his scythe and run towards the woman and the boy. In the end, he waited for them to come to him.

Anne tried to think of nothing as she walked across the stubbled field, smiling, saying hello, waving to her friends from the village. There was Meggan. There was Long Will. What would Leif say to her? And what could she say to him? What would she feel?

She was close enough to look up into his face now. He wasn't Edward Plantagenet but he was big and brown and real.

'Hello, Leif. I'm back.' Such a silly thing to say but they were the only words she had.

The big man said nothing but then he smiled and leaned down, gently wiping the tears away; the tears she was so ashamed of.

'No need for these.'

'Wissy? Why are you crying?'

Leif picked the boy up in a whirl and dumped him, laughing, on top of the harvest wain filled with sacks of unthreshed grain. 'That's not for you to ask, young man. Your aunt is tired from the journey, that's all. Let's take her home, shall we, and get this wheat to the threshing floor.'

And suddenly, as if she weighed no more than the boy, Leif scooped up Anne de Bohun and tossed her up beside her son; she was winded by surprise.

Meggan nudged Long Will. 'London's a bad place, Will. Look how thin she is. And sad too. We'll fix that though, now she's home. Maybe he will?'

Long Will picked up his scythe and his sharpening stone. 'None of your business, woman. Leave them be. Gossip is the Devil's tool as well you know.'

But as he trudged back to the village, Meggan beside him, Long Will heard the boy singing loudly on top of the harvest wain as Anne's bullocks pulled the wagon along the track to the Hall. And as Will looked back, he saw Leif join in, walking beside the open wagon. And their lady, who had looked so unhappy only moments ago, was giggling on her perch, high up on the mountain of sacks. And then she began to sing as well and all three voices – the man's, the woman's, the child's – made harmony together for a moment; until Edward lost the tune and they all laughed.

Meggan looked at him in sly triumph. 'Told you so. All will be well. You'll see.'


## Chapter Seventy-Nine

In work there was healing and, as the year finally began to turn towards winter, Anne de Bohun pushed herself ever harder so that she would have no time or energy to think. Each day she joined the women from the village on the threshing floor in the largest of her barns and, like them, flailed the wheat to detach the ripe grain from the husk. Then, with all the women standing in a circle, together they tossed the grain to separate it from the chaff. These women had become her friends because she never asked them to do what she did not do herself.

Each evening saw the chatelaine of Herrard Great Hall stretch her weary back as she shovelled the last of the clean grain into sacks she'd sewn herself. And, because she was hungry, truly hungry at last, she ate ravenously at night – which pleased Deborah and made Leif smile, to see her so greedy – and fell asleep in front of the kitchen fire as she sewed yet more sacks, oblivious of her itchy clothes. More than once Leif carried Anne up to her own great bed and placed her, fast asleep, beside her dreaming son.

One night Deborah was settled before the fire in the flagged kitchen, a pile of sacks beside her, as Leif joined her. 'Ale, Leif?'

The man sat beside the old woman on the settle and gave her a grateful nod. He said nothing as he drank deep. Then, wiping his hand across his mouth, he ventured an opinion. 'She's better, I think.'

Deborah squinted in the light from the fire; it was getting harder to thread the big sacking needle. That was a worrying sign of old age. 'Can you see to do this, Leif?'

'Of course.' Like all seamen he was good with rope and deft with his fingers. And what was this thread but a jute rope made very small?

'Do you agree with me, Deborah, about Anne?'

Taking back the needle, Deborah flashed a

glance at her companion. 'In body, I agree she's mending well. Time is the solution to...'

Leif's face was grim. 'Edward Plantagenet.'

The old woman laid a hand on the man's knee. 'Will you wait, Leif?'

He smiled faintly. 'What choice do I have?'

'All the choice in the world.'

They both turned. Anne was standing, barefooted but dressed in her working kirtle, at the bottom of the stone stairs that led down to the kitchen from the rooms above.

'You were asleep.' Leif stood, abashed. He was embarrassed to think Anne had heard them discussing her.

'I woke.' Anne was short. She would not tell them about the dream: wolves and eagles fighting. Always, every night. She spoke urgently. 'Leif, I would not hold you here for the world. You have been so good to us, helped us so much. We have no right to–'

Leif put his hands on Anne's shoulders and gently pressed her to sit in his place beside Deborah.

'Yes, you do. Every right. Mathew Cuttifer asked me to come here and make sure you were well prepared for winter. There's still a lot to do. I'm not leaving. Not unless you want me to?'

Anne shook her head. 'No. Never.'

Why had she said that? She smiled at him, embarrassed.

'I mean, it's true. We do need you here. We can't finish all that needs to be done without you. Can we, Deborah?'

Her foster-mother nodded placidly, eyes on her

work. This was between the two of them; she did not speak.

'Ale, Lady Anne?' Leif diverted Anne's confusion with instinctive kindness.

Anne stretched and shook her head. 'I'm aching in every muscle and bone. And itching!'

Now Deborah spoke. 'It's the chaff. It gets into everything. You need to wash it off. I'll boil water for you and you can bathe in front of the fire. You'll sleep better, I promise you that.'

Leif swallowed the last of his ale hastily. 'Well then, I'll be off to my bed.'

And that was what he intended to do. And yet, later, he found an excuse to wander past the kitchen on his way to inspect the horses – to see if they'd been fed properly, that was what he told himself – and happened to cast one glance through the small kitchen window, which was open to let the steam out.

He saw Anne from the back, naked but for the bath sheet wound around her hips, holding her arms high as Deborah gently washed her body. It was just a glimpse – the line of one shoulder, the supple curve of her back as she bent, the grace of an arm as she held it extended. Love and pity overwhelmed Leif; it was not right that her ribs were so clear beneath her skin; not right that grief had made Anne so slender.

He fed the confused horses a second supper that night, thinking deeply. He knew what Anne de Bohun needed, even if she did not. She needed him.

It was his task to make her see that.

# Chapter Eighty

Two days later, when the harvest was all gathered in and they'd burned the stubble in the fields, the first rains began. Anne stood at the door to the stable, Morganne's reins in her fingers, and watched the puddles forming in the inner ward. This was perfect timing. The country was parched and the rain would soften the soil; some of the strips they'd just harvested would be left fallow to rest, but a third of them would need ploughing so that the winter grain could be planted. At last, at last, things were going well.

She squinted up at the sky. The rain was setting in. She would need her hooded cloak today to ride to the village; there was planning to be done for the Harvest Home feast she would shortly hold in the threshing barn. She stroked Morganne's nose and the horse whickered, tossing her head.

'Yes, we'll go very soon. I'll just get my other cloak.'

Ducking her head, Anne set out from the stable to run across the inner ward, but a voice called out to her, a man's voice. *'Anne de Bohun!'*

She turned, the rain blinding her for a moment... 'Moss!'

The gate to the Hall had been left open and, as if to mock her earlier happy mood, Brother Agonistes – the former Doctor Moss – had ridden through, surrounded by a group of armed men. With the exception of the monk, they were all dressed in the York livery of murrey and blue. Agonistes held an ivory cross high, flourishing it as he rode towards Anne, his red eyes burning with unnerving fervour.

'You know that is not my name. I am God's servant now. And you are a witch who has been found out.' His voice was very cold.

Anger brought energy to Anne's tired body. She stood straighter and stared back at him, unblinking. 'And *this* is deluded nonsense. You are not welcome in my house. But, plainly, you must be very frightened of me – or yourself – to need so many men about you.'

She turned her back on him and strode towards the door of her Hall. Nearer, nearer, if she could just get to the door…

Agonistes spurred his horse forward across her path.

'Stop! I have authorisation to take you from this place.'

The monk pulled a small scroll from the sleeve of his habit. Anne turned and looked at the man, wiping the rain from her eyes. The monk waved the scroll as he danced his horse forward.

'Oh, I assure you, all is in order, witnessed and signed. You have broken the terms of your exile from this country. The king himself has given me this task.' He was riding around her now, circling, taunting her.

Anne's heart jumped behind her ribs. 'Let me see this thing.'

Deborah had been collecting eggs from the

hens in the orchard and chose that moment to enter the inner ward on her way to the kitchen. She nearly dropped her basket as she hurried towards her daughter. 'Anne?'

The monk ignored the interruption. His horse curvetted closer to Anne de Bohun. 'Ah, so you can read, *Lady* Anne? Too much education in a woman is a useless thing. Except today. Read what is written here. If you really can.' He sneered as he offered her the document. Anne saw the dangling seal. The king's seal.

There was triumph in the man's eyes but Anne ignored it, twitching the scroll from his hands. Turning her back, she unfurled it; the rain fell on the parchment and the letters began to run, but she grasped the sense. All of it.

*We, Edward, by the Grace of God, Sovereign Lord of the Kingdom of England, France, Ireland and Wales, Duke of ... decree that the woman known as Anne de Bohun, of Herrard Great Hall in the county of ... having broken the terms of exile ... shall be banished from our Kingdom, never to return... In this matter, my agent, the Dominican monk known as Brother Agonistes ... shall remove the said Anne de Bohun from our Kingdom at his pleasure and escort her to a place of his choosing so that she may be placed in the hands of the Church to answer certain other charges.*

Above the dependent seals there was a signature at the foot of the little scroll: E. Rex. The ink trickled mournfully, staining her fingers.

Anne rolled the scroll tightly. 'This is a fraud. This is not the king's signature.' She faced

Agonistes squarely but heard the tremor in her voice. So did he.

Agonistes held up his crucifix once more, waving it in her face, back and forth, back and forth. He spoke very softly; he had no need to shout. 'I am the servant of the Lord and also of the king. Willing or unwilling, you will come with me. Now!' The last word was a bellow as men sprang down from their horses.

'No!' Anne turned to run towards the Hall, towards Deborah, but rough hands caught her, hauled her up and threw her in front of a waiting soldier on his horse.

'*Anne!*' Deborah's wail was terrified. Dropping the eggs, she ran forward, fighting to get to Anne, hitting out and running between the men, the horses, but they were too fast. They wheeled as a disciplined group and were gone, cantering over the drawbridge, gathering speed as the rain blotted out the sky.

Deborah ran towards the Hall. 'Leif, Leif! Where are you? Help me! Help Anne!'

It was a blur, a nightmare. What was she doing here?

Anne sat up in the box bed and regretted it immediately. Her vision was partly obscured – one eye was swollen almost shut – and her head was ringing with an intensity that made her want to vomit.

Now she remembered. She'd fought them, slashed at the eyes of the man who'd held her on the horse. They'd stopped the cavalcade and then she'd tried to hit Moss. They'd beaten her for

563

that. Painfully, she closed her eyes and swallowed. There was blood in her mouth.

It was so tempting to slide down into the dark...

No! She would count to three, and then...

It was the dress that claimed her attention first in this shadowed, wavering world. Earth-coloured and clumsily made from coarse wool, it was a penitent's garment, draped over a coffer placed directly in front of the bed; she couldn't avoid seeing that dress.

And then she saw that she was naked. And cold. Shivering, half closing her one open eye against the pain, she groped for something to cover herself. There was only a sheet.

'I'm over here, witch.'

Where was he? Where was the voice coming from?

Anne swallowed as she tried to speak; even her throat was painful. 'I can't see you.'

He laughed. An unpleasant sound. 'Open your eyes. Both of them.' That was cruel. And bracing. Anne forced herself to focus.

'Ah yes, there you are, Moss. Hiding in the shadows as usual. What are you frightened of? It can't be me, surely, after what you had them do.' Her tone held the flick of a whip.

He stood at the end of the bed, the crucifix held up before him like a weapon. 'A woman should be reverently silent when a servant of the Lord, or any man, indeed, is pleased to give instruction.'

'Silent reverence?' Anne shook her head. 'I suppose you call this' – she indicated the bruises and the blood – *'instruction?'*

The monk signed the cross over the bed. 'The Lord guides me. By mortifying the flesh you will be brought to salvation.' Momentarily, his face twisted as he looked at her: the shape of her body was clear beneath the sheet. He threw her the penitent's robe. 'Your worldly clothes have been stripped away. Cover yourself. We have lost time waiting for your recovery. If we are to catch the tide, we must ride fast.'

It hurt Anne to laugh. 'So it's no easier if I'm unconscious? What are you worried about? People talking?'

'Dress. You offend God with your nakedness.'

'It won't work, Moss. You can't do this.'

He looked at her with his head on one side, eyes jackdaw bright. 'The man you call Moss is dead. You killed him. Dress and veil yourself. Men will never see your face again, not as long as you live.'

There was a cold, dark chasm opening. 'No. I will not go with you. I will go to my home.' Her voice wobbled.

Agonistes smiled; he had broken her spirit at last. 'But I have the signature of the king, your sometime adulterous lover, on the deed of exile. You saw it. You are bound for France. And burning.'

Anne shook her head. 'Why are you doing this, Moss? *You* betrayed *me* all those years ago. From the very first. Ambition and lust were your downfall; they were *your* sins, not mine.'

*'Silence!'* Concentrated venom. He thrust the crucifix towards Anne's face but his eyes dropped further down her body.

A moment, a frozen moment, and he'd ripped the sheet away from Anne. Her eyes locked on his. She made no move to cover herself.

'Face the truth, Moss. Here it is. My body is the truth. You want to kill what I would not give you.'

She saw shame in his eyes for an instant, and then he slapped her. Her eyes blurred with agonised tears as he whispered, 'Try to tempt the servant of the Lord again and I promise you such suffering that the stake will be a relief.'

There were two roads now: defeat or rage. Anne chose rage. She threw the penitent's gown across the room. 'I will not wear that thing. *I am not a witch or a penitent.*' She reared up and the crown of her head connected with his jaw, stunning them both.

But Moss, the self-serving courtier, stood before her now; the monk had disappeared. He jerked Anne up by the hair and his face was so close to hers she could smell old wine and the rancid breath of broken teeth.

'You are lost and will do as I say.'

'I think that's unlikely.'

Leif Molnar. He'd arrived so quietly on buckskin boots that neither had heard him open the door. Leaning on the haft of his axe – double-bladed, a battleaxe – he filled the door frame.

Moss turned, one hand entangled in Anne's hair. 'You have no business with this woman.'

Leif snorted, picked up the axe and settled his grip. 'A bad choice, monk, and a worse one. That's all *you've* got for certain.'

Moss's eyes were suddenly wide and blank. He smiled broadly and dropped Anne's hair, wiping his bloodied fingers against the skirts of his robe. 'Foolish man.'

He launched himself from the balls of his feet, a bright dagger in the fist of one hand. He had courage when he thought the odds were on his side.

But they weren't. He was out of practice.

Leif, the servant of Thor, seasoned by much fighting, stepped neatly to one side as Moss closed the gap. Revealed behind him was a silent party of men from Wincanton the Less. Anne's people. Armed with billhooks sharp from harvesting.

There was no need for the battleaxe. The billhooks did their work and Anne did not try to stop them, though she turned her head away and closed her eyes.

Perhaps she would do penance for this killing at another time, but not now. By the grace of a different God, she was free to go home.

## Chapter Eighty-One

It was nearly two weeks since Anne's rescue from Moss and the orchard was littered with the last windfalls of the season. The need to get the harvest in quickly had interrupted the final picking, and the first autumn gales had caught them on the boughs.

Anne was slowly moving from tree to tree, seeking the best of the damaged fruit and putting them in her apron. Deborah had taught her well

567

as a child: nothing must go to waste.

'What will you do with them? Aren't they too bruised for use?'

Anne stood up carefully; parts of her still hurt, though the pain was less with every new day. She smiled at Leif as he came towards her with another empty basket. 'Would you say that I am too?'

He smiled nervously. It was a black joke after all she'd been through. 'No. You're sound. Lots of use in you yet. Deborah asked me to give you this.' He put the basket down and Anne allowed the contents of her apron to tumble into it.

'Anne?'

She turned to him. 'Yes?'

'Show me?'

Trustingly, she allowed him to cup her face in one hand. He turned it, very gently, this way and that. 'Can't see much any more. You heal well.'

It was true: most of the discoloration had faded and the cut over her eye had healed cleanly.

Anne patted his hand in a distracted way, then bent down to gather more apples to fill the new basket. 'Arnica and woundwort. And comfrey poultices. Very basic treatment really, but I'm feeling much better.'

Leif started to say something, but stopped himself. Anne was spending too much time alone. That was not healthy. Her body was healing but her spirit was another matter; it was burdened by the monk's poison and the shadow of Edward Plantagenet. He would lift the shadow and drain the poison. If she'd let him try.

'Deborah sent me to bring you back to the Hall. She has hot food for us all and Edward's hungry. You can fill that later. Or I can.'

Anne dropped a few more apples into the basket. Already it was half full. 'Alright. I'll leave it here. We can come back after we've eaten and fill it together if you like.'

Leif brightened. At least she'd said 'we'. He bent down and shouldered one of the full baskets that were placed neatly beneath a naked pear tree.

'What do you want all this for anyway? Windfalls won't preserve well.'

Anne matched her pace to his long stride. Part of her wanted to reach out and claim one of his hands; part of her didn't.

'Meggan has told Deborah of an apple wine they make here. You peel the apples, crush them and add honey and water, then leave them to ferment. The longer you leave them, the more potent the wine becomes.' She smiled up at him. 'They use it at weddings. The guests become cheerful very fast, or so they say in the village.'

'Well then, I think you should make as much as you have crocks for. I'd like to see you cheerful again.' He took a deep breath. 'And I'd like to see you married. To me.'

Anne stopped and so did Leif. They turned towards each other and she gazed up into his eyes but said nothing; he could not read her expression.

'Anne? Did you hear what I said?'

'Wissy, Wissy, you have to hurry or it's all going to get cold. And I'm very, very hungry. Come *on*.'

Edward, spying Leif and Anne from the kitchen, had hurried out to meet them. He pulled hard at the skirt of Anne's apron, trying to shepherd her towards the kitchen.

Anne spoke very softly. 'I heard you, Leif.' But she picked up her son's small hand and allowed him to lead her towards the Hall. 'We're coming, Edward. We're hungry too, I promise you.'

Leif called out to Anne's departing back. 'And?'

She turned for a moment, but was helpless to resist her son's determination. 'Talk to me tomorrow, Leif. Let me think. I need to think...'

But she smiled at him. It was tentative, but still a smile. Leif's heart lifted. Tomorrow could not come too soon; it would be a good day. He was certain of that.

Whistling, he hefted the basket and followed the woman and the small noisy boy towards the Hall.

## Chapter Eighty-Two

The sudden shiver of winter banished the long golden summer from London. Trees shook in the pitiless east wind and the air was swirling, full of dead and flying leaves. At Westminster, it was cold again in the greatest rooms and fires and braziers were lit to ward off the damp chill and the gloom as the days drew in.

The people of London looked forward to Advent. This year, this year of triumph, the court would celebrate in style, especially now that the king seemed so secure on his throne with all his enemies vanquished. Yes, it was good to be English once more. It was said the baby prince thrived so close to this, his first birthday, and there was even a rumour that the queen might be with child again. Perhaps another son would be born, making the future of the dynasty a certain thing? The Londoners all liked the little princesses of course, but, in the end, a country needed boys, needed princes. And that was what the queen was doing for them. That was one thing you could say for Elizabeth Wydeville – she *was* fertile – and there was every hope for more children now that Edward was back in the saddle; in every way. Meanwhile, the people of London cheered the royal couple whenever they appeared together in public, which was often, and wished them well, for all their sakes, now that the spectre of the old queen and the old king had vanished away.

In the splendid nursery, as the shadows of the blustery evening lengthened, Edward Plantagenet waved the seven nursemaids, the two wet nurses and the three cradle-rockers away. He gazed down on his sleeping son and lightly touched the baby's face. There was such sadness in that touch.

'Your Majesty?'

The lord chamberlain whispered, not wanting to wake the child. The king turned towards his oldest friend and William Hastings drew a short breath. Dark circles under Edward's eyes told the story. Exhaustion. Desolation.

The king put a finger to his lips and signalled they should leave. There was a rustle like wind through standing corn as the entire silent suite of servants sank to their knees and bowed their heads to honour the king as he left his son in their care.

'Has it been drafted as I requested?'

'Yes, sire. The Lady Anne's son has been invested with the titles as you required, and the lands. He is now a baron in his own right, and, as instructed, when he reaches his maturity, will be honoured with the title Earl of Carlion. He has the French titles also, against the day you take France back into the kingdom of England. A person of great consequence.'

'And his mother?'

'She too has the grant of extra lands. Her estate will be substantial now.'

The king nodded as he took the parchment to scan. He appeared satisfied. If he'd looked at his old friend in that moment, Edward would have seen a strange expression on the chamberlain's face. Fear, perhaps? Regret?

'Very well, come with me, William. I will sign it in my closet. Then you must see that all is done as I expect it to be. I wish too that you will give the Lady Anne this new grant of arms as quickly as can be arranged.'

William said nothing. He had seen the new heraldic device: the leopards of Anjou were still there, but instead of two drops of blood there were now three and the whole was surmounted by a broken sword.

Edward sighed like a weary man and walked with a heavy tread. William attempted to buoy up his spirits.

'It will be good to have a proper winter court, sire. A tournament, perhaps? With a queen of beauty to award the prizes? Perhaps Her Majesty would graciously honour the court in this way?'

If he could not say it, who could? It was time the estrangement between Elizabeth Wydeville and the king was ended, for the good of the country.

But the king turned to his chamberlain. 'The queen of beauty? She's gone. By my actions, I sent her away.'

Something beyond politics made William Hastings speak the truth; his words came from somewhere he had not expected: his heart. 'I do not think the Lady Anne would have enjoyed living at court, sire.'

The king was puzzled. 'Why do you say that, William? How could you possibly know?'

Regret and shame chased themselves across the chamberlain's face, and this time the king observed them.

'I know, Your Majesty, because I hold the Lady Anne in the highest regard. She has real courage and it was her choice to live another kind of life from that which you offered her. We must wish her well in it. She has escaped many dangers,' – the king's look was quizzical; he rarely heard his worldly chamberlain so fervent – 'and has come home safely, at last. She has earned her peaceful haven, away from the glare of the court.'

The king gazed down on the river far below as it slipped towards the sea. They were so high in the palace, it was almost an eagle's view.

The chamberlain crossed himself behind the king's back. If Anne de Bohun prospered now, she did so despite his betrayal. A betrayal he

573

deeply regretted, not least for its being un-necessary – for it was some time since he'd heard about the death of the monk. Perhaps, one day, he would tell the king the full story. Not yet, however. Certainly not yet. Please God the false papers had been burned.

Edward turned back to his friend, eyes huge and haunted. 'I hope she will be happy, but I miss her. I'll always miss her. She was enchanting.'

The chamberlain nodded. 'Enchanting is the correct word, sire.'

Enchanting in the way of a beautiful woman. Not in the way of a witch. William Hastings allowed himself to acknowledge that truth as he followed the king to his closet. Witchcraft? That was the queen's domain. He'd fallen for Elizabeth's brand of sorcery once and only once, when it had suited them both – in trying to dispose of the Lady Anne – but never again. She was his queen, but he was not her ally or her friend. To be either was too dangerous altogether.

He had chosen his allegiance. The king, not the queen. He would hold that faith now, open-eyed, until death.

## Chapter Eighty-Three

Advent again. And it was cold. A bitter rain dripped down his neck and back as he rode and that did not improve Louis's temper in the murk of descending night. Then he remembered what had been bothering him all day. He shot the words impatiently over his shoulder.

'Le Dain! What happened to the monk? I've heard nothing.'

The barber had been dreading this particular conversation. He kicked the flanks of his cold and miserable horse and rode up beside the king.

'Your Majesty, there is bad news. I have only just received the despatch.' He was lying of course, he'd known the news for some days. 'The monk, Brother Agonistes, has disappeared.'

The king reined his horse to a stop. 'Disappeared? How? Where?'

'The events are cloudy, sire. The report I have says he attempted to remove the Lady Anne de Bohun from England and ... er ... has not been seen since.'

'But why should he do such a thing?'

Le Dain was confused. 'Your instructions, sire? You requested information. Perhaps he felt that the lady knew things about the king which would be of advantage to your cause and that if he removed her to France, he would hurt the ... the Earl of March.'

Louis snorted. Lately the pain in his legs had returned and to lose the monk at such a time was an annoyance; distinctly an annoyance!

'He's always been unstable, my "brother-monk", but in this, he's exceeded his authority. Abducting a woman from her own country? Idiot!'

The king pouted at the thought of the monk's stupidity. Le Dain licked his lips nervously. Pouting was always a bad sign.

575

'Le Dain?'

'Your Majesty?'

'I want another monk. A sane one. My legs hurt.'

'Immediately, Your Majesty. And see, there is the hunting lodge. We're nearly home.'

'But I won't eat goose tonight, do you hear me? Goose never agrees with me. It unbalances the humours. Go and tell them that. They know what happened to the last goose cook.'

Le Dain bowed reverently at the ominous words and galloped off ahead of the party towards the distant lights of the hunting lodge. Unbalanced humours? God preserve them all from Louis's humours, unbalanced or not. And just where would he get another monk, or a leech who would pretend to be a monk, at this time of night?

Leeches? Now, there was the beginning of a good idea. Leeches and the king's legs. That might work. Anything to distract Louis from asking the most frightening question of all.

The fate of the little monster, Louisa.

'What are you writing, wife?'

Margaret, Duchess of Burgundy, turned at her writing table and smiled at her husband.

'I want to give my family in England the good news we share, Charles. My mother will be delighted. So will my brother, the king.'

Charles strolled over to his wife and bent to nuzzle her neck, kissing and nibbling. She squirmed; he knew just how to excite her.

'Stop that! I can't concentrate.'

576

'But that is good. Perhaps we can make another little person tonight to share your womb with our son?'

Margaret blushed, but the bright eyes of her husband gave her such pleasure. 'But Charles, we shouldn't. It's wrong. This is the gift of life, it's not for pleasure – the Church says so. And now we have engendered a child. That is enough for the moment. Isn't it? We would not want to hurt our baby.'

She turned in his embrace, looked at him pleadingly. Charles sighed; he could see she was serious. Sometimes it was a nuisance having a devout wife.

'My darling is right, certainly. But...' He could not resist caressing her neck, she had such beautiful skin. 'Is it not a little early to be telling your family?'

Margaret turned back to her letter; she had never felt so confident, so certain. She patted his hand lovingly as she wrote. 'It is certainly ten weeks or more.' She pulled one of his hands down to her belly. 'This time, this time I have a good feeling.'

She leaned back against her husband's chest, dreaming. 'And if we have a son, we could call him Ed–' She flicked a glance at her husband. 'No. I think he should bear his father's name. Charles. In time, he will be the second king of Burgundy, now that Louis has no allies to speak of.'

Charles smiled and bent to kiss his wife. 'Never underestimate a Valois, wife. Never underestimate the King of France. We have no kingdom yet.'

Margaret turned her shining face to his. 'Ah, but we will, husband. And I carry the heir. I'm certain of it. The heir to the kingdom of Burgundy.'

Charles prayed that she was right – about the child and about his kingdom. But they'd both been wrong before.

## Chapter Eighty-Four

'I think you're ready now.'

Margaret Cuttifer stood back beside Deborah and the two women looked critically at Anne. Soft light bloomed through the thick glass of the casement and found highlights in her shining, unbound hair. Though she was very pale – all brides were pale on their wedding day – her eyes were bright and her skin was radiant. The green dress was a novel choice, of course, as were the soft red shoes, but Anne had made the gown herself and would listen to no argument about the colour. And today she was wearing the Cuttifers' wedding gift, a massive rope of matched pearls and emeralds. Jewels fit for a princess.

Anne caught her breath under their critical gaze and smiled. 'Yes. I'm ready. I really am.' She said it confidently. She meant it.

It was a brilliantly fine day as late autumn shaded into winter, and now the moment was close, the moment when Anne de Bohun would marry Leif Molnar. Soon they would say their vows in the porch of the newly refurbished church dedicated to the Mother of God, the blessed Lady Mary, Empress of Heaven.

The people of the entire village would be there and some of the gentry from the surrounding properties; however it would be a small celebration, as these things went, for it was widely perceived in the district that Anne, an heiress honoured by the king with even more substantial grants of land on her marriage, was throwing herself away on a man much beneath her in station. The bride knew better.

'Anne, are you ready yet? We can't leave the poor man standing there, not in front of the whole village.' Sir Mathew Cuttifer knocked at the door of Anne's room, and all three women giggled.

'Yes, Sir Mathew. I'm dressed. Come in.'

'I'm sorry to hurry you, Anne, but really I'm worried we'll be...' The great merchant looked at the bride and a new expression crept over his face. Awe.

Wordlessly, he held out his arm to Anne and, before she placed her hand in his, she turned to the two women who were her closest friends. She tried to speak, but Margaret hurried forward, breaking the moment.

'The veil. We nearly forgot the veil! Deborah, help me.'

Between them, the simple square of finest silk gauze edged with tiny pearls was dropped over Anne's head and an unadorned circlet of gold was gently pressed down to hold it in place. The material was so delicate, so fine, it flowed around her shoulders and down her back like a cloud.

'There. On your way, Mathew.'

Outside, in the inner ward of Herrard Great Hall, the stakes of the harvest wain had been twined with ivy and holly – the red berries standing out like rubies amongst the mass of darker green. A velvet-covered bench was placed ready for the bride and the man who would shortly give her away, in place of her dead father, as was a fur rug, in case the day should turn cold. And standing proudly by the horses' heads, one on each side, were Wat and Ralph in new livery of Anne's own colours: red and forest green.

For Anne, the journey to the village passed in a swift and nervous dream. They travelled past a blur of faces, with the din of happy shouts and barking as all the village dogs tried to welcome them at once.

And there, standing in the porch of the church, was the man she would marry; Leif was waiting for her, as nervous and pale as she was. Mathew, who was not insensitive, sensed Anne's state and before he lifted his ward, the beautiful Lady Anne de Bohun, down from the wain, he patted her hand and whispered, 'Courage, my child. *Courage!*'

Anne took a deep breath and, as the great merchant proudly led her to her groom through the people of her village, she found she *was* smiling. It was alright. It was going to be alright.

And when Mathew placed Anne's hand in Leif's much greater hand, and they both turned to face the priest who would join them together as man and wife, she twined her fingers through his and made herself think only of him. She would see only her husband's face today; she owed him that much.

But later, as Anne stood in the church, hearing the words of the nuptial mass, she looked down at her red shoes, her green dress, and she remembered, just for a moment. Once, long ago and far away, she had worn another green dress, and a rope of emeralds and pearls as well, and another man had looked at her as longingly, as lovingly as Leif now did, standing beside her at the altar.

She smiled at the tall man by her side, her new husband. For him she had sewn this wedding dress with her own hands, and with each stitch she had set in the leaf-green velvet she had consciously created a link to the future and severed one more thread from the past.

Yes, the colour was unconventional but it was her choice, for green was the colour of new love. She smiled tenderly as she linked her fingers once more into those of her new husband and looked up into his proud face. Love was a tender plant, but it would grow between them well for they would both treat it with care and tend it faithfully. This was her promise to him, and his to her.

The wedding feast of Anne de Bohun and Leif Molnar went long into the night, but finally it came time to put the bride to bed – the villagers would not be cheated of the high point of the evening.

Leif, however, was dizzy with panic and unwatered wine. He knew he looked the part of the bridegroom, for he was dressed as finely as a man could be for his wedding feast – in a long black gown of best English broadcloth with sweeping sleeves of figured gold damask, a wedding gift from the Cuttifers, topped by a padded hat the size of a wheel, fashioned from red velvet – but now the time had come to more than act the part of husband, and all his confidence fled.

Mathew smiled. Somehow it had come to him to coach both the bride and groom through the complexity of this ordeal. Sitting in the place of honour to Leif's right at the high table, he made it his business to inject some propriety into the increasingly rowdy proceedings and rose to his feet.

'Dear friends all, yes, it *is* time.'

Much hooting and pandemonium rolled around the hall from the delighted, tipsy guests.

'No, my friends. A little quiet is called for, if you please.'

The groom earnestly studied each one of his fingers in turn, and Anne, eyes modestly lowered, tried hard to smile calmly, though her head rang with the noise.

'It seems our bride and groom are bashful, as is proper...' Laughter rippled around the hall as Leif Molnar blushed. 'So we must help them to their task! A toast!'

This was the signal they'd been waiting for: all the guests scrambled to their feet, beakers in hand, yelling, 'A toast! Yes, a toast!'

'To Master Leif Molnar and his bride, the Lady Anne. Long life, and many children!'

'*Master Molnar, Lady Anne! Long life, many children!*'

'Why not start tonight!' Ralph of Dunster surprised them all, bellowing from the back of the hall, but his voice certainly carried and soon the chant became unstoppable. *'Start tonight, start tonight, start TONIGHT!'*

Leif's hand stole across the stretched white linen of the festive board and found Anne's. Her eyes were closed and for a moment her hand lay slack in his. But then her fingers twined with his own and he felt their strength.

'Yes, it is time, my husband.' Anne took Leif's face between both of her hands and kissed him sweetly, to the raucous delight of the crowd. Leif closed his eyes to savour the moment and only Deborah saw tears like jewels spike Anne's lashes.

Hand in hand, the bride and groom ascended to the upstairs room, the room with three doors, but when they turned at the top of the stairs it was the bride who spoke first, on her new husband's prompting, and this change in custom was remembered long, long after their wedding day.

'My dear husband and I, and my nephew, Edward...' She waved to the little boy who was standing on one of the tables so he could see, with Deborah trying to hold on to him, and her words were lost in the cheering. 'We thank you all for this wonderful day. This is our home and, as long as we live, you are welcome inside our doors.'

She felt Leif's arm encircle her waist and all the tension, the anxiety, drained away; for a moment she leaned against his body, resting there, gathering strength.

He tightened his grip discreetly and, though Leif rarely spoke in public, tonight he found an uncommonly loud voice. 'But now, if you've eaten and drunk your fill, my wife and I would be just as happy to be left in peace!'

Good-natured laughter swept the hall like a warm wind. 'No, no, no!'

'Yes, yes, YES!' The groom cut through the din, suddenly self-assured.

He turned to Anne. 'Are you ready, wife?'

She found the words as she smiled at him, her eyes bright with more than tears. 'Truly ready, husband.'

'Very well then. From this day, no more sorrow for you or for me.'

Bending down, he swept her up as if she weighed no more than a lamb or a small calf, and kicked open the door to the bed chamber, calling out over his shoulder, 'And now, goodnight!'

And that closed door began their life together. They had earned their peace.

## Epilogue

On the night of Anne and Leif's marriage feast, something remarkable happened in the skies over Herrard Great Hall. Meggan saw them first as she and Will wandered back towards the village, well fed and content, with the rest of the people from Wincanton the Less. A pair of sea eagles was riding the warm air as it rose from the chimneys crowning the Hall.

'Since when do eagles fly at night?'

They all stopped and looked upwards as the

birds crossed and recrossed the radiant face of the Advent moon.

Will shook his head. 'Never seen that before, dame.' He crossed himself. 'What do you think it means?'

Meggan turned back and looked at the Hall. High up, one light still shone out into the night. Then it blinked out.

Above them, the eagles called to each other and a moment later they were gone, heading towards the coast and the empty, silver sea.

'Good times. And happiness. That's what it means.'

They trudged away into the night, singing.

And Anne, lying awake beside her now sleeping husband, heard them as they went.

She turned to look at Leif's face in the moonlight slanting through the casements; moonlight had always been lucky for her.

And then Leif moved and the light touched his face in an odd way. For that moment he was a stranger, a man she'd never seen before; but then he turned again and reached out, searching for something in his sleep.

For someone.

Her.

The fingers of Leif Molnar's great hand found those of his wife, Anne de Bohun, and he sighed contentedly.

Anne curled up against the body of the giant in her bed. His warmth comforted her. As he did. Yes. They would be happy. She would see to that.

This time, it would be a good winter.

# Acknowledgments

Having lived with Anne de Bohun and Edward Plantagenet in my head for quite a few years, I would dearly like to thank all the kind friends who have helped me so much as I've written their story in *The Innocent*, *The Exiled* and now, the last book in the trilogy, *The Beloved*.

Judith Curr, executive vice-president and publisher of Atria books and Jon Attenborough, publisher and managing director of Simon & Schuster Australia. You have both believed in these books from the beginning. Thank you for your patience, interest and untiring support. I hope the trilogy repays your trust. It has been a privilege and a great pleasure getting to know you both.

Carolyn Caughey, Hodder and Stoughton, London. Many thanks to you, Lucy Hale and everyone at Hodder also, for your enthusiasm about the Anne trilogy. It's a real thrill that these books are being published in the United Kingdom. I've thoroughly enjoyed the champagne and the lunches 'around the corner'.

To Nicola O'Shea, Australian editor of *The Beloved*, Kim Swivel, Australian editor of *The Innocent* and *The Exiled* and to Suzanne O'Neill, US editor of all three books. I've so appreciated working with each one of you. You can have no idea how encouraging it is to have such kind, experienced and professional people to learn from and work with. It makes my job so much easier. Thanks, too, to Jody Lee and Clare Wallace who were at Simon & Schuster Australia, when it all began.

Many thanks also to Julia Collingwood, managing editor, Camilla Dorsch, marketing manager and Glenda Downing, senior editor, again at Simon & Schuster Australia. You must constantly be driven mad by distracted authors who just can't resist meddling with the work of experts. Thank you all so much for humouring me and holding my hand when I got anxious (which has been often!).

To Susan and Phaedon Vass. Three books later and I still owe you the most enormous debt for introducing my first book to Judith. I'm blessed to have such lovely friends.

Another friend, and important influence in my early life, is Emeritus Professor Ralph Elliott, AM, world-renowned expert on medieval literature and the kind of teacher that every callow student should meet just once in their lives. Dear Ralph, your brilliant lectures helped me fall in love with medieval England – and sometimes it feels as if I've never left!

Carol Gerrard, Julie Redlich and the Richard III Society of Australia. I'm enormously grateful for your encouragement and your interest in these books. Your hero is the brother of mine – so we're sisters under the skin. Carol, many thanks, particularly, for agreeing to read *The Exiled* and

*The Beloved* and for giving me the benefit of your expert knowledge and opinion.

Debbie McInnes (Australia), Angela Stamnes and Justin Loeber (New York), Lucy Hale (London). The oxygen for books is publicity. Thanks so much for all the work you have done to encourage coverage of my work. I'm very grateful.

To that most cheerful and witty equestrienne (and agent) – Rachel Skinner. You've stuck with this trilogy for years and years and *years* and I'm just so thankful for your support and friendship.

Finally, I'd like to thank some very important people in my life. My mother, the novelist Eleanor Graeme-Evans, my children Emma MacKellar, Emma Blaxland and Julian Blaxland and Hayden MacKellar, our dear son-in-law (and Emma and Hayden's sons, Rohan and Toby). You must all feel that these books have been going on for ever and ever in our joint lives. I hope you enjoy reading *The Beloved*.

And, Andrew Blaxland. Dear friend, husband and creative partner in all senses and all enterprises. Thank you, in particular, for putting up with my distracted state when I'm writing. I'm very much afraid there's more to come!

My love to you all.

The publishers hope that this book has given you enjoyable reading. Large Print Books are especially designed to be as easy to see and hold as possible. If you wish a complete list of our books please ask at your local library or write directly to:

**Magna Large Print Books**
Magna House, Long Preston,
Skipton, North Yorkshire.
BD23  4ND

This Large Print Book for the partially sighted, who cannot read normal print, is published under the auspices of

## THE ULVERSCROFT FOUNDATION